69 99 ONWARDS
134 -139 -143
158 159 - 236
260 265 272
305 DNA

PSYCLONE

Shyam Mael

MAELSTROM

Published by Maelstrom

Copyright © Shyam Mael 2008

Shyam Mael asserts the moral right
to be identified as the author of this work,
in accordance with the Copyright, Designs
and Patents Act 1988.

This work is licensed under the Creative Commons Attribution-
Noncommercial-No Derivative Works 3.0 Unported License. To view a
copy of this license, visit http://creativecommons.org/licenses/by-nc-
nd/3.0/ or send a letter to Creative Commons, 171 Second Street, Suite
300, San Francisco, California, 94105, USA.

You are free to share – to copy, distribute and transmit this work under
the conditions set out in the above license.

A CIP catalogue for this book
is available from the British Library.

ISBN - 978-0-9560181-0-6

Printed and bound by Short Run Press Ltd, Exeter.

Dedicated to all the fallen innocent,
and freedom fighters past, present and future.

Acknowledgements

The way has been long and arduous in parts. But for the help of others I might not have made it; but for the support of others things would have been much more difficult.

I would thank Claire Philips, Ross Heulin, and Tori Nicholson for ferrying me over the torrent when I might have gone under; Anna and Hamish Wynn for lending me shelter when my world went dark; Miche for the rescue, and J&J for much appreciated hospitality; Tim and Deb Challern, Diane Topple, Angus McLeod, and Cliff Alderton for support and patience; Chris Hammond, Bruce Mattheson and Candy McLeavy for alternative medical support; Alex Macallister and Jody Oruesagasti for friendship and nimble fingers who, as well as Molly Strover, typed the early drafts of the manuscript; Kim Bowyer for 'making sure I did not lack'; Jac and the clan for love and tears of laughter; Sandra Gilbride for faith and daring; Vicki Sandy for embracing the vision (and the lunatic), and always looking on the bright side; Jem Turpin for the use of the casa, and for the invaluable professional proofreading service; Denise Blagden for help with the cover artwork; Colin Parker for the safe harbour; Chris Durant for the woodland retreat; and lastly, but by no means least, Pearl Wharton for willing patronage.

Thanks to those whose names I've omitted (you know who you are), whose support and words of encouragement helped during the marathon that this became, and to those who believed in me, even when I lost my way.

My gratitude and respect to those dedicated and brave individuals whose words, wisdom, and 'out of the box' research are threaded through this work.

Disclaimer

The characters in this novel are fictional. Any resemblance to any person living or dead is coincidental and unintentional.

The information, technology and techniques revealed in this novel are not fictional. The responsibility, or credit, for what happens to an person as a result of utilising any of them rests solely with that person.

For evil to triumph it only needs that the good do nothing.

– Edmund Burke

... the absolute right not to be tortured or subject to treatment which is inhuman or degrading.
— Article 3, European Convention on Human Rights

The sound he made was more feline than human, a soft high-pitched whine falling to a low, mewling wail.

He hung from the ceiling by a chain, hands above his head, his thumbs red-black bloated plums above the toy-like cuffs. The big toe of his left foot traced tight, meandering grooves in the slimy ochre-tinged puddle on the grey concrete floor.

Again the sound, longer this time, pleading. He passed out again. A thread of spittle dribbled out of the slack mouth and fell in viscous slow motion into the puddle.

Footsteps echoing in the corridor snapped him awake. His trapped eyes swung to the door as they stopped outside it. Pins pulsed through his arms and hands with each thudding heartbeat.

Metal scraped in metal and the door opened. A man in a grey suit stepped in, blinking in the bright glare. He pulled out a pair of dark sunglasses and put them on. Behind him a short, muscular man in black combat trousers and tee shirt entered and closed the door.

Ignoring the suited man, Jared stared at the other, hatred and panic twisting his guts. The man smiled back and then stepped forward, his smile widening.

Jared's eyes leapt toward the suited man. 'I told you, I don't know anything!'

The man's face remained frozen in what could have been a smile or a sneer.

Renewed panic gripped Jared's chest, constricting his breath.

The little man unclipped a black stubby shape from his belt.

Jared began to struggle, panicking more as the motion swung his field of view past his torturer. His toes, barely touching the floor, made futile skating movements as he tried to turn himself around.

The man, still smiling, brought the baton up and touched him below the ribs.

The current kicked through Jared's flesh, jack-knifing him violently, snapping his jaws shut. The man stepped to the side and stroked the baton down his spine. Again his body spasmed, arching forward. Hot bile flooded his mouth and nose as his stomach turned in on itself. He choked and spat.

The man stood in front of him again and pointed the baton at his crotch.

Jared swung wildly, ignoring the searing pain in his thumbs. Spray from his flailing kick spattered his torturer. The man scowled and wiped his face, then lunged, eyes shining. Jared grunted as if hit on the head. A wave passed up his body, squeezing out a sudden whooping scream, lungs joining bladder in convulsive evacuation before he slammed into unconsciousness.

***

They were coming. He could sense their fast approaching menace. The sound grew quickly above the cheering and whistling of the crowd. The wind seemed to be playing with the sound, pushing it around so that the cheering rolled like surf, hiding the harsh chopping sound and then returning it louder. His dry mouth tasted metallic and sharp, and his legs trembled with the urge to run.

Suddenly there they were, two matt black military helicopters, giant hornets, deafening wings punishing the air. People started running. The pounding stormed closer. A frantic voice shouted his name from somewhere out of sight. Gunfire slashed through the air. Instinct overrode disbelief and he dived onto concrete, hitting his face above the eye.

He reeled back, arms swimming, blankets tangling his feet, bedside table swimming in and out of focus.

'Dan, Dan!'

'Alright!' Dan shouted, clutching his head with one hand.

The banging stopped. In the chastened silence that followed he walked unsteadily across the room to the door. On the small screen by the door he saw a woman pacing to and fro across the narrow corridor. He lifted the bar from its brackets and unlocked the door.

'What the fuck is wrong with you,' shouted the woman, pushing the door open and striding in, 'how long does it take to open a fucking door?'

Dan closed the door and dropped the bar back into place.

'Mornin' Pat. Something important was it?' He rubbed the growing lump above his eye.

'Yes, Jared's been arrested.'

Dan's hand fell from his head.

'What? Shit! When, how?'

'An hour ago, maybe more I'm not sure.'

Dan grabbed a pair of crumpled jeans off the floor and began pulling them on. Pat carried on pacing.

'We were on our way to the multi-storey to pick up the mobile. They must've been following us or waiting, I don't know. As soon as we turned off near the derelict pub they were all over us.' Tears welled up in her eyes. 'Jared swung the car round, but they were behind us too. He just put his foot down and drove at them. They started shooting…he hit one of them…' Tears rolled down her face. 'They shot him, Dan.'

Dan froze, trainer in hand. 'Dead?'

Pat shook her head. 'Badly, in his shoulder, but now they've got him.'

Dan pulled the trainer on and then grabbed a bag and began stuffing clothes into it. A laptop followed a rain of discs.

'Okay, let's go,' he said, spinning round.

Pat looked confused, but allowed Dan to usher her out of the room. At the door he turned and looked around the room. He sighed. 'Shit.'

At the street door he held Pat back. 'Stay there, I'll bring the car round.'

He stood by the car and went through a pantomime of finding his keys, feeling in each pocket as he checked the street. Except for a couple of youths on skateboards it was empty. He jumped into the car and reversed quickly.

'There's a blanket there, get under it,' he said, as Pat climbed into the back.

'Dan, what are we doing?' Pat shouted, as they accelerated away.

'You could have been tracked. Thought it might– '

He swung the wheel and the car swerved, narrowly missing a large black van careering round the corner, blue lights flashing.

'Shit, shit,' he panted, checking the rear view mirror.

'What's going on, Dan?'

Dan didn't reply. His eyes flitted from the mirror to the road.

'Dan?'

Dan looked in the mirror again. It didn't look like the van had turned to follow them.

'A van full of cops.'

Pat didn't reply.

'That was fuckin' close.'

'I'm sorry, Dan.'

'Not your fault. You'd need to be invisible to get past the cameras. That was fuckin' close though,' he shook his head. 'Can't believe how close that was!'

In the mirror he saw Pat sit up.

'Best if you stay down, I reckon. All the cameras in the area will be scanning for you. Be a good idea to ditch these wheels soon too.

'Tell me what happened to Jared.'

Jared felt the hammer blow from behind, saw his jacket explode outward and the windshield shatter into filigree opaqueness splattered with crimson, all in the same moment. There was a sudden roaring in his ears and what felt like flames running down one arm and the side of his neck.

4

His hand still gripped the steering wheel, but he couldn't move it. He let go with his other hand and punched the windscreen. Shards of glass showered into the car.

'You okay?'

He glanced round. Pat was crouched down sideways, surrounded by white mosaic. She nodded.

He took a quick look in the mirror. The bulk of a Squad van seemed to fill the road and was bearing down on them. He wrenched his hand off the steering wheel, slammed the gears and pulled the brake on, shouting as pain ripped through his shoulder and neck.

'Next corner and you bail out. I'll meet you at Dan's!'

Getting no reply he glanced round again. Pat sat staring at the ragged bloody hole in his jacket and the limp arm.

'Pat!'

'Yeah, okay!'

He looked back to the mirror. The van shot into view, skidding wide and slamming into a parked car.

'Okay, this one, there's gardens on your side!'

Pat was flung into the door as Jared cornered the car and skidded to a halt. She spilled out and immediately over a wall, and fell crashing through greenery. Her feet hit soft soil and she buckled to her knees. Sirens screamed by above.

She stood and looked around the garden. The walls were lined with neatly pruned dark green bushes, and rows of vegetables bordered a small lawn. At one end of the lawn three elderly women, their iridescent saris like giant jewels against the verdant background, sat around a low table, their actions freeze-framed; cup raised to mouth, hand in mid-gesture, all staring at her. In the instant she registered the scene it blinked into animation; the cup returned to the table, hand to lap, and one of the women rose slowly and walked toward her.

'I'm really sorry,' said Pat, stepping onto the path.

The woman shook her head gently and indicated behind her slowly with an open hand.

Pat walked around her, past the silent, staring women and along the side of the house. At the gate she stopped and looked to the end of the road. Two cars sat crumpled, accordion-like, across the middle of the junction. Beside them the blunt shape of the security van. One black jumpsuited figure was standing legs astride, both hands outstretched pointing at a shape on the floor. Another moved in close and made quick movements around the shape. Pat grimaced as they lifted the figure upright.

'You friend?'

Pat looked at the woman and nodded. They watched the figures bundle Jared into the back of the van and drive away, leaving two dayglo-jacketed figures directing traffic.

Pat felt the woman move behind her and looked round.

The woman indicated with a tilt of her head. 'Go, quick.'

Seeing her reflection in the mirror, Pat made a face, spat on her sleeve and rubbed the blood from her cheek.

'I need to sort some ID out. I think mine's in the rhododendrons.'

Dan looked at her in the mirror. Pat shook her head at the silent question.

'Nah, I don't reckon she would, even if she found it.'

'Let's hope she finds it and bins it. Sid's first then, and then ditch the car and find somewhere to crash.'

He struggled to concentrate on the road. Pedestrians, motorists, traffic lights, cameras, there was too much to concentrate on to think about Jared nicked...shot even.

He looked in the mirror. 'You okay?'

Pat opened her mouth, hesitated, then burst into tears. She hid her face in her hands.

'Pat?'

'I'm alright,' came the mumbled reply.

Dan stared at the road, his mind working at high speed. They weren't out of it yet. Pat must have been tracked. Which meant they were probably still being tracked. Probably definitely. He fidgeted in his seat, feeling like a specimen under a microscope.

A car park sign caught his eye. He slowed and turned down the ramp.

'What're you doing?' Pat asked, looking up.

'Ditching the car.'

At the barrier he took the ticket from the machine. The barrier rose and he drove in. He parked the car close to the entrance and rummaged in his bag. He pulled out a cigarette packet-sized black box and a baseball cap. He put the cap on and took a deep breath.

'Set?'

'Yeah.'

They got out of the car and walked toward the entrance. Dan fed the ticket into the machine and put a coin into the slot. The machine buzzed and the ticket returned. They walked back toward the car. Dan fumbled with the box and pressed the button. Beeps and clunks sounded around them, and lights flashed on several cars.

'Silver Audi on your left,' he said.

He slipped quickly into the drivers seat, reached under the dashboard, grabbed a handful of wires and pulled them out. Singling out two wires, he pulled them out of the connectors and touched them together. The engine rumbled into life. He let his breath out noisily and wound the wires together. He pulled out carefully, anxious not to stall. The car moved forward like a reined in racehorse. At the barrier he fed the ticket into the slot. The barrier rose and they drove out.

He turned back the way they'd come. Five hundred yards down the road he drove round the block and looped back again. The action felt futile, but it had to be done. He drove in silence wondering about moving goalposts and about Jared.

He parked the car as far away as he could without giving them too far to walk. They walked hand in hand, Pat hunched over with her chin near her chest.

'Chill out for fuck's sake,' Dan mumbled. 'Keep acting shifty and we'll get a tug.'

'Doesn't help having no ID and my face possibly digimatched to every camera and patrol in the city.'

'Well even if it's not there's still the behavioural recognition, so relax eh.'

He paused and pointed to the window they were passing.

'Rhubarb, rhubarb, rhubarb.'

Pat looked at him. 'You what?'

'Rhubarb, rhubarb. Pointing in shop windows and talking bollocks.'

Pat laughed and pulled him, and they carried on walking. She squeezed Dan's hand and he returned the squeeze.

They stepped into a print shop. It was empty except for a man loading paper into a machine. Dan nodded to him, then gestured to the door behind the counter. The man nodded and returned to feeding the machine. Through the door at the end of a corridor was another door. Dan pressed the intercom on the wall.

'Hey Sid, what's cooking Doc?'

'Hiya Dan,' replied a tinny voice, 'come on down.'

The door lock buzzed and Dan pulled the heavy door open. Dimly lit stairs led down to a low corridor with a door at the far end. The door opened into a tiny room. Dominating the room from the centre stood a long table lit with low hung lights, giving the impression of a gaming room. The table was covered with piles of leaflets and other printed sheets. A figure sitting at the far end looked up and squinted at them through thick lenses.

'Welcome to the afterlife for trees,' he said, swinging an arm over the piles of paper.

Dan squeezed past printers and photocopiers and shook hands with Sid who then stood to accept Pat's embrace, patting her back firmly. Pat squirmed.

'I know, I know, don't pat me,' he chuckled.

Pat propped herself against one of the machines.

'So, what's on?' Sid asked, looking at Dan.

'I need a new ID card,' said Pat.

'Lost your card eh?'

'Yeah, can you sort another, like rapid?'

'Bit careless wasn't it?'

'Not really. I'd say I was lucky that's all I lost. I was with Jared who's now with the Squad.'

Sid's smile vanished. He looked from Pat to Dan and back.

'Bollocks,' he said quietly, reached behind and switched off the music. The room was silent but for the hum of machinery.

'Well, are you going to give me the details or do I have to ask?'

Pat's eyes narrowed and she pushed herself off the machine. 'Fuck you, Sid!' She stabbed a finger at him. 'You've got no fucking idea, stuck in your fucking hidey hole, playing with your machines and bits of paper while some of us are out there on the frontline. How fucking dare you!'

'Easy, Pat,' said Dan.

'Well,' she glanced at Dan, then back at Sid, 'fucking bullshit! Come on out and dodge some bullets for a change!'

Dan looked at Sid and shook his head.

'Pat, you're right, that was crap of me,' said Sid. 'I'm sorry okay? Okay?'

Pat stared at the table saying nothing.

'Come on Pat, it sounds like you've got shit to sort, let's do it. Tell me about Jared.'

He sat not moving except for the rapid blinking of his eyes, tiny behind the owl-like specs, as Pat spoke.

'Having blag ID is one thing,' he said as soon as Pat finished, 'but snatched with a transmitter, not to mention running one of them over – '

'But we hadn't got to the transmitter before they jumped us.'

'Whatever,' said Sid. 'If the Squad's got Jared then they think he's something to do with it, which he is. It's only a matter of time before they're kicking our doors down. Not dissing Jared, but we all know how it is. He'll hold out as long as he can, but we should get moving. Pass the message on and drop out. I'll tat down here and be gone in an hour. You got a place?'

Pat nodded.

'Okay. Contact through the Vineyard then, but stay off the streets. And I think it's time you reviewed your broadcasting practices.'

'Yeah? Well thanks for the advice,' said Pat. She turned to Dan. 'C'mon.'

'Give me three days for the card and keep me posted on Jared,' said Sid.

'Will do,' said Dan. 'Be lucky.'

'Yeah, yous too.'

The man in the shop stopped them on the way out and handed them a large brown envelope.

Dan looked puzzled.

'Shop sample pack.'

'Oh yeah. Thanks.'

Pat stared at herself in the bathroom mirror. She rested her head against the cold surface, listening to her heart pound. Sounds echoed through her, screeching tyres, breaking glass, the thud of flesh against metal...his face... She straightened up quickly and took a deep breath.

'That's enough, snap out of it,' she said to her reflection.

She ran the shower hot enough to make her wince and forced herself to stand under it, moving so that the water needled her neck and shoulders. She groaned as tension flowed out of her muscles, and then without warning started to cry, the noise barely audible above the shower. She crouched and hugged her knees, letting the emotions wash through her, joining the tears and snot running over her arms and legs.

Finally the crying passed. She stood and spun the tap to cold. The icy spray made her catch her breath. She leaned forward against the tiles and screamed.

The vodka had been working on Dan's adrenaline-scoured nerves, but Pat's scream made him tense up again. Sounded like she was cracking up. He decided against knocking on the bathroom door. She'd shout if she needed anything. But what was he going to do? He couldn't go back to his flat, that was for sure, and was probably already on a Squad 'wanted for help with their inquiries' list. Already a file would have been put together, beginning with his postcode, comprising a huge amount of data on him. His parents would get a visit and probably be watched. Another good thing about not having a phone was that they couldn't plot his movements, or question calling history numbers.

The sun slanted through the wide windows running the length of the room, lighting the dark wooden floor. He looked around trying to visualise the owner of the flat. They were into fitness judging by the multigym in one corner, and a technofreak for sure, with that biometric laser lock and the voice-activated alarm

On a long green glass desk sat a small laptop and the bulk of some complex looking hardware. Half walls, clean, shoulder high lines of khaki green and white bisected the airy warehouse space, making alcoves for kitchen and office space. A gold cube, nearly reaching the ceiling, occupied one corner and housed the bathroom where Pat was showering. He hadn't ventured up onto the bedroom platform, although he'd climbed partway up the stairs. The fact that they came straight out of the wall with no other support begged at least one try, but, not wanting to invade his host's privacy, he'd stopped halfway. Pat had said it was a friend's place, but the TV puzzled him. People he knew in the Resistance didn't expose themselves to television.

The switch to digital television was seen by some to mark a milestone in the rise of the Resistance. Ironically, what had been put in place as one of the last invisible bars in the population's prison had also triggered an intuitive realisation in certain sensitive individuals that their minds were being messed with.

Maybe she, or he, wasn't part of the Resistance. Or maybe they had one just to be on record as having one to avoid the suspicion not having one would generate.

He walked over to the window and looked out over the river, and thought about what Jared would be going through. Like Sid said, they all knew how it was. Everyone knew how it was.

Pat came out of the bathroom and padded silently behind him. She put her hands gently on his shoulders and began squeezing the tense muscles. Dan slumped, moaning appreciatively.

'You okay, Dan?'

'Yeah, I'm alright,' he turned. 'How about you? You look better.'

'Yeah, I feel it.'

'So, come on, whose is this place?'

'Papa's.'

'Didn't know he came to this country that much.'

'He doesn't anymore. I've used it more than him these past

years, and that's not much.'

'Nice pad. Feels safe.'

'Safer than you know, a proper bolthole. Nobody gets in here that's not invited. He designed the alarm system himself. It's got a sub-bass intruder immobiliser that shuts down certain neuromuscular functions. And it feeds him data wherever he is. He already knows I'm here.'

'What's he got in here then?'

'Nothing he couldn't replace…except me at the moment. He's just into privacy and personal security. He also doesn't like the fact that I'm in this country on my own without any family to look after me, as he puts it. When we were kids we even had a nanny that was ex-military.'

'Didn't know you had any brothers or sisters.'

'Just one brother.'

'Where's he then?'

There was a pause and a vibe that told Dan he'd just overstepped Pat's personal territory boundary.

'Him and my mum were killed a few years ago.'

The phrase struck Dan as strange, but he didn't pry. It was weird, you could know someone for years and still not really know them. He knew Pat's dad was some kind of a diplomat, but didn't understand how he'd not heard about the rest of her family. Knowing Pat though, it was likely that she would have sidestepped any questions.

Pat shivered.

'You okay?' Dan asked

'Mm, yeah…dunno, think so. Actually, no I'm not. I feel sick and I can't stop shaking. But I am, a lot better than Jared must be right now. There must be something we can do for him.'

'Such as?'

'Such as…well I don't know. Something though, instead of just standing here.'

'Maybe we could wander over to the Yard and see if they'll let us see him.'

'I'm being serious!'

'No you're not. The Squad have got him, there's nothing we

can do for him. Right now us here is the only thing we can do.' He sighed. 'Say a prayer maybe.'

***

Jared flexed his wrists, trying to ease the grip of the plastic ratchet cord that fixed his arms and legs to the chair. The tension was creating an excruciating, bursting pressure in his hands.

'I wouldn't bother.'

Jared looked up at the black lenses. 'Jus' tryin' to get comfortable,' he mumbled through swollen lips.

'As I said, I wouldn't bother. You're not here to be comfortable.'

'What am I here for?'

'Oh, various motoring offences, attempted murder of a Squad officer, ID fraud, conscription evasion. Plenty for you to worry about.'

'That's reassuring,' said Jared, still squirming. 'I was beginning to think I'd fallen in with some bondage freaks.'

The man's expression didn't change. 'Save your humour, Jared, it gets worse.'

Jared's torturer stepped from behind the chair. In place of the electrobaton he held a small, black pistol-grip shape, like a voltage tester. Four tiny electrodes protruded from the end like snake's tongues. He held it up for Jared to see and squeezed the button. There was a snapping, buzzing sound and a blue-white line arced across the points. He moved it slowly down to Jared's hand.

Jared struggled in the chair, sending it toppling sideways. Lights exploded in his head as it bounced on the floor.

The man struggled to right the chair, cursing. He repositioned it then, holding the back of the chair with one hand, swung the stun gun hanging from his other wrist, caught it and held it so that Jared's forefinger was between the electrodes. The gun crackled again and Jared sat bolt upright, the veins standing out in his neck as the current raced through him. He screamed an out of control falsetto, which ended abruptly as the gun was withdrawn. He slumped forward in the chair, panting.

'These rather Neanderthal methods are just a morale boosting payback. One really can't go round running down members of the Security Services. As for finding out what you know –'

'I want to see a solicitor.'

'I don't think so.'

'I have the right to see a solicitor.'

'You are a communist terrorist, Jared, a non-person, and as such you don't have any rights.'

'I need to see a doctor, I've been shot.'

'As I said Jared, it gets worse. Now, I'd like the names of all the other people involved in this little propaganda exercise.'

'There isn't anybody else.'

The man nodded to the waiting electrocutioner.

'There isn't anybody else, I built it myself!'

He threw his body from side to side, but the man held the chair. The stun gun pressed against Jared's neck and he froze. He sat not daring to move, eyes and mouth wide, as the man moved it slowly down to his hand. His hand bunched into a fist, reflex overriding fear and pain.

Jared looked across to the man in the suit. 'Look, I'm sorry about the man, it was an accident. The transmitter I made myself, it's no big deal, just a bit of pirate TV for fucks sake! I'm not a terrorist!'

There was a sudden movement and the stun gun was at his chest, snapping and buzzing. He screamed again; pierced all over with white-hot needles, razor blades running down his arms, and the sound of his blood boiling in his ears. His nipple was being twisted and ripped off his chest. Every joint in his body ground against the next, twisting out of their sockets, jerked every which way by his spasming muscles. There was a rapid wrenching along his spine.

'Aaah...stop! Stop!'

The snapping and buzzing stopped.

'Fuck...fuck!'

'You were about to give me the names of your accomplices.'

'You can't do this...aah...fuck! You can't do this. I'm a British citizen, I've got rights, you can't do this.'

'As I've said, you're a non-person Jared, a terrorist,' the man spoke as if he was addressing a child. 'You relinquished what rights you may have had the moment you began working towards undermining the security of the State.'

'I told you, I –'

'I know what you told me, Jared. I also know that you're lying. There was a passenger in the car prior to your arrest. I'd like their details. Your ID card is a forgery; I'd also like the details of who did it. Starting with the passenger.'

'They were just along for the ride; they didn't have anything to…aah!

The electrodes spat. His vision fizzed like an out of signal TV image.

'A name.'

'What, so you two can have some fun with a fresh victim?'

He struggled in the chair, but the man held it tight. There was nowhere to hide; the current invaded every cell, blistering his body and mind. The word lobotomy flashed through his head. His brain was being fried. He could smell burning hair as well as the sickly sweet odour of his cooking flesh.

The current stopped and he flopped forward, retching and gulping air.

'You can't do this,' he panted, 'it's against the law.'

'I am the law, Jared.' Again the gentle tones. 'I am doing this, and I will have a name.'

The electrodes spat again. Jared's throat constricted, strangling the scream.

2

We humans are the most exquisite device ever made for the experiencing of pain: the richer our inner lives, the greater the varieties of pain there are for us to feel – and the more recourses we will have for mitigating pain…Never forget how painful pain is – nor how fear magnifies pain.

– Oxford Handbook of Clinical Medicine

He could hear the sea, the slow crumple and hiss of waves breaking and retreating. Everywhere was dark. Wherever everywhere was. Definitely a beach, the sound of the surf was really close, but where? And what was he doing sitting on a beach in the middle of the night?

Well, at least he wasn't hurting any more. Actually he couldn't feel a thing. He looked down at his body, invisible in the dark. He reached down, but couldn't feel anything. Why couldn't he feel his legs? He lifted his hands up to touch his face. Nothing.

The surf boomed closer.

He looked up at the rapidly reddening sky. It was the wrong colour, blood red…and getting closer, collapsing, bearing down on him. He tried to move and realised he was, silently catapulting toward the sky.

Light sliced into his brain. Weight and pain poured in through his cracked shell of a body. Galloping on the back of the rush of physical sensations came memories of how they got there. His body jerked spasmodically, dragging the clammy skin of his face on the floor of the cell. They must have got bored when he passed out again and just dumped him back in the cell. He lifted his head. The bench looked like a ten-foot wall.

Still lying on his side he drew his knees up to his chest,

16

snorting and yelping involuntarily, and levered himself onto his knees. Forehead resting on the floor he began to cry quietly.

He seemed to be three people, one, broken on the floor, listening to two arguing in his head.

Get up; you look like you're praying to the bog. I can't, it hurts. Well, it's not going to stop hurting stuck there, lie on the bench and hurt. I can't. Course you can. I don't want to move, I don't want to hurt, I don't want them to hurt me any more. Forget that, come on just get up. Fuck you. Come on. Fuck you. Fuck you.

'Fuck you,' he bubbled quietly, and rolled slowly back onto his side.

The cell door slammed open. A guard rushed in and began kicking him in the back and buttocks.

'Get up on the bench you lazy cunt, where d'ya think you are!'

Jared struggled onto his elbows and knees. Another kick punted him against the toilet. He crabbed round and held his injured hands out in front of him.

'Alright, alright!'

The guard stepped closer. 'Not fast enough, move!'

Jared scrambled up backward using the toilet for leverage. His body kept twitching and drawing out high-pitched gasps.

'Sit down and shut it!'

The sitting was easy, a barely controlled collapse. There was no question of conscious control over his body though, and the jittering and whimpering continued. The guard moved in close and raised a fist. Jared flinched and cried out. The guard chuckled and walked out.

Jared waited until the door of the cell banged shut then sat up slowly, shame and defeat adding to the pain. His insides felt wrenched and broken. He tried to take a deep breath to stop the shaking, but it made it worse. His head shook like a demented marionette complete with clacking jaw, as if he were still being electrocuted. Every pore screamed. He could still smell his burned flesh. Even the air felt taut, and threatened to strangle him, tightening with every out-breath.

The room shimmered in the glare of the light and exploded toward him like a smashed mirror. He closed his eyes against the glare and the hallucinations, but they didn't stop. Behind his closed eyelids points of coloured light kaleidoscoped into fractal shapes, bulbous geometry, and weird laughing faces melting in and out of each other.

He started to panic. His mind was coming apart. He had to do something; he couldn't let it go the same way as his body. He tried to picture Dan's face, but the hallucinations persisted. Screaming, bloodied visages melted and reformed and the gory miasma settled into Dan's barely recognisable form, twisted and bloody, sprawled on the pavement punctured with multiple bullet holes.

Jared opened his eyes and looked frantically around the tiny cell. The blank plastic walls bounced the harsh light back at him. His heart was tripping over itself and forcing its way up into his throat.

His panic deepened. He stood unsteadily to relieve the pain in his coccyx from the guards kick, and realised with a small feeling of triumph that his feet were actually pain-free.

A sound at the door made him look up. The spy hole opened and the door became a bizarre, rectangular Cyclops. Just as suddenly the cover slid back and the door swung open. The guard muscled in again and stood in front of him. Jared stood frozen, looking at his feet.

'Thought I told you to sit on the bench.'

'I was just –'

The guard stamped on his foot and punched him in the stomach. Jared doubled up and fell back onto the bench.

'Just sit on the fuckin' bench!'

He stared at Jared lying sideways fighting for breath, and looked to be debating another blow, both fists bunched at his sides. Eventually he turned back out of the cell. The door slammed shut sending vibrations through the wall and bench.

Jared sat up slowly, painfully gulping breath, his short-lived triumph shattered, broken like at least one of his toes. Tears stung his eyes and he gritted his teeth.

The sharp pain rose up his leg. He gingerly shifted his weight from one buttock to the other, hissing at the pain in his hands as he put weight on them. He fought back miserable tears. He couldn't think straight.

When were they going to stop? They had to stop eventually. Were they purposely trying to wear him down, or was everybody just venting their sick power fantasies?

The cell door slammed opened and two guards muscled in. Both wore latex rubber gloves.

'On your feet!'

He stood unsteadily, trembling.

'Strip!'

He reached automatically, but then stopped and held up his hands.

'I can't.'

'That's just the beginning, toe-rag. Turn around!'

He limped round and closed his eyes, expecting the blow. He flinched as something was run up his back. There was the sound of tearing fabric. Then again up the outsides of his legs.

'Turn around!'

He shuffled around again. His top opened, slit up the back, and his jeans flapped like chaps momentarily before crumpling around his feet.

One of the guards grabbed the front of his top and yanked it down and off. Jared cried out as the fabric dragged over his hands.

The guard chuckled. 'Just the beginning.'

Both guards turned and walked out of the cell, leaving the door open.

Jared stood there exposed and confused, goose pimples playing over his naked flesh. What now? Was he supposed to follow them?

One of the guards reappeared in the doorway with a fire hose under his arm. The jet hit Jared in the belly, winding him and slamming him back against the wall. He stumbled against the toilet, slipped on the slick floor, and went down. The rim of the toilet scraped the length of his spine as he fell and wedged upside down between it and the bench. Water rushed up his nose.

He lost all sense of direction and flailed his legs trying to get himself loose. The jet kept catching his legs and forcing them back into the air. He breathed water, choked and cried out.

The water ceased pounding him. A guard grabbed his leg and jerked him out of the bind. He lay coughing and spluttering.

The guard barked at him to get up. He struggled up as quickly as he could. He had barely got to his feet when the jet hit him again. This time he was more ready for it and lurched into the corner beside the toilet. He crouched down and forced his head into the corner. The water felt like somebody hitting his back with sticks. The jet was aimed at his neck and head, but not enough water reached his face to bother him. It felt like it was scouring the skin off his back though.

Eventually the pummelling stopped and the guard barked at him to get up. He stood and looked round cautiously. The hose was gone. The remaining guard threw something at him. He flinched and covered his face with his arms. Something lightweight hit him and fell onto the floor.

'Get dressed!'

The door slammed.

He looked down. A small white bundle lay slowly soaking up water. He picked the thing up with both hands. It unravelled to reveal a kind of boiler suit coverall made out of hospital gown material.

The sight of the suit distressed him more than he could explain. Something in him rebelled at the thought of putting it on. He wanted to shout and refuse to put it on, but he knew he couldn't. He stood frozen, staring at it.

A sound at the door made him jump and nearly piss himself. Ignoring the pain in his hands, he struggled into the suit. He tried leaning a shoulder on the wall for support, but had to sit on the bench. He didn't try to do up the buttons on the front.

The cell door opened.

'Out!'

He got up and shuffled out. Two guards stood in the corridor, one slapping a nightstick against his palm.

'Wrists!'

He lifted his hands and a pair of handcuffs was clamped around his wrists. He winced as the cuffs clamped the bone.

'Walk!'

He limped after the guard, nearly stumbling as he tried to keep up with him. He had to walk using the heel of his injured foot with a halting, bird-like motion.

He passed what looked like other cell doors, all closed. There were no sounds other than their footsteps.

He hesitated at the bottom of a flight of stairs, unable to work out how to position his foot. A stinging blow against the back of his legs made him fall forward. His hands went out instinctively to break his fall before he realised what he was doing and moved them and hit the stairs with his shoulder.

'Stand up and get up those fuckin' stairs,' growled the guard.

He pushed himself onto his knees with his elbows and managed to stand up without having to use his hand on the banister. He climbed the steps one at a time, taking his weight on the heel of his foot turned at a right angle to the other.

At the top of the stairs they went through into another corridor and stopped outside a door. The guard knocked and put his head round the door, and then motioned Jared inside. Jared limped in and the door closed behind him.

A square table and two chairs sat in the middle of the windowless room. A woman in civilian clothes sat in one of the chairs reading a file. A man, also in civilian clothes, stood leaning against a wall, arms crossed, staring at him.

The woman looked up. 'Come in,' she said, and went back to reading the file.

He shuffled over. On the table was a large envelope. The woman closed the file and put it on the table on top of the envelope. His name was printed on the front.

'You're here to answer some questions,' said the woman. 'Once you've answered those questions we can get you sorted out.'

He lifted his hands. 'You mean fix the damage?'

The woman's eyes remained on his face.

'No, that's not what I meant.'

'There's a man seriously ill in hospital after you ran him over,' said the man, suddenly close behind him, making him jump and stiffen.

'It was an accident,' said Jared, looking at the woman.

'Okay, Jared,' said the woman. 'It is Jared isn't it?'

He nodded.

'The reason I wasn't certain is because the ID card you were carrying is a forgery. The first thing I want to know is who did it.'

He'd spent some of the time in the cell thinking about credible answers he could give that wouldn't compromise anybody. The nature of the ID black market, and of the brutal Squad, made it easy for him to come up with a story in which he didn't know any of the players by name.

He told a story of a man in a pub who was known to arrange forged ID for draft dodgers and refugees. Both the woman and the man kept interrupting with questions, some of which seemed totally unrelated.

He began to find it increasingly difficult to concentrate because of light-headedness caused by a combination of the pains and from standing up. Maintaining his balance was made difficult by the damage to his foot. His spine ached and his legs kept trembling. Dots and stars appeared and disappeared in his vision.

'So why couldn't you just refuse the draft like the other gutless whiners?'

Jared glanced round, but couldn't see the man still positioned behind him. 'Look how they're treated.'

As far as most people were concerned, conscientious objectors were cowards, traitors, and supporters of terrorism and communism. Through the resistance network he'd met several who suffered. Sometimes it was easier to go underground than to face the smashed windows, petrol through the letterbox, abuse in the streets, and the more subtle refusals for jobs, etc, that began to form a pattern for most.

The questions turned to the transmitter, which he said he built himself. Luckily he'd helped Dan build it, so could explain it as if he knew more of what he was talking about than he did. As he spoke the man walked from behind him and stood in front.

'Who's your contact in the PLO?'

The sudden tangential question stopped him mid-sentence.

'The PLO?'

The man sighed. 'And there I was hoping the room wouldn't develop an echo.'

He grabbed Jared by the front of the boiler suit and bellowed in his face. 'You heard me, the People's Liberation Organisation! You have heard of them, haven't you?'

He let go and Jared staggered back, struggling to stay upright.

'What makes you think I'm in contact with them?'

The man stepped closer. Jared looked down.

'You're getting a bit confused now. We ask questions, you give answers, get it.'

'I don't have any contact with the PLO,' said Jared, still looking down.

'Where do you get the war footage from?'

'Off the Internet and from refugees.'

'You expect me to believe that?'

'No, but it's true. The footage of the wedding party getting shot up by the patrol was someone's home video. The dead bride was his daughter. The pictures of kids with phosphorus burns, or mangled by cluster bombs, were taken by the medics that –'

'You still haven't told us your method of contact with the PLO,' said the man.

'That's because I don't have contact with them. They're major league, bombs and stuff. All I'm into is a bit of pirate TV, no big deal.'

'Working against your government is treason, Jared. That is a big deal.'

'How can working for peace be treasonous?'

The man jabbed a finger at him making him flinch.

'I told you, we ask the questions, not you!'

'Okay,' said the woman, 'let's calm down a bit shall we?'

The man straightened up and stepped a few paces back.

'Have you got a girlfriend, Jared?'

He looked at the woman and shook his head.

'Nothing in the pipeline, not got your eye on anybody?'

He shook his head again. An insight presented itself. He'd not thought about it before, but it stood to reason that there was going to be a method to the process. First the abuse to wear him down physically, then the questioning. And the questioning itself, the empty, windowless room, the good cop/bad cop routine all slotted into place. The realisation did nothing to help him.

The man moved in close again. 'Are you gay then?'

He didn't answer.

'I said, are you a bum boy?'

He looked up slowly into the man's face.

'Why, you cruising?'

The backhanded blow caught him across his cheek and knocked him to the floor. Aside from the pain from the half-expected blow and the fall, it was actually a relief not to be standing.

'Hey, come on, take it easy,' said the woman.

'I'm handling this,' growled the man. 'I've broken scumbags like this before, and I'll break this one wide open! On your feet scum!'

Jared manoeuvred himself onto his knees and elbows and struggled to his feet. He glanced over at the woman, hoping that she'd step in and stop the abuse, and immediately hated himself for it. That was their game. She was the enemy too.

The abusive pantomime continued with the man alternately bellowing into his face and asking him questions about things he knew nothing of. Answers to that effect produced more verbal abuse.

The man stood with his hands on his hips, and then leaned toward Jared suddenly. Jared jumped and flinched.

'Repeat after me, I am a lying scumbag.'

Jared didn't speak.

The man slapped his face. The slap stung but, compared to recent pains, was nothing. Shock and humiliation rated higher.

He cringed inside, tensing, waiting for the next one. His hands twitched with the urge to lift and protect himself.

'Repeat after me, I am a lying scumbag.'

'I've told you what I've done, and I've –' he flinched again as the man cuffed him around the head.

He lifted his hands and the man slapped them away. The sudden return to the pain in his hands and all that went with it hit him like a punch in the kidney, kicking aside his flimsy defence. He yelped. The yelp stretched into a whimper that he couldn't stop. Tears streamed down his face.

The man chuckled. 'I knew you were a pillow biter.'

Jared shook his head slowly, and the whimpering turned to words. 'Please…don't…'

The woman's chair scraped on the floor and she cleared her throat. The man turned round.

'I could use a drink. Why don't you get a coffee while I have a word with Jared.'

The man turned back to Jared. 'I'll be back.'

The woman waited until the door had closed.

'Sit down, Jared.'

He sat down. Relief flowed up his legs and back. He tried and failed to control his tears.

'I apologise for my partner, but you're making this unnecessarily hard for yourself, Jared.'

'I told you – '

'I know what you told me, Jared, but there are several things wrong with your story, and it's getting to be a bit frustrating for all concerned. I'll let you into a secret. We picked up your passenger friend.'

Jared's heart banged. He wiped his eyes with a sleeve to hide any change in his expression.

'He'll have told you it's not a terrorist plot then.'

The woman stared at him before replying.

'He told us what we wanted to know, eventually. So hats off to you for holding out as long as you have, but there's no point. We've got all the time in the world, and we will get answers out of you too, eventually. Spare yourself any more pain. Look at the state of you, there's no need.'

'Tell that to your mates.'

'It's up to you, Jared.'

'I've told you what I know.'

'Okay, tell me again.'

He began repeating the story, relieved for Pat and that his story was safe from comparison. As he talked he replayed the scenes he'd crafted along with the story in his mind, trying to see it as he first 'saw' it, trusting his visual memory over his word memory.

As he spoke someone entered the room behind him. He stopped talking and glanced to the side.

'Carry on,' said the woman.

He shook his head. 'Can't remember where I was.'

'You've just gone into a pub and given a man you've never met thirteen hundred pounds, a photo and a thumbprint on some Sellotape.'

He didn't know why he'd included the Sellotape. When he'd visualised the story as it unfolded for the first time, the image of his thumbprint on a piece of Sellotape had been really vivid. After he'd said it he'd realised the bizarreness of the detail had in fact made the fiction seem more genuine.

'Did it not occur to you that this man you'd never met might just take your money and run?'

'Course it occurred to me. But I'd been told that's how it worked.'

'By who?'

'A bloke in a pub.'

'You little twat!'

Jared flinched.

The woman looked over his shoulder and shook her head. She looked back at Jared.

'What did he look like?'

'Dark brown hair, brown eyes, kind of crooked teeth…'

'Long or short hair?'

'Short.'

'How short?'

'Like a crew cut.'

26

'Accent?'

'I couldn't place it.'

'Northern or southern?'

'More southern than northern.'

'And his name was Oscar.'

'He said I could call him Oscar.'

The woman lifted the envelope off the table. She pulled out a large colour photograph and showed it to him.

'This your man?'

The print was a blow up of a regimental portrait and showed the upper body of a soldier in fatigues. Jared shook his head.

'Ever seen him before?'

'No.'

'Take a good look.'

He looked closer. The soldier was either mixed race or very tanned, he couldn't tell which, and was nearly a full head taller than the soldiers either side of him. He wasn't smiling. Did they want him to say it was him? Should he say it was? He couldn't bring himself to though, even if the man was a State-paid killer. He shook his head again.

The woman sighed and put the photo on the table. She stared at Jared, then looked over his head and nodded.

Jared tensed. The door behind him opened and closed. He swallowed against the pulse beat of panic. What was coming next? The panic swelled and he began to tremble. He didn't try to stop it, he felt so weak. It was hopeless to try. It was all hopeless. They were going to keep tearing bits off him until he went mad. His trembling muscles forced little snorts from his nose. He heard the door open again. The trembling got worse.

The woman glanced past him and nodded. 'You've been less than cooperative, Jared. I'll think you'll wish you'd been more.'

Someone gripped his shoulder, and he turned to see another uniformed guard. He started to cry. He couldn't help it. His tense stomach cramped. He shook his head. 'I've told you…I don't…please…I don't know anymore.' The tears were beyond control.

The guard pulled him up.

Jared's eyes stayed on the woman. 'Please…'

The woman gestured to the guard with her head, and the guard pulled his arm.

Bad Cop stood by the open door, arms folded across his chest, shaking his head, smiling. Jared looked down and shuffled out of the room.

The guard, there was only one this time, held onto his elbow as they walked, leading less than supporting.

'This is wrong,' said Jared.

'Just tell them what they want to know,' said the guard quietly.

Jared looked up. 'I've told them everything I know.'

The guard didn't respond.

'They're electrocuting me.'

'The prisoner is advised to speak only when answering questions,' replied the guard, staring ahead.

The reply jerked Jared inside. He thought he'd felt sympathy in the man's touch. But again, what was he thinking? The man was part of the meat grinder he'd fallen into. Sympathetic he might have been, but he was doing his job anyway.

His pace slowed rapidly. He was light-headed and had no strength in his legs. They felt shaky enough to give way. He felt like an old man.

The guard led him back downstairs and along another corridor. He stopped and knocked on a door. There was a reply from inside. The guard opened the door and stood back without looking into the room. Jared looked at him as he shuffled past, but the man avoided his eye.

Jared's bladder loosened and his feet faltered to a standstill. The door clicked shut behind him.

Standing beside a chair in the middle of the room were the dungeon master and the gimp. The dungeon master unclasped his hands and motioned to the chair.

'Do come in and sit down, Jared.'

Jared shook his head, fighting back tears.

The gimp took his hands from his hips.

Jared's feet jerked him forward. He shuffled slowly, focusing

28

on the chair away from the sneering of the two men. Each stumbling step took him closer, but with each step the distance left seemed huge. Tears sprang into his eyes.

He reached the chair, still avoiding the men's eyes. The wooden seat was stained. He sat down.

The gimp moved to the front and secured his wrists and ankles to the chair with ratchet cord. The trembling and twitching continued.

The dungeon master walked in front of him.

'So, here we are again. I hear in the interim you've been, what was the phrase, less than cooperative. No matter. You may have some idea that the facts you're withholding are important in some way. Allow me to disabuse you of the notion. Anything you know is, like you yourself, worthless.

'Finding out what you know will be simplicity itself with the drugs and equipment at my disposal. At present I'm not interested in what you may know, although I intend to scour your mind most thoroughly, make no mistake. No, I find the human organism's capacity for pain fascinating. As a species we're uniquely predisposed to pain in so many forms, so much more so than pleasure. For example, even in your most pleasurable moments, were the sensations anywhere near as intense as these?'

Jared looked up and tried to project all his pain and hatred through his eyes.

The man smiled. 'Come on, speak up.'

'I was right about the bondage.'

A fist slammed into the side of his face. His neck cracked as his head spun. His hair was grabbed and something hard jammed into his mouth. He opened his eyes, nostrils flaring. The baton jutted out of his mouth. A smiling, Harpo Marx face shimmered at the end of it. Jared's eyes widened and he made pleading noises through his nose, shaking his head.

Harpo's eyes widened and he nodded rapidly.

There was a dull explosion. Boiling heat filled his mouth, searing his cheeks and tongue. His throat closed, shutting off his breath. Both eardrums popped and sizzled. Then sudden, silent nothing.

Drifting unwillingly back into consciousness, his vision blearily resolved into a double image of himself, stubbled and bloody. He sat back quickly. A thin, wet smile hovered beneath the dark lenses.

'So, where were we?'

The inside of his mouth felt blistered. He cleared his throat, wincing at the pain.

'I was unconscious and you were getting your jollies,' he croaked.

The man leaned forward and put his hand on Jared's shoulder.

'Your mouth has already got you into trouble, Jared.' He dug his thumb into the bullet wound.

Jared's breath hissed.

The wet smile widened and the face moved closer.

'I'll bet your mouth's got you into trouble before that though,' the thumb dug harder, 'hasn't it?'

Jared squirmed and twisted his head away. 'What is your problem?'

The man let go, stood and walked behind him. He bent down and put his mouth close to Jared's ear. Jared leaned his head away as far as he could, which wasn't very.

'My problem, Jared, is people like you. People who think that they're outside of the law, people who think that they can transmit propaganda into the homes of innocent families; spineless cowards, happy to let others go off and fight for them. It's not enough that the Communists and Muslims are trying to destroy our country from without, your kind are a threat from within too. Fortunately, that's my problem. Society trusts me to keep its streets safe from the likes of you.'

'Who keeps the streets safe from the likes of you though?'

'There's that mouth again.'

The man straightened up, gripped Jared's head and pushed his groin against it. Clawed fingers dug into Jared's face as he strained forward. The man's grip slipped and Jared rocked forward, nearly toppling. The chair was tipped back, dragged across the floor and slammed against the wall.

'Sick bastard!'

'As I said Jared, it gets worse.'

The man stepped closer and kicked him in the stomach. Jared saw it coming but, restrained, could do nothing. The kick knocked the breath out of him.

The man stood astride the chair and shoved his groin against Jared's face. Jared struggled, his head forced back against the wall, trying to turn his already battered mouth from the pressure of the man's now bulging crotch.

The man gripped tighter and thrust harder, his zip tearing Jared's lips. Saliva spattered on Jared's head, falling from the man's open mouth.

He stood back suddenly, his face flushed, moved to the side and slapped Jared across the face, then stood back breathing heavily, adjusting his jacket and trousers.

Jared licked his lips tentatively. The bitter taste of the blood seemed to clear his head.

'Someone should show you what a proper blowjob is. You really haven't got a clue,' he said, making his voice as calm as he could, while revulsion, rage and humiliation tore at him.

'Think you're smart, eh? Well you're not finished here yet, not by a long shot, but when you are you're mine. I'm going to rape your mind, Jared, and then I'm going to turn you into somebody else. You just think about that.'

He turned and walked out of the room.

Jared shook his head and spat blood. They were going to kill him, that much was obvious. Or was it? What the fuck did he mean, 'rape his mind and turn him into somebody else'?

He wasn't sure how much more he could take. He could give them any name. The others would have gone to ground by now anyway. He could give the print shop address and a fake description. Sid was bound to be out of there by now.

Something in him knew though that nothing he could say was going to stop anything. It'd gone too far.

The door opened and the electrocutioner walked in, smiling.

'Right then, boy racer.'

He hit new heights of pain and vocal pitch as the man took his time and expertly applied the stun gun to a variety of points. No matter how localised the pain, the current was transmitted across every synapse in his body. His blood contorted and fizzed like food in a microwave. Hysterical outbursts turned to screams that ended gasping in the silence.

After a while his grip on consciousness and reality began to slip. For a while it seemed that his screams were made with no effort, fuelled instead by the current, with both scream and rictus collapsing as soon as the current was switched off.

His head slumped forward and stayed there. The man grabbed his hair, lifted his head and slapped his face again and again. Jared felt and heard the slaps from far away, as though he had sunk inside himself and was no longer close enough to the surface to feel properly.

He felt water splash on the back of his head and neck. It was warm. It ran down his face and the smell reached him, but he made no effort to move. He heard fading footsteps, and then the door.

Blood and feeling pumping back into his hands brought him back to himself with a pained moan. Somebody was releasing his wrists and legs. He was lifted off the chair and dragged out of the room by his arms. He registered the floor sliding past under him before losing consciousness again.

A door slamming vibrated through the ear that was pressed to the floor, shaking him back into the present. He was back in the cell. The memory of the guard followed the sound. Fear of his reappearance forced him to his knees.

His hands and feet felt like sponges filled with pins. Tremors shivered through him as each muscle group fought a tug o' war. He closed his eyes against the glare, but lost his balance and had to open them.

He managed to get his forearms onto the bench and lever himself up. He was still whimpering. He couldn't stop. He was exhausted, but still twitched and cramped as though all his muscles had shrunk and now strained against every bone in his body.

He passed out and woke later to a feeling of having been

shredded. Taut pouches bulged on his tongue and the sides of his mouth. His bones and muscles ached as if he'd been beaten with sticks. His hands and feet throbbed relentlessly. A yawning emptiness in his stomach suggested days without food, but the electrobaton had emptied him of everything anyway. He stank of piss. Vague, dim memories returned. What kind of person pissed on another? He'd heard of soldiers pissing on prisoners before. What kind of people were they?

Out of that context and out of uniform, they looked just like everybody else, standing at the bar joking and talking about football, holding doors open for old ladies. Maybe the capacity for cruelty was hardwired into everyone, the Inquisitioner lurking in the shadow, the adult version of pulling the legs off spiders, or putting salt on slugs. But spiders and slugs by their very non-human nature made them game for torture. It was easy not to identify with the victim. But other human beings?

Maybe any excuse or opportunity to feel more powerful was seized on, including inflicting pain on someone else. Maybe it somehow lessened the impotence of daily life, like one slave beating another. Did they wonder about their actions, lain in bed at night? Did they ever think how they would feel if it were being done to them or theirs? Did they think about it at all?

He suddenly and urgently had to piss. Standing wasn't an option, but he didn't have to, he already stank. He relaxed against the urge. Razor blades slid down inside his cock. His mouth opened to scream and he only just managed to jam his forearm in it. The scream wailed through his nose. He tensed to stop the flow and pain exploded in his groin. He lost control. Hot acid pumped through. He yelped on the in breath and the out breath, panting and cursing as quietly as he could. Throbbing pain spread through his lower back and belly.

By the time the flow stopped he was slick with sweat. He caught a movement on the floor out of the corner of his eye. He shifted his arm to see, stiffening and hissing with the pain. A thin line of watery red trickled slowly away from where he lay toward the drain hole.

Hot tears welled up and slid across his face.

Each time a man stands up for an ideal or acts to improve the lot of others or strikes out against injustice, he sends forth a tiny ripple of hope and, crossing each other from a million different centres of energy and daring, those ripples build a current that can sweep down the mightiest walls of oppression and resistance.

– Robert Kennedy

It is a peculiarity of man that he can only live by looking to the future... And this is his salvation in the most difficult moments of his existence, although he sometimes has to force his mind to the task.

– Viktor E. Frankl

Dan was the first to spot the sleek shape of the pursuit vehicle. He felt the familiar lurch in his stomach that happened every time he came close to the police.

'Cops.'

'Shit!' Pat muttered behind him.

Dan glanced round. Pat's face was pale. Fear flowed from her like an invisible fog.

'No sweat, Pat, they're not looking for you. Your ID's cool.'

Pat stared out of the window biting her lip.

'Pat!' Dan hissed. 'Chill.'

He turned back and saw a patrolman waving them down.

'Everybody be cool,' said Angie, slowing down. She lowered the window.

The patrolman walked round to the driver's side, both hands on his hips above the collection of bulky shapes and pouches that festooned his belt. Beneath the standard issue shades his heavy face was flushed pink in the heat.

'Problem, officer?'

'Just a routine check, miss,' said the patrolman, still standing away from the car. 'If you wouldn't mind turning off the engine and showing me your ID.'

Angie switched the engine off and passed her card, smiling. 'I don't mind.'

The patrolman swiped the card on the hand unit.

'And if you wouldn't mind presenting your thumb for a biometric verification, Miss Forrester.'

Angie held out her hand. 'Again, I don't mind,' she placed her thumb on the scanner. 'I think it's really clever.'

'Saves me having to ask more questions for verification. Someone might have stolen or copied your card. It would be a lot more secure and convenient for you if you had it bio-personalised,' drawled the man, sounding bored and robotic.

The machine beeped. He gave the card back and walked round to the passenger side, making a show of examining the tyres and front of the car. Dan lowered the window and handed over his card.

The patrolman swiped the card.

'Where are you headed, Daniel?'

'Oxford,' replied Dan.

'And why aren't you overseas with the rest of our boys, defending the country?'

Dan frowned. 'Is that a professional question or just curiosity?'

The patrolman drew himself up.

'Step out of the vehicle,' he said, stepping back and resting a hand on the holstered gun.

Out of the corner of his eye Dan saw the other patrolman move quickly in their direction. He clenched his buttocks against the sudden urging in his bowels.

'Now!'

Dan opened the door and stepped slowly out of the van.

'Face the vehicle with your hands on the roof and your feet apart.'

Dan complied. His fear vanished, replaced by a biting anger, as the patrolman began patting, feeling and squeezing up his legs and body. He felt his face heat up. He stared over the roof of the van at the motorists glancing sidelong as they passed.

When the patrolman had finished, he turned Dan round.

'What's in the back?'

'The doors aren't locked.'

'That's the second time you didn't answer my question,' sneered the patrolman.

'As if you'd take my word for it anyway,' said Dan, turning and walking to the back of the van.

In the dim, suddenly stifling interior, Pat wiped her hands on her jeans, her pulse racing. She listened to Dan walk around the van and stop beyond the doors. Light spilled through the opening doors. Dan stood back, lips pursed. Gravel crunched as the patrolman walked around the door, still staring at Dan, who kept his eyes on the van.

'Well, well,' crowed the patrolman, looking into the back. 'And would you mind explaining what you're doing in there?'

Pat slid down off the sacks and stepped out of the door.

'Where am I supposed to sit?'

'ID!' snapped the patrolman.

'No.'

The patrolman drew himself up again. 'Refusing to show identification.'

'No,' replied Pat. 'I'm saying no, you will not talk to me like that. You will address me politely and make requests in the proper manner, otherwise I'm straight on the phone and reporting you.'

The patrolman laughed weakly. 'And what do you think that'll achieve, there's a war going on you know.'

'I'm well aware of that, and my colleagues and I are doing our bit. You are dealing with us in an improper and offensive manner.'

Dan fidgeted in the silence. The second patrolman looked on from the front of the van. The first patrolman stared at Pat for a moment longer.

'I'll see some identification please, miss.'

Pat handed him her card and held her breath as he swiped it. He held the machine out and she placed her thumb gingerly on the scanner. The machine beeped and the patrolman handed the card back. Pat kept her face expressionless as relief flooded through her.

'Thank you for helping us with our enquiries,' said the patrolman, leaning into Pat's face.

Pat held his stare momentarily and then climbed back into the van. Dan closed the doors and took his card while keeping his eyes averted.

Nobody spoke as they drove away.

'You two are a fuckin' class act!' Angie exploded finally. 'What the fuck was all that? Is that a professional question,' she mimicked. ' My colleagues and I… are fuckin' brain damaged –'

'Angie, stuff it,' said Dan quietly.

'Fuck you, Dan! You could've got us busted or shot. Yes sir, no sir, smile sweetly and we're gone. The dense fuckers aren't programmed to cope with more than two syllable answers, it just confuses them or pisses them off!'

Pat leaned over. 'Can we stop, I'm going to wet myself.'

Angie glanced in the mirror at Pat's expression. 'Sure,' she said quietly.

They turned into a lane and stopped in front of a gated field. Pat jumped out and over the gate.

'Got any bog roll?' Dan asked.

'Some tissues in the glove box.'

He pulled out the tissues and stepped out of the van.

Again no one spoke as they drove away. Dan sat feeling the fear and rage leech out of him, leaving him shivery. He held up his trembling hands.

'Bastards,' he said, clenching and unclenching his fists.

Pat reached over and squeezed his shoulder.

'Do me a favour you two,' said Angie. 'Ignore everything I said back there. It wasn't you two, it was that power-hungry, anal fuckwit. You did right, especially you Pat. I wouldn't have had the guts. All that crap was just…crap. I'm sorry.'

'Don't worry about it, Angie,' said Pat. 'We all did well.'

The Vineyard had been a vineyard in a former life, but had since been turned over to general organic produce. The farmer employed itinerants; Romanies, travellers, and refugees, and provided park up space and facilities for the nomadic staff. Given that the groups were marginalised and generally hounded, he had a steady flow of workers, which meant that the labour intensive processes of the farm were easily taken care of.

Born to gentry the farmer had discovered socialism during his time at Cambridge. Although the farm wasn't run as a cooperative, it's energy was unlike other modern agricultural businesses due to the fact that economic incentive wasn't the primary reason for the workers turning up. Staff had the choice of being paid in cash or with credits. The credit system logged the hours worked which could then be exchanged for rent, produce, or saved to be redeemed in the future, for winter rent for example, when there was little agricultural work to be had.

The system also provided a support for those keeping a low profile. Although he refused to directly engage in any political activity that would jeopardise his home or business, the farmer looked with favour on those politicised elements that passed through, and through his strictly need-to-know policy had 'unknowingly' harboured many a fugitive. One type of fugitive that he openly welcomed was soon to be parents avoiding the compulsory vaccination of their newborn child. His daughter, a qualified midwife, was kept busy advising and overseeing births for that kind of resister.

Once a month Sunday roast was a potlatch. Families and individuals gathered around the banqueting table in the hall, or around trestles in the orchard in the summer, each bringing a dish or two, and more than enough drink to wash down the cross-cultural smorgasbord.

Dan got out at the big house, and Pat and Angie took the deliveries down to the farm. He found Sid with his machines in the basement. It looked like he'd brought the lot with him. They all looked to be semi-retired though, stacked against one wall. He wondered how it was that Sid always ended up in basements. Talk about an underground press.

Sid stood peering at a slip of paper in his hand. By the look of it he'd been sleeping in his clothes for days. Thick creases made a crazy paving stretching from shoulder to ankle. The grey skin of his face was baggy and dishevelled. He looked up and squinted at Dan, head tilted back and top lip drawing up revealing large and discoloured teeth.

'Hey Sid, how's it goin'? What's the stress?'

'No stress, Dan. It's goin' good,' he inhaled dramatically. 'I feel a change in the air. Yep, there are times when I see the hand of the universe in motion,' he waved his hands in the air like a puppeteer, 'know what I mean?'

Dan shook his head.

'Anything on Jared yet?' Sid asked.

'There's a brief on it, but he's being held under the Anti-Terrorism Act so there's no chance. We can't even find out where he's being held.'

'Wanna hear what I got?' Sid rubbed his hands together, flapping his bony elbows like a giant bird. 'Got word from a contact in the Yard –'

'Sid,' Dan exclaimed, 'for a man who never sees the sky you've got friends in the maddest places.'

'As I was saying,' Sid continued, looking pleased, 'a contact in the Yard says they're holding someone. It's supposed to be hush-hush, but people know. They say he hit one of them with a car.' He nodded at Dan's expression. 'Sounds like he's getting done over pretty bad.'

'That's the good news. The bad news, and the reason I needed to see you urgently, is they're moving him to Wallingford tonight.'

'Shit!'

'Which is not the worst thing that could happen.'

'Pretty fucking bad though,' grumbled Dan.

Wallingford was an old army base that had been turned into a 'temporary detention facility'. It was said to have a one-way revolving door. People arrested under the ever-extending anti-terrorism laws, or for what were deemed 'politically motivated' or 'treasonable' crimes were held incommunicado without trial indefinitely.

'Agreed, if he gets there.'

'Will you quit talking in riddles, Sid!'

Sid sighed. 'The van taking Jared will be intercepted,' he said, enunciating the words slowly, 'en route by a gent whose details I'll give you in a minute.'

'What?'

'Come on, Dan, keep up.'

'Keep up? You've just jumped to ram-raid, it's no wonder I'm falling behind. What do you mean, will be intercepted?'

Sid shrugged. 'The mechanics of the job are Leon's bag. He's the bloke you meet tonight. Ex-army, and by the sounds of it, doesn't fuck about.'

'Ex-army?'

'Got a problem with that?'

Dan stared at Sid without replying.

'Anyway,' Sid went on, 'he's not just willing, he's keen. And it's not as if there's a queue of people waiting to ruck with the Squad. I've not seen him in action, but he sounds hardcore.'

'Great. One ex-army psycho against a vanload of Gestapo.'

'Hey, who said anything about numbers? Leon's not alone. He's with the PLO.'

Dan raised his eyebrows, but said nothing. The People's Liberation Organisation was a paramilitary group said to be responsible for a series of bombings of military and government targets. Stories circulated from the media about the organisation being a communist terrorist cell that brainwashed their members. He'd been in on Resistance discussions where attempted contact with the organisation had been decided against because of the rumours.

'You'll need to arrange a safehouse to take him to, preferably out of the city.'

'And how much is it going to cost?'

'They don't want money. He said the debt was in the flesh.'

'Meaning?'

Sid hunched his shoulders and lifted his hands like claws 'Ask him yourself,' he hissed in a vampire parody. 'Tonight, eight thirty. He'll pick you up behind Zulla's. Know it?'

'The deli up the Grove?'

'The same.'

There was a pause.

'Is that it?'

'What else do you want?'

'How will I know him?'

'He said he'd pick you up.'

'Okay, better get on. Nice one, Sid.'

'Yeah. Regards to Jared.'

'Will do. Be lucky.'

'I don't know, Pat,' replied Dan as they drove away from the farm. 'You know as much as I do. We're going to intercept the transport taking Jared to Wallingford. 'We' being the PLO and me. Just the thought of being near those lot freaks me out, never mind taking the Squad on. There's going to be guns, people might get killed. I might get shot!'

'Well, on the positive side of things, there's a chance we'll get Jared back,' said Pat, sympathising with him, having recently been shot at herself.

'There's a chance we might all get killed!'

'Yes, but there's a chance you might not. Come on, Dan, this is actually positive. A couple of hours ago we still didn't have a plan.'

Dan seemed not to hear. 'What am I going to do if they put a gun in my hand, if I'm forced to shoot someone?'

Pat sighed. 'I don't know, Dan, what are you going to do?'

There was a moment of silence.

'This is a non-violent resistance. Violence is one of the things we're opposing. It makes us just as bad as them if we start shooting people at the drop of a hat.'

'This is hardly at the drop of a hat, Dan. Jared's life's at stake here. If there was another way, some legal recourse, we would've taken it by now. But there isn't. The authorities have got it all sewn up. They can do anything they want, and we can't do anything about it. So where does that leave us? I hear what you're saying, but really this isn't a resistance. We're not resisting anything, except maybe our facing that fact. Where's all the action mobilised through pirate transmissions? I dread to think what state Jared's in, although he's lucky he's still alive, but for what? Fifteen minutes of cobbled together footage and subverts, that ninety nine percent of people who see it will ignore and switch over anyway. Face it; the non-violent response isn't working. This is the twenty first century. Gandhi and Martin Luther King would get detained indefinitely, no appeal, no representation, no doubt about it.

'We have to get Jared back. If we don't we'll never see him again, he'll just disappear like all the rest, or like Phil come out in a couple of months not being able to write his own name or hold a spoon. No, I'm sorry Dan, I hadn't really thought about it before, but the non-violent angle isn't where I'm coming from any more.'

'You're not serious,' said Dan.

'I'm dead serious, Dan. And you know why? Because if I was in Jared's shoes I'd be praying for a rescue party to bust me out of jail, not to stand outside waving placards and collecting petition signatures!'

'I think you're letting your emotions get too involved here.'

Pat wiped her eyes roughly with her sleeve. 'Go on then, tell me your ethical, non-violent answer to this.'

'All I'm saying is violence breeds violence.'

'That's not all you're saying. You're saying that armed struggle is the result of too much emotion.'

Dan opened his mouth to reply, but Pat cut him short.

'Alright then, in the face of it's near hundred percent ineffectiveness, how rational or logical is this non-violent resistance? Surely it's not rational if it doesn't work.'

'Maybe we've just not found the right action for the circumstances.'

Pat shook her head. 'Yeah? Well while you're shopping around for the right action, why don't you buy the Devil a pair of ice skates?'

'Pat, what's got into you?'

'What's got into me? How about the fear of death, of imprisonment without recourse, of disappearing, and of my friends being killed or disappearing? Anger that I'm no longer fearful of muggers, rapists or terrorists more than I am of the people that are supposed to be protecting me from them. Angry that my civil rights have been stolen wholesale. Angry that slowly but surely my back has been forced against the wall so much that it's brought me close to doing things that are contrary to my nature and ethics. That's the condensed version. Give me a minute and a sheet of paper and I'll give you the rest.

'You're right, my emotions are involved here, my emotions and instincts. And no Judeo-Christian society programmed pseudo-ethics are going to override this feeling for self-preservation that's coursing through my veins right now!'

The Grove was busy. The heat and humidity had driven most people outdoors where the air was marginally less viscous. Those indoors hung out of windows and over balconies, their shouts and laughter falling to mix with that of the traders in the stalls that lined both sides of the street. Thick tendrils of greasy food aromas snaked among the slow moving people. Raucous laughter and loud, bantering conversations punctuated the air, the voices jostling with the music that bounced between the dilapidated buildings.

Dan stood opposite the arabesque front of the deli. He looked at his watch. Ten minutes. Time enough to get some food. He ducked under an awning and traversed the stream of people ambling along the street to a food stall on the corner in front of the deli. He took the hot, damp package and turned down an alley. He picked at the hot food, watching people flow past the alley mouth. Most looked to be out for the sake of being out, taking advantage of the later curfew time at the weekend.

He was just finishing the food when a van pulled out from behind the deli. He walked toward it, wiping his mouth.

'You Tommy?' said the driver, his face obscured by shadow.

'Nah mate,' replied Dan, deftly sidestepping around the front of the van.

'Dan!'

Dan turned back. 'Leon?'

'Yeah, let's go.'

Dan climbed into the van. The air inside was laden with the caustic tang of bodies.

'Glad you made it,' said Leon, holding out a hand.

His voice was deep, but surprisingly quiet for someone so big. His square head and thick neck sat on wide shoulders above a barrel chest that filled the space between the seat and the steering wheel. Dan reached out to shake hands and was momentarily confused when Leon gripped him around the thumb rather than the fingers. The hand was huge, and dwarfed his own.

'We've gotta wait for word about his movements before we pick your mate up, so we're gonna park up out of the city,' said Leon, ignoring Dan's obvious confusion.

'You make it sound totally normal,' said Dan. 'Just picking a mate up.'

'Would, before we attack the Squad and rescue your mate, sound any better?' Leon asked as he eased the van out into the road.

'Sounds more like what it is. Picking up a mate doesn't sound that serious.'

A figure leaned over the seat from the back.

'Don't you worry about serious, mate.'

The man spoke while looking at the road. His close-cropped black hair cut a zigzag contrast down the side of his face. He turned to Dan and held out his hand.

'Sol.'

Dan gripped the hand.

'Question is, how serious are you?' Sol asked, maintaining a grip on Dan's hand and looking at him intently. 'I mean, how far are you prepared to go to get your mate back, 'cause we aren't just going to pick him up…we are going to take on the Squad.'

Dan didn't answer straightaway. He'd been worrying the question since hearing of the arrangement from Sid. He didn't even know how they were thinking of getting him back? But what could he do against trained and armed militia anyway? He couldn't really know what he'd do until faced with it. He'd finally concluded that the situation itself would be the decider.

'I'll do whatever needs to be done to get Jared away from them,' he said, meeting Sol's stare.

'Well hopefully they'll be sensible and just hand him over,' said Leon. 'Your part will just be identifying your man.'

Dan relaxed a little, relieved to hear that he wasn't expected to get hand-to-hand. Tension still trembled through his guts though. He tried unsuccessfully to remember the questions he'd intended to ask about the organisation.

'Sid said you're involved in some pirate TV transmissions,' said Sol.

Dan nodded, relieved for the opening.

'What sort of stuff?'

'All sorts,' said Dan. 'The transmitter that Jared was busted with had anti-war stuff loaded. Pictures smuggled out from the front, armed forces careers subverts. But we do other stuff, corporate watch, censored news, anything that exposes what's going on.'

'The Voice?'

Dan nodded.

'Seen it. Class agit-prop.'

'Thanks, but how many people just change channels?'

'Probably most, but that's not the point. Gotta give them the chance. Fed government media lies it's no wonder they think like they do. Uncensored footage gives them a chance to see behind the lies. What they do with it is up to them, not your bag.'

'I don't know. I've been thinking for a while that it's the wrong way. The opposition's too big. We're fighting companies who've got access to everyone's psychographic profile. They know whose interactive buttons to press, where and how. People are used to that system. They've forgotten how to think for themselves, and definitely don't want to be different from their group. Sometimes I feel like saying fuck it, let them have what they want.'

Leon glanced round. 'Dan, people's apathy and inactivity is one of the biggest problems. If you're not part of the solution, you're part of the problem.'

'I know, I know. I'm just tired of fighting the machine.

Especially with limited backup.'

'The limitations are in your head,' replied Leon without looking round. 'Which, paradoxically, is your best weapon.'

Leon seemed to be avoiding the major roads, but they still passed a number of patrols. Before long they pulled over and parked in a lay-by.

'We'll stay here till we get word that he's on the move and what he's in,' said Leon.

'Question,' said Dan.

'Yeah?'

'What do you mean, the debt is in the flesh?'

'We don't deal in cash unless we have to, stuff's bad energy. What we're doing now could cost our lives or freedom. How much for those? And by the sound of it we're gonna save your mate's life. How much for that? One day he'll get the chance to do something for us, that's the way it goes.'

'Well, if we get him back, he won't be the only one. I'll take that on too.'

Leon looked at Dan, his eyes seeming to lock onto a point behind Dan's head. Dan shifted uncomfortably, but didn't look away.

'Okay,' said Leon finally. 'No 'ifs' though. We are gonna get your mate back.'

Tension quivered through Dan again. It looked like they actually were going to intercept the transport, Dick Turpin style. He thought of Jared and what he must be going through, and what they were about to do to free him. The knowledge clashed with his philosophy. Before this he'd held that freedom had no value if violence was the price. But as Pat had said, what other way was there? The sense of moved goalposts had him thinking back to the car he'd stolen after Jared's arrest. That too had gone against his ethics, but what other choice had he had? Sat there between the proverbial rock and hard place he began to see what Pat had meant. His ethics came from the false luxury of an artificial civilisation. What of the other individuals and groups around the world that were fighting the military-industrial machine, surely those cultures and individuals had their own ethics around violence and killing. But those conflicts were so blatant that the choice of action seemed much more clear-cut. It was only in so-called civilised countries where repression took on subtle and unseen forms that the lines were blurred. Which was why those forms were used. Propaganda was to a democracy what violence was to a dictatorship, only much more powerful.

But what was the pacifist solution? He had to admit that Pat might have been right, there didn't seem to be one. They had it all sewn up, the security services, the legal system, the media, all of it. Which was why there was an underground resistance movement.

Most of the resistance actions he knew of were of a non-cooperative nature, the easiest form to keep hidden, although the risks involved in any actions meant resisters had to be very secretive about their activities. The PLO were the most well known group, but were in a class of their own because of their militant activities. Nobody seemed to know much about the organisation itself though, probably because of the level of secrecy needed by their activities. Non-cooperation was one thing, blowing up armed forces recruiting centres and other military and State property was another thing completely.

He turned to Leon. 'Another question, why did you take this on?'

'Various reasons, but basically because we're fighting the same enemy. Freeing a comrade, a brother-in-arms, is a move the organisation hasn't made yet. Doing so is a demonstration of the need for, and advantages in, networking. It also fits with our objective to destroy the myth of the State's invulnerability and invincibility. I could ask you the question, what would you have done had we not offered our support?'

'I don't think there was anything we could have done.'

Leon nodded. 'Which is what we as a guerrilla organisation stand for, the logical consequence of the reversal of parliamentary democracy by its own representatives, and the unavoidable response to the emergency laws, the police shoot-to-kill methods, and the readiness of the system to use all means necessary to liquidate its opposition.'

47

He stopped as if listening to something. Sounds of movement came from the back.

'Okay,' he said, sitting up, 'you ready for this?'

'I thought we were waiting for word about the transport.'

'Yeah, we were.' He gestured over his shoulder. 'Us two in the back.'

Dan climbed into the back and sat on a mattress. Leon sat next to him.

'When it kicks off, you stay here till I whistle.'

Dan nodded, frowning.

'Something?' Leon asked.

'Yeah, weren't we waiting for word about – '

'Like I said, yeah, we were. We just got it,' he added after a pause.

Dan moved aside as a man passed Leon a Kevlar vest. Dan noticed that he, like the woman now driving, had averted his face when he'd looked at him. Feeling that he was in the way, he moved and jammed himself in a corner. As he turned he caught sight of the man frowning at Leon. Leon shook his head, but stopped when he saw Dan looking at him. He smiled at Dan and shook his head again.

'Don't stress it, Dan.'

He reached into a small pack and drew out two small black discs, which he handed to the man and Sol.

Dan's stomach churned as the van raced through the night. Nobody spoke. There was a moment when something seemed to pass between Leon and the man in the back, indicated by the man turning and nodding to Leon. Leon turned and caught Dan's eye. Dan looked away.

'Contact five hundred metres,' the driver shouted.

There was a shuffling, pulling down of masks, and positioning by the door.

Dan watched the non-reflective black doors of the security van get larger. A motorbike roared by, overtaking the two vans. As it drew level with the security van, the pillion rider twisted in its seat. A compact submachine-gun spat yellow stars and the security van jerked and slewed into the verge. The van accelerated past and skidded to a stop in front of the security van. Sol slid the door back before they'd stopped moving and both he and Leon leapt out.

Sol slapped one of the discs on the driver's door. He was scarcely past it when it exploded, swinging the door open. The man behind him reached it before it swung back and yanked the concussed, reeling guard out and onto the ground. Two more sharp retorts told of the same happening at the back and other side.

Seconds later Dan heard Leon whistle. He jumped out of the van and ran past the face down guard. Leon was crouched in the back next to a stretcher. A man lay in it restrained with wide straps. Leon loosened a strap, gripped the man's clothes and pulled him upright, supporting his head with the other hand. The man groaned.

'This your man?'

Dan pulled out a torch and shone it in the man's face. Jared whimpered as the light stabbed his eyes.

'Easy matey,' said Dan, turning the torch off and nodding to Leon.

Jared stopped moaning. 'Dan?'

'Let's get him out of here,' said Leon.

'Dan?'

'Yeah, it's me. You're gonna be okay, hold on.'

They pulled the stretcher out and hurried past the still prone guard. Moments later Sol jumped back into the van and slid the door shut.

''kay, let's go!'

Leon moved over, bracing himself against the acceleration, letting Sol crouch beside Jared lying sobbing and moaning on the bench. Sol opened a flight-case on the floor, the hinged front folding down to reveal rows of buttons, lights and readouts. He took a long wand from the side of the box and passed it over the length of Jared's body, his eyes fixed on the readouts.

'Just one,' he said.

He replaced the wand and drew a fat pen-like tube from the box.

'Hold his head still.'

Leon took Jared's head gently.

'What's going on?' Dan asked.

The two men ignored him. Sol brought the tube up to Jared's face and pointed it at his forehead, between the eyes. The machine gave a series of rapid clicks.

'Got it,' murmured Sol. He pressed a button on the machine and repositioned the tube.

The van lurched sending him sideways. Leon grabbed his shoulder.

'Steady as she goes, just for a minute,' shouted Sol.

There was no answer, but the van slowed. Sol held the tube up to Jared's face again. A click sounded from the machine. He replaced the tube and withdrew the other, which he passed over Jared's face. The readout on the machine remained static. Both men relaxed visibly.

''kay, step on it!'

Jared called Dan's name.

'I'm here mate, no worries,' said Dan, moving forward and reaching under the blanket to take Jared's hand.

Jared yelled and snatched his hand away.

'Careful,' Leon said, folding the blanket back.

Jared held his injured hands to his chest. As well as the damaged thumbs, each fingertip and the webbing in between the fingers was burned and blistered.

Dan's stomach creased. What had they been doing to him?

'Thumb cuffs and stun-gun,' said Leon.

Sol leaned over. 'Jared, we're taking you somewhere safe. I'm going to give you something for the pain.'

Jared nodded without opening his eyes, the muscles in his jaw jumping spasmodically. Sol took his wrist gently and slowly straightened the arm. The needle sank in easily and seconds later Jared's contorted face slackened and his spasming body stilled.

His eyes opened to slits and looked at Sol. 'Nice one,' he said, his voice barely a whisper. His eyes closed and he gave a juddering sigh.

Dan sat overwhelmed by the rush of thoughts and emotions

produced by the sight of Jared's hands. The images ate into him like acid. Sure, he'd seen pictures of torture injuries. so wasn't wholly ignorant. But the lack of experience had been a diffusing layer between him and the grisly reality. A layer now removed like a rug from underneath him.

'There are people in the world who live under this twenty-four seven.'

Dan looked up.

'You alright?' Sol asked.

Dan nodded. 'What was all that you did around his face?'

'Security services trick. Microchip implant, usually into sinuses or ears. Use them for all sorts, the least of which is satellite tracking. The first bit was a detector to find the chip, the second bit a maser I used to record its frequency and then blow its fuse. Can't get it out easily, but at least it can't do anything now. Luckily for him we've got this. Mine had to be dug out with a knife.'

He twisted his head around to show a nasty scar at the base of his skull.

The idea of someone gouging a chip out of their body with a knife shocked Dan to silence. Sid was right, they were hardcore. They were fully kitted out too. Variable amplification electromagnetics wasn't something you came across outside of a lab. A maser was a laser that operated on an electromagnetic wavelength rather than the visible light spectrum. The closest he'd come to a laser was in a CD player.

'So it's not like a regular ID or RFID chip then?'

'Don't know. It might be a straightforward tracking chip. Given where he's been though it's probably a bit more complex than that.'

'How do you mean?'

'Well,' Sol raised his eyebrows and sighed heavily, 'given that everything that goes on in us is fundamentally electromagnetic in nature, any, and I do mean any, body or mind activity can be electromagnetically altered or stimulated. Mood and behaviour can be modified right across the board, up or down. Paralysis, heart attack, audio-visual hallucinations, you name it. And with a microchip implant all that modification can be done remotely and covertly, as easily as programming a scrambled satellite TV channel from TV headquarters. Political targets can be dealt with, killed, disabled or discredited.'

'As far as tracking goes though', said Dan, 'isn't there still a risk of us being picked up by satellite?'

Sol looked at Leon.

'Oh for a vehicle with stealth technology, eh,' said Leon. 'Yes there is a risk, but it's unlikely that the transport was specifically under observation. The guards won't have been able to raise the alarm, and as we speak are being driven in the direction of their destination. If there is any attention given them, say because of lack of radio contact, a satellite check will show them heading in the right direction, and the lack put down to radio failure.'

He lifted a hand to show crossed fingers.

Dan thought about the risk for the person driving the security van, and wondered what arrangements they had, if any, for evading capture. He looked at Jared's face. Bruising shadowed both cheeks, and one eye was swollen closed. His lips were blackened and swollen. He wasn't sure, but he thought he'd seen one of his front teeth missing too.

His doubts about the ethics of the mission faded. They'd done the right thing. The people who had done, and authorised, this were criminals. The same bunch of criminals that were breaking human rights laws around the world on a daily basis.

Before long they turned off the main road and down an overgrown and potholed track. Dan made out the rough outline of a cottage, its crumbling walls streaked with ferrous stains from the cracked corrugated roof, hedged in on one side with poplars that strobed as the van lights played over them. A garage built onto the side was in better condition, though the roof was pitted with holes. A new-looking courier van was parked in the garage. They pulled in and parked next to it.

'Ready?' Leon asked.

'In a sec',' grunted Sol, bent over the machine. He pressed a button and a row of red lights lit up then winked out almost immediately, replaced by a single green light. Another button brought a drawer sliding out. He withdrew a small phial.

'Let's make it quick then,' he said, passing a slip of paper to Leon. 'Put that in the glove box.'

Leon's eyebrow rose. He unfolded the paper and read the bold print, then looked at Sol and nodded.

Sol hoisted a small rucksack onto his back and picked his way along the side of the house through the tangle of brambles and waist-high nettles. Glass and rubble crunched noisily as he clambered into the musty interior. In one room the ceiling had partially collapsed, exposing the pink and blue wallpapered bedroom above. He crouched and took a black plastic-wrapped package out of the rucksack. From his pocket he took a roll of tiny telescopic aerials. He gripped one with his teeth and extended it, drew it out of the roll, and pushed the spiked end into the soft block. He walked around the edges of the room to the small fireplace. He reached up into the flue and wedged the block between two bricks. He moved from room to room, leaving a package in each fireplace. When he'd finished he returned to the first room and placed the phial, a button-sized photocell and a wafer thin transmitter in a corner.

He joined the others waiting in the courier van.

Mist hung in thick wedges across the road creating a ceiling that stretched between the stonewalled sides, a dim, undulating gullet along which the van was swiftly sucked. Sat in the back Dan felt his stomach twisting with tension and apprehension. He leaned forward.

'What if we hit a road block?'

Leon smiled.

'That's a funny question?'

'No, it's not,' said Leon. He drew a deep breath. 'If we hit a roadblock, then we hit a roadblock. Unlikely though. They think they're so smart, they'll just track that chip and figure on taking us by surprise. The surprise is all theirs though.'

'How do you mean? What chip?'

Sol turned to Dan. 'Like I said, using the maser I recorded the frequency of the chip before blowing its fuse. When we arrived back there I programmed that frequency onto another chip and left it in the house.'

'I get it. They'll track the chip there and find no-one,' said Dan.

'What they'll find is a band of Semtex demons.'

'You mean like explosives?'

'I mean like explosives.'

'What for?' Dan spluttered, the sinking feeling returning.

Sol frowned. 'How do you mean?'

'Well, you could've just left the chip. Nobody had to get hurt.'

'Need I remind you that somebody's already been hurt,' Sol motioned with his head to where Jared lay, 'badly?'

Confused, Dan looked at Jared.

'Get this,' Sol went on, 'we're fighting a war, a guerrilla war. So far you've been engaged in the propaganda side, and good on you. Sure, this close quarter stuff is unpleasant, but what did you expect?' He held Dan's gaze a moment longer and then looked away.

Dan looked at Jared's face and thought of the men about to die or be injured. Weren't they supposed to be fighting against that? Didn't violence breed violence? He knew what Sol was saying, but there was still no need for more violence. He opened a hand and rested it on Jared's chest and sat, eyes closed, juggling the conflict between ethics and necessity.

A grey-blue dawn was breaking by the time they reached their destination. They drove down a tree-lined road. Large sandstone houses sat back from the road.

Dan leaned forward. 'At the end of this road there's a big gate in some high walls, in there.'

They turned through the massive wrought iron gateway under thick overhanging rhododendrons.

'You sure this is the right place?' Sol asked.

'Yeah, this is it.'

'What is it?'

'Estate. We're going to the gatehouse…just there,' he pointed to a set of high wooden gates.

They stopped at the gates and Dan sounded the horn twice slowly. Beyond the gates dogs began barking. Dan, calmer now, felt the anxiety of the group. Eventually the gates opened and Leon drove through. As they crunched up the short gravel drive to the ivy-clad cottage, two large Rotweilers danced around the van, barking loudly.

'Fuckin' big dogs,' said Sol.

Dan smiled, feeling a slight advantage for the first time since stepping into the van the night before.

'Stay in the van until I tell you to come out,' he said, opening the door slightly. The barking echoed around the interior as he slipped out.

Both dogs bounded up to him and stopped about six feet away from him, still barking. A thin, blond man walking back from the gate spoke to the dogs. They stopped barking, but remained where they were. He shook hands with Dan and the two men approached the van. Dan opened Sol's door.

'Come out and let the dogs smell you, then we can go inside.'

The dogs walked quickly around the group taking sniffs of each.

'They probably won't be loads friendly, but they'll let you walk around the place now,' said Dan.

The man motioned the dogs into the van where they smelled Jared with more interest before bounding out and away to watch at a distance.

Dan helped Leon carry the stretcher out of the van to the cottage where a woman stood in the doorway. Once inside they climbed a short flight of stairs and into a small, antiquely furnished bedroom. Jared was lifted onto the bed and the woman moved in close, rolling up her sleeves. She drew the blanket back slowly, and took a deep breath.

'Okay, what do we know?'

Leon answered. 'Shot sometime ago, hung by the thumbs and given electroshock. Probably not fed or allowed to sleep. More than that we don't know. He was semi-conscious when we picked him up.'

The woman slowly prised back the blood-soaked dressing. The skin around the hole was an angry red. The hole itself was crusty with blood and rimmed with thick green pus. She grunted quietly, put the dressing aside and began feeling Jared's scalp, taking her hands out occasionally to check her fingers. She felt around his neck then, skirting the bullet wound, slid her hands under his sides and down his body, all the while watching his face. She paused each time a frown flickered over his face. When she reached his feet she straightened up.

'As far as I can tell he's got a couple of broken ribs, maybe spinal injuries, and bones broken in one foot. I'll have to get him to move to find out more. Possible internal bleeding. That wound's septic and he's taken a major beating around his genitals. They're quite burned too, as are his hands and nipples. On top of the physical damage his nervous system's going to be in bits.'

She looked round at Leon. 'I'll set up a nutrient and water drip, and clean that hole up. How long will he be out for?'

'What I gave him won't keep him out for long,' said Sol, 'but his body will want to sleep. They've probably had him awake for days. The pain will probably wake him though.'

'Okay, I'll be able to do a proper examination when he wakes up. There's eats in the kitchen. I'll join you when I'm done.'

'Er, maybe not leave him on his own,' said Sol.

The woman nodded.

They filed out and down the wide stairs, and along a wood panelled corridor to a large flagstone-floored kitchen. There was no one in the kitchen, but at one end of the dining table a small spread of bread, cheese, slices of meat and salad waited. The smell of coffee came from a pot on the range.

Leon and Sol immediately helped themselves to food.

'Where are the others?' Dan asked, realising he'd not seen the other two since he'd entered the cottage.

'Outside keeping an eye out,' said Leon.

'Do you think that's really necessary? That's what the dogs are for.'

'I presume the dogs are for burglars, the Squad's our concern.'

Dan said nothing. He shook his head at Sol's offer of coffee.

'I'm wired enough.'

'He'll be okay I reckon,' said Sol. 'I've seen worse.'

'Worse?'

'Yeah, much.'

Dan shook his head. 'How do you sleep at night?'

'Sometimes I don't. So who lives here?'

'Just Aled and Kay.'

'Aled met us and Kay's with Jared?'

Dan nodded. Sol seemed about to say something when Leon walked quickly out of the kitchen. Sol put his cup on the table and followed. Dan stood there, puzzled and suddenly uneasy, then walked to the kitchen door and listened.

The end of the corridor showed a section of the hall, neither men were in sight. The slow ticking of the long case clock at the bottom of the stairs amplified the ominous and suddenly threatening silence. He crept along the corridor, stomach knotting with every step. He reached the end and peered round the corner. Leon stood crouched by the door, looking through the stained glass panel. Sol stood opposite on the other side of the hall, away from the door. Both held handguns.

'What's goin' on?' Dan hissed.

'Someone at the gates,' said Sol without looking round. 'Aled's answering it.'

Dan's guts clenched. He'd thought they'd got away with it. It was easily possible that they had been tracked and were now surrounded. Images rose in his mind of soldiers with automatic rifles scaling the walls and taking up positions around the house. His fear deepened with the realisation that he knew nothing of the layout of the grounds, despite having been there before. But if they were surrounded there was nowhere to run. He thought of Jared unconscious upstairs and how he could move him, even if he found somewhere to hide.

Leon moved swiftly away from the door and motioned to the corridor. They filed quickly back into the kitchen, immediately finding different positions and tasks in a silent choreographed complicity. Moments later Aled appeared holding a sheaf of letters and a parcel.

'How's your friend, Dan?'

'Awake,' said Kay, coming in behind him. 'Says he wants to

see everybody. He's quite distressed.'

Jared was sat up, propped up with pillows. His eyes were tightly shut, but not tight enough to prevent two steady streams rippling down either side of his nose, glistening over his swollen lips. His eyes opened on hearing the group enter.

'Kay?'

The word was forced out. Tremors tugged at him and he twitched violently.

Kay moved in and held the shaking figure against the pillows, until the spasming had subsided. Jared eyes were shut and his breathing shallow. When he'd stilled, she let go. Jared opened his eyes and tried to clear his throat.

'Water,' he croaked.

Kay raised a glass to his lips. He took a mouthful and lay back, panting. He cleared his throat again with difficulty. Kay raised the glass, but he shook his head.

'I…I wanted to...I wanted to say…' he groaned and shook his head.

Kay put her hand to his shoulder.

'No,' he hissed, jerking away from her touch.

Visibly shocked, Kay let her hand fall. Jared looked away, his head movements jerky, his eyes wide. The words when they came out were stiff, the voice of someone struggling with a heavy weight.

'I…wanted to…say…thank-you,' he said looking around the room.

Still nobody spoke.

'I…' he closed his eyes and shook his head. His quiet keening filled the room.

'I think he said what he wanted to say,' said Leon. 'Let's leave him rest.'

Out on the landing Dan sat on the stairs, tears in his eyes. Leon sat on the stairs below.

'Where do you go?' Dan asked. 'Even if you could find out who did it, who's going to try them? The courts are as bent as the government.'

'When a long train of abuses and usurpations, pursuing invariably the same object, evinces a design to reduce them under absolute despotism, it is their right, their duty, to throw off such government and provide new guards for their future security,' intoned Leon. 'United States Declaration of Independence. But I think that goes anywhere.'

Dan was silent.

'Note, 'throw off' not vote out, protest or grumble. Fuck right off.'

Dan said nothing. He was still seeing Jared's shaking face. Like how many others the world over, raped of trust and innocence and the bloody vacuum filled with horror and betrayal; guardians turned oppressors, neighbours turned torturers, the whole lot upside down and back to front.

'Dan,' said Leon.

Dan blinked and refocused on Leon's face.

'We're gonna check outside, let the others get some cram.'

Dan nodded, unable to talk. Leon and Sol seemed unaffected by events, where he was stunned or confused. Maybe because they'd seen stuff like it before. He leaned his elbows on his knees and held his head in his hands.

'You okay?'

He turned and saw Kay standing behind him.

'Just trying to keep up and not doing so good.'

Kay snorted. 'How are you supposed to be doing with all that's gone on?'

'I'm not reacting fast enough.'

'I reckon you should save the crit' Dan. We're all here, so we can't be doing that bad.'

'We had help.'

'So? Sometimes help's needed. Tell me about the rescue anyway.'

He described the action. 'They're probably pulling bodies out of the rubble now.'

'Serves them right,' said Kay without hesitation.

'What?'

'Well it does. I'm as much a pacifist as you are Dan, and I'm a medic, but I think I'd be prepared to kill anybody trying to do to you what those bastards have done to Jared.'

Dan flushed with the same feelings that had come with the conversation with Sol.

'Don't think I'd have said that a couple of hours ago,' Kay went on. 'That could've been you Dan, or me, or any of us. No, maybe the world's a better place minus a few paid killers and torturers.'

Jared looked at his hands lying in his lap. He seemed to be wearing a pair of joke latex gloves with grotesque bulbous fingers and sick colouring.

Leon was sitting on the bed, Sol standing behind him. He looked at them and then at the two standing at the foot of the bed. Their eyes held him calmly without flinching and without expressions of concern or sympathy, so different from Dan's palpable distress and Kay's concern. He looked at Leon.

'I've seen a photo of you,' he croaked. He swallowed painfully. His throat felt raw and scaly. 'When they questioned me, they showed me a photo.'

Leon nodded. 'I saw your face in a vision a hundred years ago,' he said quietly. 'We've got to go.'

Jared shook his head as tears welled up. 'So many questions.'

'Get better, then come find us and get some answers.'

Sol put his hand on Jared's shoulder. Jared sat motionless, eyes closed, tears dripping onto his chest.

He hadn't moved when Kay came back in after seeing the group out. She checked the drip levels.

'You need to sleep Jared, the more the better. I'm going to give you a sedative, okay?'

He nodded without opening his eyes. He barely felt the needle and a warm honey slowly flooded his body.

He woke later, struggling out of a dream in which he was drowning, fighting to a surface too far away to reach. He lurched upwards, pain banishing the last strands of sleep. He slumped back on the damp pillow, feeling his heart pound, each pulse beat sending pain surging through him, throbbing in his hands, groin and back. The pain was less though; quietened with the shots Kay had given him. And anyway, pain meant still alive. Pain he could stand. He hadn't known it before, but now he knew.

He tried to swallow, but his mouth was sandpaper dry. There was a jug of water and a glass on the bedside table, but they might as well have been on the moon. He couldn't pick his nose, never mind pick up a jug of water.

The curtains were still drawn and no light showed behind them, so it was possible that everyone was asleep. He didn't want to wake them just for a drink of water. But he needed to drink; the dryness was beginning to make him gag.

He looked at the water again. On the table beside it was a packet of surgical dressing. Grimacing, he inched up the bed. He lifted a hand and scissored two fingers slowly. The blistered, cracked webbing between them began to weep immediately. Gritting his teeth against the protests from his shoulder, he reached over and picked the packet up with his fingers. He dropped it onto the bed.

After a moments rest he picked it up again, brought it up to his mouth and, taking one corner in his teeth, tried to rip it open. His fingers weren't up to it though and the packet slipped through them. He lifted the other arm, moaning uncontrollably, clasped the packet with his forearms and tore at it with his teeth, and succeeded in exposing the lint. Taking the lint again with two fingers, his hands pounding, he dipped it into the water and brought it back to his mouth. He sucked at the cool moisture, breathing through his nose in quick breaths.

Coming in later, Kay found him asleep, propped up with the lint still in his mouth. She scolded herself after eventually working out what he'd been doing. She cut some IV-tube, placed the jug on a chair by the bed, fixed the tube into the water, and then slowly and gently taped the other end to his wrist. Jared stirred and moaned, but didn't wake.

Time passed in chunks, warped by opiate painkillers and sleep. The painkillers created a fog that rounded off the sharp edges of his mind and body. Inside the fog he could hear both still screaming, but the sound was dull and distant. His dreams were touched too, blurred and indistinct nightmares.

He lay not wanting to move. The stillness and weight of the quilt felt safe. Movement just set off a chain reaction of physical sensations that went on to trigger feelings of anxiety. He had to move though. He felt soiled, and not just because he'd been in bed for days. Sharp tangs of urine and sour, old vomit mixed with a vaguely rotten smell wafted up from under the cover every time he moved. He felt vile inside too, but it was going to take more than a hot bath to fix that.

He pushed the quilt back and sat up, holding his arm against his chest. His head swam and pressure throbbed in his hands and feet. His foot was swollen and green, purple and yellow. He stood and limped to the end of the bed. He lifted the gown off the bedpost with one hand, and managed to get it over first one shoulder, then the other.

He levered the door open with his elbow and went out onto the landing. He hobbled past large paintings of eighteenth century gentry hunting and shooting hung at intervals along the wood panelled walls. The antique theme continued in the bathroom, although it didn't look like a theme, it looked like the real deal. The marble floor was cool underfoot. A deep bath stood on gold claws that matched the fittings. Using his wrists to turn the taps, he ran a bath. He sat on the toilet and stared at the steam rising from the tub, mixed feelings pinballing through him; the urge to scream, the urge to return to the safety of the bed, panic lurking at the fringes of his awareness, heaving like a pool of molten lava, ready to rise and swamp him again. The rumbling of the water bothered him because it blocked out any other sounds that might have been around. He tried to force his body to relax, but it remained clenched and hunched. The bath was definitely a good idea.

He shrugged the robe off, wincing again as it dragged over his hand. Goose pimples played over his naked body and feelings of vulnerability constricted his already tense muscles painfully.

'You're safe, its cool, you're just having a bath. You're safe, its cool, you're just having a bath,' he chanted, trying to keep a lid on the escalating panic. 'Come on, you're safe; you're just having a bath. You're just having a bath.'

He gave a half laugh, half hiccup, and tears ran down his face.

His battered hands and foot made climbing into the deep tub difficult, and the bullet wound meant that he couldn't take any weight on that shoulder. Once in he crouched slowly. The water touching his groin made him gasp, stop, and steady himself against the sides of the bath. He put his hands under the water tentatively, hissing at the painful throbbing the heat produced, but keeping them there.

He could really smell himself now. He smelled sick.

He sat down slowly, wincing at the pain in his spine. The hot water sent prickly sensations racing over his skin. The liquid heat was bliss. He tried to lie back, taking the weight off his spine on one buttock, but felt exposed and vulnerable. He sat up quickly, creating a wave that rushed to the foot of the bath and back. The moving water intensified his skin's agitation. His head started to pound, and a nameless fear took hold of him.

He looked around the bathroom even though he knew no one was there. He stood quickly, cascading water, and put his back against the wall. His breathing was shallow and fast, and his eyes felt like they were protruding out of their sockets. A tiny witnessing part of him knew he was being irrational, but the fear that gripped him overrode any rationality.

He climbed out of the bath, steadying himself on the side with his forearms, his jerking, cramping stomach forcing tiny gasps as he struggled to balance. He picked at the towel ineffectually with his stiff hands, and then roared with frustration.

He walked over to the open window, tears streaming down his face, and sat on the tiled ledge. His mind wouldn't work and was just bouncing around inside his head. He shook his head. A moan quickly became sobbing. He gripped his stomach with his arms and rocked slowly. The motion fitted with the feelings of helplessness and wrung deeper and deeper sobs.

The sound of another crying voice behind him lifted the hairs on his neck. He turned and looked through the window into the garden below and saw both dogs looking up at him, one pacing and whining fretfully, the other howling softly.

There was a chiropractic clunk in his chest and his sobbing anguish poured out.

Both dogs began howling quietly and steadily.

Feet noiseless on the thick carpet, he shuffled slowly back to the room. He shut the door and leaned against it, then slid slowly into a squat. A dark heaviness dragged at him, pressure squeezing his skull.

The stun gun crackled next to his ear sending him diving into the room. He landed on his hands and crumpled face first onto the carpet. He spun round and looked wildly around the room.

He flinched again. But he hadn't heard anything. His body began to twitch.

He gasped as pain from a twisted nipple lanced through him. He shoved himself back across the floor and cracked his neck on the bed. His vision filled with stars and then his own bulbous face reflected in dark lenses. Wet lips smiled and parted.

'That mouth…'

He let out a hoarse scream, threw an arm onto the bed and tried to lever himself up. The twitching was getting worse. He had to get up, keep moving. His arms and legs seemed to be on the wrong way round though, and incapable of making anything but random movements. He supported himself on the bedstead and tried gimping around the bed, but gave up and curled up on the bed, pulling the quilt over him. The quilt covering his ears made him immediately anxious, so he pulled it down.

Was he hallucinating? He must have been. But the pain was real. It wasn't possible to hallucinate pain, was it? Whatever was going on he hadn't escaped. The bastards were still in his head.

He tasted blood and realised he'd bitten his lip. The blood brought him back to himself. The blood was real, the bed was real, everything else was just another nightmare. He was having the longest fucking bad dream of his life. When was he going to wake up? How was he going to escape if they were in his head?

An image of Leon rose into his mind. With it came feelings of calm and solidity. The dreamlike quality returned, confusing the boundaries between what he remembered and his nightmares since.

What had he meant when he said he'd seen his face in a vision? He definitely remembered him saying it, although it hadn't fully registered at the time. A vision? What had he meant?

Maybe he would go and find them and get some answers.

He registered the thought as the first he'd had about what came next. Not long ago he'd thought there wasn't going to be a next. He shuddered and quickly turned his attention to remembering the faces of his rescuers. Of the four, Sol's and Leon's were the clearest. The other faces were indistinct and shadowed. All of them had given off a rock solid, unflustered vibe.

He relaxed slowly without noticing as he lay wondering about the mysteries that had appeared in his world. Under the quilt was warm and safe. He slipped into sleep with a frown creasing his forehead.

He woke up later, instantly wide-awake. He looked around the room for whatever it was that had woken him. The room was still lit by the bedside lamp and nothing had changed. He looked down at his sleeping face. Disorientation hit him like a buffeting wind. The motion blinked him to the other side of the room. He stared back at the bed. From where he stood (*stood?*) he could see the top of his head and the mound of his body under the quilt. Leading from the mound to him was a faint silvery thread-like line.

A slow wave of calm washed over him. Apart from that he didn't feel anything. He should have been freaking, but he wasn't. He wasn't hurting either, for the first time in what seemed like a lifetime. No pain, no fear, just calm. There was a quiet logic to the realisation that he left unexplored. He didn't care why or how; it felt good.

He lifted his hands and looked at them. Apart from being pale they looked normal, pre-Inquisition normal, no burns or bruising. He flexed the fingers and turned them around. The fingers began to melt away like ice under a blowtorch. The hands dissolved to stumps. He looked up at the bed. No change. He looked back at his hands. Solid and pale. Seconds later the fingers began to melt again. He watched the hands melt to stumps then looked up to the bed and was beside it again, looking at his sleeping face.

He looked back at the door, and was pressed against it, the close-up grain of the wood filling his vision. He reached for the handle and drifted through the door, passing slowly through what felt like thicker air out onto the landing. The lights were out and the landing black, but everything was visible. He thought about the stained glass front door and was there, hovering a little above head height in the hallway. He approached the door and pressed through its thickness out into the garden.

Cloud covered the sky, but the garden glowed with a dusky mauve light that seemed not to have a direct source. Movement was as easy as thinking in that direction. He moved around the garden, tingling with feelings of freedom and exhilaration as the trees and bushes blurred past him.

A thought stopped him. Was he just dreaming? The experience was so real that he'd not questioned its reality. Maybe it was just another opiate-tinged dream. How could he tell if it was a dream or not?

The sensation of somebody behind him made him spin round. A few paces away, sniffing the air, stood the dogs. Both were glowing like the rest of the garden, although the light around them was noticeably brighter than that around the bushes beside them.

Jared smiled, relieved. 'Hey dogs.'

Both dogs cocked their head. But there was no way they could have heard him, his vocal chords were tucked up in bed. But then so were his eyes and he could still see.

One dog snorted and began sniffing the grass near his feet. The other dog sniffed once more in his direction then turned and ambled away. Looking in the dog's direction he noticed the silvery cord leading away from him in the direction of the cottage. He felt himself tighten all over, as if his skin was shrinking.

He opened his eyes and immediately grimaced at the pain from a cramp in his calf.

He was painfully aware of being back in his body. Pain needled all over him, everywhere throbbed and pounded. He felt like he'd fallen inside an Iron Maiden.

He stood and hobbled over to the gilt mirror above the washstand. He looked at his reflection, ignoring the damage and other changes that aged and pinched his face, and stared into his eyes. He'd never thought about it before, but here he was staring at a reflection of his face and the eyes he was looking through. Eyes that he didn't need to see. His face, but not him. Again that sense of being locked in.

An old Martha and the Vandellas tune ghosted around his mind. He did have somewhere to run though. The reflection in the mirror smiled revealing a broken tooth.

He hobbled back to the bed and sat down, the idea taking on substance quickly, no detail, just a solidifying of purpose.

He lay back wondering how to do it, dredging his memory for what he'd heard or read about out of body experiences. They were accepted phenomena that had been experimentally verified, and weren't always stimulated by a near death experience, but what else triggered them? Maybe he could just think himself out, like he could move by thinking about it when he was out.

He seized on the aim like a flung lifebuoy and spent the next few hours lying on the bed visualising himself rising out of his body or being stood on the other side of the room. Nothing he tried worked, but by the time he eventually stopped trying the pains in his body had faded to a complaining murmur and his mind was calm.

The conundrum continued to hamster wheel around his head throughout the next day. He spent most of it outside wandering around the garden and sitting in the sun. Ringing the cottage were flowerbeds overflowing with flowers, most of which he recognised although he couldn't name them all. Bees, presumably from the hive tucked in one corner of the garden, bustled around the beds and the rose-covered cottage walls. The air was heavy with variety of perfumes. Aside from a small kitchen garden, an orchard surrounded the cottage. Apples of several varieties, pear, cherry, hazel and chestnut, all bordering on ancient, dotted the neat lawn grass.

He lay underneath a spreading chestnut, the dogs sitting sphinx-like at a distance.

When he looked in the mirror he saw his reflection, but it was only the reflection of bits of his body. He couldn't see himself, the seer that was doing the seeing, the seer that could still see even when not using his eyes. He could even see in the dark. He wished he'd thought to look in the mirror while he was out of his body, and wondered what he would have seen. But the dogs had seen him, or at least been aware of him, and responded to his voice.

The thoughts continued to occupy his mind, along with thoughts of Leon and the PLO.

Occasional chance exchanges with Aled, usually passing in the kitchen or hallways, or brief interludes with Kay when she changed his dressing provided his only human interaction. They both seemed inclined not to talk and, although pleasant enough, restricted the conversation to inquiries about his health, the weather, and facts about the cottage and garden. Their unwillingness to talk and the infrequency of the meetings made him suspect that they were avoiding him. Either that or they just didn't use much of the cottage. Sometimes he'd hear a door close or faint music, but most of the time it was as though he were the only occupant. There were no repeats of his earlier flashback experience, and despite his attempts he didn't leave his body again.

Anxiety pursued him, and panic regularly threatened to overwhelm him. The reassuring safety of the oasis with its canine guardians was a line of defence against his fear. He got strength and comfort from the dogs who followed him around the garden and sat with him quietly at a distance, never too friendly or interested in being stroked, but there anyway. After what had happened when he'd first tried to have a bath, he felt that they understood him somehow, or at least knew what he was feeling.

The connection felt like the one he remembered from Leon and the others, calm, quiet, and sure of themselves. Or was that just the way he'd seen them in his battered state, his rescuers pumped up to superhuman proportions?

Doubts about the validity of his memories went unchallenged. To challenge them would have meant summoning them for cross-examination. The last thing he wanted to do was think about what had happened. Whenever a memory forced itself on him he would busy himself with some physical activity, anything, or failing that plunge into some mental task like algebra or reciting the alphabet backward, anything to avoid the thoughts.

He thought about the insane world outside and the forces that had brought him there. Society was regressing steadily, lumbering downhill, gaining speed, and heading for certain catastrophe. There they were living in the twenty first century with all its potential benefits in accumulated knowledge and capabilities, but they might as well have been living in the Dark Ages. As capabilities had grown and knowledge expanded there'd been a reduction in personal awareness and freedom. Way different from the vision of the mid-twentieth century when World War Two ended, or at least seemed to, and a bright tomorrow was seen where advances in technology would free societies from the drudge of labour and release them to pursue activities of a higher order.

The Second World War hadn't really ended though; it just changed names and became the 'Cold War'. Different enemy, same principle. When the Soviet Union imploded, the focus shifted again. On the surface it looked like different wars, but in reality it was the same routine being replayed over and again, one following the other, some overlapping in a barely noticed consecutive order; with the same key factions in the financial-military-industrial complex involved and the same agendas being pursued. War was the U.S.'s biggest industry and export. The U.S. had overthrown, or attempted to overthrow, no less than sixty-five governments since 1949.

The U.S. defence budget the previous year was close to seven hundred billion dollars. Seven hundred billion dollars divvied up among the good ol' boys network in the congressional-military-industrial complex. And what was being defended? The world wasn't in danger of being taken over by Muslims or Communists.

The only reason why the Federation formed and joined with the Arabs had been because of U.S. military and economic expansion.

Since 1945 UK forces themselves had been involved in actions in Korea, Palestine, Malaysia, Kenya, Cyprus, Aden, Suez, the Falklands, the Balkans, the Middle East and the current one, with Northern Ireland filling in any gaps. In recent years the UK had been the third largest military spender in the world, giving the lie to the media reports of 'defence cuts'. Over £27 billion of taxpayers' money was poured into the military and a further £900 million subsidised the UK arms industry in one year.

A classic doublethink situation existed where the top five United Nations nations were the world's top five arms dealers. In fact it was likely to the point of certain that the baton and stun gun used on him were manufactured overseas by British companies.

The thing was, the general population of a country didn't make war; it was the leaders of the country who determined the policy. It was always a simple matter to drag the people along though. All they had to do was tell them they were being attacked, and denounce the pacifists for lack of patriotism and exposing the country to greater danger.

The public were so conditioned to war as a political recourse that they left their homes and families and went off to fight, to defend the motherland, the empire or the faith, uphold national honour, protect the national interest, prevent enemy attack, in fact for any reason that their leaders fed them. Nowadays they went to war to uphold democracy and establish peace. And those that didn't fight directly supported by keeping the wheels turning at home, and by not taking a stand.

The thousands working for Royal Ordnance, for instance. Okay, the people didn't get to see the effects of the 'products' they made because it wasn't shown on television, but what did they think they did? It was hard to imagine. Did their children know what they did for a living?

Apart from their ignorance of facts and their conditioned

beliefs about conflict resolution, there were other reasons why the public was so compliant. One of the biggest reasons was a complicit media which, when it wasn't feeding the public biased socio-political information, was conditioning them into lifestyles that supported the governmental agenda of production and consumption, and discouraged growth in awareness, personal responsibility and community.

A prime example was the news war reports. Very rarely were dead bodies shown. Blown up buildings and vehicles, even soldiers or tanks firing at some unseen thing, but never the result. Maybe one body shown per fifty or a hundred thousand dead. Maybe if they showed pictures of that day's dead, every day, with a little counter in the corner clicking away, people might start to get a real impression of what war was about, especially when they saw how many women and children were on the list.

Or the fact that a footballer, TV presenter or soap opera actor was paid more than say, a teacher or a nurse? Was it that their role in society was somehow more important? How could sports or entertainment be rated as more socially important than education or healthcare though, unless the distractions served a larger purpose?

They'd been cheated out of that utopian vision. There was the potential in western culture for everybody to work short hours, have somewhere to live, enough to eat, and their own ecologically sound transport. If that were the case though, society would change. So mechanisms had been put in place to make sure it didn't happen, state education, and the wage and taxation systems being among the most effective.

But the improvement of the general standard of living by the increase in technology was inevitable. For the purposes of the minority that controlled the country there needed to be other structures present to divert the potential within the population down either dead-end or coercive avenues. Intense media exposure inclined the population into behaviour that revolved around the production and consumption of material goods. Ever-changing fashion standards and an emphasis on 'the latest', coupled with peer pressure and fear of ostracism made sure that it was a never-ending carousel that hardly anybody jumped off.

The other structure was the manufactured presence of an external threat. In the years leading up to the current military action against the Federation and since, it had been the spectre of the terrorist, fanatical, barely human individuals and organisations intent on delivering death and destruction to the civilised world. The terrorist, real and imagined, was created by groups far older, more established, and more insidious than those the terrorist was said to represent. Groups whose agendas could be traced back into last century; power-based agendas focused on control, of information, finance, natural resources and whole populations. Terrorists wearing suits and ties.

The threat of terrorism was good for business. It maintained an environment of fear and state of crisis necessary to keep the population compliant, and to encourage their handing over of power into the hands of the government. People willingly gave up their rights and freedoms if they thought that's what was necessary to keep them safe. One of the most blatant and tragic cases so far had been the scrapping of the United States Constitution by the Patriot Acts. But even then, the compliance of an entire population wasn't guaranteed and the laws had to be passed in secret. The fabricated threats to society paved the way for the moves.

It took an acute perception to see the gradual habituation of the population to being governed by surprise; to accepting decisions planned in secret; to believing the situations were so complex that the government had to act on information which the people couldn't understand, or so dangerous that, even if the people could understand it, it couldn't be released because of national security. The process was so subtle, each step disguised as a temporary emergency measure or associated with real social purposes. And all the crises' and reforms so occupied the people that they didn't see the slow motion underneath, the process of government growing remoter and remoter. Not only that but each measure, each reform was introduced in such a way as to make any opposition to it seem unpatriotic or sympathetic with the enemy.

Each successive move built on the preceding one, with the powers that be learning from the previous attempts and perfecting their techniques, all the time depending on the stupidity and short attention span of the masses. And well they might, because that lack of perspective itself was contrived through education and the media, and was a known neurological effect of watching television.

It was the fight against the media mouth of the machine had brought the three of them together. He thought about Dan and Pat, out there somewhere, hiding. He wondered where they were, and how many others had gone to ground.

The unstructured days suited him as much as the isolation. He didn't want to do anything or talk to anyone. It also meant he could catch up on sleep lost during the night. Not only was getting to sleep difficult, he would waken several times in the night, wide awake without knowing why. In his sleep his dreams haunted him, being chased, smothered or crushed, or sinking in quicksand.

The silence of the cottage and garden was welcome. Unknown sounds were threatening. Sitting under a tree one day, a wood pigeon's clattering takeoff above him startled him so much that a squirt of piss ran down his leg. Instantly he was on his feet and furious, at the bird, at himself, at everything and nothing in particular. The rage refused to fade for a long time. Anxiety and anger jostled him daily making him doubly glad he wasn't around people.

He gave up trying to project himself out of his body. It didn't work, although the attempts relaxed him.

The infection in the bullet wound cleared up much quicker than he'd expected, using silver colloid. The virtually tasteless liquid was apparently made by Aled. Jared took it orally and Kay put it on the dressings. Slowly the swelling on his foot went down and it became easier to walk. He picked the scabs off the burns leaving mottled patterns all over him. At first glance his hands looked like he had a skin pigmentation condition. A closer look at the regularity and precision of the scars soon corrected the impression.

Eventually the limbo isolation began to press in on him, the lack of stimulation forcing him back on himself, pushing at the locked doors in his mind. He realised it was time to go.

The dawn chorus was in full swing and saturated the morning air. Jared crouched and scratched behind the dogs' ears. He was going to miss them and their communion bond. Neither reacted to the gesture, just sat staring at the gates. Jared stared too, waiting for the PLO pickup.

For a moment he stopped worrying about what waited for him in the world beyond the gates and immersed himself in birdsong. Whatever waited for him in the city it was unlikely to be a dawn chorus.

His pulse jumped at the sound of a heavy vehicle approaching. It stopped by the gates, revved its engine twice and beeped once. He took a deep breath and stood.

'Okay, later lads. Don't be eating any dodgy meat now.'

At the gates he turned back to the cottage. The dogs were where he'd left them, looking at him. The cottage looked as solid as it's double century age. Anxiety sank its claws into his guts and he felt the urge to return to the safety and companionship of the dogs and their surreal oasis.

He slipped through the gate and closed it behind him.

The driver of the truck was a woman that had been in the group that rescued him. Although he'd only seen her once just before the group left, her olive green eyes were unforgettable.

'Alrighty?'

'Better than I was the last time I saw you.'

'I'll bet.' She gestured behind with her head. 'Jump up on the bed back there and shut the curtains.'

He climbed into the back. 'You expecting trouble?'

'Trouble's a permanent fixture these days. Could be we'll get a tug even though the wagon's permits are on the ANPR system. It gives the Stazi something to do being as there's so many of them on the streets. I've got papers too so there shouldn't be a problem. There's always the risk of some frustrated little fascist wanting to have a look in the cab or the back though. If it looks like we're going to get stopped, the bed base lifts up and you get in sharpish. There's a bolt underneath to lock it shut.'

The smouldering anxiety in his guts sputtered into flame. He swallowed hard against the heartburn.

'And if they find me?'

'They die and we run. Enough of the negative though, you look a lot better than the last time I saw you.'

'I should hope so, I probably looked like shit then. I'm feeling loads better. Bit worried about my mental health at times, but I'm okay.'

'You been spinning out?'

'Guess you could call it that.'

He mentioned the shakes and crying, and the panic attacks and dreams, realising as he spoke that he'd missed conversation with another human being. He laughed self-consciously.

'Sat behind here it feels like I'm in a confessional.'

'Tree Hail Mary's and an Our Father and you'll be as roight as rain.'

They both laughed. The action felt strange to Jared. He thought about it and couldn't remember the last time he'd laughed or smiled.

'It's not surprising you've been spinning out,' said the woman 'We'll sort that out though.'

'How?'

'You'll see.'

The statement sounded ominous even though he felt it wasn't meant to. He sat back. The uncertainty swelled and filled the booth. Here he was again in the darkness of a truck not knowing where he was being taken. His heart thrashed against the back of his ribs. He sat up, breathing quickly, and drew the curtains halfway. The woman glanced round and immediately her expression changed.

'You okay?'

He licked his dry lips. 'Bit claustrophobic.'

'Okay. Stay back though eh.'

He sat back and tried to relax.

'Shrug your shoulders a few times and take long, deep

breaths.'

He shrugged his shoulders. They were tense, but then he was tense all over. The deep breathing seemed to clear his head. He brought the image of Leon to mind and focused on the feeling of solidity to counteract the anxiety about the unknown life he was being driven into.

The traffic build up as they neared the city mirrored the build up of tension in him despite the breathing and focus. There seemed to be more Squad patrols on the streets. He had the sensation of having been away for ages.

Driving down off the flyover into the city he saw a line of stationary vehicles at a checkpoint ahead. Uniformed men were walking around them, inspecting inside and underneath. A Squad man with a machine gun across his chest looked up in their direction.

Jared moved to the end of the bed and reached under the mattress at the same time as the woman muttered for him to hide. He fumbled around for a catch or something to lift the base up with, but couldn't feel anything. Immediately he began to panic. He ran his fingers along the edge of the base. On the edge closest to him he felt a small indentation. He jammed his finger underneath it and lifted. Stuck on the underside of the wooden base was thick rubberised foam.

He slipped inside and pulled the base down. The sound of the engine rumbled loudly in the cramped space. He found the bolt and slid it across. The gloom was total but didn't stop him from looking around wide-eyed. The ridged metal floor cut into his knees and calves. Cold sweat ran down his sides.

The engine slowed and the truck stopped with a squeal and hiss of airbrakes.

The questioning voice of a Squad man came from disturbingly close by his head. He heard the woman answer, and then silence. The man spoke again and the cab moved.

Jared tried to slow his rapid breathing.

The cab door slammed. Moments later he heard the rear doors open.

The space started to press in on him. The air grew thick. He shook his head.

The rear doors slammed.

Just a few more minutes, all he had to do was hold it down for a few more minutes.

The cab moved as someone climbed in. Jared held his breath. There was a muffled rummaging and then tapping directly above his head. He jammed a knuckle into his mouth and bit down.

More knocking, this time behind him. He tensed against the urge to piss.

The cab moved again, and then again and the door slammed.

He let his breath out slowly.

The engine started up and the truck pulled away.

He counted to ten and slid the bolt back. He pushed the base up and looked over the edge. The woman had one hand in the air wagging her finger. She made zipping motions over her mouth.

He climbed out as quietly as he could.

She turned the radio on and lifted the mike out of its cradle.

'Eight eight three.'

There was a static-filled pause and then, 'Go ahead eight eight three.'

'Running a little behind, got delayed at a checkpoint.'

Another pause. 'Problem with the paperwork?'

'No, just bored Stazi. Even checked out the décor in the cab.'

'Roger that. See you shortly then.'

She hung the mike back, turned to Jared and made zipping motions again. He nodded understanding, but the she didn't see him. Given their rabid obsession with surveillance and information databasing it was quite possible that the cop who searched the truck had planted a chip in the cab. He thought about the neutralised chip in his sinuses. Not a pleasant thought, even though he knew it had been disarmed.

4

*Education is the most powerful weapon you can use
to change the world.*
– Nelson Mandela

Sometimes the blackness fitted. A black velvet that pressed gently, occupying spaces and crevices, wrapping in a second skin, soft and deep. Sometimes. Other times the embrace turned vicelike, crushing with a suffocating weight, the absence of light rendering the air a different element. That fitted too with his sense of floating, adding a confusing vertiginous harmonic, disorientation lapping at the edges like a threatening tide. It was an old friend though, ancient, pre-form.

He inhaled deeply. Blackness flowed into his lungs, embalming his already immobile body. The harmonic twanged through him again, constricting and expanding.

A door opened sluicing light into the room. Sol stepped inside quickly and shut the door.

'You okay?'

Leon inhaled slowly and deeply. 'Hmm…'

'Thought I'd look in on you.'

'Just looking. Nothing doing.'

'The policy is no soloing, remember.'

'Like I said, just looking. I want to know what they're up to.'

'What're you up to?'

'How do you mean?'

'You know what I'm talking about, Leon. Shut me out if you have to, but don't treat me like a deadhead.'

Leon sighed again. 'Just processing, don't sweat it. Thinking of Jared too.'

'Still think it was a sketchy idea letting him go and try to recruit his friends.'

'Suggested ways of stopping him? No, their connection's too strong, better to bring them in.'

'Yeah, and a whole bagful of variables. I still think it's risky.'

'It's all risky. We've got to take the risks.'

'Well, we have, Jared's on the streets. So maybe a good idea to keep an ear out?'

Silence.

Sol turned and walked out.

Leon clicked on a small desk light. The action drew his thoughts. What was the point in lights if you could see in the dark? Then again what was the point in eyes if you could see through space and time?

He had been treating Sol like a deadhead though. Even though he'd buried the awareness that had been insisting since the Jared job, conflagration and shock echoing across time, there was no way Sol wouldn't be aware of it and its association with Jared.

He clasped his hands behind his head and leaned back. Sol was right about Jared too. The sooner they had his friends in the better. It was too risky for him to be on the streets.

**

The fire escape steps rang as Dan took them two at a time. The stairs stopped in front of a narrow, featureless steel door. He looked back and checked the alley mouth.

A key inserted into the brass cylinder lock brought it out revealing an aperture inside which a blue light pulsed. His finger in the hole produced a quiet beeping sound, followed by a hydraulic hiss from around the door. He withdrew his finger and the lock slid back. He leaned away from the heavy door to pull it open and stepped inside. Immediately a pulsing alarm began, a low, bass growl that set his teeth and guts on edge even though he knew its source.

'Chill home, it's Dan,' he said, pulling the door closed.

The alarm stopped. He tapped a combination onto the console

on the wall, and the door relocked with a hiss. He took off his trainers and walked over the scratchy coir matting to the office. He flipped open the computer and typed in his pass code. A message appeared on the screen.

Hi hon. Back around three. See file labelled Psy-Ops.

He looked at his watch and wondered whether Jared would make it.

The file was a graph showing a complex layout of what he recognised as high pass frequency signatures, along with dates, times and other figures. The signatures were new, and there was no indication of cluster identity. He checked the times. The transmissions had appeared about five days ago. He stared at the lines, then gave up and walked over to the kitchen.

On the black marble worktop stood a bottle of Polish vodka, a jug of tomato juice and three glasses. He smiled and poured a drink. He raised his glass in a silent toast, then ambled over to the stairs on the other side of the room.

He steadied himself with one hand against the wall and climbed the castellated olive-green blocks. At the top he turned and sat. He sipped his drink remembering sitting there the day Jared had been taken. Seemed like a hundred years ago. Things had stepped up a gear since then. On that score Jared had been right to go to ground. Even the option of a detailed virtual identity was becoming less sure as the military service exemption criteria narrowed to keep up with the demand for cannon fodder. The run in with the patrol had been the last straw for Pat. He didn't blame her for opting out; he wasn't far off it himself.

Anxiety buzzed around his stomach like an insect fretting against a window. It was ages since he'd seen Jared and then only briefly before he'd hooked up with the PLO. There'd been word saying that he was okay, but there'd also been talk of paranoia, anger attacks and uncontrollable shaking. He wished again that there was a sympathetic psychiatrist in the Resistance. There were a couple of medics who were willing to take the risks involved with treating people in the Resistance, but it sounded like it wasn't Jared's body that had sustained the lasting damage.

A tone from the computer drew him from his thoughts. He climbed back down the steps, leaning away from the mild vertigo that tugged at him, hurried across the room and rapidly tapped in switching instructions. The saver fractals blinked off, replaced by a view of the fire escape. He walked to the door, unlocked it and pushed it open. Jared jumped through. Dan closed and relocked the door then turned to Jared.

'Hey.'

'Alright mate.'

Jared indicated into the room with his head. 'Nice pad.'

Dan nodded. 'Drink?'

'Anything cold.'

'Bloody Mary?'

Jared chuckled. 'Nice one.'

He moved slowly around the room. He stopped in a square of sunlight in the middle of the room stretching up to the blue wedge of skylight, yellow diaphanous walls slowly shifting with golden dust motes.

Dan turned, drinks in hand and stopped. Jared was stood, the light haloed around his head, scything his arm slowly, disturbing the carousel of particles, palm upturned as if trying to catch the dust. Dan's stomach creased, seeing the tattoo-like markings on the moving hand. He walked over and stood in front of Jared. Jared looked up and smiled a lopsided smile.

'Simple things and simple minds.'

Dan eyes were suddenly hot with tears. He set the glasses on a half wall, then turned to find Jared had moved closer and was standing, still smiling, open armed. They embraced for long moments, dust dancers weaving in the stillness around them. Finally Dan drew away, embarrassed, but Jared held onto his shoulders, looking into his eyes.

'Good to see you, Dan.'

Dan retrieved the drinks and handed one to Jared. 'Yeah, you too. Pat'll be here in a blim.'

'She's doing all right for herself by the looks of things. What's she up to, body guarding for pop stars?'

'Don't take the piss, Jared. She's let us use this place. She wasn't happy about you coming here, but wanted to help.'

'Well excuse me!' Jared put his glass down. 'Maybe we should have arranged somewhere else.'

'Maybe, but like I said, she wanted to help.'

'But wasn't happy about it.'

'I'm glad you're here, Jared. You know Pat, private and touchy.'

Jared didn't smile at the old joke. He'd wondered whether unresolved stuff between him and Pat would come up. After leaving Aled and Kay's he'd seen her once before he'd joined Leon. She'd argued that the PLO didn't sound right and that his friends were there for him and would look after him. He'd known what she was saying, but had gone anyway.

He shook his head as all the old feelings bubbled up again. He'd done what he had to.

'I'm glad I'm here too, Dan.'

Dan didn't answer.

'How is Pat anyway?'

'She's okay. She took your leaving hard, man. Felt like we'd let you down. Thought that's what you felt. She's okay though. Bit stressed. She's been talking about leaving the country.'

Jared shook his head. 'She should stay. We need all the people we've got, especially now.'

'What do you mean, especially now?'

'What do you mean, what do you mean? Don't you feel it?' His face became animated. 'It's like leaning back in your chair, teetering on that point where it could fall either way. Look around you. Soldiers in the street, curfew, folk pissed off with chronic taxes and the war taking all the country's men. It's on the edge. Leon's right –'

'Leon's on a crusade, Jared. We can't build a peaceful future on the wreckage of violence.'

'Hippie bullshit!' Jared exploded. 'This fucking system needs to be torn down! Wreckage is just what we need to build on. As long as it's still standing, there's no room for change. That's why this war has been good –'

'Eh?'

'No,' Jared raised his hand, 'listen. Of course the war's a fuck up. But the way things were going nothing was going to change. Now though, things are different. The whole thing's really unstable. We could start something here, an avalanche that'd bring the whole stinking lot down,' he laughed sheepishly. 'It sounds a bit dramatic, but you know it's true.' He mimed reading something. 'All the underlying, immediate, socio-economic and trigger mechanism causes are in place.'

Dan walked to the window. Beyond the rows of red brick warehouses, the river stretched away, a silted silver-brown snake weaving sluggishly toward the hazy horizon. From this vantage, the city looked so peaceful. But Pat wasn't the only one. He was sick of it too. Maybe it was time to leave, head for the hills.

'Thing is,' said Jared, quieter now, 'you've no idea of what kind of a force we represent.'

Dan turned. 'We?'

'Yes Dan, we. The People's Liberation Organisation and the other bits of fragmented resistance, because despite what you say, we are working toward the same goal, people's liberation.'

Dan turned back to the window.

Jared sighed. 'Look, things are changing, and fast. They've changed loads since I've been with the group. You say Leon's on a crusade. Well, he does have a mission, and it's not that different from yours. The difference is how he's, how we're, prepared to get there. You should come, it'd pop your head. Everybody's so organised. That's the trick, organisation. That and a little willingness to take part in some radical, revolutionary actions.

'I'd really like you to come, Dan. I miss you. Really, there's not a day goes by when I don't wonder where you're at. And worry about you. There's bad shit going on and most folk aren't protected, including you.'

'Talking of bad shit,' said Dan, anxious to change the subject, 'check this out.' He walked over to the computer. 'Access Tech-Storm.'

The screen saver blinked off, replaced with a map Jared

guessed to be Russia from the upper semi-circle of the Arctic Ocean. Dan tapped some keys and layered an isobar map over the landmass of the Siberian Plains.

'The moving arrows show wind direction patterns consistent with the local land forms.'

More tapping highlighted two areas. Upward from the south moved a wide red wedge, lapping against a smaller green swathe above.

'NATO and the Federation just before NATO's 'big push' when the Federation got shoved back into the Gobi. Watch the weather.'

Jared had heard about the action. The media had gone on about the 'victory' for a long time afterward. He watched as the clouds coalesced and formed a huge slowly spinning spiral. The vortex swelled as the storm moved with a slow serpentine certainty. Dan tapped some more keys and opened another window showing the weather system in primary coloured patterns.

'Radar animation. Watch around the nine o'clock position next to the tornado.'

Four straight blobs like the shortened tines of a fork appeared briefly and then were gone.

'Now watch the tornado's trajectory.'

Instead of continuing along its path the vortex moved away almost at right angles and seemed to speed up. Dan tracked forward.

'And again, this time at twelve o'clock.'

Again the blobs appeared momentarily and again the tornado changed direction.

'Always directed southwest, never further north than Astana where the Allied line was. Totally fucked the Red Line, bodies and equipment blown all the way back to Mongolia. And when it got switched off…'

He tapped some more keys. The spiral speeded up then abruptly disappeared. He tracked back and let it run again.

'…and it did get switched off. One minute huffing and puffing and blowing your house down, the next…nothing.'

84

The spiralling clouds suddenly lost their concentrated coherence and broke up into smaller, slowly whirling patches moving steadily away from the loosened centre.

'Right on the back of it came the biggest airborne attack of the war, with the grunts waltzing in after to mop up.'

Jared shook his head. The implications of power necessary for that level of manipulation, not to mention the domino effects on the global weather, were boggling.

'Reckon I could get a copy of this?'

'You'll have to ask Pat.'

There was a toning from the computer. Dan brought a window up showing the fire escape.

'Talk of the Devil.'

'She-Devil.'

'Now now.'

He walked over and unlocked the door. Pat stepped in.

'Sorry I'm late, I've had a bit've a mad day.' She kissed Dan's cheek and then glanced at Jared. 'Jared.'

'Pat.'

She swung her bag off her shoulder and placed it carefully on the floor.

'Had to give Fran a lift. Her ID card failed for some reason, so she couldn't get anywhere or do anything, totally screwed. She reported it and all they could say was that she should have had it bio-personalised. She now has the choice,' she drew speech marks in the air, 'of waiting around a month for a replacement or getting chipped this week. One of these days they're going to phase cards out all together, and then everybody will have to get chipped.

'So I drop her at home and I'm on the way here, stopped at some lights, and the next thing some junkie shithead's put his fist through the passenger window and tried to take my bag off the seat.' She shook her head and bent to reach into her bag.

'And?'

'And I grabbed his hand, pulled, bounced his face off the side of the car and drove off,' she laughed, 'through the red light too. What I really needed was one of those BMW's they make for the

South African market with the three sixty degree CS gas spray and six foot flamethrower.' She reached into the bag and lifted a brown parcel. 'Mexican?'

'Yum, yum,' said Dan. 'How do you know he was a junkie?'

'Aren't they all?'

She laughed, pointing at Dan's expression. 'Not really, tracks. Come on, let's eat.'

Jared watched her walk around the half wall to the table. Her lithe body was just how he remembered. She still moved with that sinuous feline grace that made the long legs and androgynous close-cropped hair, gymnastic, sensuous and compelling to watch,

'How's it going then, Jared?' Pat asked, turning and catching him looking.

Jared shrugged. 'It's going.'

Pat tore open the greasy parcel and inhaled appreciatively with her eyes closed.

'Mm, I do like Mexican food. I wouldn't mind a Chinese takeout once in a while though. Actually the place I got this from used to be a Chinese takeaway. The Mexicans probably got it cheap after the owners had ducked out, or got chased out.'

She handed Dan a burrito. 'Did you check the transmissions?'

'Yeah, couldn't make any sense of them though.'

'No, I need to get into the file at work. Thing is I can't get at it without them knowing. Just accessing it means I've got to come up with a reason why, and if it's not part of my workload there'd be questions. It was a fluke getting that Tech Storm data. Should've needed clearance just to look at it. Fucking government sponsors.'

Jared accepted his food with a nod that Pat didn't see as she seemed to be having trouble looking at him.

'Well don't go risking. It's handy having you there,' said Dan.

'Not sure I'll be there much longer.'

'How come?'

'Been getting the feeling some very hectic smelly stuff is about to hit the spinning thing. I'd rather not be around.'

The food acted like butter on cat's paws, and they ate in

silence. It reminded Jared of times before when their friendship was such that they were comfortable enough in each others company without the need for speech.

'You were talking about bad shit going on,' said Dan finally. 'What did you mean?'

'The whole country,' said Jared. 'It's so on top. Talk about a climate of fear. Street spies, ID checks, stop and search, curfew. What's next? Look at America, martial law in most states. Coming soon to Airstrip One. Although the British were always slyer about things, with their fist-in-the-glove approach. What do you know about the PLO?'

'Not much,' answered Dan. 'Militant. At least one individual with high level info-tech. Rescued my friend from the jaws of death, claimed him for their own.'

Jared smiled. 'Like you said, not much. Remember the problems I was having after the torture?'

'I heard.'

'Kay said it was post-traumatic stress disorder. Leon agreed, said he'd seen the same thing with guys in Russia. He gave me some things to do, mental and physical exercises, ways of separating the part of my mind that was freaking out, so it couldn't pass those impulses on to other parts like my breathing and muscles. How to draw in energy, move it about, and release it. I still have the attacks, not so often now, but I can handle them. That was just the beginning though,' he paused. 'One of the reasons I've not been around is that a group of us have been into some serious training for the past while.'

'Serious training?'

'Yeah,' replied Jared looking pained. 'Thing is, I can't tell you about it right now.'

'What d'ya mean, you can't tell us about it?'

'I just can't, Dan, not now.'

'So if you weren't going to tell us, what was the point in mentioning it?' Pat said.

'Because I want you in on it. That's how I convinced Leon. In fact, Leon and Sol weren't happy about me coming here, but I insisted. You two are family; Leon gets that. But there are security reasons for not talking about it now. Come and visit, talk with Leon and Sol. Really, this is the best –' he broke off, catching a look that passed between Pat and Dan.

'What?'

Dan turned to the window. Pat stared at the floor.

'What, Dan?'

'Just sounds spooky, is all,' Dan answered quietly.

'Spooky how?'

'Well, you disappear for months living with a pretty insular group that looks like some kind of militant black magic mind-cult, then reappear saying you have been doing some serious training with them, but you can't tell me for security reasons, and want me to come and meet the boss and his sidekick, so they can tell me how it is. Spooky, no?'

Jared nodded. 'I hear what you're saying. Leon's not the boss though. It's a non-hierarchical group, kind of. Yes, most of the group's structures and movements are his and Sol's ideas, but they, more than anyone, know what we're up against. They know what tech the authorities have, how to protect ourselves and fight back. I know what you're saying, Dan, but they, you know, them,' he stressed the word, 'have ways of making you talk.'

Jared's intense stare kept Dan from glancing down at his hands.

'Trust me,' said Jared. 'This is the best thing.'

'What kind of training can you talk about then?'

Jared turned to Pat. 'Well, there's an emphasis on physical fitness. Everybody does gym workouts, and we do all sorts of group stuff like rock climbing, sometimes at night, pot holing, that kind of thing. There's theory and ideology that cover guerrilla history and techniques, State control techniques, including the media, the Squad and its methods, that sort of thing. There's other sorts of training too, role play stuff that gets you used to the interrogation methods they use, including sleep deprivation, nudity and shitting in front of each other.'

'Shitting in front of each other?'

Jared laughed at their expressions.

'Yeah. Not all the time, just as part of the training. We use sensory deprivation and hypnosis for deprogramming and reprogramming –'

'Jared,' said Pat, 'do you realise how wrong this sounds?'

'Weird, yes, wrong, no.'

'Hypnosis, sensory and sleep deprivation, and shitting in front of each other sounds more than just weird. It sounds wrong. I agree with some of the things the PLO are doing in terms of resistance, but what does nudity and shitting in front of each other train you to do? All those things add up to brainwashing in my book.'

'You're right, Pat. My brain has been washed. It feels fresh and clear and shining instead of flabby and dirty. It's like a film's been removed from my eyes, I can see clearer.'

'Oh boy, you'll be chanting Haré Krishna next!'

'No, next I tell you to take a running jump.'

'Jared, normal people don't do what you described. It's deviant. And if its not the Kinky Club, what's going on?'

'Basically it gets you over any hang-ups you've got about those things.'

'What are they, resistance fighters or psychotherapists? So what if you've got reservations about public nudity.'

'Ever had a complete body cavity search?'

'You know I haven't.'

'Yeah, I know you haven't. Imagine it then, you've been arrested, they've got you in a room and told you to strip naked. Down to your top, bra, knickers, and then you're stood there bare assed naked, and they're walking around you smirking and making comments. How does it feel? If beforehand you'd got used to being naked in front of people other than your lover of the moment, your sense of self wouldn't be as battered as someone who hadn't.'

'I reckon I'd still feel as vulnerable as.'

'For sure, but definitely not as vulnerable just because of your nakedness. There are stages to their techniques. Strip search is one of the first that's supposed to soften you up. Take away somebody's clothes and you strip away a psychological layer of defence. Because we've grown up in this society, we've inherited its Victorian memes. They have to be gotten rid of before they can be used against us. Same goes for toilet habits. They'll let you go to the toilet, eventually, but then they'll stand and watch you. How do you think that feels? If you've not prepared for it, and it does take practise, that's another layer of defence broken down and they've not even laid a finger on you. Try and imagine how empowering it would be to be forced to do those things and for them not to achieve the desired effect.'

'I'll take your word for it. What were you saying about hypnosis?'

'In a way it's linked to what I just said. As we grow up we're infected by the memes of the society we grow up in. Language, education, religion, the media, all program our minds in specific ways and seriously affect the way we see the world and ourselves. Most of that programming is designed to confine us to a certain places in society and to be productive cogs in the machine. All of the programs are designed to keep us away from the awareness of our full potential, to make sure that we're distracted, obedient and happy little cogs. Techniques like hypnosis are fast-track methods of rewriting those programs…'

'Yeah, and replacing them with what?'

'Whatever you like. I know what you're hinting at, but you're way off the mark. We have so much potential as individuals and as a species, but most of it gets hobbled when we're kids and manipulated as adults. Hypnosis is a key to unlocking those chains. It gives us back control of our minds. With it we can get rid of self-limiting programs and mind viruses, clean up our softdrive, free up some space and install some amazing programs that allow us to access our full potential. Actually I'm surprised at you, buying into that dreary old smear campaign.'

'Forget what the media says, Jared, what you describe sounds very Branch Dravidians.'

'Two answers to that. First, you should check out the behind the scenes FBI and government actions that led to those people, those women and children, being incinerated in that Waco siege before making a judgement, and second, Victorian sensibilities like I said. Because what I described is so removed from your conservative centre, you label them weird or cultish. Thing is though, it's society that's labelled them like that, you're just parroting those value judgements as if they were your own.'

'Conservative judgements?'

'Yes, conservative. Take your feelings on public nudity and shitting. There are some cultures that don't have hang-ups about those things. If you'd grown up in those cultures, your feelings on the subject would be different, like it'd feel weird to cover yourself in clothes or to insist on shitting in private. It's really difficult to see how our past shapes our perception now, but it does in very deep and powerful ways.'

'Point taken, but it still sounds weird,'

'Have you learned how to make bombs yet?' Dan asked.

Jared looked at Dan for a moment before answering.

'Dan, even if I'd not teamed up with these lot, I'd still be talking about armed resistance. They'll not take me alive again. But the PLO is something quite special. They're, we're, freedom fighters in every sense, not just political. Like the man said, we've got to emancipate ourselves from mental slavery. The nightmare that's going on in the world is because people's minds have been co-opted. With freed minds people wouldn't stand for the shit that's going on, and would know what to do about it. Free your mind and everything else follows.'

'Free your mind using sensory deprivation and hypnosis?'

Jared turned to Pat. 'Using whatever works. Hypnosis, NLP, Mimetics, whatever wakes you up to how the mind works and is controlled, and gives you a way to take control of it yourself. Our personal power is constantly eroded, given away and taken away. The State doesn't want empowered individuals. Plenty of mechanisms have been put in place to prevent people from realising their full potential.'

'And to find out about this serious training we've got to come and meet your leader.'

Jared sighed. 'Come on, Pat. This isn't like you. It's like you've made your mind up already. What's really going on?'

Pat stared at Jared without answering. The stare held.

Dan cleared his throat. Pat broke the stare and looked down at her hands.

'Pat?' Jared persisted.

'I don't want to talk about it anymore,' said Pat without looking up.

Jared stared at Pat, willing her to look at him again. She didn't. He sighed and walked over to Dan.

'I'm gone.'

Dan nodded.

'Look after yourself Pat,' said Jared quietly.

Pat glanced up and then away again. 'Yeah, you too.'

At the door Jared stopped and put his hand on Dan's shoulder. 'Please come. It's important.'

Dan nodded again. He closed and locked the door and turned to Pat.

'What do you make of all that then?' Pat said.

'Don't know what to make of it really. Sounds a bit weird.'

'Sounds cultish to me.'

'But Jared's no fool. He'd see through something like that.'

'Who knows where his head's at after what happened to him. He was really animated and intense when he was talking about it. And some of the things he said didn't sound like him. He was broken and vulnerable when he joined them, maybe he wasn't thinking straight. Maybe he wouldn't have joined if he'd not been in such a state, or if he'd had us with him.'

'Maybe. But how about considering that he knows what he's talking about, or taking what he has to say at face value? You know he's right about the social programming bit.'

'But you heard what he said about having to get naked and shit in front of the others. That sounds like some weird cult behaviour.'

'I didn't hear him say that he had to. And the reasons that he gave for doing it made sense. Jared knows, more than any of us, about their methods. And I've met some of the others in the organisation and they don't fit my picture of a cult. Maybe like he said it's our cultural hang-ups that make it sound cultish. He's definitely picked up on their militancy though, "they'll not take me alive again". Talk about hardcore.'

'Well that at least I can understand.'

'Maybe we should meet up with them and see for ourselves.'

'No thanks. I'll conduct my ablutions in private thank you. Go for it. Like you say, you've met before.'

'The scat thing's really got to you hasn't it?'

'It all sounds a bit too weird for me.'

***

Watching the way he walked, an observer might have thought it was raining or blowing a gale. It was neither. The night air was still and humid. A heavy shower had sluiced through the clammy mouth that had been pressed over the city for days. The relief had been instantaneous and brief, and now the concrete exhaled steaming moisture, adding to the already damp air.

Dan walked as briskly as he dared, head down, baseball cap peak low, feet longing to match pace with his mind and run through the emptying streets. A few others hurried by, caught up in the pre-curfew tension. On the spot fines, overnight lock-up or up to a month in jail for repeat offences were risks few dared to take. In theory there was a degree of leniency in the hours immediately after curfew to allow for extenuating circumstances. The reality included bribery, which wasn't always successful, or wasn't possible in the case of the fine that arrived in the post courtesy of the facial recognition programming of the CCTV, which automatically scanned faces and checked the database for authorisation.

He was jerked out of his thoughts by an amplified voice.

'Warning – You are being monitored by CCTV.'

The voice came from loudspeakers positioned on a pole beneath the cameras.

'I repeat; your behaviour is being monitored by CCTV.'

Dan looked around to see who was being singled out. He wasn't the only one. Other people were looking around too. A group of youths nearby were looking guiltily at each other. One of them stuck his fingers up at the camera, and the group slunk off.

Dan carried on, disturbed at the intrusion and reminder of the constant presence of the CCTV watchers. The weirdest thing was that the voice that came from the speakers was a child's voice.

The sick psychology of the use of children's voices was supposed to make it harder to show defiance to the cameras, the theory being that it was harder to be defiant to a child's voice. The warped psychological warfare aspect meant that children recruited from schools for the scheme and shown around the CCTV centres were indoctrinated into the concept that forcing people to behave in certain ways in public was normal in a free society. Just as disturbing was the fact that the public, manipulated into law-and-order hysteria in their predictable sheep-like way, accepted not only the intrusive surveillance and its aspect of public humiliation, but also the perverted use of their children.

He turned the corner and came face to face with Bellevue. During the Federation infrasound weapon retaliations, for reasons probably known to the twisted experts in that field, the shock waves had razed the area that Dan now approached, instantly flattening to rubble a half mile wide doughnut and left a perfectly circular area about half a mile in diameter in the middle. The intact area had probably been the area directly below the UAV drone plane that housed the 'bomb'. Undamaged buildings rose from the centre of the flattened expanse like a gothic crown, reminding him of pictures he'd seen of Las Vegas squatting in the desert.

He stepped off smooth tarmac onto the desiccated surface of Bellevue. As well as buildings being pulverised in the attack, tarmac and paving slabs had fractured to dust.

Among the bulldozed banks, once temporary, now semi-permanent camps mushroomed. Rows of canvas tents and wet facilities filled the squares. Fires burned in drums despite the humidity. Women moved around them, while men lounged in knots looking on. Further in the Government Issue tents gave way to tin and cardboard in predictable shanty style. The radical change in environment was echoed by the figures populating it, suspicious, sallow-eyed refugees wearing charity clothes of thirty-year-old fashions. No one here seemed concerned about the curfew, but then this was a police no-go area. With no cameras and a hundred places to duck into, the Zone was the place to run should you get caught on the streets after hours.

Feeling he was being followed he speeded up his pace, resisting the urge to check behind. He ducked into the dim interior of a marquee. Once inside he ran through the yellowy light between rows of beds. A group of men in a corner looked up suspiciously from their card game. He ducked through another flap back outside, then stopped and stood beside the flap, fist raised.

Someone barked a question inside the marquee in what sounded like Russian. He heard no response. He stood almost overbalancing, waiting to slam down on his pursuer's head.

'Dan,' said a voice from inside the marquee, 'I'm going to walk through the flap and I don't want you to hit me.'

A figure ducked through before Dan had a chance to think. Sol straightened up and nodded at Dan's raised fist.

'Thought you were a pacifist.'

Dan lowered his hand. 'Fuckin' cloak and dagger bullshit.'

Sol smiled and motioned with his head.

A wide dirt track skirted the perimeter of the surviving circle of buildings, a radial road around what remained of the commercial buildings and old city pubs. Those that hadn't been demolished during or after the event still stood, amputee buildings, their heavily graffiti'd walls fringed with stalls and shacks, most selling cheap meals and drinks, the 'kitchens' of Tent City. One wall held a large graffiti mural, a futuristic scene of a fortress city in the middle of a battleground wasteland, and the words 'Welcome to Hell View'.

They stepped back onto smooth tarmac and Dan had the repeat sensation of entering another world. He turned and looked back over the flattened plain at the horizon of buildings on the other side of the zone, a ring of concrete and brick mountains surrounding the ruined plain.

Bellevue had a ghetto air to it. There was very little traffic and lots of people just hanging around. Here and there small groups of sullen men loitered, smoking and spitting, and heckling the bored prostitutes. Piles of rubbish, and household items littered the gutters and fronts of boarded up businesses.

Halfway down a back street they mounted some stairs to a doorway in the side of a warehouse. Locks clicked in the door and it swung open.

Behind the door sat a man in what looked like a motorised cart. The chair was low-hung, and the back of the car curved around and slightly over the seat, giving the impression of a gothic racing car. The driver's posture was twisted in the bucket seat, his head in constant uncontrolled motion. One hand lay twisted, flamingo-like, in his lap, the other grasped a joystick on the seat arm.

'Wotcha,' said Sol, squeezing the man's motionless arm. 'Dan, Cleve, Dan.'

Hanging around Cleve's neck was a large glass medallion. It lit up with green letters.

HI DAN

'Hi,' said Dan, unsure whether to shake the man's hand or not. He decided not to.

He turned and followed Sol across the loading bay to another door. Beside it a woman was sitting on a crate swinging her legs. A machine gun lay on the crate beside her.

'Dan, Nicole, Dan.'

She nodded at Dan, who nodded back.

'Nicole was with us when we lifted Jared.'

'Yeah?' Dan puzzled momentarily trying to place her, and then remembered the machine gun. 'Er, thanks.'

Nicole smiled and nodded again, then without breaking eye contact gestured with her head toward Sol who seemed to be in a rush and was already through the door.

Dan went through the door and caught up. 'What's Cleve's story?'

'He's our doorman. Cerebral palsy. Classed as a useless spastic by society. His speech-related brain impulses are translated to analogue and displayed on the readout. The screen changes colour with his mood.'

Dan thought for a moment. 'I hesitate to say it, but isn't he a bit of a liability as a doorman, I mean, security-wise?'

Sol held a door open. 'Don't you believe it.'

The office looked like that of a typical haulage company, if a little smarter. Leon was sitting at a desk looking at a sheaf of papers. He laid the papers down as they walked in and stood up. Dan noticed how fluid and seemingly effortlessly he moved for such a big man.

'Good to see you again, Dan,' he said, gesturing to a chair. 'Glad you made it. Get you a drink?'

Dan shook his head.

'Okay, down to business then. What do you know about the People's Liberation Organisation?'

'Not much really. The authorities say you're responsible for various bombings and kidnappings. You're definitely hardcore, you saved Jared. Other than that I don't know what you're into, or up to,' he ended, sounding more challenging than he meant to.

Leon nodded. 'I can tell you don't trust us, and that's okay. Like you said, you don't know us, and just because we've worked together once, it doesn't mean were on the same side, right.'

Dan didn't say anything.

'Well, we are a secretive bunch, but considering the state of things, you've got to be, as I'm sure you'll agree. Basically our aims are similar to what I think yours are. I know you've been involved in trying to balance the media input out there with transmissions of data that's being kept from them, and like Sol said, good on you. Our plan is geared toward removing the more covert, destructive influences involved. We want to tear down some walls.'

'Justice isn't achieved by force.'

Leon smiled. 'Tell that to Jared. Where did you get the idea that justice isn't achieved by force? And what do you mean by force? The labour force, force of circumstance, force of habit?'

'I mean violence.'

'Then say what you mean, the language we use builds the map

in our head. Because force is exactly what's needed. The physics definition of the word is a measurable influence tending to cause the motion of a body, the body for the sake of this conversation being society, and in particular it's system of governance. Going back to Jared's liberation though, I would agree that force was used. I wouldn't agree that it was violent.'

'You call bombing people non-violent?'

'No, I call that violent. But I didn't include that in Jared's liberation. Jared was liberated with the minimum force possible. The guards would have experienced minor and temporary discomfort. The rigged explosion was aimed at what would have been armed individuals, combatants, intent on doing my people and me serious harm, and was indeed violent. Two very different actions. But we digress.

'You say the means are the end. Where do you think this ends? Some peaceful utopia where everything's rosy? In my book there is no end, only process. We can go in a promising direction or we can go in a wrong direction. This country, in fact countries the world over, are being led in the wrong direction, in ever decreasing circles down the drain. Trying to change that direction with anything but force is a waste of time. The State only recognises one coinage, power.'

'So trying to buy justice with that currency doesn't work because the Government has more than we'll ever have. We have to use what we've got.'

'Which is what, the democratic process?' Leon scoffed. 'So show me the democracy. A democratic society is one that facilitates the best possible individual and social growth. In a democracy supreme power is supposed to be vested in the people collectively, and administered by them or officers appointed by them. If it isn't the will of the people, is it really democratic? What we have is a system of representative democracy where the decision-making power falls overwhelmingly into the hands of the privileged class. Representative democracy is a fiction designed to pacify the masses while limiting their voice in the system. The will of the people has been, at best, ignored, but overall it's been manipulated and perverted.

98

'Society is run like a pyramid, control ascending from the plebs at the bottom into less and less hands, becoming increasingly centralised until at the top you have the elite of the mega-corporations and the military-industrial complex, not called moguls and barons for nothing. The illusion of choice between political parties is just that. Behind the different coloured facades, they're all funded and steered by those same international groups. Whichever party is in is kept in place to further the aims of a select few, those aims being social and political control. Even were there a party that would change the status quo, it wouldn't get a look in. What we've got, and had for years, is effectively a single party state.

'The human race is approaching one of its biggest challenges ever, the survival of the species. Forget terrorists or communists, the planet's going through some huge changes. You've seen what's happened already, wait until it really kicks in.

'I think its safe to presume that we're aware of the more obvious methods being used to further the aims of the Forces of Darkness. I want to talk about the less obvious, but infinitely more sinister.'

'Remember this?' Sol held up the flight case.

Dan nodded. 'The maser.'

'That and more,' he took a deep breath. 'If I sound patronising, it's not intentional, but I'm going to assume you have no knowledge of what I'm about to tell you.

'Everything that goes on in us is electrically generated. I say electrical meaning low-level electromagnetic energy. Every thought, reaction, motor command, auditory event and visual image is an electromagnetic impulse or cluster of them in the brain, the frequencies of which can be singled out and recorded. Not only can they be recorded, they can be transmitted too, using equipment like this, a sort of synthetic telepathy.

'It works on the same principle as a laser. You can fire a laser against a window and pick up the sound vibrations on the glass from people's voices inside and translate them to analogue. Old hat surveillance stuff. The maser picks up electromagnetic impulses instead of sound vibrations, like EEG machines in hospitals. The secret services use it to communicate with their operatives in the field, extrapolating or transmitting audio-visual information directly from or to the auditory and visual cortex, bypassing the inner ear and optic nerve. All that's needed to do that is a catalogue of the person's excitation potentials.'

'That's spooky,' mumbled Dan.

'There's more. Just like your sub-vocalised thoughts, et cetera, your emotions have specific brain patterns, or signature clusters. If I recorded your signature clusters while you were in a pissed off mood then transmitted them at Leon, he'd feel the exact same emotion. All that's necessary is to transmit it with another frequency that stimulates brain entrainment. Transmitted on a carrier frequency above or below human audibility, he wouldn't even know that the feelings were coming from outside him.

'The technology was developed way before the end of last century, and its uses ranged from voter manipulation, political assassinations, and PsyOps in the early stages of the Arab-American conflict. Here it was initially transmitted televisually, injecting emotion into films and dramas, but was soon adapted to selectively manipulate public feeling and opinion. The problem with that was even though people were already completely attached to their digital drug, it had a relatively limited scope for targeting individuals or affecting large groups of people simultaneously or over long periods of time. So they developed and aggressively promoted another form of communication, one that uses frequencies which are perfect for brain entrainment.'

'Phones!' Dan blurted, verbalising the realisation as it came.

'Pretty sharp,' Sol nodded. 'Microwave communication technology is one of their biggest and most effective social control mechanism to date. A totally invasive surround loop, supersaturating the individual in bioneural control. Virtually everyone from rug rat to wrinkly has got a phone on them or near them twenty-four seven. Not only can large numbers of people be targeted simultaneously, each user can be targeted individually. The phone against the head gives direct transmission via bone conduction, giving easy access to anybody's mind.

'Also easy for them to catalogue and database a whole slew of data. By law the phone companies have to database for a minimum of five years, and release on demand, all user data as well as real-time user location to within three feet. And even if you don't use a phone, there are few places that don't come under the range of ground-based transmitters. I've even seen them blatantly disguised as trees, and with the Whore riding the Beast, there's transmitters in church steeples too. In short, in every fucking nook and cranny.

'Now bearing in mind what was just said about brain entrainment, is it any wonder that despite the fact that this war has been going on for years killing millions of innocent people, despite the ever increasing taxes, the bankers blatant blagging, et cetera, et cetera, nobody is making a fuss? People on the streets, in the factories, prisons, right across the board, nobody is saying anything.'

'And you think that apathy is being transmitted?'

'What do you think, Dan?'

The atmosphere in the room tensed slightly.

'I think the powers that be are dodgy enough to use this kind of technology. I'd like to see some hard data though, that's a pretty radical claim.'

'I can give you reams of data, but right now we have a more pressing need.'

'Dan,' interrupted Leon. 'I'll carry on Sol, you can tell me if I get it wrong.'

'Okay, so we know that our thoughts can be affected using equipment that we know the security services have. Kind of problematic if you're not into the idea of being controlled like a puppet, or if you want to keep the contents of your mind to yourself. So our very own tech wizard here designed a micro-transmitter that created an electromagnetic field that basically scrambled any incoming, which meant that the spooks couldn't ponce your brains and you weren't affected by covert microwave saturation. Something wasn't right though because suddenly our people started getting pulled. Luckily our ID card sources are top notch, as you know, and the ones who were pulled stayed cool. Couldn't work it out though. It was unlikely that they were dressed or acting wrong. Part of our training is on how CCTV behavioural recognition programs work. But then we sussed it. The field produced by the device was interrupting police remote monitoring. They couldn't get a reading from the card's chip, so presumed the people weren't carrying one and pulled them. Luckily the cards worked when they swiped them and the biometrics were tight, so they let them go. Very nearly fucked things up though.

'Lifting Jared was a real risk and potentially could've revealed us. As it is, it's brought us attention we could've done without. As far as you're concerned the authorities can potentially associate you with us, which increases the risk to you too. Of all of us you're the most at risk. That's the reason we want you to join us, for everybody's protection.'

'And what do I have to do to be in your gang?'

'Inside this building you're protected from the kind of brain-rape mentioned earlier by the kind of tech mentioned,' said Sol. 'Out of the building and without protection you're wide open. Which means you're vulnerable and a security risk. What I want to do now is essentially download a security programme into your brain.'

He paused, but Dan said nothing.

'Think of it like any other encryption programme, only this one protects your wetware. Kind of like the transmitter Leon described, but this works in a different way. Instead of generating a field this actually entrains your brain to a set of frequencies that, lyrically put, can't be beat. All incoming gets entrained too, which then adds to the strength of the beneficial signal. There's no danger to your mind, the only effect it has is to stimulate receptiveness to those frequencies. Being tuned in to those frequencies is what provides the protection.'

'Okay, let's see if I've got this right,' said Dan. 'You want me to let you rewire my brain to make us all safe.'

'Cynically put, but that's about the gist of it. And safer is what it makes things, not safe. Whilst you're unprotected they can take stuff out or put it in without you knowing about it. Once you're protected they'd have to resort to other more mundane ways of extracting information from you, like they did to Jared. Action could then be taken.'

Dan stayed silent. He didn't like the thought of anyone tampering with his mind, whatever their intentions. But what were their intentions? What if they were trying to control his mind? What if he said no, would they let him walk out? What if they were right?

'I don't suppose I could get back to you on this.'

'I like your caginess, Dan, it's healthy. Right now is not the time for it though. We need to bring a little more trust into this to move forward. Your decision has a bearing on how we proceed from here. Things are happening really fast. Like Leon said, lifting Jared upped the stakes, and now the authorities are doing everything in their power to find us and stop us. At the moment they can only suspect who we are and our capabilities, and can't know our intentions, so we still have the elements of stealth and surprise on our side. Pretty soon though the shit's going to hit the fan and when it does there won't be time for thinking or talking. We've taken a big risk allowing you in this far, but we trust Jared's judgement. If you don't want to, it's not compulsory, but this is as far as we go.'

Dan wished Jared were there. He'd been a bit disturbed to find out that he wasn't going to be, and had to work at ignoring his suspicions and taking Sol's explanation of Jared being away training with another group at face value. In that respect, he'd already brought some trust into the deal. That was before they wanted to mess with his head though. He wished he had more time to think about it.

He wondered if Jared had done it, and guessed he probably had. Maybe that had been the reason why Jared wouldn't talk about certain things when he'd seen him last.

'Dan,' said Sol, 'I know what it might look like, and you've got the disadvantage of not knowing this stuff or us. If we had a plan to take over your mind though, we could have done it when we first met or since then from a distance without you knowing. You trusted us once and you'd never even met us then. One reason why we're all still alive is because of this box of tricks.'

'Dan,' Leon's voice rumbled, 'don't stress it; decide with your heart. The head can be too full to get a clear picture. The heart knows the truth of a thing.'

The change of tack confused Dan. What Sol said was true though, Jared was alive because of them. So why the mistrust now? Where did it come from? He thought of the brainwashing cult rumours and the ones about the group being backed by the Pan-Asians, even Sid's vampire jokes. Leon was right; his head was full of stuff. He smiled without intending to, and nodded his head.

'Good comment that.'

Leon nodded once and returned the smile.

Dan took a deep breath, turned to Sol, and gestured to the flight case. 'Shall we?'

Sol smiled. 'Good man.' He opened the case. 'Back when we lifted Jared, I used the maser to record the frequency of the chip they'd implanted in his sinuses. We use the maser for this too, only this time it transmits the, call it the encryption algorithm, to a specific part of the cortex. The area we focus on that acts as an antenna sits in between the two hemispheres of the brain. You might feel a little dizzy, but it's nothing to worry about, just the strength of the transmission. All you have to do is sit still.'

He aimed the maser at the middle of Dan's forehead.

Dan closed his eyes. This had to be the strangest thing he'd allowed anybody to do to him. Doubts about what he was doing nagged at him despite his decision. What if it affected his brain in other ways? Was there a way to undo it once it was done?

A soft pulsing sensation began in the centre of his head, and what felt like warm liquid slowly spreading over his scalp.

'Feel anything?' Sol asked.

'Yeah, feels like you're pouring warm treacle over my head.'

'That's an indication of increased electromagnetic activity in that area. Any vibrations?'

'More a kind of pulsing.'

'All good.'

The pulsating slowly increased in pitch to a low hum that sent goose bumps up and down Dan's body. The hum became a buzz briefly before levelling out into a tinnitus-like hiss. Moving clouds of multihued purple washed through the blackness behind his closed eyelids, wave after slowly moving wave.

'And that's all there is to it.'

Dan opened his eyes.

'Those sensations might persist for a little while, but they'll have smoothed out by the time you leave.'

'Dan,' said Leon. 'I have to say thank you and well done for trusting us. If I'd been in your shoes, I would have had a tough time making the decision. It was the right decision though. There are other side benefits to the process that develop over time as your brain integrates the entrained frequencies.'

'What kind of side benefits?'

'I'd rather let them develop in their own time than prompt you. It'd be good if you came back after today, say in a week or two. The frequency shift will have been integrated by then and it'll be easier to demonstrate it. We'll synch the visit with Jared being here next time. I know he was excited about showing you stuff. For now I'll show you some of our practical arrangements.'

He led Dan out and upstairs.

'The majority of our funds come from the distribution and courier business. Financing aside, there couldn't be a better front. It provides the authorisation needed for movement around the country, larger fuel quota, vehicles, and a building that provides space for all our needs. The template has been replicated with slight variations in other parts of the country with other groups.'

Persistent pulsating sensations distracted Dan as Leon showed him round the living quarters. His head felt as though it was being massaged on the inside.

One noticeable thing about the space was its tidiness. Although the shower room looked able to accommodate a dozen, as did the dorm-style rooms, the lack of clutter suggested that it was underused. Leon explained that although there were currently six in the unit, they could accommodate many more if necessary.

He opened a door and they stepped into a room painted in a similar muted tone to the others. A set of low filing cabinets sat in one corner next to a desk with a computer monitor. Several rows of shelves held more books and papers than Dan expected to see. Desks formed a square horseshoe in the middle of the room. A woman and a man wearing headphones were sitting at the desks reading. Both looked up as the group entered, and Dan recognised them from the rescue. They removed the headphones and Dan heard faint music.

'Ash, Cheddar, Dan, who you met briefly. Just showing him around.'

Both nodded a greeting, replaced the headphones and returned to their books.

'What these two are doing demonstrates our ethos, practically and philosophically. Practically there's an academic side to the training that requires the taking in of quite a bit of information. Stuff like guerrilla history and tactics, current and historical politics, survival in a range of environments, behavioural science and certain forms of self-development. To speed up the process we use accelerative learning and preconscious processing techniques. The technique they're using uses certain sounds that stimulate brain states conducive to rapid data processing. Combined with specific reading techniques, it's possible to take in well in excess of twenty thousand words a minute.'

Dan watched them as Leon spoke. Neither seemed to be reading at all, just staring at the book and turning the page every other second in a steady rhythm.

'I say twenty thousand because that's the initial target for someone new to the process. For someone who knows the process or practised other forms of preconscious processing, speeds over a hundred thousand words a minute aren't unusual.'

'A hundred thousand words a minute? Even if it were possible to read that fast, surely it's not possible to take it all in.'

'Why surely? Actually at those speeds we expect around a seventy percent comprehension rate, although our expectations are based on our experience and not what's possible. A hundred percent recall is possible, but in practise there's a fluctuation slightly below that.

'Take languages for instance. The population of this country

106

are famous for being crap with other languages. In countries other than the U.S. and Britain though, conversance in two or more languages is almost the norm. Why? Blame the education methods and their psychological bias that encourage cultural separatism by making bilingual comprehension much more difficult than it need be. Using these methods it's possible to learn a language in under a month.'

'And this works with everybody?'

'Everybody,' said Leon. 'Every one of us has genius potential.'

'So why isn't it taught in schools?'

'Why do you think? The State can't have people developing their full potential. It's harder to use or manipulate intelligent, aware and high functioning people. They don't make good consumers or workplace fodder for industry. The modern state education system was designed by industrialists in the late eighteen hundreds to program individuals for their socially allotted roles in industry, and in doing so deactivate the genius potential in them. Schools themselves are factories in which raw materials, children, are shaped and formed into finished products, manufactured like nails, with the manufacturing specifications coming from industry and government.

'Private education differs only in that the person is programmed to fit into the higher echelons, slightly bigger cogs in the machine. But their full potential is deactivated in the same way and for the same reasons. In fact, every teacher should realise they are a social engineer in place for the maintenance of a specific social order.

'Here, using techniques that are only given any serious application in military and commercial settings, we remove the culturally imposed blocks to learning and activate that innate genius potential. We get rid of the old, restricting programs and install new ones that access abilities you can't imagine. And not just mentally, right across the board, physically, emotionally and spiritually. Achieving our full potential as individuals, and as a species, is fundamental to our philosophy.'

They stepped back out into the corridor.

'But that's us. Now back to the situation we're in, and what needs to be done. The world has suffered a silent fascist coup. Hitler and World War II were just one stage in a long-term vision based on theories of eugenics and world domination. A preparatory stage to test techniques, set the world military scene physically and psychologically, and establish military-industrial structures that have been expanding ever since. The vision has been slow to develop, but we're fast approaching its realisation. It's taken so long because of its breadth, nothing less than the complete control of the planet's resources and inhabitants.

'Hitler was a puppet funded and manipulated by people a lot smarter than he was. I.G. Farben was the company that made it possible for Hitler to go to war. Farben produced nearly a hundred percent of Hitler's needs in synthetic rubber, methanol, oil from coal, aviation fuel, plastics, explosives, and poison gas. They were the company that produced the Zyklon B gas used in the concentration camps. Without Farben there could have been no war. But there would have been no Farben cartel without financial assistance from Wall Street. Wall Street banks loaned the Nazis over a hundred and thirty million dollars.

'On the board of Farben's American subsidiary, American I.G., was the chairman of the National City Bank and the Federal Reserve Bank, the president of the Ford Motor Company, a director of Standard Oil and the chairman of the Chase Manhattan Bank. Ivy Lee & TJ Ross, the top public relations firm in New York, handled their publicity and fielded any criticism from inside America about American involvement with Farben. It was through technical assistance and support from well-known American companies that the German Wehrmacht was built, with techniques learned by Germans from car manufacturers in Detroit being used to construct Stukas. The fuel from coal technology came from Standard Oil of New Jersey. The details, which are all publicly available, are shocking and saddening. My grandfather died in that war. And what of the millions of others who suffered and died for what was a huge money making and power consolidating business exercise.

'Following the war, three members of the board of Farben

were found guilty of war crimes by the Nuremberg Tribunal. Three German directors, that is. No American directors were ever brought to trial. When Farben was disbanded by the allies, it later emerged in the guise of the companies they'd signed cartel agreements with including ICI, Carnation, Nestle, Bristol Meyers, Whitehall laboratories, Proctor and Gamble, Roche, Hoechst and Beyer and Co; mostly chemical and pharmaceutical companies. The Rockefeller Empire, old bedmates of Farben, and the Chase Manhattan Bank now allegedly own over half of the U.S.'s pharmaceutical interests and is the largest drug manufacturing combine in the world.

'Add to those facts the hundreds of Nazi scientists and their families taken out of Germany immediately after the war by the Americans in Operation Paperclip, and resettled in the U.S., supposedly so that the Russians wouldn't get their expertise. The main areas of their work were military, chemical, and biological. Josef Mengele, infamous for his ghoulish experiments on twins, is the kind of scientist we're talking about. The SS officer Wernher von Braun who led the team that developed Germany's V-2 rocket masterminded the U.S. moon missions. Herbertus Strughold, the man later called 'the father of space medicine', who designed NASA's on-board life-support systems, had been involved in human experiments at Dachau and Auschwitz.

'Chemical and pharmaceutical companies are knowingly, and with the backing of government legislation, exposing the population to substances that are known to cause a variety of cancers, primary organ toxicity, gland dysfunction, immune system corruption, brain modification, et cetera, et cetera.

'The population is moulded from an early age, brains and bodies deadened and compromised by mass drugging and by long-term exposure to chemicals that, particularly in the case of aluminium compounds, affect behaviour. The first time fluoride was added to drinking water was in the Nazi concentration camps. Now they didn't give a shit about the prisoner's dental health, so why did they go to the trouble of adding it to the water supply?

'Research shows that fluoride actually has negative effects on dental health. Aluminium, and its compounds like fluoride, also inhibit brain growth and regeneration, and act as a behavioural modifier, which is why Prozac is a fluoride-based drug, and maybe why governments are so keen to fluoridate water supplies. Aluminium also just happens to be the perfect molecular antenna for the bioneural manipulation of their HAARP frequency weapons.

'There's a chemical that, when added to a tank of tadpoles, inhibits the maturation of the tadpoles and stops them turning into frogs. That chemical, like everything else, including say a virus, has a specific frequency. That frequency when transmitted at tank of tadpoles inhibits the maturation of the tadpoles.'

Dan waited for Leon to continue. When he didn't he shook his head.

'And?'

'For years governments have been working at ways to get everybody microchipped. Phones and ID cards were their vanguard and have been extremely successful. Everybody's Interlinked, and the media are making sure that more and more people are opting for ID bio-personalisation. But there are still ways around the technology, as you know, and it's not just people in the Resistance that resort to them. The system is still too open for the controllers. Do you think that with all the advances in nanotechnology over the last twenty years that the grain of rice-sized chip is as small as it gets? And why are governments so bent on pandemic alert-induced mass vaccination programs, the shots from which repeatedly result in adverse short and long-term effects? For sure the overall and specific damage to a person's physiology is good for business for Big Pharma, but the promotion and legislation suggest that something other than just the enrichment of governmental-industrial connections may be going on.

'I mention all this because I want you to appreciate what we're up against. There's research papers in Resources that the network slipped past the filters of the Public Information Department if you've a few hours to spare. Basically these negative influences are being applied across the board in a variety of ways, chemically, electromagnetically, biologically and psychologically. Like designed viruses, they've attached to the individual and collective organism and have been reproducing and spreading for a long, long time. People's minds and bodies are riddled with them, literally. So much so that they can't be forcibly removed.

'Like the physical body, deliberately weakened to create business for the drug barons, so too the political body to make business easy for the puppet masters through their puppet politicians. The mechanisms of that suppression are now so deep-rooted that attempts at removal from outside won't work. We need to stimulate the suppressed system to mobilise a response to the infection.

'The task would be easier if we could reduce people's exposure to the behaviour modifying agents. If we could remove the blindfold, people could see for themselves. Until they become conscious of the chains that hold them, and of their own political power, people will never kick back, but until they do they won't become conscious of the chains. That's why we've got the media, the microwave muzzle, Anti-Terrorist laws, Patriot Acts, et cetera. If the lower levels of the pyramid got restless, it could bring their carefully managed structure down.'

'Yeah, crushing a lot of little people at the bottom.'

'We're not talking civil war, Dan; we're talking civil disobedience. No meaningful social reforms in history were brought about without a struggle. No struggle, no progress. Those who say they want freedom and yet argue against agitation want crops without ploughing up the ground. They want rain without thunder and lightning. The struggle may be moral or physical or both, but it must be a struggle. Power concedes nothing without a demand. It never did and it never will.

'And anyway, the routine functioning of this society is far more violent than any reaction against it could ever be. Think of the number of children that the present system allows to starve to death each day as a result of foreign policies, embargoes, and national debt, and then add to that the thousands it actively shoots and bombs.'

'So you want to start a revolution then.'

'In a manner of speaking yes, but not in the way usually considered. What we want to do is make people aware of their potential, politically and otherwise, and present the means for developing it. For that to happen certain restrictions have to be removed, most of them in people's minds.

'The People versus the Powerful is the oldest story in human history. At no point in history have the Powerful wielded so much control. At no point in history has the active and informed involvement of the People, all of them, been more required.'

***

Dylan heard the train pull in, cursed under his breath and started to run down the escalator. He dodged round two backpackers stood at the bottom, both looking from the little map they held to the wall signs and back. He skidded round the corner in time to see the train pulling away and cursed again.

At the far end of the platform stood a khaki-clad figure, assault rifle across his chest. Dylan walked down the platform. The soldier nodded.

'Don't reckon much to your camouflage.' said Dylan. 'Shouldn't it be white with black lines?'

'Hah hah,' replied the soldier. 'Missed your train did you?'

Dylan gestured toward the tunnel. 'Caught anyone in there recently?'

The soldier scowled. 'I've never seen anything in there, 'cept rats. I don't reckon there is anyone in there.'

'Which makes yours an easy job then.'

'Yeah, easy and boring.'

'Ne'er mind,' said Dylan. 'Just think about the money.'

He walked back up the platform slowly, unsettled by the soldier's presence. He never got used to seeing soldiers on the street, or underground for that matter. Soldiers and guns.

He kept walking in an attempt to cool down by moving the stale and stiflingly warm air across his body. Public Directive notices spaced at intervals along both walls kept catching his eye and annoying him again. He didn't want reminding that their watchful eyes were watching him. CCTV cameras everywhere were bad enough without eyes looming at him from posters all over town. Neither did he want to be repeatedly instructed to watch people around him. Watch and report.

Of all the signs, the watch and report directives bothered him the most. It wasn't enough that in Britain they were under more CCTV surveillance than anywhere else in the world, every individual was recruited to 'do their bit' as well. Legitimised and fed, the authoritarian personality had free rein to exercise its bigotry and prejudice. Self-righteous zealots, supported by a broad and ambiguous list of 'suspicious behaviour', kept the Squad well supplied with hapless suspects whose looks or actions 'weren't quite right'. The Public Directive policy bred mistrust between people and encouraged conformity to a vague and manipulable set of social rules that governed appearance and behaviour. The nail that stuck out got hammered down.

He looked up, suddenly conscious of his train of thought and what signals he might be giving off. Several people looking at him looked away immediately. He stopped pacing and looked back down the platform, trying to look normal.

A quickening breeze announced the next train and the people on the platform began to move. The train pulled in. He got on, slumped into a chair and opened the paper. It irritated him instantly, knowing as he did all the angles and editorial bias. It was pointless reading it. Trying to read between the lines and analyse the spin to arrive at something approximating the truth was a waste of time, never mind trying to pull in what wasn't reported. The word spin said it all; it used to be called bullshit. And if he, a journalist, couldn't decipher it, what chance did other people stand?

He turned to the Public Appointments. He didn't know what he was looking for, but it was likely there'd be something. With so many men taken by the war, any bloke in the country could get a job or get laid easier than falling out of bed.

The train doors opening made him and the other occupants of the carriage turn. They were in a tunnel, presumably waiting on a light, and the doors shouldn't have opened. Dylan's heart banged and his nostrils flared as his brain picked fire as the first possible reason. Before it had selected another, several masked figures climbed up into the train. There was a jostling as some passengers pushed their way past those next to them, away from the doors.

'Everybody sit down!' barked a figure, his bulk filling the doorway. His legs were bent to prevent his huge frame stooping, giving him a simian look.

There was a shuffling sound as people sank to the floor, some quickly, others slowly, looking around uncertainly.

'You are in no danger,' the man continued, looking around the carriage, 'unless there's any of you who would endanger the safety of their fellow passengers with unnecessary heroics.'

As he spoke other figures clambered up into the carriage. They were all dressed alike in grimed black military gear and balaclava masks, a severe and threatening contrast to the homogenous fashions and bright glare in the carriage.

Dylan's mind raced. Robbery? Hijack? Possible political reasons for hostage taking? The man had an English accent, but that didn't rule out backing from another country.

Maybe they were after someone in particular. The number of people disappearing had risen over the last few years, people ranging from influential public figures to the apparently ordinary. But they just disappeared; gunmen didn't snatch them off trains. But robbery didn't fit either. Cash was virtually obsolete these days and stolen cards were pretty useless.

The figures moved around the carriage handing out sheets of paper. The juxtaposition of bizarre and mundane puzzled Dylan. He leaned out into the isle and looked down the length of the carriage. Through the door at the end he saw the scene being replayed in the other carriage.

A sheet was passed to him. He took it, but instead of looking at it examined the figure passing it as it moved down the aisle. Though he couldn't tell by the shape, blurred as it was by the asexual clothing, he was sure that it was a woman. He made a mental note of his assumption that hijackers were male. An inexcusable assumption given all the action on the Front involving women, particularly the hardcore Chinese women soldiers.

People were looking around and directly at each other for the first time since they boarded. Some were reading. A curious fact presented itself to Dylan. He looked around to check whether he was right. Although the military clothing of the hijackers and the man's tone gave the impression of aggression, the subsequent actions were relatively ordinary and non-threatening. More than that though he'd not seen any guns or weapons of any kind. Which wasn't to say there weren't any, but so far none had been waved about. He wondered what would happen if he tried to apprehend one of the hijackers. Not that he was about to, visible guns or not.

Behind him at the far end of the carriage an old woman began shouting.

'Ya can't make me take it, go on piss off, leave me alone. I'm an old woman, leave me alone!'

The big man gave a short whistle. The other figures turned and moved toward the doors. When they'd all jumped down, he looked around the carriage.

'Thank you,' he said, then jumped down and out of sight.

No one spoke. Dylan continued looking around. Some people started getting to their feet, uncertainly meeting other people's gaze. Some were reading the sheet, several of which already littered the floor. The whole thing had taken less than five minutes.

'What the hell was all that about?'

Dylan looked round into a flaccid, pasty face. He pointed at the sheet in the man's hand without saying anything, irritated without knowing why. He was wondering at the feeling when the door warning sounded and the doors closed. He looked down at the paper in his hands. The train began to crawl forward as he read.

Once finished he sat back. So that was it, yet another conspiracy theory. He found he couldn't laugh this one off as easily though. Here was a group who felt strongly enough to risk their lives and freedom and who had the audacity and organisation to take over a train, and underground too.

A burst of brightness and echoing acoustics and they were pulling into a station, the bright blur slowing to reveal a platform empty save for armed police positioned along its length. A voice came over the loudspeakers as the doors opened.

'Your attention please, the Underground is closed for the remainder of the day. Please make your way directly to the exits. Staff will be on hand to take statements. Your attention please...'

The atmosphere in the station was heavy. Visually things looked fairly normal, except nobody was coming down the stairs or escalators. Few people were speaking and only in hushed tones. Most looked shaken and keen to get out. The sound of hurrying footsteps bounced off ceramic surfaces.

A man holding a clipboard met Dylan at the top of the escalator.

'I'm with the Anti-Terrorist Squad. We're collecting information to help us with this incident. Firstly, do you have any of the propaganda that was given out?'

'I left it on the train,' said Dylan, without breaking his stride.

The man hurried alongside to keep up.

'Could I have your name and –'

'Look, I'm sorry I can't help you,' interrupted Dylan, feigning angst, 'they were all masked and it was over very quickly. I'm in a rush. I've got to get across town somehow.'

He walked out, threading his way through the clipboard carriers and the gesticulating passengers around them.

The front of the station was cordoned off. A policeman let him under the line, watched over by another in a flak jacket holding a semi-automatic carbine across his chest.

He walked briskly up the road keeping an eye out for a taxi, while he phoned the news desk. There'd be a bonus in a scoop like this. It was highly unlikely that any of the other agencies had anyone who'd been on the scene. The word was out though, and was already displayed in a bulletin text report and Directive update on a nearby Urban Screen.

5

A human being is a part of a whole, called by us "Universe". A part limited in time and space. He experiences himself, his thoughts and feelings as something separated from the rest - a kind of optical delusion of his consciousness. This delusion is a kind of prison for us... Our task must be to free ourselves from this prison...

– Albert Einstein

In the province of the mind, what is believed to be true is true, or becomes true, within limits to be found experimentally and experientially. These limits are further beliefs to be transcended. In the province of the mind, there are no limits.

– John C Lilly, MD. *The Center of the Cyclone.*

Jared sat, eyes closed, breathing slowly in and out, alternately closing one nostril and then the other with the thumb and forefinger of his right hand. He was aware of the others around him by the sound of their relaxed breathing as they went through the consciousness-settling procedure.

His mind slowed, the incessant chatter getting less as he focused on each breath, the rise and fall of his chest and diaphragm, the insides of his nostrils cooling and warming, and the ever present hiss in his ears.

'Okay, give it five.' Leon's quiet voice.

Jared sat back and rested his hands on the desk, keeping a focus on his breathing, and imagined his body growing heavier with each out breath. Awareness of sensations drifted in and out; the chair hard beneath him, a light tingling up and down his spine and around the back of his neck and head. His right earlobe itched. Random thoughts intruded; what he was going to eat later, bits from the Zapatista module, wondering if Leon would be in the mood to talk later, the 'Identification of Overall Troop Manoeuvres Through The Movement of its Individuals', pieces of the Astral Navigation module. All the thoughts and sensations he observed as if from a distance, allowing them to pass and focusing on his breath.

The five minutes passed quicker than expected and Leon spoke again.

'Prepare for Phase One.'

Jared opened his eyes and sat up straight. To his right was a thin stack of plain paper and a pen. He took a sheet from the pile, set it in front of him and picked up the pen. A little ripple of excitement ran through him. He breathed in slowly through his nose and began the affirmation.

'I am a spiritual being. Because I am a spiritual being, I am able to perceive beyond all boundaries of space and time. My consciousness is ever present with all that is, with all that was and all that ever will be.'

The hushed voices of the group filled the room like a litany.

'It is my nature, as a human, to be able to perceive, and thus to know, all that there is to know. Everywhere, at all times, I seek to learn, and thus to evolve. To further my own personal growth, and to assist others in their growth, I direct my attention to a chosen point of existence. I observe what is there. I study it carefully. I record what I find.'

The voices faded to an expectant silence.

He began to write. Top left he wrote Type 4. Top right went his name, date and time. Top centre he wrote PS-Good, ES-Relaxed and excited, AP-None.

Leon spoke again.

'Target 9163...8425.'

Jared wrote the randomly assigned numbers and relaxed the tension in his shoulders. Vague shapes flashed to mind. He quickly sketched an ideogram of basic lines next to the target coordinates. Next to it he wrote A: moving across, horizontal flat across, diagonal downward, curving under left, curving under right, horizontal flat along; describing the movement of the pen as he'd sketched.

Leon repeated the coordinates and Jared repeated the process.

Next he moved the pen back to the first ideogram and pushed the nib gently into the paper. He searched around for a word to describe the texture and wrote Hard. A probe into the second ideogram produced a Mushy sensation. Returning to the first he probed again and obtained a Man-made descriptor. A second probe into the second drawing obtained Natural.

Under the first ideogram he then wrote B: No-B. Under the second he wrote B: Wet land. Underneath those he wrote C: No-C.

He looked up and made brief eye contact with Leon as he slowly scanned the group.

'Okay, Phase Two.'

Jared pulled a fresh sheet of paper from the pile and wrote P2 at the top. On the left he wrote Sounds and was immediately aware of a faint rustling from behind him. As he was writing the word he heard whooshing in the distance and wrote that too. Next came Textures, the associated impressions being wet.

He carried on listing the impressions for Temperatures, Magnitudes and Visuals, breaking Visuals down into colours, luminescence and contrast, getting fleeting impressions after the writing of each word. Taste came through really strong, sour enough to make his mouth water. Smells drew a blank.

He'd just completed the sensation categorising when he became aware of another. Under the other categories he wrote VF-turned on, put the pen down and took a deep breath.

'Okay, Phase Three.'

Jared took another sheet and began sketching quickly. A picture was already forming in his mind. He shaded in a wide dark mouth with a long tongue sticking out, pencil bar moustache and one oblong eye. He raised an eyebrow. The drawing didn't seem to fit with the physical descriptor clues. He shut off the train of thought quickly to avoid his conscious mind getting involved.

'Phase Four.' Leon's voice told of the other's completing the phase as rapidly. Phase Three didn't usually take more than sixty seconds.

Jared took another sheet of paper, positioned it lengthways, mapped out the data matrix and began entering data in the columns, his pen gradually speeding up and skipping from box to box.

'Probe S.'

He pressed the pen nib to the paper briefly and jotted the response.

'Probe M.'

He repeated the procedure.

Probing E made him smile. He touched the pen briefly on the Viewer Feeling box again and the smile widened. He jotted down the descriptor and sat back to let his conscious mind settle back into silence.

Leon's instructions continued, guiding the group into wider and deeper degrees of the target description. Jared was amazed at how much data he was able to access. The concept still amazed him even though the process itself was no longer as alien as the first few times. The fact that humans were composite beings with two fundamental aspects hadn't been news to him even during the initial training. He knew he wasn't confined to his body.

Although moving his awareness from physical five sense stimuli and focusing on subspace input had taken him less than a week to grasp, he found processing the data tricky because the subspace mind perceived and processed information differently from the physical mind. The subspace mind was all-pervading across time and space. It was everywhere at once, connected to, and somehow part of, everything in the physical and non-physical universe.

The remote viewing techniques shifted him away from the noise of the physical senses and allowed access to the more intuitive subspace awareness. They also provided a structure that brought him into either a closer or altered association with the target.

Finally he began to sense the flow of input lessening despite repeated probing. He wasn't surprised when minutes later Leon ended the session.

He stretched luxuriously without opening his eyes and 'watched' himself reassemble, the gestalt awareness of his body thickening and taking on detail; a stale taste in his mouth, numbness in his thighs and buttocks, and a slight pressure in his bladder. He opened his eyes slowly and looked around the squinting, stretching group.

'Everybody back…and okay?' Leon asked, walking around collecting papers.

There were mumbles and nodding all round.

Jared cleared his throat. 'Can we verbal?'

'Sure,' said Leon, 'this is just an exercise. Minimal though. I'd like to follow protocol with the analysis.'

'Nicole was target, wasn't she?'

Leon smiled and nodded.

'Her touch is so easy,' Jared went on, 'and she's always turned on!'

The others laughed. Evidently he'd not been the only one to pick that up.

Leon lined up the reports on a desk. Underneath them he put four photographs. The group gathered round.

The spot was a riverbank, the structure a road bridge over the river. All the ideograms reflected the dark mouth of the space beneath the bridge and something, a tongue in Jared's case, emerging from the space. Moving lines above the space were agreed to have been vehicles crossing the bridge, while descriptors like man-made, curving over, wet, wet land, or mushy all related to the structure and surrounding land itself.

'What about taste?' Jared asked. 'That came through really strong.'

'Lemon sherbets,' said Leon, smiling.

Nods and smiles all round showed everyone had picked that up too.

Leon gathered the reports up when they'd finished the analysis. 'Remember that this was Type Four data. Because we're so tight there's an increased likelihood of viewers extrapolating information from the monitor's field telepathically. That can be avoided if both monitor and viewers are blind. Data from then would be Type Five. We'll do it that way next time.'

Jared hung back as the others filtered out. Leon perched on the desk, waiting.

'Wanted to ask you something,' said Jared. 'It was Nicole's

emotionals that triggered it, but it's been on my mind.'

Leon chuckled. 'You were right when you said that she's permanently turned on.'

Jared didn't smile. 'Well today is the first time I've felt horny since the torture, and I was tuning in to somebody else.'

Leon's smiled faded and he nodded, but didn't say anything.

'It works alright otherwise, but it seems to have forgotten what else it's for.'

'Who have you tried with?'

'No one.'

'Maybe you should.'

'This is difficult enough without embarrassing myself in front of someone. I was hoping there was something along the lines of the other exercises you gave me before, something I could practise on my own to sort it out.'

'Take my advice and try with someone before you pronounce it broken.'

'And if I can't…get it up?'

'The right person will understand, and might be able to help.'

Jared thought about it. Maybe Leon was right. Maybe he just needed some stimulation other than himself. Maybe linking with Nicole's emotionals was a hint in that direction.

'Do you think Nicole'd be the right person?'

Leon sighed and picked the stack of papers off the desk. 'I'm a freedom fighter, Jared, not a fucking dating agency.'

The unexpected reply stumped Jared. Embarrassed, he turned and walked out of the room. Furious with himself for asking, he ran up four flights of stairs. He shouldn't have asked. How much advice did he need anyway? If he was interested there was one way to find out.

He poured his irritation into sprinting up the stairs, but was still glad to find the study empty. He looked around for something to occupy his mind. He picked up some social psychology resources he'd photoread the day before, and went to his room.

Technically it wasn't 'his' room, the living arrangements being communal. But because the warehouse had so much space, whoever wanted or needed private space used one of the empty rooms for as long as they needed. He'd used the same room since he got there, but nobody had a problem with it.

He flopped onto the couch and opened the book. The flagged sections of the text accomplished his mission.

A psychologist called Zimbardo had converted a basement at Stanford University into a mock prison and selected twenty-one carefully screened 'healthy', 'mature', and 'normal' students to take part in an experiment. Randomly eleven were assigned roles of 'guard' and ten of 'prisoner'. The guards had official-looking uniforms, while the prisoners had prison uniforms, bed linen, towels and toothbrush. No other personal belongings were allowed.

Zimbardo and the guards drew up a set of rules for the prisoners. Guards were allowed to give certain rewards for good behaviour.

On the first day the 'count' of the prisoners, carried out three times a day, took ten minutes. By the second day the 'count' time had increased as the guards started to use it to harass the prisoners. By the fifth day the 'count' took several hours as the guards berated the prisoners for minor breaches of the rules. By the end of the sixth day, the situation had deteriorated so much, with the guards inventing new and harsher rules, that Zimbardo called a halt.

More than a third of the guards consistently behaved in such a hostile manner that Zimbardo, a psychologist, had to describe their behaviour as sadistic.

Jared put the book down, reminded of his incarceration. He'd wondered then and now he knew, it was hardwired. Personalities weren't that stable and only required the simplest change of role to undergo radical changes. All it took was a costume change.

He tried to imagine himself in the role of a guard. Was there a sadist in him, waiting to crawl out given the excuse? He couldn't see it and tried to imagine further how his prison guard workmates would respond to his not joining in. How many joined in just to avoid disapproval from their group?

He remembered a seeing a cross reference and looked it up.

Social Pressure and Conformity. He scanned the jargon-laden pages and found what he was looking for. Another psychologist, Solomon Asch, and another experiment, this one to test levels of conformity that might be induced by group pressure.

Groups of eight to ten students were selected to take part in an experiment supposedly researching visual judgement. Sat round a table they were presented with sets of two cards, one marked with a single line, the other marked with three lines of different lengths. Their task was to decide, individually and out loud, which of the three lines was the same length as the single line. The right answer was obvious.

Only one student in each group was a real subject. The others were accomplices of the experimenter, instructed to give wrong answers in twelve out of the eighteen trials. The real subject was positioned to be the next-to-last person in their group to give their answer so that they would hear everybody's wrong answers before giving their own.

Thirty-seven of the fifty subjects conformed to the majority at least once, and fourteen conformed on more than six of the twelve trials.

Interviewed after the experiment most of them said that they only went along with the majority to avoid being ridiculed or thought odd. A few of them said that they really believed the group's answers were right.

Conclusions of the research were that people conformed for two main reasons: they wanted to be liked by their group and/or because they believed that the group was better informed than them. Asch also concluded that the group pressure implied by the expressed opinion of other people could lead to perceptual modification and distortion, effectively making a person see almost anything.

Social control was simple to those who knew that stuff. All they had to do was manipulate opinion in a section of the population, and the rest, lacking in their own conviction and too afraid to risk ostracism, would follow. Public opinion formed a power structure, an invisible police force that governed people's behaviour continuously. Whole populations were putty in the hands of those that controlled the media.

But it wasn't just that they were easily influenced by peer pressure, people actually tended toward blind obedience to authority, as shown by the Milgram experiment. The experiment was conducted in response to the trial of Adolf Eichmann, a senior official of the Nazi Party on trial for war crimes and crimes against humanity, who had used as his defence the claim that he was following orders.

Ordinary people from a wide cross-section of the population were recruited through newspaper ads for $4.50 for an hours work. The work was taking part in an experiment supposedly on the effects of punishment on learning. In reality the test was on obedience to authority. The participant was the actual subject of the experiment, and an actor working with the experimenter played the role of the subject.

The participant was seated in front of an electro-shock generator and given a 45-volt shock to show how it felt. The actor playing the part of the subject was then hooked up to the generator. The participant then asked the subject questions. Every time the subject gave a wrong answer, which he did according to the plan, the participant was required to give an electric shock. With every wrong answer the voltage was increased in 15-volt stages up to 450 volts. Each numerically labelled switch also had ratings from 'slight shock' to 'danger: severe shock' and 'XXX' on the last two. Unknown to the participant, there were no shocks, the actor was acting, to the point of screaming and banging and begging the person to stop. The stern, white-coated experimenter told those participants that expressed any discomfort with what they were doing that they had to continue. Ultimately, 65% administered the maximum 450 volts, and no subject stopped before 300 volts.

Two thirds of the subjects fell into the category of 'obedient' subjects. As Milgram himself said, he'd set up a simple experiment to test how much pain an ordinary citizen would inflict on another person simply because he was ordered to by an experimental scientist. Stark authority was pitted against the subject's strongest moral imperatives against hurting others and, with the subject's ears ringing with the screams of the victims, authority won more often than not. The extreme willingness of adults to go to almost any lengths on the command of an authority represented the chief finding of the study.

Jared noticed a rising agitation and put the book down. He shook his head, but the agitation didn't stop. He lay back on the couch and put his hands over his abdomen, and focused on breathing slowly and evenly. Gradually the tension eased and he slipped unnoticing into sleep.

He felt someone pulling at his arm and looked round. It was Leon. He smiled and beckoned with his head, then turned and waded into a river. The water was so silted up it was hard to tell how fast it was flowing. Jared started wading across, but the water was the consistency of treacle. He pushed against it and it thickened around his legs. He looked up and saw Leon standing on the other bank watching him. He shouted for help, but Leon shook his head and shouted back that he didn't need any.

The force against his legs began to push him over sideways. He tried to lift a foot, but it was stuck. He fell sideways slowly.

He jerked awake, disorientated and confused, emotions from the dream wrapped around him like cobwebs. He checked the time and found he'd slept for nearly two hours. It didn't feel like it, he felt sluggish and heavy. He leaned back on the couch, wondering about the dream.

A knock at the door made him jump. Instantly he was furious and slightly nauseous. He cursed quietly and shouted for the knocker to come in. The door opened and Nicole's face appeared around it.

'Hey Jared, seen Cheddar?'

He shook his head.

'You okay?'

'Yep.'

Nicole hesitated. 'You sure?'

'Yep.'

Nicole looked at him for lingering seconds. ''kay, catch ya later.'

The door closed.

126

Jared stared at the door, chewing his lip. He reached over and grabbed his gym gear and sat holding it momentarily before standing abruptly and walking out.

In the gym he racked back and forth on the rowing machine trying to out row the feelings that hounded him, the voices that mocked and criticised. He was glad the walls weren't mirrored. He didn't want to see his face. He panted through his nose and tried to bore a hole in the wall with his stare.

He pushed himself until his arms and legs were burning and too weak to do anymore, then sat, elbows on knees, head hanging down, watching drops of his sweat dapple the floor.

After showering he went back to his room and found Nicole sitting on the couch reading the book he'd been reading earlier. She held it up.

'This stuff really makes you wonder about people, eh. Hope you don't mind me dropping by, I've been meaning to for a bit.'

'Did you not find Cheddar then?'

'Yeah, I found him. I heard someone in the gym. Knew it was you. Nobody else works the rower like that.'

'Juice?' Jared waved a bottle.

'Got any vodka to go with it?'

'Afraid not.'

Nicole pulled out a half bottle. 'Good job I brought some then.'

Jared picked up two cups and sat on the couch. Nicole turned sideways, and held the cups as he poured.

'Salud.'

Jared raised his cup.

'How's your practice coming on?'

Jared frowned. 'You don't need to ask.'

'But you don't seem to have a problem with other subspace work.'

'I keep trying and it just keeps not working.'

Nicole looked at him for a moment. 'Openness and trust make it easier. Do you trust anyone enough, or want to be that open?'

Jared just stared at his drink.

'You ever clock how many miles you do on that rower?'

'Nope.'

'How come, you're on it often enough.'

'That's not why I do it. I just row my angst away, however many miles it takes.'

'Can I ask why you're feeling angsty tonight?'

'You can ask.'

'Will you tell me?'

'I don't want to talk about it.'

''kay.' She paused. 'Thing is though Jared, even though you won't talk about it, you're still feeling it. Those emotions broadcast out beyond your body. I feel them; we all feel them. The anger that comes out of nowhere, frustration humming away in the background like an abscess – '

Jared stood up. 'I said I don't want to talk about it.'

'You're not,' said Nicole gently, 'I am. Jared, your bottling it up isn't working, for you or anyone else. It's like you're carrying some ripe French cheese in your pocket, the smell's getting everywhere. Like I said, I can feel it, and from where I'm standing the feelings are getting stronger.'

Jared turned and looked at Nicole.

'Did Leon put you up to this?'

Nicole looked puzzled. 'How do you mean?'

'Did Leon send you up here?'

Nicole's green eyes blazed. 'What the fuck do you think I am? Some fucking wench the chief sends up to the men!'

'I didn't mean it like that.'

'Just how did you mean it?'

'I tried talking about it with him earlier. I thought maybe he'd mentioned it.'

Nicole stared at him, then sighed and lowered her shoulders. 'You tried talking with him.'

'Didn't feel like I was getting through.'

Nicole nodded. 'Leon's carrying a lot, Jared, a hell of a lot. Maybe he can't handle any more at the moment.'

'I wasn't asking for him to handle anything. All I was looking for were some exercises like the ones for PTS.'

'What's the problem?'

He didn't answer.

'Sexual?'

'I said I didn't want to talk about it.'

'You said you tried talking with Leon about it, why not me?'

Jared sighed. 'Okay, yes, it's sexual. Since the torture I've not been able to get a hard-on. Works fine otherwise, but it's given up in that department.'

'Who have you tried with?'

'No one,' he said, trying not to sound exasperated.

'How do you know then?'

'It never took somebody else to get me hard before.'

'Jared, after the abuse you had it's not surprising that some things don't work in the same way. This can't be the only thing.'

It wasn't the only thing. But he could deal with the disturbed sleep, the panic attacks and the rages. This was different.

'This is different.'

'And potentially sortable.'

She put down her drink, stood, and walked over.

'How about we sort it?'

'I don't think so, Nicole.'

'Do you not fancy me?'

He smiled.

'Gay?'

He shook his head, still smiling.

'Didn't think so.' She took his hand, walked backward, and sat on the bed. He pulled his hand away and stayed standing.

Nicole held her hands up. 'Okay, no pressure.'

'Sorry Nicole.'

'For nothing, mate. No stress.'

He sat on the bed and looked at his drink.

'I feel like such a cripple.'

'Huh, tell that to Cleve. Jared, you've got an erection problem, put it in perspective. And anyway, I'm not talking just sex. I'm talking massage, cuddles, sleeping with... mate, if I don't get skin to skin with someone at least once a week I go mad.

'Come on,' she put a hand on his shoulder, 'it'll be fun.'

She slid her hand across his shoulder and traced a line up the back of his neck with a nail. He arched his back.

'No pressure…'

She kissed his shoulder.

'…no expectations…'

Her lips brushed his ear.

'…just fun.'

He drew back with a pained expression.

'Okay, okay,' said Nicole, moving over on the bed. 'Backing away from the man.'

'I'm sorry, Nicole.'

'Don't be, mate. Sorry for being pushy.'

'I thought you and Cheddar had a thing going anyway.'

'We do, but it's not exclusive. That's one thing I love about this crew and our extended family, we function so well communally. It's so strong, and really empowering.'

Jared felt himself getting tense. Everybody was so perfect and right on.

'What about Cleve?' He knew he was being spiteful, but he didn't care.

'Cleve's problem's motor control. Getting kissed and stroked and sucked does it for him just like anybody.'

'Have you…?'

Nicole smiled.

'But what do you get out of it?'

'The melting joy that's to be had in real giving? The bursting sensations of love and empathy, and the super kinky turn on of rubbing myself to orgasm against a vulnerable, helpless, and totalling loving it friend.'

Jared looked down, away from Nicole's twinkling eyes, and pushed the thoughts from his mind, reminding himself that he was better off than Cleve. There was no room for jealousy.

'What if Cleve was gay?'

'One of the blokes would probably do for him.'

'Who's gay in this crew then?'

'Just Leon. Dar has bi-leanings, but he does his head in over it for ages after. That's not the point though. It's all energy. Woman, man, black, white, hale, crippled, close your eyes and its just nerve endings and electricity. All the rest is construct, and variable.

'Actually I got to Dar too late. Ash's already claimed him.'

'So you thought you'd come and try me.'

'Wrong. It was just a visit. Like I said, I've been meaning to. Then you mentioned your problem and I saw a chance for sharing.'

'Did you?'

'Jared, I'm sorry I've wound you up.'

'You haven't.'

'Feels like it.'

'Yeah? Well I also feel like being on my own.'

Nicole stared at him with a sad expression, and then stood up slowly. "kay. I'll catch ya later then.'

Jared watched her walk toward the door. Part of him was screaming in disbelief. What was he doing? Why was he letting her leave?

The door closed gently with a click, the sound of the lock on the door of the safe he'd shut himself in. He resisted the urge to throw his glass against the wall, got up and put it on the table and stood staring at the door. He could call her back, reach out with his mind and touch hers, communicate his needs and fears without words. Except he couldn't. But why couldn't he? Like she'd said, he didn't have a problem with other subspace work. None of the others had a problem with telepathy.

Her questions came back to him. Was it because he didn't trust anyone enough to let them into his head? He trusted them with his life though. There wasn't anyone he felt safer with. Maybe openness was his problem.

He noticed the bottle of vodka by the bed and retrieved his glass.

He'd read up on the literature and knew the basis of telepathy. Most people had moments of recognisable telepathy; knowing what someone was about to say or that the phone was going to ring, and who was ringing, or the classic sense of being stared at. Research showed that telepathy was normal not paranormal, natural not supernatural.

Research into morphic fields showed that morphic resonance was the principle behind the organising activity of atoms and protein molecules through to whole organisms, including the Gaian 'organism'. Social groups were organised by fields, like flocks of birds and shoals of fish. The morphic fields of social groups connected members of the group even when they were miles apart, and provided channels along which the organisms could communicate at a distance. Morphic fields were the cause of all mental activity and perception. In the same way as the fields of other material objects, like magnetic fields and Earth's gravitational field, extended out beyond their surface, the morphic fields of minds extended out beyond the body.

So what was his problem? Without trying he was aware of the feelings and mood of the others in the group. Nicole's French cheese analogy was spot on. There was no way everyone wouldn't have been aware of his moods. So why couldn't he consciously send and receive like the others? Leon said that it was as easy as allowing, that trying got in the way. How did he allow something to happen? Maybe the torture had blown more than one fuse.

He reached for the bottle and topped up his glass.

***

Alex spied his friend's crumpled form slouching against the bar. He walked over and put a hand on Dylan's back. Dylan turned with a wavering, unfocused look. His face brightened and he chuckled.

'Nice one.' He turned and shook Alex's hand. 'How'd you find me?'

'Phoned the office, said I was a friend. The woman expressed surprise that you had any, but for an old friend of the family she informed me that you'd probably be propping up this bar. Been here a while have you?'

Dylan nodded. 'As you see.'

Alex looked over to the barman. 'Large malt, no ice, and another one of what he's drinking.' He looked back to Dylan who stood leaning lopsidedly, smiling.

'When did you get in?' Dylan slurred.

'A week, ten days maybe.'

'How's it going?'

Alex shrugged. 'It's going.'

Dylan nodded. The action sent a wave down his body that jerked to a stop at his knees.

'Shall we sit down?' Alex suggested.

Dylan frowned. 'No,' he said, and pushed himself up off the bar. 'As long as I remain standing, I can drink. As soon as I sit down I'm a goner.'

'I get the feeling it's not a celebration.'

'Course it's a celebration,' Dylan slurred loudly. 'I'm alive, hurrah. Plenty of cause for celebration.' His expression darkened momentarily, then brightened again. 'But hey, so are you, and you're back,' he slapped Alex's shoulder, 'and that is cause for celebration. Welcome back mate. Bet it's good to be away from the Front, eh?'

Alex nodded. 'Kind of. I don't feel fully back yet. But like you say, I am back. Many a time I thought I wouldn't make it.'

Watching Dylan struggle to focus, Alex wished his friend wasn't so drunk.

'Actually, I'm not supposed to be back. Caused a bit of a stink really.' He leaned closer to Dylan and spoke quietly. 'No-one's allowed straight back except brass.'

Dylan's eyes appeared to find a focus. 'Course they are.'

Alex shook his head.

'Yes, six month tour, then R&R.'

'R&R in camps in Germany or Turkey. Nobody comes straight back except brass…and body bags.'

'How come?'

'Official reason, bio-contamination.'

'Real reason?'

Alex was quiet for a moment. 'Have you got a phone on you?'

Dylan fumbled in his pocket and brought out his phone.

'Do me a favour and turn it off.'

'Eh…why?'

'I'll tell you later. Just humour me.'

Dylan shrugged, switched the phone off and put it back in his pocket. 'Okay?'

'Thanks, I'll explain later. You're on the news desk, what do you say is going on in the war zone?'

'How do you mean?'

'Casualty stats, equipment losses…who's winning?'

'Minimal losses as far as I can tell,' said Dylan, struggling with his diction. 'As for who's winning, I'd say neither really. What are you getting at?'

Alex glanced around the bar then back at Dylan. 'The information being given out about the war is deliberately misleading. The troops go to NATO R&R camps and get debriefed and we get reposted around Eastern Europe. I get back here and I'm immediately placed under house arrest and being debriefed once a day by military intelligence, a bloody oxymoron if ever there was one. Call me paranoid, but I know the phone's tapped.'

'Call me thick,' said Dylan apologetically.

'I didn't get it either at first,' said Alex, his voice still low, 'all their biological contamination bullshit. But no one who questioned, who interrogated me, wore a mask or anything. Then a couple of days ago I was watching the news and the war slot came up showing scenes of a town supposedly shot that day. A town I watched U.S. troops lay waste to over a month ago. The whole town, four or five thousand people, in less than an hour. Ever seen the effects of white phosphorus?'

Dylan shook his head.

'I'd put money on it that no-one out of the war zone has. The Geneva Convention bans its use on civilians, but it's getting used on them just like napalm and depleted uranium. Wily Pete, as they call it, melts flesh to the bone. The whole town, men, women and children lying where they fell, some still in their beds, clothes intact, skin caramelised and blackened or dissolved. Women and kids Dyl'. Why can't the military stick to killing other military?'

Dylan felt himself sobering. 'How did you get back?' he

asked, sensing the need for a change of subject.

'Had to blag my way back. Like I say, there's no leave granted.'

'But you're not in the army, what's all this talk of leave?'

'We're at war, mate. The media is included in the overall strategy. Propaganda blindfold. The public haven't got a bloody clue. Millions dead, mostly civilians. I'd had enough. It took me nearly a month to find a way back, eventually helped by a group of people who don't agree with what's going on, smuggled back into my own bloody country with a load of refugees,' he gulped his drink. 'I understand them a bit more now.'

'So you're AWOL then or out of a job?'

'Both I think. Fuck 'em, I quit anyway.'

Dylan chuckled and raised his glass.

'That's the least of my problems though. With the wage I've been on and nowhere to spend it, I'm good for three years at the very least. But I'm pulling sick leave, Post Traumatic Stress,' he stared hard at his glass.

'Other problems?'

Alex grimaced and put a hand to his stomach. 'Well for a start, nothing but alcohol and coffee since dinner yesterday. Shall we get a bite somewhere?'

'Sure,' said Dylan, accepting the parry. Food was a good idea anyway and he sensed Alex wouldn't be rushed.

The walk cleared his head a little by the time they saw a pub advertising 'Good English Grub'. The bar was busy, but they found a table in a corner.

'What to eat then?'

'Er, maybe not here,' said Alex.

'Eh?'

'Without being too obvious about it, watch the door and tell me if a woman in a dark grey two-piece with a handbag walks in.'

Dylan glanced over Alex's shoulder. 'Are you saying you're being followed?'

'Call me paranoid until she walks in. I'll give her three minutes. Maybe it's my long lost aunt or Jenny's brief trying to nail me with divorce proceedings, or maybe it's just my imagination. Thing is though, I'm a potential embarrassment for the war machine, a security risk. By the way, how's Angela?'

'Don't know and don't care. Split just over six months ago. My own fault, I was hell to live with,' Dylan smiled. 'Even I don't like living with me. Hate the job, hate the society. Just can't get rid of the feeling that I'm being shafted. Most of my waking hours spent dancing to somebody else's tune, only to have most of what I earn taken in tax to line somebody else's pockets and fund their never-ending war games. Really I'm just going through the motions, and trying to figure out what next,' he sat back and rubbed his eyes. 'You were right though. Grey twin set just walked in.'

Alex swore quietly.

'Looks like a brief,' said Dylan.

'Okay, just ignore her.' He sighed. 'Sorry to get you involved in this mate.'

'Involved in what, she could be Jenny's brief.'

'Sure.'

'Well, do we eat here or not? Come on, do your ulcers a favour.'

Alex looked up. 'How do you know I've got ulcers?'

'I'd say it was par for the course you've been on. Look, we might as well eat here as anywhere else. If you keep galloping around town, they're going to know you suspect a tail. My shout.'

Alex gave Dylan a grateful look. 'The roast beef and a pint of bitter.'

Dylan stood unsteadily and went to the bar. The woman was sitting at one end of the bar looking at a newspaper. He stood next to her and looked at the specials board above her head. The woman looked up. Dylan looked at her and smiled. She didn't return the smile and resumed leafing through the paper. Dylan looked at her clothes and noted the fact that she wasn't wearing a wedding ring. She looked up again.

'Another one?' Dylan said.

The woman's eyes flicked contemptuously from his face to his clothes. 'I don't think so,' she said, looking back to the paper immediately.

'Earthquake,' said Dylan, indicating the front-page headline.

The woman turned the page and looked.

'Another one.' His smile broadened.

She looked at Dylan smiling his broad smile, then without answering looked back to the paper.

Dylan ordered the food and carried the drinks back to Alex, still smiling.

'Something funny?'

'Yeah, but I'll tell you another time.'

'Did you get a look?'

'Oh yes. Don't think she's a cop, calves are too slim. My money's on your divorce papers.'

'I'd like to think so, Dyl', but if that's the case, why hasn't she served them already?'

Dylan shrugged. 'Waiting for evidence of infidelity?'

'No need. Things were going down the pan before I left. That was over two years ago. Irretrievable breakdown, simple enough. And anyway, twin set and slim legs is just today's shadow, yesterday was someone else.'

'You tell me then.'

'Government or military, not that there's much difference,' said Alex. 'I told you, I'm a potential embarrassment, or security risk as they'd see it. The only people that come straight back are brass, dead or wounded. The brass won't talk, the wounded aren't allowed to, Official Secrets Act, national security blah. And as a grunt their perspective on what's going on is pretty limited anyway, and they're hardly going to confess their own war crimes or expose their mates.

'The press aren't in a position to report on what's actually going on either. No independent uplinks, strictly controlled press pools and all dispatches censored. Unless you're there yourself, which very often you're not, the information you get is handed out by the military and therefore suspect.

'As an embedded journo you have to sign a contract with the government that requires you to follow government direction and orders. It even prohibits you from suing for injury or death, even if it's caused by the military. You're completely controlled by the military and dependant on the troops for protection. Word soon gets around if somebody's reports are at odds with the military's. Non-embedded journo's have a habit of running into friendly fire or being in the wrong hotel during allied attacks. You remember Jerry Floyd and his cameraman Ted? Both of them and their local translator were killed, by friendly fire, essentially because they weren't part of a military organisation.

'During my debriefing they told me I wasn't allowed to talk to anyone about the war zone, not even family, without first consulting their media office. Talk about the Ministry for Public Enlightenment and Propaganda.'

'I get the picture, Alex. So now what? You're back, and they're following you to see where you go and who you talk to, which implicates me in this whole conspiracy by the way, now what?'

'Probably depends where I go and what I do.'

'What are you going to do?'

'I want to blow the whistle on the whole thing. The public should be exposed to the facts of the war, all of them; civilian casualties, flattened towns, facts about who's making big bucks out of it all.

'The defence budget, the defence committee, what's being defended? If NATO withdrew, the Federation would just go back to their rice and soybeans and goods manufacture. And all the other little men who are kicking back wouldn't have to if the U.S. and its marauding allies would take their thieving fingers out of pies that aren't theirs. The Pan-Asian Federation don't want to take over the world, they're not interested in shoving communism or any other ism down anybody's throat, except their own population. They just want the Neo-Con's thieving mitts off their natural and capital reserves, and, in the case of China and Japan, repayments on the billions of dollars of U.S. debt they've been buying for years. Financially they don't need this war, unlike the Anglo-American mob that's making trillions of dollars in munitions and construction contracts.

'Over the last few years the Pentagon's outsourced on average $150 billion a year in work to corporations. Almost half of it was in no-bid contracts and three quarters of that was to the five largest defense contractors headed by Lockheed Martin and Boeing. Lockheed is the undisputed king of contractors. But the rest are all the same. KBR, Halliburton, Bechtel, et cetera, all pigs at the trough. All get the contracts through no-bid decisions. Decisions made by politicians who have links to the industry. It's them and their cronies that are behind this global expansionism. They're a private, for profit, off-the-shelf, regime-change industry. They fight the wars, organise the occupation that follows, rebuild the ruined infrastructure, recruit new governments, and manage the post-war economy.

'But most of all the public needs to be told how NATO's weapons of mass destruction are poisoning other countries around the world including this one. The U.S. has permanently contaminated the global atmosphere with radiation that has a half-life of two and a half billion years. Under the right conditions one alpha particle of uranium causes cancer. A pinhead of DU releases 12,000 alpha particles a second. I've seen a buried report that shows that uranium aerosols have been blown up here on wind currents from the war zone resulting in concentrations of uranium over Reading high enough to alert the Environment Agency, who decided that nobody needed to know.

'I have nightmares about the children I've seen with horrific birth defects caused by the tonnes of uranium that's been used in the war. And I mean horrific Dyl', mutations a special effects crew would find hard to replicate.' He shook his head. 'I've cried so hard, for those kids, for their poor families. And it's going to happen here too, it's happening already, look at the exponentially rising cancer statistics. Wait until we start getting babies born in Berkshire with their intestines on the outside.

'And guess who's making money out of it. Pulled the rug out from underneath my royalist feet I can tell you. The largest uranium mining company in the world is Rio Tinto Mines, a company that's poisoning great swathes of Australia, Africa, Ecuador, Papua New Guinea, et cetera, et cetera. The Royal family privately owns investments in uranium holdings worth six billion dollars through Rio Tinto Mines.'

He put a hand to his head.

'Something's very wrong Dyl'. It's like I've just woken up. None of this is happening by accident. Everything, everything's been analysed and risk assessed, and long-term battle and contingency plans drawn up, and I'm talking about the global financial situation as well as the war. This has been going on for a long time.'

'Hmm, cheery stuff,' said Dylan. 'Where to now then?'

'First get out of the business. We're part of the problem. What's going on is in effect a criminal conspiracy under international criminal law in violation of the Nuremberg Charter, the Nuremberg Judgment and the Nuremberg Principles, defined by wars of aggression, crimes against humanity, and war crimes that are legally like those perpetrated by the Nazis in the Second World War. International law is being broken every week, yet the public isn't hearing about it. It's no wonder people don't understand what's going on in the war zone. And to make it worse, deliberate misconceptions and theories about fanaticism and fundamentalism are being encouraged and propagated. I've forgotten the amount of times I've heard it said that suicide bombers only take that recourse because their religion promises them a fast track to heaven where wait more virgins than they can shake a stick at.

'Napoleon once said three hostile newspapers are to be feared more than a thousand bayonets. I'm scared Dyl'. More scared now than I ever was sitting in an APV wishing I had another set of body armour to go on top of the set I was wearing. It's easier to dodge a bullet. This is so much bigger than us. And how the hell do you fight it? There's no friendly fire to worry about, and thank God there's no family for them to threaten me with, but they could just snuff me out, or lock me up and lose the key. Mumia's still in jail nearly thirty years later, and look how blatantly fixed that case was, never mind all the journalists and celebrities that went public in his support. The authorities don't give a shit. They're so blatant and smug because they know that even if the facts get past their media filter nobody will do anything.'

Plates of steaming food arriving ended the conversation. The food took the edge off Dylan's inebriation and gave him time to think. He knew what Alex meant when he said it was like he'd just woken up. Lights were going on in his own head; thoughts, snippets of information, glimpsed patterns and links, previously ignored, left unopened, filed under Don't Go There.

It wasn't that he was ignorant of the things Alex had spoken of, but it was as though he hadn't seen them properly. Going round with his eyes wide shut. It was scary though, and bigger than them, a sleeping dog that he'd so far managed to tiptoe around. Which was the smart move. Nobody talked politics except the party pantomime kind. He supposed there were others that thought as he did, but they, like him, wouldn't be stupid enough to risk exposing themselves.

Alex sat back and wiped his mouth. 'Here's my plan. Find a way of doing a piece and getting it shown. Take a page out of Michael Moore's book, not that his work has made the slightest bit of difference. Then I'm off, leaving this stinking, sinking ship, and going back. Going back to give something back. Help pick up the pieces instead of feeding off the Empire's road kill. Voluntarily, although not as some kind of penance, more as a show of gratitude.

'Being witness to those people's suffering has exposed me to myself. Their pain has shown me my shallowness and selfishness; their strength and tenacity under the most despicable treatment has shown me how weak I am. Because of that weakness I've been guilty of complicity. I didn't just stand by; I joined in, telling myself that I was performing a valuable service through journalism, even though I knew I was just a whore in the entertainment business. No, get out Dyl', do your self-esteem a favour. At best we're intellectual prostitutes, tools of rich men behind the scenes. Worse than that though, we're part of the control mechanism, their weapon of mass deception.'

Dylan watched his friend's animated face as he talked. Alex had changed, which wasn't surprising considering where he'd

141

been. He definitely looked older, greyer, with deepening crow's feet, but he also seemed more youthful somehow. Vitality had replaced the slightly stiff reserve and predictability. Vitality verging on righteous anger.

He glanced over Alex's shoulder at the bar. Twin set and slim legs had gone. Two men in suits stood where she'd sat.

Alex noticed Dylan's attention and stopped talking. 'What?'

'Nothing. Just noticed twin set and slim legs has gone.'

Alex sighed. 'I am sorry for implicating you in this mess, Dyl', but you're the only family I've got. I trust you, and you know the industry,' he attempted a smile, 'my man on the inside.'

'Maybe not for much longer.'

He told Alex about the hijack and passed him the handout. Alex read it and shook his head slowly.

'See the bit about the compliant media? It's like I was saying, and now people are resorting to hijacking to get the message across.'

'Tell me about it. Campbell refused to air my report without, what he called, judicious editing. He said the emphasis on the hijacker's non-violence could be construed as sympathetic. I told him that one of the points that I was trying to make was that four people could take over a train carriage full of people simply by telling people to sit down.'

Alex nodded. 'An interesting point.'

'I argued about the decision, but got nowhere. In fact, when I got irate he advised me to go away and think carefully about things. Luckily I'd photocopied the handout beforehand, because the whole thing's been buried.

'Talking of which, it describes the phone networks as if they're some kind of mind control. Why did you ask me to switch my phone off?'

'You mean apart from doing you a favour and minimally reducing the chances of you getting testicle or bowel cancer from carrying it around in your pocket?'

Dylan laughed. 'Yes, apart from that.'

'It's no joke, Dyl'. Even with the most rudimentary grasp of biological systems, it's obvious that pulsed microwave radiation is damaging. If it interferes with aviation and hospital equipment, then it interferes with the even more delicate electromagnetism of the brain and body, regardless of whether any thermal effects occur. And then there's the carcinogenic effect of microwave radiation.'

'Okay, point taken. You were saying?'

'Ever heard of Celldar?'

'I get the feeling I'm going to.'

'Cellphone radar, hence the name. Designed by British Aerospace Engineering Systems and Roke Manor Research, a subsidiary of Siemens, that wartime Hitler funder and slave labour user. Uses GSM and 3G networks as a form of covert, passive radar that renders pictures of all real-time objects within the range of each base station, inside or outside. Essentially it's a high performance, long-range, low-cost detection system for use in C4ISR solutions. Tracks, cues, and identifies anything bigger than a squirrel on land, water and air.

'Add to that the fact that you can be pinpointed to within three feet anywhere in the world because of the regular pulsed signal the phone sends out, pulsed microwaves that are going through your body by the way. Three things then, they know where you are at all times, and can detect who and what's around you, even through walls, and your phone transmits without you doing anything. Now maybe, maybe, it only transmits a pulse to maintain a fix, but if it can do that it can transmit anything, like our conversation.'

Dylan chuckled. 'I think I detect an odour of conspiracy theory.'

Alex didn't smile. 'Is that so? Then what about the U.S. vs. Ardito? Ardito is allegedly a major mover in the New York Genovese Mafia family. The FBI used evidence collected from conversations held in the vicinity of Ardito and his attorney that were recorded using their mobile phones. The surveillance technique works even when the phone is switched off. You have to take the battery out to be sure.

'Anyway, why is it that the phrase 'quantum theory' or

'superstring theory' has the feel of respectability, but the phrase 'conspiracy theory' has the opposite? Especially as the sciences are theorising about things that are impossible to observe, while the latter is composed of easily verifiable, mostly publicly available, information. Don't take my word for it, Dyl', check it out for yourself.'

He pointed to the handout.

'This too. Behavioural modification and neural control using certain frequencies is old hat, the technology's been around for at least fifty years. The Soviets used the same frequencies and intensities used by the phone networks as weapons. There are hundreds of patents for devices related to mental and emotional influencing, and perception engineering. And they're public domain patents. What about the millions that have gone into military psychotronic technology? The phone networks would be the perfect vehicle for neurally manipulating or controlling individuals or sections of the population, just like for Celldar.'

'It all sounds a bit Nineteen Eighty Four.'

'Ever read it?'

'Ages ago.'

'Then I'd recommend another read, especially considering his descriptions of continuous manufactured war, surveillance, state control psychology, and language. Very pertinent. It was a savvy stroke to trivialise that concept like they did. Trivialised, and in doing so totally legitimised twenty four hour, seven days a week CCTV surveillance.'

He glanced around again.

'And that's another thing, I've come back to a country where every town has got government spies on the street. 'Human Intelligence' operatives. State-approved surveillance by civilians, including Junior Streetwatchers that the State pays cash for informing. Microphones embedded in lampposts and street furniture. How? It's like we've slipped back in time to behind the Berlin wall.' He rubbed his eyes. 'Pinch me and wake me up, tell me it was just a nightmare.'

Dylan didn't laugh. 'Who'd have thought, eh?'

'I bet no one saw this coming, even though all the signs were there. But it's not going to get any better unless we do something about it, while we still can.'

'What can we do about it though?'

'You could start by asking the question as if it was a real question, instead of a statement that says there's nothing you can do.'

'I mean it, what can we do?'

'I mean it too. Ask yourself the question and think about it. The answers might take some working out, but there is something you can do. There are things we can all do. People have to get off their backsides before it's too late.'

Dylan leaned forward and spoke quietly. 'Lower your voice a bit.'

Alex froze.

'You should be a bit more careful,' said Dylan.

'Seriously Dyl', said Alex, almost whispering, 'what will it take? How far do they have to go before you're moved to do something?'

Dylan looked away from Alex's searching stare, at a loss for an answer and slightly troubled that he'd not asked himself the same question before.

Alex looked at his watch.

'Hey look; I've got to get on. Still got things to do.'

He stood and pulled on his jacket. 'Bloody good to see you, mate.' He gripped Dylan's hand with both of his. 'Speak with you in a couple of days, eh.'

Dylan nodded and watched his friend walk out. Neither of the men at the bar paid him any attention.

Like a phantom limb he still kept reaching for he pulled his cigarettes out of his pocket, paused and tutted, and put them back. He finished his drink and walked out. In the doorway outside he stopped and lit up. The health warning on the packet caught his eye. He'd seen it before, but he hadn't seen it before. The cheeky fuckers. Someone should remind them that using depleted uranium weapons would harm the unborn child.

He passed a bus shelter…ad-shelter he corrected himself. The sign wasn't an advert though; it was a Public Directive notice reminding people to be vigilant.

Alex had been surprised at the state of things, yet he hardly thought about it much. Which was probably one reason why they called it function creep. It crept up on you, and not just the technology. But like Alex had said, there had been plenty of signs. The takeover of politics by corporate interests, rampant cronyism and corruption, fixed elections, obsession with crime and punishment, and national security, and the whipping up of the people into a patriotic flag-wearing frenzy. Even the recession resulting from manipulated stock market crash copied the template used in the build-up to the Second World War.

People liked the cameras though, and the ID cards or chip implants. They made them feel safe. Why wouldn't anybody like them, they would ask. If you had nothing to hide, you had nothing to fear.

***

'No use arguing your case with me, Lock, the word comes from higher up.'

There was a knock at the office door. Lock sat back. The slight movement sucked a draught of air down the collar of his shirt, chilling the film of sweat on his neck.

'Come in.'

The door opened and the secretary walked in carrying a tray. Lock watched her breasts bounce slightly under the thin blouse. As she bent to place the tray on the desk, he imagined taking her roughly from behind. His fists clenched thinking what he would do with those bouncing breasts.

'Colonel,' said the woman, pouring coffee into a cup, 'your twelve thirty appointment just phoned. Stuck in traffic, regrets he'll be late.'

'That so?' Colonel Sellar replied, staring unconcernedly over the top of the secretary's blouse.

She straightened up.

Sellar cleared his throat. 'Well, after this I'll be going for lunch. Beggar can wait until I get back.'

'Yes sir.'

She turned and walked out of the room.

'Right, now where were we?' Sellar said, as the door shut. 'Yes, you had one of the bastards, had him for close on a week, and then let him be spirited away. Bit of a poor show, wouldn't you say?'

Lock said nothing. A muscle twitched in his jaw.

Sellar stared at Lock. The power hungry little prick. A new updated armoury, bigger budget and that ponce in the chair, it was no wonder the Squad were getting ideas above their station, whining about protocol and jurisdiction. Well bigger toys didn't make bigger boys.

'If it were down to me my men would take over where your boys left off.'

'Really Colonel,' Lock sat forward, uncrossing his legs. 'I admit, I made a mistake and underestimated the organisation of this group, but no one could have foreseen this incident.'

'Foreseen no, acted on information taken from the suspect, yes.'

'We got no information from the suspect.'

'Quite.'

'Well at least there were no hostages.'

'Of course there were no hostages! Hells bells man! It was a purely propaganda move, surely you can see that. Here.'

He thrust a sheet of paper across the desk. Lock recognised it as one of the pamphlets given out by the terrorists. He thought better of saying he'd already read it and picked it up in case he'd missed something.

This information has been compiled by a group of concerned citizens wishing to bring to the public's attention moves that are being made against them. The method of delivery though potentially distressing for some was chosen because of the compliant nature of the media industry, the use of which would render the message buried and unheard.

Using techniques developed before the end of last century, techniques involving ultra-high and ultra-low frequencies

147

inaudible to the human ear, your freedom of thought is being circumvented. Covering the country are transmitters that broadcast pulse-modulated microwaves, the intensity and frequency of which pass through the skull, bypassing the ear directly into the brain. In themselves these weaponised frequencies trigger a whole range of physiological disorders including immune system breakdown and cancer (as demonstrated by the leukaemia cases and deaths following the deliberate exposure of the American embassy in Moscow). Broadcast 'piggyback' on these frequencies are low amplitude replications of specific brainwave patterns which, when directed at a subject (read: you the public), also affect thoughts, responses and behaviour.

The greatest activity on the Home Front has been mainly commercial and socio-political, influencing public spending, opinion and behaviour. It is as you read also being used on the Russian Front, falling within the category of 'non-lethal weapons', using the military's satellite, airborne and remote vehicle ('drone') capabilities. The use of the technology has not been confined to the war zone however, and has seen the technology injected into public life in a way much more insidious than soldiers and armoured vehicles in the streets.

There are few forms of protection open to non-military personnel. The military have their own combination methods.

What can you do? How can you with no military hardware or training protect yourself and your family?

- *Reduce your exposure by limiting your use of microwave technology (wireless devices in particular, which effectively place a transmitting mast in your home).*
- *Observe your feelings closely, especially during Television exposure. Are they just a result of visual stimuli, program theme, plot, etc, or are they uncharacteristically intense or alien to your personality?*
- *Demand that microwave-detecting equipment*

148

*withdrawn from the market by the government be
made available to the public. One need not be using a
phone directly to be affected by Extremely Low
Frequencies from nearby phones, and ground-based
and satellite transmitters.*

- *Contact the various communication companies
  (phone/television/Internet), informing them that you
  intend to limit your usage until the situation has been
  properly investigated and rectified.*
- *Researched information regarding the above can be
  found on the Internet using search items such as:*

*Microwave Mind Control
ELF Dangers
Remote Neural Monitoring
PsyOps*

Be aware. Your ignorance is their bliss.

Lock put the paper on the desk.

'You have enough clearance, and surely enough sense, to see
that this could jeopardise one of our most important projects.
And the bastards even had the audacity to take the time to cock a
snoot before dispensing with your backup.' Sellar waved the slip
of paper found in the getaway vehicle. '"Men in glass houses
shouldn't throw stones". You let them make a mockery of you.

'There are to be no more cock-ups. This group is to be
terminated with extreme prejudice, is that clear?'

'Quite,' said Lock.

'Quickly and quietly. Under no circumstances must the public
be exposed to anymore of this.'

He began shuffling papers on the desk, then looked up and
stared at Lock.

The muscles in Lock's jaw bunched and danced. He stood
briskly and strode to the door.

'Another thing Lock…'

Lock paused with his hand on the door handle.

149

'I expect seamless integration with this department, beginning with a full report of the suspect's internment post haste.'

Lock walked through the outer office, his vision red and grainy. When he reached the outer door he stopped to put his sunglasses on. His hands were clammy and bore a line of tiny red horseshoe impressions on each palm.

His driver had the car door open by the time he reached it.

'City,' he hissed between his teeth without looking at the man.

Extreme prejudice. He'd show them extreme prejudice. Domestic scorched earth was what they were going to get. He'd twist those anarchist cunts until they screamed blood. Sellar was right, they'd made a mockery of him. Well, he'd fix that. He'd have them crawling and begging before he programmed them and sent them to their death.

Tiny creaks came from his teeth as he ground them together.

And those Whitehall wankers, tying him up with that ponderous prat as if he was some kind of attack dog on a leash. Seamless integration. Yet Sellar would be the first to distance himself should things go awry. And what of it if the public got wind of anything? They were so stupid and gullible they lapped up every cover story. And those who did see through the spin were too pathetic to be concerned with. Made you understand why the country needed a strong government. Sheep needed a shepherd.

6

What difference does it make to the dead, the orphans, and the homeless, whether the mad destruction is wrought under the name of totalitarianism or the holy name of liberty and democracy?
                                                    – Mahatma Gandhi

> *He's the one who gives his body as a weapon of the war,*
> *and without him all this killing can't go on.*
> *He's the Universal Soldier and he really is to blame...*
>   – Buffy Sainte Marie/Donovan *The Universal Soldier*

Leon pierced the ration tins and set them in the sooty sand. He leaned back against the side of the crater and looked up at the sky. The sun hadn't climbed high enough to penetrate the shell hole, but already his sweat-soaked clothes stuck to him like gritty mummies bandages.

Two constants in all the fucked up inconstancy, the sun and the sand. The sand behaved like the enemy, as though they were somehow formed from the same material, slowly but surely getting everywhere; the sun shared their relentlessness, pounding them, day after day, without let-up.

Exhaustion weighed him down despite the anti-fatigue pills. No sleep for days, and the constant stress of hunting things that were invisible to eye and radar, had him perpetually on edge almost to snapping point.

He opened the warmed rations. The mess that was supposed to be stroganoff had a vaguely comforting school dinners aroma to it, while the smell of the Food Corps iron rations reminded him of tank exhaust. The stroganoff could wash the spinach down.

He looked over at Sol squatting opposite. 'I always wish I was Popeye and could down this crap in one.' He lifted the tin and squeezed it. The thin alloy crumpled and green gunk oozed out over his hand. He laughed.

Sol smiled. 'Suits you and that fucking laugh of yours.'

Leon licked at the gunk. It even tasted like tank exhaust.

Tank exhaust...tank exhaust...tank...

He scrambled to his feet, mess tins flying. Sol was beside him instantly, peering over the lip of the hole.

'What?'

'Tank.'

'Anybody else?'

'I don't see anything.'

'Nothin' on the scope.'

Leon tutted and slowly eased his rocket launcher over the edge of the hole.

'That sure?' Sol said.

'We'll be home in time for tea, Ginger.'

Tension hummed through the four men who, following Leon's example, stood ready with rocket launchers.

There was a faint hissing crackling, like the sound of an approaching brush fire.

'Ghosts at nine,' said Leon, sinking lower.

The hissing grew louder quickly, preceding a shimmering, localised heat wave moving rapidly along the track through the blasted trees. A tail of twigs and pine needles followed the haze just above ground level.

Leon pushed his fingers into the dust without realising.

A second haze followed the first, then another, and another. Stealth tanks. A battlefield specialisation used by both sides in response to the infantry-based warfare. Radar-cloaked and virtually invisible to the eye due to a coating of phased-array optics that doubled as camera and screen, recording the background scenery and reproducing full colour holographic images of its environment over the hull. The radar cloaking had enabled the tanks to carry out raids on the frontline troops undetected by Allied ordnance and jets.

'Target by sound off...one,' said Leon.

The others sounded off the numbers quietly.

The hazes halted on the track and sharpened to complete invisibility. The effect was like looking through a window. Leon marked the lead tank position on the track and waited.

Was that the lot? The last thing they needed was to be hunted down by a rear guard.

They couldn't let those move on though. He lifted the rocket launcher slowly and sighted it on the section of tree that marked the position of the rear of the lead tank's turret. The others mimicked the action.

'Ready...hit 'em!'

Four tandem-charge HEAT anti-tank missiles streaked out from the group and found their targets almost simultaneously. The tanks became instantly visible in the midst of the fireballs, materialising like phoenixes in flames. The turret hatches of two of the tanks flew back and men spilled out. A secondary explosion, probably the tanks munitions, blew one man screaming into the air. Single shots from the group downed the others. For a moment there was no sound except the crackling of flames and exploding ammunition from the gutted tanks.

Leon watched the flames, wondering how many that made. He'd stopped counting when he'd begun to feel a piece of him die each time he killed someone, as if his life were linked with theirs in some deep, inexplicable way. Airborne had an easier time of it, climb to fifty thousand feet, press a button and dump hundreds of tonnes of explosive and never have to see the bodies bursting and burning; the annihilated schools, hospitals, and neighbourhoods.

His attention was drawn back to the burning wreckage. A chill ran through him and his lungs froze in mid-breath. The burning bodies of the shot men draped over the sides of the gutted turrets. Rising slowly out of the bodies were two egg-shaped clouds. About the size of a small man they seemed to be made out of white mist. As he watched two more orbs emerged out of the smoke above them and hung motionless. A feeling of sadness reached him. More orbs drifted out of the smoke and grouped with the others, hanging like mute spectators of a traffic accident.

What the hell were they?

A hand touched his arm.

'Let's get outa here.'

Leon turned. 'Yeah, let's.' He glanced back at the scene once more before following the others.

The yomp back to the extraction point didn't allow much time to think about the apparition. Although this far from habitation there was little risk from I.E.D's, a bigger risk lay in other tanks. A static stealth tank was invisible. He led the unit off the valley floor along a goat track he'd seen on the way in. Their potential visibility when they cleared the tree line was a lesser danger than stumbling over something in the valley. The trail steepened sharply and soon they had to shoulder their weapons and climb. The forest fell away to a rustling table of green below. Out of the shade the heat built up rapidly and sweat darkened their fatigues in growing patches.

Leon flinched into a crouch as a huge shadow passed over him. Above him four buzzards circled close to the rock. Their wingspans looked to be wider than his height. Another two took off from a ledge thirty feet above him. He wondered whether buzzards were a bad omen. As if omens had anything to do with anything.

They made the extraction point without incident. The Lynx breezed in less than ten minutes later, homing in on the combined signal of the unit's chips. They ran through the wall of dust and bundled into the chopper. The door-gunner didn't even glance at them, his wraparound gaze scanning the horizon. The last man was scarcely in and they took off, sharp and veering. The pilot was taking no chances either.

Leon rested his head against the bulkhead and took a deep breath. They might still get shot out of the air with every guerrilla fighter's favourite eighteenth birthday present, the RPG, but there was nowhere to run now, so he might as well relax. He hoped this wasn't one of the rigs that hadn't been fitted with flare-launching systems because of defence budget skimming. It wouldn't be the first to have been shot down as a result. The odds on outmanoeuvring a heat-seeker weren't very high.

The buffeting draught was hairdryer hot.

As if it had been waiting, his mind went back to the phenomena at the tanks. The only thing that he could think of was that they were the souls of the tank crews. What else could they have been? But he didn't believe in life after death. What you saw was what you got. But what had he seen? The image of the orbs and the feeling of sadness were still vivid. How come he'd seen them and not the others? Or maybe the others had and, like him, were processing it on their own.

A loud clang shocked him back into the belly of the beast. One of the gunners opened up, sending empty cases arcing into the air. A barrage of clangs, something whizzed past Leon's ear and punched the bulkhead, and suddenly the air was full of red aerosol. A rifle clattered to the floor. Leon grabbed for it, but Sol reached it before him.

Seated across from Leon, Murphy, the piss-taking Irishman, was slumped over a foot wide cavity in his chest. Spongy flaps of lung released ribbons of blood into the air that caught and spun in the vortex, spraying everywhere. Leon lifted his arm to wipe his face, but stopped on seeing the gore-spattered sleeve. He wiped the blood away from his eyes with his fingers.

Murphy seemed to be peering into the hole. The chopper banked and the body fell forward into the harness. Long ropes of shiny offal spilled out of the hole and flopped between his legs. The chopper continued with its evasive action and Leon had to concentrate to keep his stomach where it was.

The Lynx's engine noise dropped an octave and started misfiring. Swirling black smoke filled the cab.

'You got a parachute?' Sol shouted through the din.

'I was hoping to borrow yours!' Leon shouted back.

Sol reached round and took the clips and grenades from Murphy's webbing and passed them around. Leon wiped the blood-slicked clip on his leg before pocketing it. Even Irish luck had to run out sometime. Or had it? A death so swift could've been a gift.

A snatch of a dream that had woken him a few nights before came back to him, fire surrounding him, consuming him; death in an explosion of fire. Maybe it had been a premonition. But the sounds and feelings that had come with it were calm and quiet, nothing like the frenzied racket that filled his ears.

Calm settled into him even as he was flung around in the harness as the chopper continued to weave and shudder. Today wasn't his day to die. He didn't know how he knew, but he was sure.

He looked over at Sol, shook his head and mouthed, 'not today'.

Sol returned a wan smile and shook his head.

It didn't sound like they were going to get very far though. The Rolls Royce Gem engine coughed and missed and revved, and seemed on a terminal spiral. The Lynx sank rapidly, lifting Leon's stomach into his mouth. He swallowed and grimaced against the acid bile.

One of the gunners crouched next to Leon and shouted.

'Fuel tank hit…convoy…ahead…hitch…base…'

Leon nodded.

The engine misfiring worsened and the chopper lost altitude swiftly and began to slow. The ground raced toward them. A line of armoured vehicles wreathed in a cloud of dust flashed past beneath. At least they weren't going to have to walk.

The engines gunned and the chopper yawed crazily as it slowed. The pilot managed to put them down without pitching it over. As soon as they touched down the gunners lifted the guns off the mountings and jumped out. Leon unzipped a body bag and, aided by Sol, lifted Murphy's body into it. He scooped up the trailing intestines and poured them back into the hole. They were warm and slippery soft, and gritty with sand. He wiped his hands on his trouser leg.

They walked away from the chopper toward the approaching convoy. The pilot stopped Leon and asked for his rifle and a grenade. Leon passed them over without question. The pilot fitted the grenade to the end of the rifle and fired at the chopper. The explosion blew it onto its side. One rotor stuck up out of the smoke and flames like a single, defiant finger.

The pilot handed the rifle back. 'Honourably discharged.'

The convoy was U.S. AFV's and APC's returning to base. The unit split up among the vehicles. Leon climbed into the back of a Hummer.

'Holy shit! What y'all been doin' out there?' said a young, freckle-faced GI opposite, scratching his leg vigorously.

Leon squeezed into a corner on top of some ammunition crates. A faint butchers shop smell wafted up from his stiff fatigues.

'Ghost busting.'

The GI nodded, still scratching. 'Sneaky slant fucks. How many dya get?'

Leon hesitated, unwilling to continue the conversation.

The soldier laughed. 'Did ya make crispy critters or did ya get ta play gook-in-the-box?'

'Can it, man,' muttered the GI next to him.

'Just making conversation. Name's Monahan, pleased ta meet ya.'

Leon just stared at him. As blood spattered as he was, he could be as antisocial as he liked. He guessed the GI's age to be around twenty. Pale blue eyes under almost invisible blond eyebrows, and an imbecilic smile, all grits and mom's apple pie. Mom probably had a picture of her l'il boy, in regimental colours, razor-sharp creases and spotless white gloves, that she proudly pointed out to all visitors. He wondered what Mom would think of crispy critters and gook-in-the-box.

The comments were typical. Reducing people to labels removed their humanity and allowed behaviour toward them that would have been unacceptable toward someone considered to be another person. A little mental sleight-of-hand and what was immoral and indefensible became morally justifiable. Nigger, Gook, Raghead, Slant; an untermenschen by any other name was still an untermenschen. The thought occurred to him that maybe it was the racist tone that had provoked the muttering GI.

'Will you quit scratchin' your boils,' grumbled the same GI.

'Fuckin' sand fly!' Monahan complained, scratching harder.

The grumbling GI snorted. 'Sand fly my ass!'

'Course it's a sand fly bite, plenty of the guys have got them.'

'Sure man, whatever you say.'

'Doc said it was a sand fly bite. I got medication for it.'

'Sure he said it was a sand fly. Don't mean to say that's what it is.'

'So what is it then professor?'

'It's what you sittin' on.'

Monahan shook his head. 'You make less sense everyday, old man.'

The GI chuckled humourlessly. 'Don't it all? What're you sittin' on?'

'You know what I'm sittin' on, what we're all sittin' on, 'cept you, you sat on your brains.'

Laughter bounced around the hot interior.

'Hah de fuckin' hah,' drawled the GI. 'Thing is we's all got shit for brains. We's here ain't we. Truckin' around in a sittin' duck steel box in a land where everybody wants to kill us, sittin' on highly radioactive ammunition.'

'I don't wanna hear this!' shouted a voice from the front.

'Find some sand to bury yo' head in then! Ain't everybody here scared to hear the facts…are they?' He looked around, but nobody spoke. 'What we's sittin' on is a weapon of mass destruction,' he went on. 'Uranium's a nuke.'

'It's depleted uranium,' shouted the voice from the front again.

The GI's voice raised an octave. 'Depleted to what? Shit's got a half-life of over a billion years. An' we's sittin' on it. No wonder half the guys got radiation boils.'

'Carter, if there was any danger to the men we'd be issued with protective gear.'

'Where the fuck you been?' Carter gasped. 'We's pawns, disposable shit for the players on this Grand Chessboard. Dumb, stupid animals if ya ask Henry Kissinger. My dad was in 'Nam. Survived ol' Ho Chi Minh's men, but didn't get past Agent Orange. Ate him up from the inside. You check out the stats from the first offensive. Near 600,000 troops made it back from the Gulf. Half of them are on permanent medical disability, an' over eleven thousand are dead. An' of those guy's kids born afterward sixty seven percent got birth defects and serious illness.'

'That was the raghead's chemical weapons.'

'Man, you eat lies like I eat Hershey bars! We used chemical weapons! The shit we's sittin' on's all three, chemical, nuclear an' biological. How many tons of this shit's been spread over this land these last years? I'll tell ya how much, enough to make more mutant babies than I ever wanna see again. Place is getting like some Mad Max nuclear desert. I tell ya, I'm glad I got my breedin' done before I came here. You try it now an' you playin' retard Russian roulette.'

Leon tried to ignore the conversation. He was struggling enough with images of Murphy without thinking about the children with bulbous heads, no eyes and gaping palateless mouths held up by women as patrols drove by, the 'look what you've done' message blatant and gutting. They were wiping out generations. Carter was right, more than enough DU had been used, was still being used, to turn most of the war zone into inhospitable land. In fact it was a guaranteed result. Was that the plan? Were they intentionally poisoning the people and the land? Given the fact that military scientists had all the information about uranium, it sure looked like it. He adjusted his position, the thought of rectal cancer almost as uncomfortable as the crate.

Carter's talk seemed to have squelched conversation in the Hummer, and the men sat sullenly staring at their boots. The youth opposite reached to scratch, and then stopped.

Leon had a fleeting impression of being in a hearse. He dug a nail into the cuticle of his thumb. The sharp pain cleared his head. This wasn't his day to die.

He thought about Carter's Agent Orange comment. Another example of the U.S. war on Earth. 2-4-D, a supposed defoliant, produced by Monsanto, those champions of genetic modification, trashed some of the most diverse forest on the planet. On top of the extermination of plant and animal life, the Vietnamese people still carried the legacy of cancers and birth defects. Just like in the 'war on drugs' in Colombia where hardcore herbicides were sprayed over the unique Andes Mountains, to the same effect. But they weren't that fussy about where they contaminated. The U.S. Navy repeatedly fired depleted uranium rounds into prime fishing waters off Washington State during routine weapons calibrations.

The U.S. military was the world's largest polluter. It produced more toxic waste in a year than the five largest chemical

159

companies in the U.S. U.S. military bases all over the world discharged toxic material directly into the air and water, and poisoned the land of nearby communities resulting in increased rates of cancer, kidney disease, birth defects, low birth weight, and miscarriage. Their knowledge of the short and long-term effects of the chemicals suggested that the use was deliberate. And like Carter said, DU had a half-life of billions of years. There was no way to clean it up, and nowhere to hide.

Alerted by a crackling message, he looked up and squinted through the dust thrown up by the lead Bradleys. Ahead was a line of low flat-roofed buildings interspersed with straggly palms. Even from that distance he could see that many of the walls that made up the traditional courtyards of the houses were collapsed and crumbling. He easily imagined the general layout of the village, replicated in all the towns and villages dotted around that part of the world; one or two main dirt roads bisecting blocks of single-story flat-roofed houses, each L-shaped and walled to give the multi-generational families a private courtyard, the more luxurious of which had a tree that gave some shade from the fierce sun.

He swallowed against the nausea produced by the diesel fumes, tension, and amphetamine.

The Hummer in front shot into the village and the one he was in peeled off to flank. They skidded to a halt and everybody spilled out. Thumbing the safety on his rifle he followed the GI in front of him, looking around for Sol and the others as he ran. Bedlam broke out behind him; the sound of a grenade explosion, women screaming, doors being kicked down, hoarse soldiers voices and gunshots.

He ran up an alley. A face appeared at a doorway and withdrew quickly. Shouts and scrambling sounded inside. Without breaking his stride the soldier in front kicked the flimsy door off its hinges. The door fell flat, throwing up dust, and the soldier disappeared inside. Leon followed.

An old woman and a younger woman cowered behind a youth in a vest and baggy trousers who raised a stick at the advancing soldier. The still moving soldier shot him and the youth doubled up. The old woman behind him made a noise and fell to the floor. The soldier jumped over the youth and through a door. The younger woman screamed after the soldier and knelt beside the old woman. Sounds of splintering wood came from the other room.

Leon knelt by the old woman, ignoring the shrieking younger woman. The shot had passed right through the youth and hit the old woman. The phrase two birds with one stone flashed through Leon's mind as he reached automatically for his knife.

The younger woman launched herself at Leon, clawing at his face and nearly knocking him over. He shoved her and she fell back against the wall, terror in her face.

He moved the old woman's hand and slashed the already blood-soaked robe exposing the hip. The bullet had smashed rather than penetrated and, although there was loads of blood, there didn't look to be any arterial bleeding. The youth gurgled beside him. He wadded some of the robe and pressed it gently to the wound, then took the old woman's hand and placed it on top.

His mind seemed to be working in fragments. Part of it was aware of shouts and explosions from the compound, and the absence of any returning fire, part was keeping an eye on the girl, still crumpled against the wall, yet another part was listening out behind him.

He turned to the youth. Blood was pooling on the floor from his mouth and abdomen.

There was a trampling of boots and the soldier returned, breathing heavily.

'Clear in there. What's he saying?'

'His prayers probably.'

'Yeah right,' the soldier grinned, missing Leon's tone. He grabbed the youth, pulled him upright and shouted into his face.

'Where's your buddies, huh?'

The barely conscious boy gave no reply. Blood dribbled out of his mouth.

'No point,' said Leon. 'Get him outside.'

'Yeah right.'

The soldier dragged the boy outside. Leon lifted the old

woman and laid her on a divan in a corner. The old woman clutched his arm with a bony, wrinkled hand as he straightened up and stared intensely into his face. He thought she might say something, cursing would have been the order of the day, but she just stared silently, as if wanting to memorise his face. Leon prised her fingers away gently, glanced once more at the girl, then walked out of the house.

The square was full of people. The women and children were being herded to one side and the men to the other. The Yanks were already 'interrogating' the only two between teen and old aged men. Rifle butts thudded against shoulders and thighs in response to vacant looks, linguistic incomprehension being taken for non-cooperation.

Another useless Coalition Force exercise and propaganda success for the Federation. Even if those locals hadn't been sympathetic before, they would have generated village-wide support by the time they left. He walked out of the square to avoid the spectacle and went to find the others.

He stood by a Hummer with 'one weekend a month my ass!' scrawled on cardboard in the windscreen, and looked out across the scrubby desert plain. Mountains shimmered in the distance. He easily imagined the men from the village scarpering there when they'd seen the dust of the convoy.

The old woman's creased face and stare came back to him. It hadn't been terrified or hate-filled as he'd expected. Apart from the pain fixed in her face, the look was gentle and questioning. What did they think of the men that forced their way into their houses, killing and smashing?

He pushed the image away only for it to be replaced with his own grandmother's lined and puzzled face. He shook his head to get rid of the image. Someone tapped him on the arm and he turned round.

The GI stepped back and looked him up and down.

'Shit! And I thought I was havin' a bad day. Smoke?'

Leon took the cigarette and broke the filter off before lighting it. 'Bad for your health y'know.'

The soldier laughed. 'Yeah? I'll race 'em. See if I can kill myself before Congress does.'

'Wouldn't like to put money on it.'

The soldier frowned. 'You know it. Hear about the hit on the Eighty Second?'

Leon nodded. 'Truck blew up outside the compound, killed a guy.'

'Yeah, and only our excellent defences prevented more people from being killed, blah blah bullshit! The truck blew up inside the compound and the reason only fifteen people were hurt and one guy killed was just plain fucking luck.

'They make us get on every fuckin' vehicle that enters the compound, and plenty of vehicles come. It's like playin' Russian roulette. Water trucks and gasoline trucks I understand. We need that stuff; even though there's still plenty of ways they could detonate one of those too. I'll tell you what was being delivered though, and what the guy died for. A general's decorating his office there. It's a nice office, a luxury office you might say. And it needed a carpet to go with all the new furniture. Now while we can get along just fine with field beds and folding chairs, of course the brasshole has to trick out his office like he's a fuckin' Roman Caesar or somethin'. So these furniture trucks come onto our compound when we already know that people out there want to kill us. This truck was loaded with carpet. Farrier died for a general's carpet.'

Leon didn't say anything.

'What we really need here are some fuckin' trucks to haul away all the fuckin' bullshit. And a few to get our asses to an airport pronto.'

'It's just one fuck-up after another,' said Leon.

'Ya can say that again.'

'Might get a T-shirt printed.'

The soldier pulled a small bottle out of his pocket. 'Pills?'

A GI on his other side leaned over before Leon could answer. 'What flavour?'

'Efexor, Bennies, Valium, Dexi's, morphine, whadya need?'

'Gimme some Bennies, just in case I can't get to the espresso machine, heh heh.'

163

'More mad shit,' said the soldier, glancing back to Leon, 'everything but the morph' I get from the doc. You go in with combat stress, maybe get you get seventy-two hours rest and then back into action. They don't even diagnose PTSD anymore, cuts into combat power. Three hots and a cot, and that's your fuckin' lot…if you're lucky. Usually just sent on your fuckin' way with a bag of pills. It's getting so's I'm looking at the driver's eyes before I get in an AV or chopper. We got guys out there who're stoned outta their skulls day and night. One guy even ran his tank over a family. A whole fuckin' family! Ain't safe, if ya ask me. Have to keep a tight asshole. Things're fuckin' surreal enough without trippin' out on those fuckers. What the fuck do they care though, as long as they've got fingers on triggers they ain't too bothered about how stable the fingers are. Sayin' that, my fingers'd be a lot more unstable without a little help from my friends.'

The other soldier laughed. 'Yeah right. Interest any of you guys in some Khash, guaranteed top quality.'

'The man I've been lookin' for,' exclaimed the GI. 'What's your guarantee?'

'Fell off the back of a Hercules?'

The GI chuckled. 'Right on.'

Watching the two men's furtive heroin deal, Leon felt a sensation of moving backward at speed. He blinked rapidly and stood up straighter. He thanked the GI for the smoke and went to find Sol.

Something seemed to be squeezing him deep inside. The pressure was so strong that he felt he should have been struggling for breath, but wasn't. He could have passed it off as fatigue, but memories and facts gripped him irresistibly, forcing his mind's eye open. He'd wondered what Monahan's mother would have thought of her son if she'd known the truth of what he was doing. But what of his own grandmother, whose face he'd seen in the face of the latest collaterally damaged innocent, what would she have thought of his own involvement in the military securing of international oil and drug monopolies? What did he think of himself? Part of the neo-fascist monster that was strangling the world, annihilating and taking over, poisoning everything with it's touch. A lackey for oil and drug barons, corporate and secret service warlords who enslaved their own population with the drugs that funded their takeovers.

He spotted Sol, Jock and the chopper crew by their bloodstained fatigues and smeared faces, grouped away from the Yanks at the perimeter.

'Feels like I've fallen into a fucking Hollywood film,' said Jock as he joined them. 'You'd think because we speak the same language we're the same, but we're not. They're from a different fucking planet.'

The Yanks wound up operations and they hauled out, leaving the jackboot imprint of tyranny.

Leon sat with his eyes closed, the heat inside the Hummer adding to the slowly crushing pressure. Something had broken the lock on the door in his mind that held back all the things he didn't want to think about, and the previously suppressed thoughts, images and knowledge hamster-wheeled around his head.

As squad leader he'd had orders not to engage what he knew were heroin labs, and knew of the no-fly zones over opium growing areas. But he was a soldier, strategy was for the higher-ups. But what about heroin and cocaine being transported in military planes? He was a soldier, what was he doing working for murderers and drug traffickers? He hadn't joined the army for that. And he had volunteered; he couldn't blame conscription. But he hadn't known the hidden realities of the U.S.-led world dictatorship then. He knew now though and had for long enough, it was obvious to anyone who looked, and yet he was still part of it. Denial wasn't a river in Egypt. Was the prospect of a dishonourable discharge and possibly prison as a conscientious objector that bad? How long was he going to carry on being part of it?

Another fact he'd buried slunk into view, government contractors involved in human trafficking. It was common knowledge that the Yanks ran the prostitution scene with the help of the local mafia. Again, it made strategic sense. Thousands of troops wanted that kind of R&R, and a service had to avoid the men being compromised by foreign interests. The fact that women were bought and sold like cattle, and that the tastes catered for included little girls made the knowledge harder to handle and easier to forget. And how easy it was to forget, willingly distracted with work, TV, and socialising in the bar. That war was primarily a business run by men in suits in public office, men engaged in illegal arms dealing, international drug trafficking, slavery and paedophile prostitution was too much to think about. But knowing and not taking a stand meant he was guilty too. His continued silence and inactivity made him accomplice to the crimes he knew were being committed. How many times could a man turn his head and pretend that he just didn't see?

The convoy pulled over at a checkpoint. The comet tail of dust overtook them like a visual echo. Leon climbed out wearily and looked around. The sun was at its height and intense white light bounced from every surface. A wedge of concrete bunkers and buildings flanked the road. Leading from it the inevitable halted queue of buses, cars, and taxis. Small barefoot boys ran up and down the line selling drinks and pastries. Everything shimmered in the heat. Two Bramham tanks sat either side of the point, watching the traffic. Soldiers stalked around the zone. Compared to the natives the troops looked like a different species of animal. Their height and girth wrapped in desert fatigues and body armour gave a sense of impenetrableness. The Empire's Imperial Storm Troopers.

He was so hungry his stomach was imploding, twisting into gripey knots. The rest of his muscles still fizzed with amphetamine, but felt calcified and wooden. But for the hit on the chopper they would have been back and squared away by now, instead of fannying around…he stopped the moan as it began with the thought that had he been in Murphy's seat, or had his head been half an inch to the right, he wouldn't be fannying around anywhere, anytime. He had nothing to moan about.

Tantalising smells of spicy food drifted from the setups grouped around the zone. Sol and Jock appeared, reminding him of what he must look like.

'There's a fuckin' wind up,' muttered Jock.

'What's that?'

'Nice smells, shame about the place. Buyin' from one of they stalls is asking for dysentery.'

Leon sat on the ground in the shade against the wheel of the Hummer, exhaustion and his wooden muscles making the action a real effort.

Sudden tension in the zone made him look around. A car was approaching at speed, overtaking the line of waiting cars. A soldier near the checkpoint walked into the middle of the road and signalled for the car to stop. The car had just begun to slow when shots rang out. The windscreen shattered and the car veered and skidded to a stop. Soldiers converged on it rifles trained. Out of the corner of his eye Leon saw the guns of the Bramhams zero on the car.

The driver was shouting and waving one arm. The soldiers were bellowing at him to get out of the car. One moved in, yanked the door open and dragged the man out. The man struggled and pushed the soldier away, only to be grabbed by another and slammed against the side of the car to be searched. Soldiers on the other side of the car lifted two bodies out and laid them on the ground, both looked to be dead or unconscious. The driver started shouting and pushed past the soldiers to go and kneel beside the bodies.

Everything went silent momentarily. All the soldiers that weren't scanning the terrain nervously were looking from one to another mutely. The occupants of the other vehicles began to get out. The driver launched himself at the nearest soldier, punching and screaming. The soldier shoved him roughly with his rifle. The man staggered back and was caught by one of the locals. On turning and seeing who was holding him, the man's waving hands went to his face and he began wailing. Other locals formed a group around him, while others took up the angry tirade against the soldiers, all witnesses, all gesturing around the zone.

A stretcher team arrived from the checkpoint and lifted the bodies onto the stretchers. The air and movement pulled at the robes of the largest body. It was a woman and her size wasn't fat. Her abdomen had the swell of the last stages of pregnancy.

A silent sledgehammer smacked Leon in the forehead. For long seconds his only movement was his eyes following the progression of the stretchers; a pause as though he'd just witnessed a distant explosion, seen the flash and was waiting for the sound to catch up. His chest tightened and he realised he was holding his breath. He let it out slowly, still waiting for the shockwave. Two birds with one stone. More non-combatants. Women and unborn children. More innocent dead. A family's life ruined. Family in this context being the extended type of that culture. Was it their first child? What would the bereaved father spend the rest of his life doing? He knew what he'd do.

He rolled under the Hummer and lay on his back with his head against the warm tyre. He didn't feel hungry anymore, and the GI's morphine was becoming more attractive by the minute.

By the time the debacle had been sorted and the convoy was approaching base it was nearly sunset. The slanting sunlight lit up the interior of the Hummer painting everything crimson. Leon looked down quickly to shut out the visions of phosphorus-scorched faces. Light splashed his hands coating them in blood. He turned them over. The light turned the smears of Murphy's blood a deeper shade. How many ways could a man have blood on his hands?

'Home, sweet home,' said Carter.

Leon looked up at the approaching base. It looked immense, a huge concrete and steel fortress squatting in the middle of the desert.

'How big?'

''Bout ten, fifteen square miles.'

Leon raised his eyebrows.

'Houses 'bout twenty thousand troops, an' we don't slum it neither. Swimming pools, gyms, miniature golf course, an' a movie house. We even got a Burger King an' a Pizza Hut. One of over a hundred forward operation bases we got out here.'

The massive sections of prefabricated concrete rose out of the desert like something out of a Dune novel or Mad Max film.

Leon tried to picture a hundred bases like it connected with the thirty or forty between there and Poland that had been built since the fall of the Berlin Wall, fortress garrisons along the Empire's frontier. It was no wonder the American economy was on its knees. The cost involved was unimaginable, even without the billions of dollars scammed in cost-overcharges by military contractors. Lives and money squandered by businessmen in comfortable offices.

The convoy was marshalled through the defended perimeter. The image of a space age garrison intensified. Ranks of armoured personnel carriers, tanks, rocket launchers, and trucks segregated block after concrete block in all directions. They made their way along dusty roads between the buildings, office blocks, shops, and barracks, all with thick mortar-proof walls. Leon started to estimate how long it would take to drive across the base and then gave up, his brain was too tired.

They drove out into the open alongside an airfield equally bristling with armaments; ordered fields of bombers, fighters and assault helicopters stretching into the distance, watched over by regularly spaced anti-aircraft missile emplacements.

Not believing his luck, Leon spotted an RAF Merlin. He got the driver to patch through to the other vehicles and a few minutes later they were walking over hot tarmac toward the chopper. The chopper crews immediately fell to. It turned out to be their lucky day; the Merlin was taking off in ten and returning to base.

'Well lucky,' said the gunner relaying the news. 'I couldn't have stood another day in Hollywood.'

Night fell quickly, as if keen to cover up the day's damage; one minute it was light, the next it was black. Leon sat in the Merlin, cursing the politicians who'd sent him there. If it wasn't the UKUSA Mafioso using NATO as their own private army to seize resources and strategic positions, it was the other fascists in the EU using the RRF for their own gain. Less a Rapid Reaction Force than a Rapid Robbing Force, protecting export interests and ensuring freedom of movement for trade and the supply of raw materials for the corporate connections in government.

But he'd volunteered, and every day he stayed there was his choice.

The amphetamine finally caved in against the mounting pressure of fatigue, and the chilled desert night air did nothing to stop his eyelids falling like steel shutters. He was vaguely aware of the noise and buffeting, but sat catatonic, temporarily unhooked from the grid.

The sound of the chopper slowing dragged him up from the well he'd slipped down. The lit up camp stretched out beneath them.

A stretcher crew met them on the pad and took charge of the body bag. The weight of the day rushed in on Leon as he trudged toward the store squinting against the lights. A bow wave of silence preceded them. Men looked, but gave them space. No shouts, no whistles, not a word.

They checked their weapons in and walked wordlessly to barracks.

Sat on his cot, Leon filled his cup with rum and added a splash of coke. He paused mid-pour, looked at the can in his hand, and shook his head. The sun really didn't set on the new Empire.

Sounds and images pounded his brain, audio-visual reports in a mental debriefing of the last forty-eight hours. One fuck-up after another. He swallowed hard against the bile rising into his throat. A slug of rum and coke sealed the action. The rum burned. He welcomed the fire like a penance. If only he could bathe in the stuff, open every hole to it and sear the black tide that was slowly rising and filling his head with wailing and screaming.

He wished the Valium would hurry up and kick in. The amount he'd taken guaranteed him at least twenty-four hours dreamless unconsciousness, all the respite he could expect for a while. Maybe he should have taken the GI's heroin.

As if at the end of a tunnel he heard a barking voice.

'Ten-HUT!'

He didn't move. He had no intention of moving for as long as possible. Curl up in a corner and lie so still he'd be taken for a pile of laundry and be left to fester.

A pair of boots materialised above the lip of his cup.

'You got a hearing problem soldier?'

He thought the question over. Maybe he did. Either that or the speaker was speaking through a tube at him. He was tempted to look up and check, but didn't move. Movement entailed energy and he had no more, and he liked the mystery anyway.

'Ignore me once more, soldier, and you'll be cleaning latrines with your toothbrush. Ten-HUT!'

Another pair of boots materialised between Leon and the barking voice. The boots were well worn down at the heel.

'With due respect sir, I think it would be best if he was left alone. We've just got in from a real heavy one.'

So it was him, Leon mused, unless Sol was talking through a tube too.

'You expect me to accept that as an excuse for blatant insubordination?'

'I hope you'd accept the reason as it's more along the lines of combat fatigue than insubordination, sir.'

'No such thing as a fatigue that'll keep a man on his arse when told to stand to attention, and if you don't stand aside and your malingering friend stand to attention you're both going to pull a double dose of the shithouse blues. Now I said, ten –'

Another pair of boots materialising beside Sol's cut off the order. The barking voice turned disbelieving.

'This is mutinous!'

'Call it what you will, sir,' said Sol again, 'but it's a majority decision that'll take more than just you on your own to overrule.'

A wave of fondness for his mates eased through Leon and he blessed them silently.

There was a moment of silence before the first pair of boots disappeared from view and stomped out of the room. The other two turned to face each other.

'He'll be back with the MP's.'

'Unlikely. He'll report us for sure, but he won't be back in a hurry.'

'Hope you're right, I can't take anymore either.'

Leon felt both of them looking down at him before their boots moved from view. The creak of their cot springs telegraphed stereophonically across the floor and up his legs.

His vision started to close in like the end of an old silent movie. He still held half a cupful of hooch. Opening his hand to let it fall would have been the easiest way but, summoning all his concentration, he lowered it slowly to the floor; slowly because it's meeting the floor was the only way he was going to gauge where the floor actually was. He sat up and collapsed back in one fluid motion and sank into black nothing.

He came to instantly wary with a sense of wrongness. It was pitch black and there was no sound. Even at night there was the ever-present sound of the camp; heavy motors, vehicles, shouts, the general hum of the war machine. Right now though there was nothing.

He opened his eyes, but there was no change in the light. The solid black around him offered no visual reference. He looked down at a glow that seemed to be coming from his body. He seemed to be shining. Realisation turned his head.

Earth, huge and radiant, hung suspended in the blackness, bright blue expanses mottled with brown and swathed in swirls of white, growing to fill his vision as he hurtled toward it. He sought a landmark, in vain. There seemed to be more water and less land. Most of the islands had disappeared and the larger landmasses had shrunk. None of the coastlines were familiar. The Iberian Peninsula had definitely shrunk, or the Mediterranean grown, and looked more like an island. North America too was smaller, around the perimeter and inland where the great lakes formed a single enormous puddle, a vast inland sea connected to the Atlantic. The continent itself looked skewed somehow.

He didn't have time to ponder the riddle as his curved trajectory slung him through the upper atmosphere. Clouds momentarily whited out his vision and just as suddenly he was bursting through over land, and stopped. He was denied the disorientation of the sudden change in speed by the scene below. Something big had happened, earthquake by the look of things. Whole sections of the land stretching for miles in all directions had concertinaed and corrugated. All buildings as far as he could see were damaged and collapsed, and the roads buckled and pitted. Truck-sized chunks of tarmac and concrete jutted out of pools of oil-slicked water. Power lines were down and littered the land like untidy spider webs. Traffic was almost non-existent and comprised mainly military vehicles. Near some of the collapsed buildings people were gathered in clumps near fires burning in oil drums. Others stood in sullen queues in front of trucks guarded by armed soldiers.

What had happened? The wrecked roads and buildings suggested an earthquake, but what kind of earthquake skewed continents?

He moved further into the city between collapsed and semi-collapsed city blocks and buildings. He could hear shouts and glass smashing and the sound of heavy engines, but couldn't see anyone. He followed the sound. Out of the corners of his eyes he glimpsed curtains twitching in several upstairs windows.

As he got closer, the sound got louder. He rounded a corner. A row of tanks advanced down the road ahead of him, with infantry units dressed in urban camouflage following crouched behind them. Black smoke from burning cars overturned in the road filled the air. Ragged knots of civilians lobbed bottles and stones from behind walls and piles of rubble. The tanks progressed inexorably along the road, pushing aside the burning barricades with rending screeches of metal on concrete.

A shot sounded from an upstairs window. The gun of one of the tanks turned, rose and fired in the direction of the shot. A whole section of the building exploded outward in a cloud.

The scene blurred and shifted to a dimly lit room. Stark shadows thrown by candles and paraffin lamps spaced around the room shifted on the walls and etched in sharp relief the faces of around a dozen adults standing and sitting around. Flickering flames reflected in the bottles and glasses in people's hands. The men were unshaven and the women dishevelled. Some had sores and red eruptions on their faces and mouths. The expressions on all the faces were strained. Several women were crying, and the streaked, blotchy faces of the others said they had been. In a corner, being studiously ignored by everyone in the room, three figures stood around a body laid out on a sheet. One of the figures was pulling the other one away, crying. The remaining man held a saw. He crouched and began sawing.

Leon moved closer. Laid out on the sheet was a dead man, a bullet wound in his temple. It was the cadaver's leg that the man was removing with the saw. The saw cut through to the bone quickly and began to make slick, grating noises. The man had to stop more than once to hold down the reflex that visibly pumped his stomach.

He laid down the blood-smeared saw when he'd finished, lifted the separated leg, stood and turned to the room. His red-eyed stare met with the eyes of one of the others. The man stared back at him, his mouth tight and grim. The man holding the leg sighed, turned and walked through a doorway into a kitchen.

The scene blurred again and resolved into the grey doors of a wide elevator at the end of a rock-hewn corridor. Two blank-faced soldiers with assault rifles across their chests stood either side. The elevator doors opened slowly and a technician stepped out steering a laden lifter. He passed Leon without seeing him. Leon moved into the elevator and the doors closed behind him.

The elevator sank. He looked above the door for an indicator, but there wasn't one. There weren't any buttons either. The elevator descended rapidly. Long passing moments had him trying to picture the skyscraper depth of the elevator shaft. Eventually it began to slow and stopped. The doors opened into a wide, empty hall. The walls and the ceiling looked like black glass. Through open sets of double doors at the far end of the hall Leon saw an auditorium filled with soldiers. He moved across the hall keeping close to the wall. The soldiers looked to be intently watching something. Their stillness made them look like cardboard cutouts.

He slipped into the auditorium. The walls and the ceiling here too seemed to be fused rock. At the far end was a raised platform with podium and chairs arranged. A soldier moved around the platform adjusting the props, nothing interesting enough to hold the complete attention of hundreds of servicemen.

He studied the seated soldiers. Straight backs, hands on thighs, all looking ahead, alert but expressionless, and totally silent.

'Ready Sergeant?'

The soldier on the platform turned in the direction of the voice.

'Yes sir.'

'Good, let's roll 'em.'

'Yes sir.'

The Sergeant approached the podium, leaned on it with both hands and looked at the seated soldiers with a vague smile.

As if animated by a thrown switch the entire auditorium erupted into laughter. The soldiers looked around at each other as if in response to a hugely funny shared joke. The sergeant straightened up, smiling, and moved away from the podium.

'So listen up.'

The laughter quietened.

'This morning your commanding officer will speak to you on the subject of Russia and the Middle East. He's been there, I've been there, and as in forty eight hours from now you'll be there wondering what the hell's going on, I'd advise you all to pay close attention to what he has to say. Anyone I catch sleeping will wish to hell he was already taking incoming in a Gobi foxhole. Ten-HUT!'

As one the soldiers rose to attention. The officer strode crisply through the door to the podium. Another bark from the Sergeant seated the soldiers.

'Thank you, Sergeant. Gentlemen, your zero hour has arrived. You will now take the interests of the United States under your protection as your comrades did before you. The men of this battalion who have gone before you have proven without doubt that we are the perfect blade to excise the creeping communist cancer. We march further, penetrate deeper and strike fear into the heart of the enemy everywhere.

'You are charged with upholding democracy throughout the world and maintaining security at home. We will pursue no other ultimate aim than to maintain freedom for the American people and to secure a living space for the American family. Your families are proud of you, the nation thanks you, you who risk

175

and give up your lives to win for your people a greater future and surer peace.

'It's with a feeling of pride that I look out at all those assembled here today, ready to prove themselves not unworthy of the days of yore and not unworthy of those great men, the fathers of our land, who laid the foundations of our laws and shaped the greatness of our country.'

Leon moved to the back of the auditorium, away from the oddly familiar speech and through another set of double doors. He found another fused rock-walled hall identical to the first, also empty, but with the doors on the other side closed. He crossed the hall and opened one of the doors slightly. A low-lit corridor stretched off into the darkened distance. Light from open doorways spaced at intervals striped the corridor. He moved into the corridor and through a doorway into a room. It was empty, sort of.

Lining the walls, five high on an industrial stacking system, were tanks filled with pale blue liquid. Submerged in each tank, floated a naked man suspended by a gauzy hammock. Assorted IV tubes led from each arm, catheter and colostomy tubes trailed between the legs.

The bodies were completely motionless and gave no indication of life. Neither did they look dead though, despite being fully submerged and not breathing. EEG pickups stuck to their chests suggested that there was a heart rate to monitor. Leon peered at one of the bodies, looking for a pulse, without seeing one. Nothing. Just an inert, apparently healthy body.

He moved out of the room and down the corridor to the next room and found the same scene. All the rooms contained the same collection. He wondered if it was some kind of cryogenic storage without the ice? The thought didn't fit though. Since when could blacks and Latinos afford cryogenics? And these were young men all in their early twenties.

The answer came to him, abruptly and dreadfully. He backed out of the room, away from the bodies and his deduction. It couldn't be. But what else could it be?

He moved down the corridor quickly. Corridors linked off it in each direction, each low-lit and striped by the light from open doorways. Room after room stretched on in Gigeresque repetition. The thought of it being not only possible, but actual was boggling enough, and what it looked like the technology was being used for even more so, although there was a sense of sickening inevitability to it as well. The scale of the operation though was numbing.

A shape further along the corridor turned out to be what looked like a baggage train; a chunky tug attached to a train of low flatbed carts parked outside one of the rooms. Laid out crossways on the carts, looking like freshly made mannequins, were rows of bodies. A bored-looking orderly sat in the driver's seat picking his nose intently.

Another orderly backed out into the corridor with a hydraulic lifter and placed a hammock-hung body next to another on a cart.

The scene blurred again into what looked like a cross between an operating theatre and an industrial production line. More bodies were laid out on conveyor belts that stretched off through a hatch at one end of the room. Wires trailing from ceiling conduits attached to the temples of each body. Technicians sitting behind monitors overlooked the lines.

Leon heard a whistling like close incoming and excruciating pain stabbed through the centre of his forehead. Instantly everything went black and he was tumbling backward. He screamed, but heard nothing over the pain of his head being sliced in half. He panicked, losing himself, coming apart, forced apart by the high-pitched whine drilling through his head. The thought flashed through his mind that maybe he'd been pronounced dead but wasn't, and the mortician doing the autopsy was removing the top of his skull with a circular saw.

He screamed again. His mind. He was losing his mind. Something was ripping his mind apart. White-hot fishhooks of pain dragged him in every direction. He screamed, became the scream, was the scream, falling through darkness. Falling, falling...

Just as suddenly as it had begun, all sound and motion ceased. Pain thrummed away from him like the echo of a guitar string, leaving a mausoleum silence.

Someone was in there (*in there?*). A presence. He strained for a sound. The void and silence surrounding him was so absolute that whoever or whatever it was could have been right next to him.

Movement flickering at the edge of his vision caught his attention. Gradually he made out a twisting, multicoloured tube snaking out of the blackness toward him. Slowly twisting, rapidly growing larger and larger, its translucent walls coruscating with moving colour images.

The subway-sized tunnel finally overtook him and sucked him in. Images raced past him, around him; an overturned van, a man with a single, large earring, people marching in a city, a deformed man in a racing car, the man with the earring, sewer tunnels; microsecond snatches of people and places he'd never seen.

The images deconstructed into streams of colour and he was surfing inside a rainbow. Electric liquid light; violets, greens, blues, overlapping tones and hues; getting lighter, whiter and whiter. A point in a sea of light, a light so bright it should have been blinding, but wasn't.

Light and unbelievably peaceful. Unbelievably peaceful.

How long had he been there? The question had the rumble of eternity. Before though, something had happened before. But that was fine. He was there. Everything was so bright and peaceful.

But where was there? He couldn't remember how he got there. Where had he been before then?

Before then? Every when was then. That was fine. He was.

He'd never experienced such a profound and deep peace. He never wanted to leave. He couldn't remember how he got there, but that was okay.

He floated in the white light not thinking. He didn't need to think. It was enough to be, thinking was difficult there.

Where was there though? Where had he been before?

The questions bothered him, and not just because thinking was difficult. He was glad he was there…and yet. There was something he had to do, something he hadn't finished. He couldn't remember what.

Gradually the thought took on the solidity of certainty. He hadn't finished.

He opened his eyes. The corrugated ceiling of the hut dipped into focus. From outside came the sound of heavy engines and gantry cranes. He looked down. He was fully clothed on his bed.

Time disorientation hit him. It could have been anytime of the day or night. He felt like days had passed. How long had he slept?

He swung his feet off the bed and sat up. A giddying gestalt awareness of cause and effect expanded away from him, branching rapidly, fanning out in a psychedelic latticework of fractal whorls; patterns in the chaos. He stood, cleaving the air as if passing through smoke, sensing the displaced air currents around him and other currents propagated by the simple movement. The sensations were so strong that he froze in an attempt to lessen the effect. With the pause came the knowledge of its futility and he relaxed. A smile formed on his lips. He felt effervescent. Excitement and the urge to laugh tingled through him.

Sol and Jock were curled up on their beds, also fully clothed. So he hadn't been gone that long.

He crept toward the door.

Sol raised his head. 'You okay?'

Leon stopped mid-stride, but didn't reply.

Sol raised himself up higher. 'You okay?'

Again Leon didn't answer.

Sol sat up warily. 'Leon.'

Leon looked around as if expecting there to be someone listening, then silently gestured outside.

Blue-white floodlight lit the camp. Dust kicked up by vehicles swirled in the light. Leon stared up at the massive steel hulks of two Challenger tanks as they rumbled past. The wealth, ingenuity, and creativity of the race co-opted into bigger and better ways of maiming and killing. He shook his head slowly.

Sol was looking at him.

'We've got to get out of here.'

7

Piss. Piss and rubbish. The sweet, decayed, clinging stench of humanity. Dan's head swam with the Escher-like repetition of clothes, cans and bottles, piss stains and graffiti as he picked his way through the debris. The asphalt walkway rippled under his feet.

He stopped at a mound of rubbish; distended black plastic bellies stretched and burst, spilling out rancid guts. Sticking out of the top of the pile were two legs. The jeans were blood-soaked and burgundy, as were the trainers.

'Way fucked,' said Sol behind him. 'Nobody's even tried to hide the body, they've just carried on dumping their shit on top.'

Dan walked on, shaking his head. He stopped at the top of a flight of stairs and turned to Sol.

'I'll be two minutes.'

The graffiti'd wall-light barely lit the cave-like gloom. He stepped down the stairs, avoiding bits of broken glass, steadying himself against the greasy wall. At the bottom of the stairs was a steel plate-clad door. He kicked it twice. The sound bounced around the space. He was just about to kick it again when a flap slid back behind the letterbox. He bent down and looked in. Darkness obliterated the face behind it.

'Nick?'

'Dan?'

'Yeah.'

The flap shut and bolts slid back. The door opened out into the cramped space and Dan stepped around it into the flat.

The warm hallway was only marginally brighter than the landing, though the orange-tinted light painted a womb-like rather than subterranean air.

Nick's gaunt, pallid complexion made him look like an extra

in a zombie movie.

'The resident's association should empty your bins more often,' said Dan.

'It was the residents association that put it there,' said Nick, his voice gravely and wheezing, 'the other RA that is. Bloke raped a twelve-year-old girl. Word got back and he got put out with the rest of the rubbish.' He shrugged. 'Call it self-policing. What's your story?'

'I was passing and thought I'd call by, see if you'd seen Big Chris.'

Nick shook his head. 'You've come to the wrong place, mate. I haven't seen Chris since he did rehab. That was like nearly a year gone.'

'He was working at the Manor detox project, but vanished about a month ago. I thought maybe he'd had a relapse.'

'Maybe he has, not here though.'

Dan looked into Nick's pinned eyes.

'Not gonna preach, Nick, but I've gotta say something. There's a war going on, and not just in Russia. What you're doing, that's one of their weapons too y'know. Doesn't have to kill you dead, on the nod's good enough. Which also makes anyone who sells the shit a government agent. You're more than that, man, come fight with us.'

Nick shook his head. 'Fight for what? It's all fucked. The planet's dying. Next stop extinction, mate.'

'The planet's not dying, she's being raped and murdered. But the rapists and killers have names and addresses.'

Nick shook his head again. 'Too full on for me.'

'One day you won't have the choice, but by then it'll be too late. Think about it.'

Walking back through the complex, passing the legs again, Dan told Sol the story.

'Harsh,' said Sol, 'but then so is being raped, especially at twelve.'

The park was also on the other side of the tracks. Not that any tracks existed. Had there been though they would have been

181

ripped up and sold for scrap long ago. It was a park in the loosest sense of the word, a fenced-off area paved with reconstituted tyre rubber slabs. Plastic-coated industrial pipes formed climbing frame, slide, seesaw, and swing frame from which a single car tyre hung on chains. A recreation area in need of recreating.

An old woman stood beside it, gripping the railings fiercely with one hand, marching on the spot with trembling, hesitant steps. Her voice rose and fell, muttering, whispering and complaining. Her free hand shook in the air, offering a fist to ephemeral agitators.

A group of youths blustered round the corner. Their pace slowed and they looked from the woman to each other. One swaggered toward the still ranting woman. The woman stopped ranting and her feet stilled as though she was aware of the approach, even though she faced away from the youth. He turned back to his mates at the sound of their muffled laughter. The woman turned too and began babbling loudly. The other youths moved up behind the first.

Sol motioned to Dan to hang back.

The youth said something that prompted wild laughter from the rest. The woman stopped talking and looked confused. Encouraged, the youth continued his heckling, strutting up and down beside the woman. She shook a fist at him and turned away, muttering to herself. He walked around her and pantomimed her fist shaking. The woman turned away again.

'C'mon,' said Sol. 'Oi!'

The youths spun round. 'What?'

'Just wanted to ask you a question,' said Sol.

The youths looked him and Dan up and down. More than one of them spat.

'How many of you got family?'

The piss taker seized the question. 'What're ya sellin'?'

Sol shook his head. 'What would happen if someone hassled you or your brother or sister?

'We'd have him,' bristled the youth. 'No one messes with my family?'

Sol nodded. 'So what would happen if someone messed with

182

your granny?'

The youth glanced at the old woman. The others busied themselves polka dotting the pavement.

Sol nodded. 'She's maybe somebody's granny, eh?'

The woman seemed to have forgotten them already and stood, still gripping the railings, talking into the air. The youth stared at Sol, and then said something over his shoulder. The others slouched off. He looked back at Sol, nodded once then turned after the rest.

Dan thought about the youths and their type as he and Sol carried on to the soup van. One of the State's self-generated, homegrown justifications for ever-stricter social control, grown in a mulch of confused and destructive domestic situations, teenage pregnancies, gangs, dead-end opportunities and alienation. With the vacuum created by the decay in family values, moral structures and positive role models filled by the media vomit of sex, crime and disaster, it was no surprise that dissatisfaction and social dysfunction were the results.

Faced with the hyped up problem of 'anti-social elements' the pliant public willingly accepted massive invasions of privacy. The so-called solutions of increased CCTV surveillance, ASBO's, and more prisons didn't solve anything. Nor could they ever have intelligently been expected to. Issues weren't addressed, the alienated kicked back in the only way open to them, with more vandalism and violence, and the only ones to benefit were in the thriving surveillance and crime-control industries.

Draconian punishments had repeatedly been shown to have no significant effect on the crime rate, which was directly linked to levels of poverty and unemployment as well as to less quantifiable but equally obvious factors like racism, the destruction of urban communities, and the general alienation produced by the system. But like so many other irrational social policies, the trend persisted because it was reinforced by powerful vested interests.

Despite a lowering of crime statistics, the UK led the field, just behind the U.S., for prisoners per head of population, well ahead of other dictatorships like Zimbabwe, Turkey, Burma, and China. In recent years there had been more prisoners serving life sentences in the UK than in the rest of the EU put together. The practise created massive profits for Parliamentary-connected private security companies. Privatised facilities needed high occupancy to be profitable, and because so many of the country's male workforce were drafted into the Forces, full advantage was taken of the captive workforce. But prior to the war the financial advantages of using taxpayer subsidised prison labour had driven the practise to the point where it had become a multi-million pound industry.

Prison employers paid no health or unemployment insurance, no holiday pay, sick pay, or overtime. Prisoners received minimal wages, oftentimes below the national minimum level for their manufacture and handling of electrical and machine parts for the likes of IBM, Microsoft, and Honda. And since the war, helmets, underwear, ammunition, flak jackets, and a whole range of other basic items for the war effort rolled off penal production lines. Such a lucrative and productive practise didn't encourage prison reform. Quite the opposite, under a regime where more bodies equaled more profits, prisons had taken one big step closer to their historical ancestor, the slave pen.

The soup van was parked in the car park of a boarded up discount furniture store. It was voluntarily run by the residents of a local squat who communally worked several organic allotments and distributed cheap veg and free soup to the homes of the elderly and on the streets. Various groups used the squat itself for meetings. The soup queues themselves also served as Resistance drop points.

They'd been there for about ten minutes, getting and passing on messages, when Sol looked up and saw Dan walking over looking concerned.

'Bloke by the van, asking about TV pirates. Says he's a journalist.'

Sol glanced over Dan's shoulder. 'Brown Harrington?'

'Yeah.'

'Okay, I'll see to him. Go rhubarb with some of the others so he doesn't zero on me.'

He watched Dan walk around while he relaxed his awareness and felt around. There was a hint of a wrong impression at a distance, but the man himself seemed kosher, and there was a positive feeling in the thought of approaching him. Sol watched him watch Dan as Dan moved around the knots of people.

He threaded his way over.

'Heard you're looking for some TV pirates.'

The man turned. 'That's right.'

'What's your interest?'

'Sort of professional, sort of personal. I used to work in media.'

'That media as in Licensing Bureau?'

The man laughed. 'No, but I guess you've got to ask. I used to be a journalist. I realise, given the nature of the business, that I'm not going to have a queue of people wanting to talk to me, but that's all I want to do, just have a chat really.'

As he spoke a motorbike pulled onto the waste ground and up to the van. The rider dismounted, pulled off his helmet and wiped the hair back from his ruddy face. He unzipped his leather jacket revealing a priest's collar.

'Good day to you,' he boomed jovially.

Sol nodded. 'Mornin'.'

'Name's Roderick, I'm from St Bartholomew's.'

'St Bart's, that's the one that backs onto Bellevue.'

'That's right. Know where it is, but don't come that often eh?'

'Don't go at all. Come here often enough though. Right little oasis, innit?'

'That's why I'm here really,' said the priest, projecting his voice to the knots of people around the van, 'because it's a place people come for sustenance.'

'If you need a bite, you've come to the right place, everybody's welcome here,' Sol said, also pitching his voice louder, and stressing the word 'everybody'.

The priest gave an exaggerated laugh. 'It wasn't that kind of sustenance I was thinking about. After all it is written that man cannot live on bread alone. He needs his spirit nourishing too,

185

with God's word,' he winked at Sol. 'That's where I come in.'

'Isn't it also written,' Sol hesitated, 'thou shalt not kill?'

The smile left the priest's face. 'That's right.'

'Then why are your colleagues blessing tanks and troops?'

The priest's scowl deepened. 'The Federation consists of godless communists and heathen Muslims who are waging a war not only against the western nations, but also against God. It is our duty as citizens and Christians to resist them.'

Sol nodded. 'Surely any god worthy of the name should be able to fight it's own battles. But don't you think that it's immoral for the church to be profiting from the manufacture of equipment used for war?'

The priest snorted. 'I'm not aware of any such thing.'

'Maybe you're not paying attention. It's said there's none so blind as those who won't see. Perhaps you could ask the Bishop why the church has shares in companies that make those things.

'But here's one closer to home that you might know about. The water supply to the standpipe behind St Bart's, the one used by the refugees. Why did the church turn it off?'

The priest flushed and looked around at the silent, mostly refugee, audience.

'The church has expenses as everyone else does,' he blustered, 'and things being as they were with the Water Tax it was decided that it was no longer financially viable to supply water to all and sundry.'

'Not as financially viable as fighter planes or armoured vehicles eh?'

'Now look here – '

Sol held up a hand. 'Let me remind you of another passage from your book. Matthew twenty-five: "Then he will say to those on his left, 'Depart from me, you cursed, into the eternal fire prepared for the devil and his angels. For I was hungry and you gave me no food, I was thirsty and you gave me no drink, I was a stranger and you did not welcome me, naked and you did not clothe me.' Then they will answer saying, 'Lord, when did we see you hungry or thirsty or naked and did not minister to you?' Then he will answer them saying, 'Truly, I say to you, as you did not do it to one of the least of these, you did not do it to me".'

He held the priest's gaze momentarily and then turned his back on him.

The priest looked at Sol's back and around at the watchful faces, and appeared about to say something, but then turned abruptly and walked quickly back to the bike.

Sol shook his head. 'We're fighting gods wars now.'

The man held out his hand.

'Name's Dylan. I'm going to lay it on the line because I think you'll be sympathetic to my cause. A journalist friend came to me a few weeks ago after getting back from two years on the Front. Smuggled back, wasn't really supposed to be here. Mentioned being in trouble and that he was going to blow the whistle on things. He wanted to get some alternative war reports out. I'm pretty sure they were taking him seriously, the first day I saw him we were followed. I'd heard of some TV pirates operating out of this area a while ago, so I've just been asking around.'

'And your friend?'

'Dead.'

'Sad news. Excuse me for prying, but how did he die?'

'The post mortem said overdose.'

Sol nodded, but said nothing.

'They're saying it was depression and post traumatic stress.'

'Two years in the war could seriously fuck you up.'

'He wasn't depressed and certainly not suicidal. He was angry and he was going to do something about it. Looks like somebody had other ideas.'

'And now your idea is to pick up the baton and finish the race.'

'Something like that.'

'Is your will up to date?'

'He was like family, I can't just leave it.'

'I'm not suggesting you do. You should consider the arrangements for your dependants though, in case of your having a sudden heart attack or unexpected suicide.'

Dylan shook his head. 'How did it ever get to this?'

'People let it, just like always. So self-centred and superior, and insensitive to how it might feel were they in the shoes of those it was happening to. There's a famous quote from Pastor Niemoller.'

Dylan nodded. 'I know the one.'

'Another question should be, what are we going to do about it?' Sol went on. 'A week from now start having breakfast at Mona's, round the corner from the market in Vauxhall. Once or twice a week, about seven o'clock, and leave your phone at home.'

'I've stopped using one.'

Sol raised an eyebrow. 'Smart move. Okay, do me a favour now though and go and chat with some of the others round here, just in case you are being watched.'

Sol joined some of the refugees who were having a laugh about the priest, and surreptitiously watched Dylan walk around the group. One of the older refugees spoke.

'What you say is true. If we all treat each other as family, then is no problem, you know what I'm sayin'. Each man is you brother and each woman you sister, especially for the woman. Even the woman you want to sex. Not that you would bed you sister, but you treat each woman as you would have another man treat you sister, yes?

'One time I know this man, he not like this. All the time he lookin' at the woman and takin' off her clothes in his mind, you know what I'm sayin'. Plenty time I say this no good, but he don't listen. Then one night we is standin' around. All the prostitutes are walkin' around, but they no look at us, they know we not business. All the time this man say, lookit them legs, lookit them tits, what I would do, and so fort'. I say what if you sister, what you say to the man who talk like you? But he laugh and say, she not my sister, she whore only good for fucking. I think to myself what am I doin' standin' with him?

'Then this woman appear, walkin' to us. An' is like my eyes is goin' strange, she look small like a child an' tall like a man at the same time. She look at me an' is like her look go right inside me. Right away I get this strange feelin' and feel scared, then not scared, then scared some more. She look at the man with me who stand up and push out his chest. Is like her eye's flash and I feel scared for the man. He already walkin' to her like a rooster. I see her smile. Is a smile like a knife blade. The man say, I like the way you walk. She say, walk with me then. In her voice I hear is like many screamin' voices. I think to call to him, but am frozen, like the animal in the car lights. I know in my deep self that bad things gonna happen. She look at me one time more an' smile. Is like I know her and she know me, but I sure I never met her.

'That is the last time I see both of them. Nobody ever see them again. The man he disappear. You ask me, I think she not human, she devil woman, Lamia, come to clean the world of men like this man, you know what I'm sayin'. Men disappear all the time now. For sure is mostly government, just like in many other places, takin' away anybody who would make trouble for them, but how many time this devil woman possess women and walk the streets?'

The assembled men raised eyebrows and looked at each other, nodding.

Sol walked over to Dan. 'Let's go.'

'What's up?'

'Tell you in a minute, c'mon.'

He whistled an approaching taxi and they both bundled into the back.

'Where to mate?'

'Back the way you came, in a hurry, then the docks.'

'Wanna lose somebody is it?'

'Yeah, and I'm betting cash you're the man for the job.'

'No problem.'

The taxi u-turned and took off.

'Was it that…' Dan began.

Sol frowned and shook his head. 'You got a radio in here?'

'Sure,' said the driver. 'What you wanna listen to?'

'Anything.'

The driver smiled and nodded.

'I think he was genuine enough,' said Sol, once the music filled the cab, 'but I think it's likely he was under surveillance

189

though.' He related Dylan's story.

'Shit,' said Dan softly.

Sol grimaced. 'Yeah. Hopefully it was just one person tailing him. Hopefully they didn't have a camera. We've got to consider both of us and the soup van compromised though. And it's going to be tricky getting home. That's why we're heading out this way. We'll split up. I should've listened. I had a vague feeling about talking to him, but went for it cos he felt okay.'

'Maybe they didn't pick up on us. He did talk with some of the others.'

'Too many hopefuls and maybes. It's done now though. Might get some mainstream media exposure out of it. We can use Mona's as a message drop without having to meet him again.'

The driver seemed to have taken Sol seriously, driving with bursts of acceleration, aggressively changing lanes, braking sharply, cornering, accelerating and cornering again. Eventually their speed slowed, but the driver kept checking his mirrors.

Sol was in two minds as to whether the evasive driving was a good thing. Definitely a bonus to find a driver that, by the looks of it, could. A tail would be having difficulty maintaining contact. But the ANPR could track them effectively enough through CCTV and satellite. He pushed the negative train of thought away. The driver was a good omen. Every evasion was helpful, no matter how small.

He leaned forward. 'Where d'ya learn to drive like this then?'

'Bosnia,' answered the driver without taking his eyes off the road. 'Was chemist. Have chemist shop with family. One day no more shop, no more family, and I learn quick to drive like this to stay alive.'

He glanced at Sol in the rear view mirror.

Sol put his hand on the man's shoulder briefly, then sat back, old anger displacing the compassion.

Bosnia, Beirut, Baghdad, a world of casualties. Little people ground under the wheels of the empire. The rug of family and business life pulled from under them, leaving them bloodied and bruised or dead. The collaterally damaged.

He looked at the meter, took out his wallet and counted out

190

some notes, then passed them to the driver. The man took the notes and spread them deftly with his thumb. He glanced at Sol and nodded once. He passed Sol a business card.

'When you need, you call, okay.'

Sol took the card.

'Thanks, I will. One last thing please. After the lights up ahead turn right and let us out, and then take off again quickly.'

He turned to Dan.

'We bail out and into that pub on the corner. We can phone from there.'

The driver stopped at the lights, but didn't pull away when they changed to green. Horns sounded behind them. He caught Sol's eye in the mirror and winked. The lights started to change to red and the taxi shot forward and round the corner. Sol and Dan jumped out and it took off again.

***

Jared found Leon in Resources.

'There's timing for you,' said Leon, nodding to him as he came into the room.

'Jared, as you know, has had first-hand experience of what we're talking about.'

'Both hands actually, and the rest,' said Jared, not meaning to frown. He sat down and nodded to Leon to continue.

'The whole purpose of detaining an individual in isolation is to destroy their sense of themselves, and to confuse and disorientate by keeping permanently off balance. It also severs their connection with other people and information, allowing those in charge to warp their awareness of the world outside their confinement with misinformation and lies.

'Don't underestimate the effects of sleep deprivation. Using only that technique it's possible to impair a persons cognitive faculties to the point of psychosis. By that I mean complete mental and physical breakdown. Isolation and sleep dep' are two techniques adopted worldwide as the cheapest and easiest way of breaking a person.'

Jared stood up. 'I think I'll pass on this class.'

'Understood,' Leon said. 'And you did pass this class, with distinction.'

Mumbles of 'hear hear' came from the others.

He went down the hall to the other resource room and sat on a desk looking out over the canvas and rubble of Hell View. It looked like they were under siege, surrounded by an army encampment. Maybe he was getting too militant like Dan said, always thinking about things in militaristic terms. It went with the territory though. They were urban guerrillas, there was a war on, and they were constantly surrounded, unlike rural guerrillas like those in Latin America who could slip away into the mountains or jungle.

Tactics were essentially the same though. Surprise, mobility, local superiority, and knowledge of the local terrain.

Mobility was important because of the increased risk in urban centres of being easily and quickly surrounded. Head-to-head direct confrontations with professional armed forces were avoided. Hit-and-run actions were the order of the day. Actions were meticulously planned to take a matter of minutes – arrival at target, attack, and melt back into the city. Targets were various points of the military-industrial network: military property and manufacturers, police stations, government offices and communication hubs. Targeting took into account the organisation's strict code regarding personnel, which maintained a definite line between combatants and non-combatants.

Knowledge of the local terrain aided mobility. Streets, alleys, structures of all kinds, and the layouts of the sewer and underground systems had to be known in detail. The resistance fighter's familiarity with the terrain was an advantage, even against the GPS technology used by the security services. Knowledge of the subsystem, essential due to the surveillance cover of satellite and CCTV, meant someone could disappear into the systems and reappear on the other side of the city, or shelter below ground for periods.

Of all the impressive talents that developed through the group's broad-spectrum training, he'd been amazed at his rapid intake of detailed and complex subsystems. Map reading and remembering directions had always been a weak point. Using the preconscious processing techniques he'd found he could retain much more much quicker. Nicole had devised a game where one person described directions, above and below ground, to a point that then had to be identified by the others. He got an adolescent pleasure from giving her correct answers.

The tactic of surprise was a necessity because numbers were so small compared to superior state forces. Most operations took place so quickly that the police didn't have time to react. Attacks choreographed with other groups served to further dilute the response.

Support of the population, once seen as an aspect of the resistance fighter's inventory, was no longer considered a general option because of the majority having been coerced by media brainwashing. The term 'resistance fighter' was never used by the media. All actions were tarred with the same 'terrorist' brush. The Public Order Directive had surpassed the intrusion of the street spies by legally requiring individuals to report all and any behaviour deemed to be 'anti-social, treasonable, or suspicious'. Innuendos, hints and statements from various authoritative sources as to what actions were defined by the terms meant that all sorts of behaviour was reported by the zealous and the vindictive.

What sympathisers there were mainly consisted of relatives of resisters and a surprising proportion of professionals who had the position and acumen to see what was going on and the integrity to resist it.

The security vulnerability of the organisation was dealt with by compartmentalisation. Information was shared on a need-to-know basis. Because of the level of state surveillance of electronic communications, most information moved around the network by courier-carried encrypted mail. The courier system itself was heavily compartmentalised to provide security. Messages to be communicated were given to an intermediary, who then passed the message to a courier. The courier didn't know what the message meant, who it was from or to. Their job was simply to transport it to another intermediary, who passed it on to the recipient. That way, no single element in the chain, if captured by security forces, was able to compromise the entire network. The cryptosystem used by the organisation was a hybrid that combined conventional and public key cryptography. Any electronic transmissions were anonymised and used a shift-cipher rotation.

The sun glinted off the glass towers of commerce beyond Hell View, barons overlooking the peasants. And there lay the problem. Even though it looked like it, in reality there was very little difference between the slave and the worker. Slaves might not have been paid, but they were given what they needed for survival. But workers had to pay most of their wages to survive. The fact that some jobs were less unpleasant than others, and that individuals had the right to start their own business, buy stocks or win a lottery, disguised the fact that the vast majority were collectively enslaved. Forced to give over most of their lives to employers who made more money out of their workers than they paid them, while the government took much of what was paid, directly and indirectly, through taxes.

The system reduced people to spectators of a world over which they had no control. The more alienation it produced, the more social energy had to be diverted just to keep it going; more advertising to sell unnecessary commodities, more ideologies to deceive people, more spectacles to keep them pacified, more police and more prisons to repress crime and rebellion; all of which produced more frustration and antagonism, which had to be repressed by more spectacles, more prisons, ad nauseam. The vicious circle continued and real human needs were met only incidentally, if at all, while virtually all labour was channeled into absurd, redundant or destructive projects that served no purpose except maintaining the system.

The secret to capitalist success was 'creative destruction'. The dynamics of capitalist competition generated modernisation at a rapid pace. Products were soon superseded by the latest model and became obsolete. Old rapidly gave way to new in an unending cycle of growth and prosperity. Media and advertisers used every psychological and technical trick in the book to fuel the cycle.

Renewables in any sector fundamentally threatened capitalism. That's why they were suppressed by various means.

The whole thing was down to money, the biggest scam of them all and one that allowed the banking cartels to control whole countries in the form of their government, businesses and general populace. Money that didn't exist was given out in the form of credit, loans and overdrafts in return for interest. But the 'money' was just numbers typed into an account. From that moment the account holder had to pay the bank interest on those numbers on a screen. Failure to repay resulted in the bank legally taking possession of the actual, physical wealth of the debtor; cars, homes, land, and possessions to the value of whatever figure was typed onto the screen, plus interest.

Banks controlled how much money was in circulation through credit. The more loans they made, the more money was in circulation. But that 'money' wasn't actual physical money, notes and coins. It was virtual, represented by numbers passing from one computer to another electronically via transfers, credit cards, and cheques.

The more 'money' in circulation, the more economic activity took place, the more products were bought and sold, the more income people had, and the more jobs there were. What was seen by most to be natural economic cycles of boom and recession were the results of systematic manipulation by the families and groups that owned the banks.

During a boom, people got into more debt. Businesses borrowed more to invest in new technology to increase production to keep up with demand. People borrowed more to buy a bigger house and more expensive car because they felt confident of their financial prospects.

Then, at a carefully chosen moment, the major banks raised interest rates to suppress the demand and began calling in outstanding loans. Less credit meant less money in its various forms in circulation. This curbed demand for products, which, as time went on resulted in fewer jobs because there wasn't enough money in circulation to generate high economic activity. Eventually the people and businesses that couldn't keep up the repayments went bankrupt. The banks then took their real wealth in return for a loan that was only ever numbers on a screen. And not just businesses and people, whole countries too fell prey to the same system. Instead of creating their own interest-free money, governments borrowed from the private banking cartel and used taxes obtained from the people to repay the loans.

Globally the world's poorest countries were forced to hand over control of their land and resources because they couldn't repay the loans calculatingly given by the world banks. The 'Third World' debt was manufactured to replace physical occupation of resource-rich or strategically placed countries. Once a country was indebted to foreign banks, they were forced to hand over control of their affairs to the bankers, the World Bank and the International Monetary fund, which then dictated economic and social policy at every level.

Along with that there was the profitability of war. No other method of control had yet been tested in a complex modern economy that had been anywhere near it in scope or effectiveness. Bomb a country to rubble, capture its natural resources, then make the people pay for rebuilding it. The people living in the camp below knew all about that.

The ending of capitalism would eliminate the conflicts of interest that served as a pretext for the State. Most present-day wars were ultimately based on economic conflicts; even seemingly ethnic, religious or ideological antagonisms usually derived much of their real motivation from economic competition, or from psychological frustrations that were ultimately linked to political and economic repression. As long as desperate competition existed, people could easily be manipulated into reverting to their traditional groupings and squabbling over cultural differences they wouldn't bother about under more comfortable circumstances. War involved far more work, hardship and risk than any form of constructive activity; people with real opportunities for fulfillment had more interesting things to do.

For over a century the U.S. had done everything in its power to prevent the development of a working alternative to the capitalist model. All attempts were quashed immediately, by any means necessary, lest they serve as inspiration or example to others. Other victims of the imperialist military-economic fist were those countries who, although retaining free enterprise to some degree, were unwilling to allow the U.S. hegemony to dictate what went on within their societies; reluctant to let the WTO/IMF/World Bank stomp in and privatise and sell the country's social assets to multinationals, to deregulate, erase their border, drive local industries and farmers into impoverishment, trash social services and safety nets, develop a cheap labour force, cheap raw materials, and a market for corporate goods, in the name of globalisation, that natural extension of capitalist growth and control.

A knock on the door interrupted his ranting thoughts. Leon's head appeared round it.

'You okay?'

Jared nodded. 'Just wondering how you get rid of capitalism?'

Leon stepped into the room. 'I'm not sure it is possible to get rid of.'

'So what are we doing then?'

'Just trying to clear a bit of space, like around a shoot being choked by weeds. Given the chance the shoot will grow, it just needs some space and light.

'The most important place we have to clear a space is in people's minds. If people could be given pause from the frantic work and consumption cycle, and I'm not talking statutory holiday; if the blinkers could be taken away, even momentarily, that glimpse of open space around them might reach in and wake up the freedom-loving soul.'

'Then what though?'

'Who knows? It can't be known. There are too many variables, not least the reaction of the ruling powers to the threat of the removal of that power. We just have to trust that given the space the shoot would grow naturally. In nature all systems develop toward balance if left alone. Hatred, intolerance, consumerism all have to be artificially generated to push out the natural tendency toward harmony and balance. What we need is a system that would encourage diversity, decentralisation and local autonomy, and self-management and personal responsibility. Those things in themselves reduce the need for hierarchy, and remove aggressive competition and exploitation. Look at past revolutions –'

'That all failed.'

'To ignore them because of their failure is missing the point. Given the repressive environment they came out of, it's hardly surprising that they didn't go further than they did; what's inspiring is that they went as far as they did. What should also inspire us are the dreams and visions that fuelled those struggles, because they were fighting the same hierarchical, repressive, exploitative monster.

'And anyway we shouldn't be striving to create yet another situation. Stagnation is part of the problem here. The whole of human existence is one of change. What we should be looking to do is change the direction we're moving in, like a rudder on a ship. A continuous process of small changes in the right direction, growing with and adapting to our world.'

Jared opened his mouth to say something, but Leon silenced him with a gesture. He stood frozen with his hand still in the air, his eyes fixed on a distant point.

'What?' Jared asked, suddenly tense.

Leon blinked and looked down.

'Trouble, let's go,' he said, turning for the door.

By the time Jared reached the door Leon was running down the corridor. He ran after him and caught up on the stairs. There was the sound of running below.

'What's going on?'

'We've been made,' said Leon.

Everyone was in the bay when they got there. Sol looked like he'd been running. Everyone except Cleve was armed.

Leon walked over to Cleve and knelt on one knee. He took a hold of Cleve's hand and put a hand on his shoulder. Cleve's readout cycled through a rainbow of reds and greens. His face was still as he stared at Leon.

Leon stood and turned to the group, his eyes wet. 'Make it brief.'

Jared watched the others say goodbye. Nicole leaned over and hugged Cleve, then stroked the tears from his cheeks.

Jared knelt and gripped Cleve's arm. Words appeared on the readout.

IT'S A BIG FEELING, EH

Jared's sight blurred and he nodded. 'Too big for words.'

He joined the others at the courier bikes. Sol and Leon were talking urgently. Silent tears streamed down Nicole's face. Ash and Cheddar were pale.

'We'll head for the Boarding House,' said Leon. 'If it comes on top, get underground. Regroup at the Manor, assuming it's not been compromised. If it has, go to ground. Subspace communication only.'

Jared grabbed a helmet off the peg and climbed on behind Leon. Ash and Nicole went pillion with Cheddar and Sol. The bay door in front of them began to crank up slowly, remotely operated by Cleve. Jared turned and waved once as they drove under the door and down the ramp.

They raced across Hell View, raising dust, and into the city. Leon threaded aggressively through the traffic. At the sound of multiple sirens Jared looked round and saw the flashing lights of a Squad van and behind that the flashing lights of a car.

Leon torqued the bike and Jared had to lean forward against the acceleration. They dodged between buses and cars, weaving in and out into the oncoming traffic. He looked round again. The others were keeping up, leaving their pursuers floundering through the traffic despite their sirens.

In his mind he saw a railway embankment bordered by allotments. The image was part of a knowing where they were, what route they were taking and the approach to the line. He felt an affirmative response that didn't come from him at the same moment that he realised that the others knew too. Another realisation followed the first; he had access to the groupmind.

He was pressed forward hard as Leon braked and then had to grab Leon's jacket to keep from falling backward as they accelerated away again.

Different sirens, closer, made him turn again. Two motorbike cops had joined the chase and overtaken the lagging vans, and were arrowing along their trajectory.

He felt the affirmative response again. They needed to split up.

Leon throttled off and raised his head. The flashing lights of another Squad vehicle showed above the traffic ahead. They accelerated around a corner, leaning so low that Jared had to tuck his knee in. Tyres screeched behind as the others took the corner.

They raced past garages and workshops built into railway arches, aiming for a switchback under an arch that he'd never seen, but knew was there.

A temporary roadwork sign said the road ahead was closed. Jared looked up. The arch over the road that they were presumably aiming for was clad in scaffolding. The road underneath was blocked off with wooden panels and fencing.

He heard Leon swear as they braked and skidded to a stop. The others were right behind them. Jared jumped off and looked around for an escape route.

'There!' Ash shouted, and started to run across the road toward an alley.

Machine gun fire raked the tarmac in front of her. She skidded, fell backward, and scrambled to her feet. Somebody behind Jared returned fire. The Squad men took cover behind the car.

'Here!' Leon shouted.

He ran at the garage closest to them and kicked the door. It didn't move. More gunfire carved a line above their heads across the front of the garage. The plate glass window fell out of the frame in long stalactite chunks. Nicole, down on one knee, and Cheddar, returned fire.

Sol dived through the window and slid across a glass-strewn desk. The others piled in after him.

'Cheddar, check for an exit!' Leon shouted. 'Jared, gimme a hand with this!'

He pulled a filing cabinet away from the wall and tipped it onto its side. Jared took the base and they hauled it onto the desk in front of the window. Another cabinet and a desk followed that.

Cheddar came back in shaking his head. 'An office, a kitchen and a bog, no exits.'

'Right,' said Leon. He nodded at the two cars beside them in the workshop bay. 'See if either of those is working. It wouldn't have to get us very far.'

He walked over to Jared and Nicole at the barricade, glancing at Ash crouched against the wall with her eyes closed. Jared was crouched across from Nicole looking through the barricade.

'Status?' Leon asked.

'Two behind the car, four behind the van. Bike cops are blocking off the top of the road.'

Leon peered over the barricade, and then ducked back down. 'I'm gonna reccy out back.'

Jared watched Leon walk to the back of the garage, looking around as he walked. Ash was still crouched with her eyes closed. He heard/felt a voice/touch, and turned to Nicole at the same moment she turned to him.

'Cleve.'

Rubber screeched and smoked boiled from the wheels as the cart leapt forward, seconds before the warehouse door exploded. Mortar and steel shrapnel lashed the cart canopy. It skidded to a stop and spun round. Cleve watched the soldiers emerge crouching out of the dust.

He smiled. He could feel them, his tribe.

His eyes insisted his consciousness back to the warehouse, where more figures were emerging from the dust. Energy fountained through him. The groupmind was filled with a rushing like nearby water and he felt held in enveloping warmth. His whole body buzzed and felt huge, but light, lighter than he'd ever felt. His hand on the joystick jerked and the cart swung around. The death's head on the back leered at the soldiers, lightning gleaming in its mouth.

One soldier beckoned to two others. 'You two, get the spas', you, get those bay doors open.'

The two soldiers straightened up and walked toward Cleve.

The staccato bark of the machine gun mounted under the cart hammered the bay. One of the soldiers jerked backward into the air, the other threw himself to the side. Rubber screeched again, immediately answered by the rattle of assault rifles. Bullets ricocheted off the cart canopy adding to the din as it sped toward the door. The door swung open, Cleve zoomed through and it swung shut immediately, reducing the sounds to dull thuds.

He angled the cart toward the open freight elevator, trundled inside and turned in a slow circle.

'Cleve.'

'Leon, don't cheapen this with words. I'm ready.'

He felt Leon sigh.

'Journey well, man.'

'I'll see you all later, friends.'

The bay door exploded. A grenade skittered along the floor toward him. The lift doors slid swiftly shut. The shock rattled the steel box and the air pressure jabbed at his ears, but the box rose. At the floor below top he stopped and rolled cautiously out of the lift. The sound of a helicopter motor filtered down from the roof.

He closed his eyes and opened to the groupmind. He was with them all and they were with him. Never alone. He moved a fragment of his consciousness forward. The readout lit up.

NEST DESTRUCT FAILSAFE OVERIDDEN

His twisted body slumped in the chair. The charge in the cart detonated at the same time as the lower two floors of the building exploded. The warehouse sank quickly, collapsing in on itself, the helicopter with it, the spinning rotors snapping and twisting as it burst into oily flames.

Shifting quickly out of groupmind disorientated Leon momentarily. He could hear Ash shouting. He ran to the front of the garage. Ash was standing near the door, her eyes clamped shut, arms and fists straight down, the tendons in her neck standing out. Leon looked to see who was on the barricade. Nicole caught his eye, then turned back to the street.

'Lousy fuckers!' Ash screamed. She ran up to the barricade. 'You lousy fuckers!'

Jared grabbed her jacket and pulled her down. She sank into a squat.

'Lousy fuckers...'

Leon crouched down to her.

'Ash ... Ash,' he shook her gently, 'Cleve's still with us, don't stress it. C'mon, save it.'

He led her away.

'You okay Nicole?' Jared asked.

Nicole glanced round. 'Scared shitless.'

Jared gave a grim smile and turned back to the street.

Another Squad van was pulling up in front of the first. It stopped, but nobody got out. Minutes later roof doors opened up slowly and a shape rose out of the van. It looked like a large satellite-receiving dish except the dish was square. It was pointing at them.

'Oh shit,' said Jared slowly.

He'd seen images of the device in a State weapons module. The Active Denial System. Produced a focused beam of millimetre wave energy that travelled at the speed of light and penetrated the skin, causing unbearable pain, neurological dysfunction and organ damage. Classed as a 'less-than-lethal' weapon it had applications from the battlefield to the street, with described uses ranging from border and crowd control to covert assassinations, 'mysterious' plane and car crashes, and induced psychosis and suicide.

A figure in a suit stepped out of the van and spoke to one of the militiamen.

Jared's throat constricted and he whirled round to face the back of the garage, eyes wide.

'Jared?'

He ignored Nicole and looked out at the street again. He

looked away quickly, then at Nicole. His face was flushed.

'Leon!'

Leon strode over.

'What's up? Shit, when did that arrive?'

'By the van, bloke in the suit.'

Leon looked. 'Guy with the shades?' He looked at Jared. 'That's him?'

Jared nodded and winced at a grinding in his guts. 'Leon, I'm really scared now. We've gotta get out of here.' A griping pain shot through his belly. 'I think I'm gonna shit myself,' he licked his dry lips and shook his head.

'No sweat, we'll sort him,' said Leon. 'Go shit.'

Jared glanced out into the street, but didn't move. Leon put his hand on Jared's shoulder and Jared turned. Leon stared at him intently.

''kay?'

Jared nodded.

''kay.'

Leon watched Jared's receding back.

'Ash, go with Jared would you, make sure he's okay.'

At the sound of her name, Ash, sitting propped up against the wall, Ingram across her knees, opened her eyes. 'Where'd he go?'

'Out back. I think he's on the edge of a spinout.'

Ash pushed herself up. 'Join the fuckin' club.'

Leon looked at Nicole. 'Keep an eye on that vehicle.'

He walked quickly and found Cheddar under one of the cars.

'Any luck?'

'No chance. Drive shaft seized.'

'You got the Semtex?'

'Oh yeah, blow the fucker loose.'

'For me you donk.'

Cheddar slid a bag across the floor.

'Cheers. Stay on it eh.'

He walked through to the back and into the empty office. He closed the door, leaned against it and took a deep breath.

He opened the bag. In it were binoculars, a bag of electrical components, a Tower Buster wrapped in a toroidal coil, grenades, and blocks of Semtex. He out took three plastic-wrapped blocks, three percussion caps, wire, and a squeeze-action detonator.

He pushed a cap into each block, slipped them into the inside pockets of his jacket, and fed the wires up his sleeve. He stripped the wires and connected them to the detonator, making sure the safety was on.

He leaned his head against the door and closed his eyes. He sighed. So today was the day. Well, he was ready too. He'd been ready for a long time.

The weight of responsibility lifted from him. They would take care of themselves. Goodbyes could come later. He took a deep breath and nodded once, then pushed himself away from the door.

Back in the garage there was no sign of Jared. He walked up beside Nicole and passed her the satchel.

'Anything?'

'No change.'

He jumped up onto the barricade and scrambled over it out into the street.

'Leon!' Nicole screamed, overcoming her paralysis.

He began walking without looking back.

Nicole's scream reached Jared in the back, and jerked him toward the door. He grabbed the Ingram out of Ash's hands and ran down the corridor.

Everyone was at the barricade. Leon was walking down the middle of the road, hands out to the side.

The faces at the barricade appeared and disappeared in Leon's mind like a set of photographs. Their confusion and concern reached him like clutching fingers. He wondered briefly how each of them would deal with what he was about to do.

Refocusing he noticed a crowd gathered behind a police line across the end of the street. Far enough away to be shaken, but not hurt. The rest of the nation would get the reports of another terrorist attack. He knew it was playing into their propaganda-wielding hands, but it would save his people, and they could continue the mission. He could do no more in this war.

He saw a sneering smile formed on the face of the man in the shades. The Squad man next to him snapped his fingers.

'Shake him down.'

A militiaman moved from his position by the car toward Leon. Leon stopped walking.

'Let him walk,' demanded Lock.

'Sir, that's not procedure,' said the man.

Lock raised his hand. 'Mine is a psychological war. I fight it my way. Let him walk,' he hissed the last words between his teeth.

The man hesitated, and then nodded to the waiting Squad man who resumed his crouch. Leon began walking again. The smile reappeared on Lock's face, as the distance between them got shorter.

'That's far enough. Now lie face down with your arms and legs apart.'

Leon stopped and lowered his arms. 'The man you want called Jared...' he said, allowing his mind a whisper touch of them all.

'What about him?' Lock sneered finally.

Leon smiled. 'You can't have him.' He squeezed the detonator in his hand.

From the barricade Leon's body seemed to disappear, exploding outward in a red and black fireball that engulfed men and vehicles. The car exploded almost immediately.

A rolling wave of heat hit the barricade. Jared just stared, stunned.

A flaming fragment fell in slow motion and bounced off the burning van, dislodging a charred corpse stuck to the front.

'Go!'

Jared flinched as if slapped.

'Everybody out!' Sol shouted, vaulting the barricade.

'Go!'

It was Leon's voice.

Jared jumped onto and over the barricade and hit the street running.

Machine gun fire slashed through the oily smokescreen. He

heard a cry as he leapt into the alley. Running footsteps followed him. He pulled his jacket off as he ran and wrapped it around the Ingram. Then it was all running; across a road, another alley, another road, dodging between cars and people, pumping his increasingly leaden legs up and down, forcing air into his burning lungs, following Sol's pounding form.

He glanced behind and saw Nicole and Ash.

Sol skidded to a stop and ran back toward him. A courier van was parked at the end of the side street. The driver stood next to it struggling with several boxes and a clip frame. She kicked the door shut and walked into a building as Ash and Nicole caught up.

'Cheddar?' Sol asked, rummaging in a pocket.

Nicole, panting, shook her head.

Sol's lips tightened. 'C'mon.'

The van lights flashed once as they ran toward it, activated by Sol's sonic key. They jumped inside. Sol reached under the dash, yanked out a fistful of wires and began pulling at them.

'Jared, check for pursuit, Nicole, if the driver shows, grab her and get her in the back.'

Jared looked around and checked the mirrors.

Seconds ticked by.

Jared glanced into the back of the van. Nicole stood by the door, ready to grab the driver. Ash was staring past him out of the window.

'Come on,' muttered Sol urgently.

Jared checked the mirrors again.

The engine turned and caught, and Sol slipped the van out into the street.

'We've gotta get underground. How're we packed?'

As well as the Ingram Jared had they had another two with four clips each and a handgun with a full clip. They also had the satchel.

'Plenty. We got cash?'

They had.

'Okay, get to the cut and get underground, then split up and meet at the Boarding House. Presuming they've not been busted too, we can get some idea of how big this op' is.'

Sirens sounded behind them. Sol checked the mirror, cursed, and floored it. The van leapt forward. He pulled out onto the other side of the road to overtake two cars.

The combination of the siren's advance warning and the sight of the van approaching at speed began to clear the road. Jared sat with his feet braced on the dash, staring ahead, praying for there to be no people crossing.

Traffic lights loomed up on red. They veered out onto the other side of the road again and swerved around the lights. Hanging onto the handle above the door, Jared had a moment of sickening deja vu. Horns blared, but no tyres screeched, and they were across.

Sol stomped on the brakes and hauled the van round a corner.

'This is us,' he indicated to a black brick wall.

He yanked on the handbrake and skidded to a sideways stop.

Jared flung open the door and jumped out. He ran to the wall, jumped and straddled over it, then reached back and grabbed Ash's hand.

There was a drawn out squeal of rubber as a Squad car skidded round the corner, its doors already opening.

'C'mon!' Sol shouted, jumping down.

Jared dropped down onto the embankment and slithered after the others. A bow wave of cans, bottles and dusty earth churned in front of him. He turned at the sound of running footsteps above, lifted the Ingram, and skidded backward looking up.

Arms and legs appeared over the wall. Jared stopped and fired. The sound of the oblique ricochets twanged through the trees. The arms and legs disappeared back over the wall.

Nicole shouted that she was covering. Jared turned and scrambled the rest of the way, and ducked into the shelter of the tunnel.

They ran into the welcoming blackness. Six sets of tracks, divided in some places by walls that reached the high ceiling of the tunnel, converged in the gloom. Clinker ground and crunched under Jared's feet as he followed the others silhouetted in the light from Sol's torch. Apart from the looseness of the clinker the going was even and gently down sloping. The tunnel curved out of sight.

A burst of gunfire reverberated around the tunnel. Shots ricocheted past him and the air was suddenly full of flitting shapes and the thrumming of tiny wings as bats took off from the ceiling in a cloud.

Jared twisted and fired wildly. He ran some more and stopped to spray the tunnel again. He caught up with Nicole who was crouched, her face lit up with the tiny LED torch in her mouth. She pushed a rod into the ground and looped a length of wire around the eye on the end of the rod. She waited for Jared to pass then stretched the wire across to the wall.

Jared fired another burst down the tunnel. The muzzle flash lit his hands a fleeting yellow-white.

Nicole jammed another rod into the ground beside the wall and threaded the wire through, and then reached a black apple-sized sphere from the satchel. She hitched the wire to the pin and put it down gently at the base of the wall.

They joined Sol and Ash waiting up ahead, and ran on until Sol angled across the tracks. They all took out their torches, spread out, and carefully stepped over the shining steel rails.

The sound of the blast barrelling down the tunnel made Jared jump and nearly lose his balance. He teetered on one leg and windmilled his arms. The air grew thick with squeaking shapes. He crossed the rest of the tracks and joined the others, their partially lit faces disjointed and flushed. In front of them the tracks separated and disappeared into smaller, staggered tunnels. Distant noises from the tunnel mouths completed the labyrinthine air.

'Right, we split here,' said Sol, verbalising what Jared already knew. Sol would go with Ash and Nicole with him.

He felt close to tears at the prospect of the separation. It was all happening too fast. Cleve, Leon, Cheddar, and now this.

Sol put a hand on his shoulder.

'No worries. Just be careful coming out.'

Ash hugged Jared. 'See you later.'

The tunnel in front of him was much smaller than the space

they were in. The rails leading off into the blackness glinted in the light from his torch.

His feet wouldn't move. The wave that had been carrying him further and further away from where he'd started pushed him against the wall of fear that fought his movement into the tunnel like an invisible force field.

Nicole touched his arm and gestured with her head. They didn't have time to hang about.

The clinker changed to concrete and the tunnel swallowed them up. The walkway beside the rails inclined up into a steel box running above the base of the tunnel below the level of the rails. Jared didn't relish the thought of walking all the way to the suburbs as it was. Along a ledge made the prospect even less appealing, and that was without the electrified rails or the chance of being smeared against the tunnel wall by a train.

Nicole's quiet voice echoed through the gloom. 'Leave it out, Jared.'

Jared opened his mouth to snap a 'what the fuck do you expect' response and then stopped. Nicole was right. What was he doing? This wasn't the place to bring more darkness into. He concentrated around him. Distant sharp shrieks and rumbles echoed softly. The stale air tasted like rubber and metal. Their footsteps echoed soft and synchronised. He watched Nicole's back and trusted his feet to the ledge.

Irrational thoughts of there not being enough oxygen grew into a sensation of being crushed. The feeling got stronger as he walked, as if the tunnel was narrowing.

'Jared, please.'

Jared opened his mouth to answer, but started to tremble. His skin prickled with sweat. His heart banged and the racing pulse throbbed in his throat. He leaned his back against the wall and put his hands on his knees.

Nicole stopped and turned.

'Attack?'

'Yeah,' said Jared, trying to control his breathing.

'Fuck! Well do what you gotta do, we can't hang about here.'

Jared bristled with another response and pushed himself off

the wall.

'Anger? Good,' said Nicole, 'get angry...and let's keep moving, eh.'

She was right again. There was plenty to be angry about. He nodded. Nicole nodded once and began walking again. The anger absorbed the slippery panic. His heart still pounded, but the fear was displaced. They had things to do.

He pictured where they were in the system. He'd neuroloaded maps of the system as part of the training. The Integration and Familiarisation module meant that he had a fairly accurate awareness of not only where they were, but also every other line, splice, junction and layer. The module had involved going to his level and visualising moving around the system like a rat in a maze. The perception induced was a non-localised unitary spatial awareness. It did feel familiar, he wasn't lost. He knew where they were.

An insight presented itself. Contrary to Sol's cautions he'd visualised the system as a series of brightly coloured tubes. Maybe if he'd imagined black and grimy he wouldn't have found the atmosphere so oppressive.

Gradually a faint hum overtook the hissing in his ears. It seemed to be coming from close by. He stopped walking. The movement of air against his face continued.

'Quick,' said Nicole, and ran along the ledge.

The ledge flashed in and out of sight in the light of the torch. Jared slid one hand along the wall to balance, and squeezed in beside Nicole in one of the alcoves cut into the tunnel wall. He felt Nicole's breath in the hollow of his neck.

The hum from the rails grew louder and they heard the faint clatter of the train.

Nicole slipped her arms under his jacket and round his waist. He put his arms round her and squeezed. She squeezed back.

He felt a movement in his groin, a lengthening and thickening. Nicole must have felt it too because she pushed the top of her pelvis against it. Confused, he flinched inside while his groin returned the pressure. A pulse beat throbbed in his cock sending tingles up his back.

Nicole nuzzling his neck sent a shiver through him. He lowered his head. Her hair filled his face. She pulled him toward her and he found her questing mouth in the dark. The kiss was urgent and clashing, both of them making little sounds and squeezing and pushing.

The train rushed by, lighting the alcove and filling it with crashing, screeching sound. Flickering light played through Jared's eyelids. Nicole's breath was hot on his cheek.

The end carriage flashed past leaving a thick blackness and rapidly fading sounds.

Nicole pushed herself away with her pelvis. She gave his jacket a gentle tug. 'Ya see.'

Jared smiled. He watched Nicole's body silhouetted in the torchlight as they walked. Just like that. What had he been waiting for? But what was he thinking? Cleve, Leon and Cheddar were dead and everybody else on the run, and he was getting horny.

Life was for living though.

The phrase had been Leon's. The finality of the past tense sank through him. It didn't seem real that they were all dead. He wished he could stop and take the full weight of the day. Curl up in a hole and let life pass by for a minute.

His skin tingled subtly as if all his pores strained to hear.

Nicole's footsteps stopped and the light went out.

'Something?' Nicole whispered.

'Not sure. Maybe we should check the tunnel.'

'Here.'

He walked along the ledge until he met Nicole's outstretched arm. She pulled him into an alcove.

He took a breath and relaxed his shoulders. The inky blackness suited the focus. He went to his level and was immediately aware of impressions of movement and sounds in the space where they'd split up. The tunnel they were in felt still and empty.

'Anything?'

'Yeah, dogs in the hall, but clear in here.'

'Same. Let's go.'

The blackness stretched on. Trains passed at intervals, relieving the monotony with a squeeze into an alcove. Their clinches were easy and companionable without the passion of the first.

Jared found the presence of the trains reassuring. As long as the system was running the authorities couldn't mount a full-scale operation to flush them out. They'd probably plot potentials based on walking speed and cover exits as they came into range. The longer they were in there, the worse it was. They had to get out before curfew when the system closed. After that the Squad would have all night to work through the tunnels.

After a while the muscles in his lower back and legs started to ache and the lack of light began to affect his eyes. Impossibly towering baroque columns in translucent colours, prancing carousel horses and processions of cavorting Chinese dragons flowed by. He swapped point position with Nicole and focused on the ledge.

The torchlight bobbing in time to his step made the shadow pulsate as if he was in the gullet of a giant. He wondered what they'd find when they got above ground again. Things were so unreal anything was possible.

But what were they going to do now with Leon dead, and no base or business? He knew there were short-term contingency arrangements, but what if the Boarding House had been turned over? What if the hit on the warehouse was part of the bigger move anticipated by Leon? And what were they going to do without Leon? He knew what Leon would have said to that. He'd constantly tried to get rid of hierarchical thinking and dependencies in the organisation.

What seemed like hours later the tunnel began to angle upward, straining his already protesting calves. He concentrated on putting one foot in front of the other.

A subtle change in the air drew him out of his walking trance. It was less metallic, clearer somehow. They had to be approaching the first possible exit. The anticipation of getting out of the tunnel was tempered by the probability that the exit was covered. A probability going on certainty.

A lighter circle grew gradually in the distance. An apprehensive knot in his guts matched it, growing tighter with each step. They stopped and remoted the opening. Both returned negative impressions.

With the binoculars he made out the bottom of a narrow, steep-sided cut. Roughly five hundred metres of killing ground for anyone positioned above. They didn't have that many options – go on, go back, or stay where they were.

They ducked into an alcove as another train passed.

'Now what?' Jared asked, when the noise died down.

Nicole didn't answer.

'Nicole?'

'Shh.'

He tensed and listened, but couldn't hear anything.

'Sol and Ash are in the same position, but something's happening,' said Nicole. 'We've got to wait out and be ready to move.'

He ignored the disappointment of not having 'heard' anything and wondered what the something was that was happening. If Sol and Ash were trapped too, what could it be?

Watching the daylight slowly fade to grey he wondered why it was that he'd lost groupmind connection. Accessing it automatically as he had made sense given that he'd been in a high stress survival mode, but he wasn't out of it yet, so why had he lost it? Why couldn't he maintain it?

He was bending his legs to relieve the ache when a shape fell past the tunnel mouth and landed beside the rails with a resounding smack, like a sack of potatoes. Seconds later, two figures abseiled swiftly to the floor.

'Shit,' he whispered, bringing the Ingram up and sinking to a crouch.

Nicole put a hand on his arm. 'Wait.'

The silhouetted figures didn't move.

'C'mon,' said Nicole, 'they're on our side.'

They walked slowly toward them. One of the figures beckoned urgently. They ran the rest of the way.

'Well met, friends,' greeted a man wearing a Squad uniform.

'Who are you?' Jared asked, cycling gut reactions to the uniform.

The man seemed puzzled and glanced at Nicole. Jared tensed with a flash of anger.

The man looked back at Jared. 'Friends. Explain later. This way.'

He led them past the other uniformed figure that was stripping the inert fallen body of its uniform. Two knotted ropes hung at the side of the tunnel.

'Quick as you can,' said the man, and then turned and walked back.

Questions about what was going on tumbled around Jared's head as he climbed the rope. The knots in the rope made climbing easy, but no less freaky. Pungent perfume surrounded his head as he brushed through the buddleia bushes sprouting at intervals out of the grimy brickwork.

He looked up and saw silhouetted shapes looking over. The shapes helped them over the top and turned out to be more uniformed men. One of the men hurried them to a waiting Squad van. Moments later the man who'd met them on the track jumped in and slid the door closed. The van pulled away.

Nicole reached out her hand. 'I'm Nicole, and very grateful.'

The man shook her hand. 'Marcus, glad to be of assistance.'

Jared held out his hand. 'Jared, also grateful.'

'So,' said Marcus, 'you're Jared.'

'Explain,' said Jared.

'I heard about your rescue from Leon.'

'You knew Leon?'

'Well enough for it to be weird talking about him in past tense.'

Jared didn't say anything.

Marcus stood up. He stripped off the uniform and started pulling on civvies.

'Any word of Sol and Ash?' Nicole asked.

'They're being extracted as we speak. We've been expecting a move like this for sometime. Although we've got our sources we couldn't be sure about the extent of their intelligence. It looks like what they did have was based on surveillance data rather than internal penetration.

'Yesterday's events changed things. For a start the army's now in charge. Although Leon taking out the Squad head hatchet accelerated the move, it'd been planned before that, another stage in their creep toward martial law. On top of that the Stazi are really pissed off. There've been raids all over the city.'

The post-curfew roads were empty of people and traffic as if some apocalyptic force had captured everyone. Jared imagined how the vehicle they were in stood out, not that a Squad van would get a second look. They did have a problem though. According to Marcus, the Boarding House had been raided. They could get a few hours respite where they were being taken, but would have to find somewhere else when it was abandoned later.

He needed to stop. He felt weak and light-headed. Trying to think back to when he last ate, or sat down, made him dizzy. Trying to think where they could go only drew blanks. Sol would know.

Sol didn't. What he did know, news of other raids and arrests, didn't help much. Neither did the news of Ash's death. A sniper, who must have watched his unit get neutralised by the group that lifted Sol, had picked her and two others off as they came out of a tunnel.

Jared stared numbly at the kitchen table. His head felt encased in black stone. Sounds of activity came from around the house, as the others made ready to ship out immediately after curfew. Nicole wept quietly beside him.

The sense of unreality persisted. Get up in the morning and before you next went to bed four friends were dead. It was like living in Palestine or Iraq, go out not knowing whether your family would still be alive when you returned, and them not knowing if you would.

He took a deep breath and pulled himself out of the spiral. There was shit to sort. They had to find somewhere to hide. He looked up at Sol.

'If we can get transport there's a place we could go over near the docks.'

216

'That the woman that was with you when you got picked up?'

'Yeah. She might not be very happy about it, but she won't turn us away.'

Pat wasn't happy about it. Her frosty greeting quickly escalated into a full volume refusal when Jared told her what they needed. Sol and Nicole hovered by the door ready to leave.

Jared let Pat rant. Finally he held up his hand.

'Pat, I'm gonna stop you. Twenty-four hours, that's all –'

'Jared –'

'Will you fuckin' listen to me?' Jared bellowed at the top of his voice. 'I thought you were my friend. That's why I came here.'

A tone from the computer stopped him. Pat stared at him a moment longer, then walked over to it.

'It's Dan and another man.'

Sol moved away from the door. Pat unlocked it and pushed it open.

'Hey!' Dan exclaimed brightly as he stepped in. 'Morning coffee is it?'

'Chance would be a fine thing,' replied Jared, glancing at Pat.

Dan hesitated, catching the look and the vibe. He looked at Pat.

'You know where everything is,' she said. 'I've got a conversation to finish.'

She walked toward the bathroom, Jared followed. Dan looked at Sol who just rolled his eyes.

Walking over to the kitchen, Dan turned. 'Sol, Nicole, Taff.'

Taff nodded. 'How're you doin'?'

'I guess you had to be Welsh with a name like that,' said Nicole.

Sol tensed with a sudden feeling of wrongness. He picked up a magazine for something to look at while he processed what it could be. The man's face had seemed vaguely familiar, but his voice had dislodged a distant memory. The memory inched slowly into focus. Tashkent. Military hospital. Lying in bed heavily doped, trying to shut out the images that brutalised his

217

waking and sleeping, pain hovering around the edges waiting for the morphine to wear off. Taff, if that was his name, was an MI operative who had been there debriefing a soldier on the other side of the ward, his sing-song valleys voice an odd contrast to the threats he was laying into the soldier with in an attempt to get some information out of him. The man was dying, loudly. What time he didn't spend pleading for someone to kill him, he spent crying and moaning a woman's name. The medics couldn't sedate him into silence on the orders of MI who wanted him awake to debrief him. The incessant moaning had grated on Sol who still felt guilty about wishing the man would die quickly.

He could hear Jared and Pat arguing in the bathroom. The man was standing beside the computer mirroring his action of leafing through a magazine. Sol took a slow, deep breath and walked toward him. The man looked up from the magazine. Sol pointed to a drawer in the computer desk.

'Can I get in there?'

'Sure,' said the man, stepping to one side.

Sol bent down then stood quickly and rammed a fist into the man's face. The blow lifted him off the floor and over the low couch behind him. Glass and wood splintered as he landed across the coffee table.

Sol clambered over the couch, chasing the still tumbling form.

The man landed on his knees, already reaching under his jacket, and pulled out a pistol. He brought it up to aim at Sol who kicked it spinning across the room. The man fell back and kicked out, hitting Sol square in the groin. Sol doubled up and crashed to the floor.

The man stood, shaking his head. Fat drops of blood fanned out from his mouth. He turned and staggered across the room to the where the gun lay.

'Jared!' Nicole shouted.

Jared stood in the doorway of the bathroom behind Pat, both summoned by the commotion. His eyes darted about taking in the room; Dan by the sink, Nicole by the computer, Sol in a gurgling ball on the floor, and the man, the lower half of his face smashed and bloody, weaving toward him, his eyes fiercely fixed on the

218

gun that lay a few feet away from Pat.

Pat stepped forward quickly and kicked the gun away. The man jerked to a stop and looked at her. The flap of his top lip parted showing the smashed mess of maxilla and a mouth thick with blood. Still staring at her he lifted a foot and pulled a long, black blade from his boot.

He stepped closer and held the knife out in front of him, flicking it from side to side. Pat stared at him, face devoid of expression, hands slack at her side. He moved in close and feinted at her face. She flinched and stepped back.

He smiled and blood fell out of his mouth. He took another step and flicked the knife again. There was a blur of white and the sound of violently ruffled cloth, and his knife hand was suddenly immobile, seconds before Pat's scything hand chopped into his neck under his ear, felling him instantly.

'Somebody tell me what's going on,' she said, still holding the arm.

'Military,' groaned Sol, pushing himself up.

A tone sounded from the computer. Dan leaned over and tapped some keys. The screen blinked then showed four figures clutching assault rifles on the stairs.

'Oh come on!'

'Don't worry, the door'll hold,' said Pat.

Sol looked round at Pat, who looked from the screen to the man to Sol. Her gaze lingered with Sol, then back to the man.

She dropped the arm, knelt on his back, and took hold of his head with both hands. She bent forward then yanked the head back and round. There was a moist crunching sound. She stood, grimacing, rubbing her hands on her clothes.

'Pat,' called Dan.

Pat stepped over the body and walked quickly to the computer, giving Sol a hand up as she passed. Jared, still standing in the doorway of the bathroom, followed.

'They're gonna blow the door.'

The screen showed one of the figures attaching small shapes around the door. Another stood spooling wire, while a third crouched looking into the alley, rifle high across his chest.

Pat reached over and tapped keys rapidly. Words appeared on the screen overlaying the scene.

ENTRANCE DISABLE LOADED
CANCEL/CONTINUE

'Continue,' said Pat.

The words disappeared and were replaced.

ACTIVATE/CANCEL

'Activate.'

Outside there was a sound like a volley of shots as explosive charges blew the retaining bolts out of the wall, then a screech of metal as the fire escape fell twisting into the alley.

Pat turned from the screen to the stunned faces.

'Never thought I'd have to use that.'

'There was only thr –' Sol began, but was cut short by a loud thud from the window.

They all turned and saw the other soldier hanging from a rope, his feet against the window. The assault rifle swung up to point at them. There was a scrabble of bodies diving for the floor.

'Don't do it,' said Pat, still standing.

The gun stuttered and the soldier jerked spasmodically as the bullets ricocheted off the window and tore into his legs and abdomen. He swung upside down momentarily, smearing blood on the pane, then fell from view.

Sol stood, shaking his head slowly. Pat ran up the steps to the bed platform and began grabbing things and throwing them into a rucksack. Dan stood staring at the body.

'Would somebody sort the body out,' shouted Pat.

'Sort it out?' Dan asked.

'Out the window?'

Nobody moved. Pat stopped on the stairs and looked down.

'It's going to take them ages to break in. It is my dad's flat.'

Jared shrugged and walked toward the body. 'He's dead anyway.'

He took hold of the legs and Dan took the shoulders, trying not to look at the head. Neither of them looked after the legs flipped out of sight.

'Okay, let's go,' said Pat, heading for the bathroom.

Jared looked at Sol. Sol shrugged and handed him an Ingram. They followed Pat into the bathroom.

Inside Pat was crouched by the heating duct. She pulled away a panel exposing the inside of the duct.

'Goes down to a boiler room. At the bottom of the duct is another panel held in with magnetic strips.'

She handed Jared a head-torch.

'After you,' said Jared.

'You're the one with the gun.'

Jared stared at her; she stared back.

The square steel duct was just wide enough to accommodate a person. Jared looked inside. Hand-width rungs attached to the side of the duct disappeared down into the darkness. He lowered himself with his hands; it was too cramped to bend his legs, occasionally sliding a foot onto a rung to take his weight.

Claustrophobia pressed in on him in the confined space. The pressure was distant though, like the feelings on hearing of Ash's death, like his reactions to the other deaths. Eventually he'd have a chance to start processing, but not while everything was taken up just staying alive.

At the bottom the duct turned a right angle by his feet. There was a handle in the middle of the panel. He listened for a sound beyond the panel, but could only hear muffled, ringing footfalls echoing around him. There was no room to unsling the Ingram.

He held the handle and pushed. The panel didn't move. He put his knee against it and pushed again. The magnets parted abruptly.

The light of the head torch showed a large, brick-walled space. He clambered out of the duct onto the oversized boiler and jumped down. The others joined him and stood getting their breath back. No one spoke.

Pat walked around behind the boiler. 'Over here.'

Set into the floor between the boiler and the wall was a

rectangular block with metal loops at either end. Sol and Jared lifted it and slid it to one side, revealing a brick shaft with a ladder set into the wall. Stale, briny air wafted up.

'Smugglers passage,' said Pat. 'Leads to a building at the end of the wharf.'

Jared just stared into the black hole. Sol squeezing past snapped him out of the trance.

'It's alright, I'm on it.'

The ladder was easier to climb. The passage was vaguely coffin-shaped with a low curved ceiling. Black mould covered the glistening red brick and several inches of water lay on the floor. Judging by the depth of the shaft they'd come down, they were below the level of the river.

He heard the scrape and clunk of the block being dragged back into place and had a brief thought of slaves being shut into pyramids.

The sound of splashing footsteps filled the passage.

His vision swam in and out of focus in the weaving beam. Shadows danced. The sound of footsteps seemed to be coming from in front as well as behind. He looked along the empty passage and staggered slightly. His legs felt filled with concrete. He just wanted to stop, close his eyes, curl up, cry, scream. He stopped and turned.

'I think we're taking the underground thing a bit far now.'

The comment brought tired smiles out of Sol and Nicole. Pat just glared at him.

The humour lightened him a bit despite Pat's anger. She had reason to be angry. Her main objection to their staying had been the potential compromising of her sanctuary.

They reached the end of the passage sooner than he'd expected after the previous walk. But then they'd walked halfway across the city, not just along a wharf. Sol joined him at the top of the ladder and helped push the block out of the hole.

They climbed out into a room the size of a large pantry whose walls were lined with wine bottles in racks. The door was ajar.

Jared peered around it into a long storeroom. Light filtered in from barred street-level windows. Along both sides of the room

222

were pallets of boxes and cases.

'One of my dad's partners is a vintner,' said Pat. 'He and my dad bought this place after my dad bought the other place and found the tunnel.'

She led them to the other end of the cellar and up an inclined ramp. She unlocked the door at the top with a key hanging on the door and walked out into what looked like a freight loading area. Pallet pullers and forklifts stood waiting by curtain-side trucks.

Pat pulled the tarp off a covered shape against a wall revealing a plain white commercial van. She opened the driver's door.

'On the wall by the roller door there's a box with a key and two buttons,' she said, indicating with her head, not looking at anyone. 'Turn the key and press up. When we're through press down and turn the key.' She climbed in and shut the door.

Nicole walked toward the door, the others climbed into the back of the van.

Jared sat on a wheel arch feeling vulnerable and boxed in. He strained, expecting to hear sirens, but only heard the rattle of the roller door.

They pulled out.

Nicole clambered in.

'Clear,' she said over her shoulder.

Sol crouched behind her and looked out into the street. Jared lay down on the wood panelled floor almost tearful with relief. He glanced at Dan sitting on the other wheel arch. He was staring down and didn't look up.

Jared could feel Pat seething and Sol and Nicole's minds working furiously. His own mind seemed to have gone the way of his exhausted body and refused to do anything.

They hadn't driven very far when Pat pulled over and parked. She turned.

'This is where I leave.'

Jared sat up. 'Eh?'

'I'm on the first boat or plane off this rock.'

'Are you sure that's a good idea?'

'Jared, hanging round with you is the bad idea. I was safe in the flat, now I haven't even got that. Don't worry about me, my dad's got channels. Seriously. The van papers are in the glove box. Do what you want with it.'

Jared shook his head. 'I don't know what to say.'

'Say goodbye, Jared.'

The hardness of the voice and look brought tears to his eyes.

'Bye Pat.'

'Take care, Dan, and good luck…all of you.'

The van door slammed.

Without a word Nicole slid over into the drivers seat, started the van and pulled away.

8

Could we see when and where we are to meet again,
we would be more tender when we bid our friends goodbye.
— Marie Louise De La Ramee

J ared stared at the freight train sitting on the siding, waiting for the driver to return. Sol shifted beside him, stretching first one leg and then the other. An owl hooted in the darkness. Small black shapes flitted around the lamplights behind the station.

He checked his watch. It was nearly time. He tested the straps on the chest harness for the third time.

'Better get going then,' said Sol, barely visible in the gloom. 'I'll be in touch, but we won't move for a bit yet.'

'Okay,' replied Jared. There wasn't anything else he could say, despite the feeling of pressure in his chest.

'Look after yourself.'

'Yeah, you too.'

A door opened at the back of the station building and boisterous, joking voices spilled out into the night.

Sol gripped Jared's hand with both hands. Jared hesitated, feelings of finality overcoming him.

'Go,' Sol pushed him gently, 'go.'

He ran doubled up and ducked underneath an end carriage. He lay on his back and pulled a set of karabiners from one of the pockets of the jumpsuit, then clipped them to the undercarriage. Clinker on the track dug into his shoulder blades.

A door slammed at the front of the train.

He clipped the krabs to the straps on the waist and chest harnesses and ratcheted both straps bringing him close to the frame. He fitted his legs through the loop on the end krab.

The diesel engines coughed into life. So far, so good. He heard and felt a slow domino clunking as the couplings took the strain, and the train began to move.

225

He waited until the train had left the station before pulling a pair of headphones from a belly pouch and putting them on. He clicked them on, completely cutting off the growing din of the wheels. He pulled the hood of the suit over the phones against the chill wind that streamed over his body, crossed his arms over his chest, and hung, cocooned in silence and warmth. All mod cons, as Sol had joked while he kitted up: thermal jumpsuit, noise reducing headphones, night-sight goggles, and daypack with survival kit and disguise. The semi-automatic in a shoulder holster was a reassuring hardness against his side.

The train clattered through the night heading south with its stowaway. Gradually the motions and vibrations eased his anxiety, unravelling it like the miles that sped beneath him.

Grief caught up with him again. He shook his head and closed his eyes against the tears, but couldn't stop the memories forcing their way in; looking back at Cleve, vulnerable and alone in the echoing loading bay as they evacuated the warehouse; Leon in the street, standing with his arms out to the side, Cheddar's chuckle, Cleve's dry jokes, wasted moments with Nicole, disagreements with Leon that he'd never be able to put right.

Why was it only after someone had died that you fully appreciated who they'd been and how much space they occupied? Given their circumstances, what had he been thinking? How had he not noticed that he was holding the illusion that nobody was going to die?

He'd not been aware before that there were loads of things he wanted to do with Leon or Cheddar or Cleve, but now his mind filled with things that he hadn't done and would never be able to do, and the fleeting, unseized moments he'd let slip by. 'See you later' had meant 'I'll see you again' instead of the more realistic 'I might see you, I might not'. A door had been slammed in his face, and the future he'd presumed stretched off into the distance severed.

And here he was again, in the dark, going fuck knew where, and hung under a fucking train this time. When had his life begun to have such bizarre hiccups? He used to think of himself as fairly ordinary, if a little reactionary. That was it though, to step outside of that manufactured, media-maintained bubble was to enter the fray. Welcome to the real world.

Bitterness and frustration welled up, dragging guilt-tinged anger with it. Emotion overtook him. He clicked the phones off, gripped the steel undercarriage as hard as he could, opened his mouth and yelled, long and loud, again and again.

He let go and slumped into the harness. He clicked the phones back on and concentrated on his breathing, shutting out all other thought. Gradually the movement of his cradle rocking him gently eased him into sleep.

Several times in the night he woke when the train slowed or stopped, but none of the stops were at a station and fatigue claimed him quickly.

The train stopping again woke him. Grey-blue dawn light illuminated the tracks. He looked at his watch. This had to be the place. He put the phones back in the pouch and ratcheted himself low enough to be able to see between the wheels. The siding looked empty. He had to move quickly before they started offloading the freight. Thankfully he could count on industrial inefficiency for a time lag between arrival and offloading. Even so, he had to move fast, it was already light enough to be seen.

He unclipped the krabs and lay on his back to wriggle out of the jumpsuit. He pulled a camera and notepad out of the daypack and stuffed the suit in. Pulse racing, he stuck his head between the wheels and scanned up and down the track, then scrambled out and walked quickly away from the train. Expecting a shout at any moment, he crossed the tracks and breathed a sigh of relief when he reached the access road that ran alongside. So far, so good.

Now off the tracks the gricer disguise would legitimise his presence in the area, although he doubted that even the most nerdy train spotter would be out at this time in the morning.

He spied a dusty Land Rover standing out among the executive motors in the car park and headed for it. An old man in a shabby brown waxed cotton jacket and flat cap climbed out as he approached.

'Edward?'

'That's me, friend. Jump in.'

He climbed in. Edward shook his hand firmly.

'How was your trip?'

'Good thanks, I slept most of the way.'

'Was a tad confused, Sol said to be there at six, but there wasn't a train due until eight thirty.'

'Well, there was no way I could've caught the public train, so I kind of hitched a lift on that freight train that just pulled in.'

'I see.'

Jared waited for the next question, wondering whether it would be about the first or last part of the statement. Sol had said that the couple he'd be staying with wouldn't want to know why he was hiding out or what he'd been doing in the city.

'And how do you kind of hitch a ride on a freight train then, if you don't mind me asking?'

He watched a smile form on the old man's face as he told him.

'What, slung under a carriage, all the way down here?'

He nodded.

Edward chuckled and shook his head. 'Well I never.'

They drove in comfortable silence. The countryside unfolded before them, glowing in the morning light; gentle rolling hills in various shades of green, parcelled out into squares by gorse-topped stonewall hedges, all encapsulated under a bright blue bowl of sky.

Jared wound down the window and took a deep breath. Unexpected tears sprang into his eyes and ran down his face. Uncaring, he just sat and made no move to wipe them away. Out of the corner of his eye he saw Edward turn as if to say something and then turn back to the road.

He sat for long moments as Nature poured into him and tears ran out. Finally the tears stopped flowing and he wiped his face with his sleeve.

'Handsome day,' said Edward.

'So it is, and a handsome place.'

They breasted a rise and the land fell away gently in front of them, rising up in the near distance to the slopes of a high rounded hill. Either side of the hill, stretching away in both directions on the eye-level horizon, ran a band of blue ocean, dark against the powder-blue sky.

'Wow,' said Jared.

'Yep. One of my favourite bits of road this, on account of that view. Where we're headed is on the other side of that hill.'

They turned off the main road and the view was hidden behind the high stonewall hedges that bordered the narrow twisting lanes, some of them only just wide enough for the Land Rover. Finally they turned through a gate and into a sloping yard where a woman Jared guessed to be Lizzy was beating a rug hung over a clothesline. For some reason he expected a farm dog to come yapping, but none showed. Edward introduced him to Lizzy, who also asked how his trip had been. Edward answered for him, obviously keen to tell. Lizzy seemed less amazed than Edward and simply commented that he must have been comfortable to have slept most of the way.

She gestured to the daypack and asked if that was all he had, then answered herself saying travelling underclass he would have needed to travel light wouldn't he. Edward chuckled at the joke. Jared smiled and wondered if the couple were always so jovial or whether the joking was to put him at ease.

Lizzy pointed to the other side of the yard. 'Go out of that gate and up the track. The caravan's at the top of the field. There should be everything you need, so take your time and settle in. Drop by anytime you like.'

He thanked them both, relieved there wasn't any small talk expected and walked to the gate. The track was fringed with gorse bushes covered with yellow flowers. The spongy moss and grass of the track itself said it was a long time since vehicles had used it. That suited him fine too.

The caravan was the long static kind. The key was in the lock and he let himself in. He stepped over the threshold into the smell of freshly baked bread. On the worktop a tea towel-shrouded shape sat atop a cooling rack. He put his hand on it and found it still warm. The cupboards were well stocked with a variety of tins and packets and jars.

He shook his head, touched by the couple's generosity,

realising that Lizzy had meant it when she said he could take his time and settle in. With that much food he could lock in for a week. He wondered again what Sol had told them. He lit the cooker and put the kettle on. On the door of the fridge was a note.

Jared,

We are vegan, so you won't find any dairy in the fridge. There is what we hope you will find pleasant alternatives. Should you particularly want dairy, please come and talk with us.

With well wishes.

He smiled and opened the fridge. The sight of cartons of rice and oat milk, vegetable margarine and a block of tofu made him smile even more. He closed the fridge and walked over to the open doorway.

The land sloped away into a neat little valley, a wooded cleft he presumed led down to the sea. Squares of green stretched away from the other side of the valley. On the horizon the silhouettes of what looked like a castle ruin and a large monument stood out on top of a long, low hill.

He reached over and turned the kettle off, then stepped outside, shutting the door behind him. The grazed meadow grass underfoot as he walked toward the stile at the far end of the field reminded him of Aled and Kay's garden. He wondered if the dogs were still alive.

The gorse hedge was thronged with bloom. On the other side of the stile a track led off high above the valley through low heather and scrubby gorse. Tiny birds flitted around the bushes, weaving their needlepoint song.

His boots were soon coated with a layer of dust from the track. He felt heavy and constricted despite the heat that warmed his back and head. His heart beat harder with the exertion. He stopped and took a deep breath. His heart was really thumping, the pulse thick and loud in his throat and ears. The space around him suddenly seemed vast and he felt in danger of falling into it. Sweat prickled on his forehead. His legs began to tremble and then gave way without warning. He crouched with both hands on the track and tried to get a grip of his breathing and racing heart.

He sat on the strip of grass that fringed the track. The lowered centre of gravity calmed him. Gradually the sky ceased sucking at him.

Sol was right. Leaving the city had been a good idea, even though he hadn't wanted to. Things were stressed enough. He was a liability. He wasn't even capable of a simple walk without freaking out. Holing up in attics and basements with other Resistance members on the run from the security services had been difficult. The combination of tension and cabin fever had made things difficult for everyone, but he'd suffered several attacks brought on by the confinement and tension. He wondered if the people he'd hidden with were still alive and free.

Gradually his pulse slowed to normal. The open countryside was a welcome change from being boxed into a windowless room in the city, but the space and isolation only deepened his anxiety and feelings of loss.

He wished he had a cigarette, and wondered where the craving came from. He hadn't had one for years after it was pointed out that politically he was kicking his own ass by funding the government with his addiction. Stopping had also spared him the slow poisoning, not from tobacco which he didn't think was carcinogenic, but from all the other crap they put in the tobacco that definitely was. So why did he want one now? Not that it was an issue; he didn't have any.

He felt twitchy, a feeling he recognised from the time he'd stopped smoking. Maybe that was what it was about.

He breathed in deeply and put his hands flat on his thighs. He was anxious, but that was understandable. He was a fugitive, on his own, in a strange place. He reminded himself again that his being in that strange space meant he was safer than his friends.

The Squad had been rounding up anyone suspected of 'treasonable attitude' or 'seditious behaviour' and detaining them in 'temporary detention centres' built by international corporate war profiteers. Most people were taken in for questioning following the online submission of their digital photograph and a statement detailing the action or conversation seen or overhead by the Intelligence Operative. Audio transcripts from public-

231

mounted microphones were also often submitted. Once the person was identified and located through digital face mapping and database referencing, they were picked up at home or at work. They had the 'choice' of voluntarily helping with enquiries or being arrested. Claims of innocence were ignored. Cooperating by pointing the finger at those said to have seditious leanings was a way those being questioned often demonstrated their innocence and patriotism. In such a climate no one was safe, least of all people in the Resistance. He was definitely better off than most. The thought didn't relax him.

He stood and carried on walking. The track led around onto the headland. An onyx-green sea stretched away, shifting slowly, shimmering shards of sunlight. Black cliffs curved away either side of him into the distance. A loose cloud of gulls soared below him in silent shifting formation, riding unseen currents rising against the cliffs. As he watched, one broke formation and dive-bombed another, seemingly at random. The two chased, twisting and turning briefly, and then swooped up and over and rejoined the back of the flock.

He looked from the gulls to the cliffs and back to the sea. A wave boomed close by. The dull, implacable vibration resonated with his heaviness. He stepped off the track and sat down.

The sun spread a shifting carpet of light on the waves. A cormorant arrowed by below, skimming the rounded backs of the waves rolling slowly toward the cliffs.

Gradually he was aware of a feeling of unease. A subtle something registered by the hairs on his neck. He turned quickly. Heather, gorse, and cloudless sky. A grasshopper buzzed. A wave boomed. He blinked back with the realisation that he was just staring, brain disengaged. He turned and looked back out to sea.

He saw himself as if from above, stopped where land met water. He'd gone as far as he could go.

Eventually he stood up and walked back along the path, eyes down.

The caravan felt like a sanctuary. He sat at the table and stared vacantly out of the window. Tears welled up, grief and separation bubbling up like marsh gas to choke him. The voices of the dead and their faces appeared to him, locked in a memory loop that was never going to change; pieces frozen in time falling away down a bottomless black hole.

Even though he'd known their position was precarious and safety tenuous, he'd still put off doing or saying things until tomorrow. Guilt and regret pulled at him. He'd wanted to get past the weirdness with Pat; to have sex with Nicole; deeper chats with Leon, another chess game with Cleve, and that drink with Dar. All put off until a tomorrow that now was never going to come.

The long days and lack of structure shifted him into a numb and timeless limbo. Being outside produced such feelings of smallness and vulnerability that he spent most of the time in the caravan staring out of the window, or just staring.

The bread and milk ran out. He didn't go down to the farmhouse. He didn't want to talk to anyone. The caravan became his shell and like a snail he drew his head in.

Sat in the doorway one morning, the sun high and hot, the heat felt good but didn't unclench him. He felt frozen in mid-spasm, stuck in a cramp. He heard someone clear their throat and looked round to see Edward, the sleeves of his faded check shirt rolled up, carrying a basket. He waved once.

'Handsome day.'

Jared shaded his eyes with his hand.

'Mornin' Edward.'

Edward lifted the basket.

'Brought you some things. There's some bread and salad and veg from the garden. There are plenty of tins and whatnot in the caravan, but if there's anything you want just write a list and we'll pick it up, save you going into the village.'

'Is the village off-limits then?'

'Well, put it like this, it's a small village so new faces get noticed. Most men your age are away at the war. You'd be reported in a jiffy. How's the place suiting you anyway?'

Jared nodded. 'Good, thanks.'

His voice sounded blunt with lack of use. He cleared his throat, thinking to add something, but no words came to mind.

Edward looked at him, seeming to expect a little more banter.

He cleared his throat again. 'Conversation's got a bit rusty…and to be honest, I'm not in a very talkative mood.'

'No, you don't look it. Anything I can do?'

Jared shook his head. 'Thanks though.' He paused, then added, 'Some close friends died recently is what it is.'

'I'm sorry to hear that.'

Again, no words came to mind.

'Maybe it's only sad for those left behind though', Edward continued. 'I mean, one could be glad for them, odds are they're in a better place.'

Maybe he'd be glad if the old man carried on his doddery way.

'Not sure what's so good about this life anyway,' added Edward, seeming to slip easily into the role of speaker.

'Okay for you to say, you're on the way out.'

'Didn't mean any offence, friend, and I apologise if there was any. And yes it's because I am probably, but not necessarily, closer to death than you that I have this perspective. I've had this view for a while though; it's not just old age that tests one's illusions. And they are illusions.

'I remember observing the birthday of someone close to me who'd recently died and realising that I'd never celebrated someone's birthday, including my own, with the thought that one day that person, or myself, wouldn't be there to share the celebration. I was nearly thirty years old then. Talk about slow. Thing is we humans have an acute difficulty accepting, embracing and living with the fact of our mortality. The reality of the situation is that when you say goodbye to someone and they go out of sight round the corner, that could be the last time you see them alive. Morbid? Quite the contrary, it's one of the few one hundred percent certainties in life, and a fact that should move us to savour every moment.

'But yes, you get to my stage in life and death does begin to have its attractions. Mind if I sit?'

234

He pointed to the chair by the steps.

'No,' said Jared, hoping the single syllable answer didn't sound rude. He just didn't feel like talking.

The old man sat and stared out over the valley.

'Used to be a doctor. A career like that gets you thinking about life and death. That's how I met Lizzy, she was a midwife in the same hospital. There was a war on then too, as it happens. Turned out neither of us were very happy about things in the medical industry. Practical things that limited our effectiveness as professionals and fundamental things that made us ashamed of what we were doing. I guess we were quite radically minded. Radically minded was one thing, acting on it within the system was another thing entirely though.

'You see, doctors, in fact most allopathic medical personnel, not to mention the rest of society, have this notion that 'doctor knows best'. Put it down to medical training and cultural programming. Rare is the doctor that will admit to the fact when the practises they're involved in are counterproductive or wrong. And any that do and try to do something about it soon find themselves victim to negative responses from their peers, railroading, and disciplinary action.

'And you could forget about support from your union. By then unions were already moveable buffer zones for the government that deflected and diffused any threat of industrial action, status quo maintainers that took their member's money and then made sure that nothing radical ever happened. And not just in the medical industry either. It was the same right across the board. At best toothless dogs, at worst parasites.'

'What things?' Jared interrupted.

'Hm, what?' Edward turned quickly.

Jared wondered whether the surprise was at the question or the fact that he was sitting next to him.

'You said there were things that you weren't happy about.'

'Yes, yes there were,' he paused, 'a vague, general dissatisfaction at first, but the more we looked into things, the more that dissatisfaction turned into serious misgivings. You see, you take a careful look at things and a dark picture emerges. No, the way things are going I wouldn't want to be around in twenty years time, never mind a hundred.

'Take cancer for one example. Cancer is big business, right up there with arms and petrochemicals. Nearly ten billion pounds spent on cancer treatment each year in Britain alone. Incidence of cancer is on the increase and getting frighteningly near to fifty percent of the population. Despite the government media line about smoking and sunbathing being the culprits, the epidemic has various causes, virtually all of them actively promoted or ignored by government health departments. The doctor-fed diet of vaccinations, antibiotics, analgesics, steroids, routine x-ray scanning; pesticides, herbicides, household detergents and toiletries, fluoride and chlorine in tap water –'

'Hold on,' said Jared. 'Okay, I've heard about the tap water thing, but some of the other things save lives.'

Edward nodded. 'That's what most people think. Take vaccinations then. As I've said, Lizzy and I were involved with the newborn and very young. Part of that management included the government vaccination program. Vaccines, a mixture of animal derived proteins and viruses, formaldehyde, mercury, aluminium, carbolic acid, et cetera, injected into infants as young as two months old. Ignoring the obvious insanity of injecting some of the most carcinogenic and poisonous to human chemicals, the vaccination concept itself is so flawed that it begs the question of how the practise began.

'For instance, childhood illnesses like measles, mumps and chicken pox produce symptoms which reflect the efforts of the immune system to clear the virus from the blood, which it does by sending it out exactly the same way it came in. When a child recovers from measles, you have true immunity. That child will never, never again get the measles no matter how many epidemics it's exposed to. Furthermore, it will respond vigorously and dramatically to whatever infectious agents it's exposed. The side benefit of measles is a nonspecific immunity that primes the child's immune system so that it can better respond to the subsequent challenges that it is going to meet in the future.

236

'Now, by contrast, when you take an artificially attenuated measles vaccine and introduce it directly into the blood and bypass the portal of entry, there is no period of sensitisation of the portal of entry tissues. There is no silent period of incubation in the lymph nodes. Furthermore, the virus itself has been artificially weakened in such a way that there is no generalised inflammatory response. By tricking the body in this way, we have done what the entire evolution of the immune system seems to be designed to prevent. We have placed the virus directly and immediately into the blood and given it free and immediate access to the major immune organs and tissues without any obvious way of getting rid of it.

'The result of this is the production of circulating antibodies, which can be measured in the blood. But that antibody response occurs purely as an isolated technical feat, without any generalised inflammatory response or any noticeable improvement in the general health of the organism. Quite the contrary, in fact. The price we pay for those antibodies is the persistence of virus elements in the blood for long periods of time, perhaps permanently, which in turn presupposes a systematic weakening of our ability to mount an effective response not only to measles, but also to other infections. So far from producing a genuine immunity, the vaccine may act by interfering with or suppressing the immune response as a whole in much the same way as radiation and chemotherapy, corticosteroids and other anti-inflammatory drugs do.

'Chronic long-term persistence of viruses and other proteins within cells of the immune system produce chronic disease. We know that live viruses are capable of surviving or remaining latent within host cells for years without continually provoking acute disease. They do this by attaching their own genetic material to the cell, and replicate along with the cell. That allows the host cell to continue its normal functioning whilst continuing to synthesise the viral protein.

'Latent viruses produce various kinds of diseases. Because the virus is now permanently incorporated within the genetic material of the cell, the only appropriate immunological response is to make antibodies against the cell, no longer against the virus. So, in actual fact, immunisations promote certain types of chronic diseases, including cancer and other autoimmune disorders like autism. Far from providing a genuine immunity, the vaccines are actually a form of immunosuppression.'

Jared watched as the old man switched gears as he spoke, from his initial slow idling to his present passionate pace.

'I apologise in advance if I bore you. This is a particular bug bear of mine.'

'Not at all, it's interesting.'

'Then how about antidepressants? SSRI's like Prozac and Ritalin. Two of the now acknowledged side effects of SSRI's are suicidal ideation and psychotic thoughts. Now call it pedantic, but there are no such things as side effects, there are only effects. So why are drugs that are known to cause suicidal and psychotic thoughts being prescribed to the depressed and potentially suicidal? How many mildly depressed people have they pushed into chronic depression or over the edge into suicide?

'I found a research paper whose authors had found that in the majority of cases in the U.S. where a pupil had gunned down other pupils and staff then either shot themselves or were shot by the police, the pupil involved was on Prozac-type medication. And when the parents of one of these children tried to sue the pharmaceutical company, the judge refused to commence proceedings and insisted that they take the out of court settlement that the company had offered in an attempt to keep it out of the news. Another paper listed cases of suicides of young people who were on these drugs.

'Hysterectomies,' he continued relentlessly, 'thousands of women have healthy uteruses completely removed and then are put on hormone replacement therapy drugs, drugs which cause cancer, bone disease and heart disease, the very things that having the hysterectomy is supposed to prevent.'

Edward's voice stopped and Jared realised that he was slumped against the doorframe, as if a weight were pushing him down. He sat up.

Edward leaned back and stretched out a leg. 'Dark, like I say.

Thing is, the people that are promoting these processes and selling these drugs have all the information, so it isn't happening through ignorance. And because it's happening on such a wide scale, negligence doesn't come into it, which just leaves design. Which is a very disturbing thought.'

'Consider me disturbed.'

'I do apologise,' said Edward, standing slowly and stiffly, 'such wasn't my intention. But as a friend of mine used to say, if you're not disturbed, you're not paying attention. In that respect ignorance really is bliss. Enjoy the sunshine, Jared, and do call by sometime.'

Jared watched him walk slowly and carefully down the path and out of sight.

There was no getting away from it. It was everywhere he looked. Dark like Edward said. Dark and heavy, and it filled his bones like concrete.

The war was being waged on all fronts. People were surrounded by a pincer movement, oil barons with their government lackeys and standing armies on one side, and their twisted pharmaceutical industry partner on the other, waging a long-term biological war, both producing a nation of immunodeficient pharma-junkies, wage slaves and cannon fodder; protected and facilitated by a global media propaganda apparatus.

Trying to liberate them was a waste of time. There was no chance of getting through to them. Drugged and conditioned into docility, people loved their servitude. Even if there had been no neural manacles, they were as unlikely to kick back as any other farmed animal. Sheep for the slaughter.

But there were the manacles. Flip-top manacles in every pocket, wireless manacles in every home, school and coffee shop. A frequency fence that controlled the livestock. And there was no way of getting through the fence.

The analogy made him think of the Animal Liberation Front. The fences they'd had to get past were physical though, and the ones they'd liberated had known they were being experimented on.

History did repeat itself, and not just in the carbon copy replication of government processes that created enemies for convenience, or bombed its own population to generate public support for illegal and immoral excursions abroad. There was also the persistent denial on the part of the general population that anything untoward was going on; the refugee camps, the prisoner of war camps where torture and abuse were the norm, the persecution of Orientals, Muslims and refugees, the war itself.

Like their predecessors in Germany, they pretended not to know. Willingly hypnotised and desensitised by the flickering box and its endless outpourings of trivia, lies and manicured images that numbed down and dumbed down so subtly and effectively that when the modern day Reichstag's burned, the knee-jerk reactions produced were predictable in direction, intensity and duration. Pavlov's people. Like sheep, they were herded in the desired direction, with just enough room for individual variations to preserve an illusion of independence.

The consumer was the product. Programmed by the programmes; news reports designed to perpetuate the current government-desired worldview, multi-layered lifestyle programming deviously contrived by linguistic and behavioural experts. Literally years of people's lives spent drinking in the poisonous 'entertainment' brew of dysfunction, conflict, humiliation, and lies that poured out of the open sewer in their sitting rooms.

Surrounded by his people it was easy to believe in the positive potential and essential goodness of human beings. Easy to believe that their hope lay in the people. Interface with the person on the street though and it was hard to keep that faith. So much conceit, so much ignorance and intolerance, and parroting of right-wing media-manufactured viewpoints and opinions. Media provided an excuse not to think for people who didn't want to think. They were worse than sheep.

He got up off the step abruptly, as if the movement might put some distance between him and his thoughts. It didn't. He stood for a moment and then pulled the door shut and set off across the

240

field.

The heat felt near tropical. The sun on the sea was a sparkling glare. He shaded his eyes with a hand and wondered how close the Gulf Stream came to the island. Close enough to make a difference to the climate, driving in from the station he'd seen palm trees.

He tried to picture the process going on under the polar ice; colder water sinking, creating the pump effect that shifted streams and currents around the globe. He wondered, not for the first time, how it would be when the pumps stopped as a result of the polar ice melting.

At that latitude the winters were definitely going to get colder. Not that they were going to get off as lightly as a mini ice age though. Eventually the melting ice would change the weight distribution of the planet and, like a spinning top once poised in perfect balance, the whole planet was going to wobble. When that happened the crust floating on the magma core would slip.

It was all fucked. And perched on the edge of the island was definitely not the best place to be. Or wasn't it? The thought of a giant wave sweeping in was actually quite attractive. No running away, just sitting there watching the swell move in and getting swamped by a hundred foot wall of water. Game over.

That's what was needed, a flood of biblical proportions to wash the shit off the face of the planet. Nature responding to the infection with a shiver and sweat. Extinction for humans and a blessing for everything else. It would serve them right, they'd flirted with it long enough. What was so good about Hopeless Sapiens anyway, with their reverse Midas touch that turned everything to shit?

A wave boomed below. Along the cliff edge was a rocky outcrop, a blunt, diamond-shaped wedge jutting out over the sea. He made his way carefully across the heather to the rock. The exposed flat was about two feet square. He stood on it with one foot and peered over. Far below waves foamed around a hump of slick, green-black rock. It would probably take about four seconds to hit the sea. Four freaky seconds and he could be out of there.

The thought surprised him, but didn't shock him. Why not? It was his life and it was shit. If there was one thing in this fucked up world that was for him to decide, it was when he left. His vision blurred and he stepped back and sat down in the heather.

Why was he crying? Fucking crap bastard. Four seconds. It was his life and it was shit. Pack it up and start again.

The voice in his head jeered him. Crap bastard. Left up to him he'd just wander round snivelling.

He breathed in deeply and suddenly. He had to get a grip. He stood and moved cautiously back to where he'd been sitting, leaning away from the edge as he walked.

He stared at the outcrop. Had he lost it? It wasn't that mad though. He'd had enough.

He shut his eyes and tried to imagine what would go through his head in that four-second freefall. He didn't care and it didn't matter anyway. Like vomiting, the worst bit was getting there, the actual vomiting was a relief. Relief. No more pressure. No more pain or weirdness nipping at his heart and his head. The fish could have his fucked up body.

He sat staring at the rock and then got up and walked back to the caravan, feeling strangely lighter. He'd found a door in the wall. He wasn't trapped; he could leave anytime.

His mind kept returning to the rock for the rest of the day.

The following day he talked himself into going down to the farmhouse. Even though he didn't feel that sociable, he needed to hear voices other than the one in his head.

'Come in, come in,' said Edward putting the rifle he was oiling onto the table. Jared ducked through the low doorway into the kitchen. It was warm and smelled of yeast. He shook Edward's waiting hand. It was rough and dry like an old weathered fencepost.

'Alright my 'andsome?' Lizzy chimed, stood at the range stirring a pot, rolled up sleeves and floury apron the picture of Victorian domesticity.

Jared nodded at the wine glass next to the gun. 'Bit early isn't it?'

'Not at all,' said Edward. 'Join me. Anytime of the day is a good time for a glass of kvass.'

'Kvass?'

'Tea wine.'

'Tea wine?'

'Strange acoustics in here all of a sudden,' said Edward tilting his head and smiling.

Jared laughed. 'Sorry, it is a bit early. Maybe a glass of kvass is just what I need to bring me round.'

Edward stood and reached a miniature tankard from the shelf above the ingle-nook. He sat it on a coaster and poured a drink. Jared sipped the golden, slightly sparkling drink.

'Is it supposed to be vinegary?'

'Slightly, or according to taste. The longer it's left to ferment, the more vinegary and the more effective.'

'Effective at what?'

'Well it'd be easier to say what it's not good for. Biochemically speaking its an adaptogen, which means that it normalises general body metabolism and brings all processes into balance. For instance, if you have high blood pressure, it'll lower it, and if you have low blood pressure it'll raise it.

'Not only that, it stimulates a detoxification throughout the whole system, and is especially good for flushing toxins out of the liver, both metabolic and environmental toxins. Because of that it's effective in a wide range of diseases and conditions, and I mean a wide range. Research over the last hundred years or so have shown it to be effective for over thirty-two different conditions.

'It deals with the arthritis I get at times, and eases my mind about the heavy metals I can't avoid ingesting, like the mercury and other metals in my fillings, fertilisers and pesticides in the fruit and veg we buy, et cetera, et cetera. The daughter in-law swears by it for cystitis, and it sorted out her dad's irritable bowel in no time.

'What's on today then?'

Jared shrugged. 'Ad-libbing.'

'Very good,' Edward replied, making it sound like one word.

'Wanted to say thanks for the vittles.'

243

Edward guffawed. 'Now there's a word that you don't hear much nowadays.'

Jared smiled. 'It's the kitchen and Lizzy, and you…quite Dickens.'

Edward laughed again.

Jared turned to Lizzy.

'That bread was the best I've ever tasted.'

'Oh there love, you're very welcome,' she said, rewarding the compliment with an appreciative smile. 'There's more where that came from.'

'You see that,' said Edward, 'compliment her baking and she's instantly flirting. I'll have to remember that one.'

'Tuh,' Lizzy looked at Edward and tossed her head back. 'Just giving the man a lift to antidote your tirade of doom and gloom.'

She turned back to the range, winking at Jared as she did.

'I apologise again for dragging my cloud over to you the other day,' said Edward.

'I was interested.'

'And considerably more glum by the time I left. But that's the way of it sometimes, things don't look pretty and for a while they just get uglier. Take me for instance.'

Jared smiled and hoped the smile didn't look as brittle as it felt.

'How did you get on with the dairy alternatives?' Edward continued.

'Fine. I have vegan friends, so it was pretty normal.'

He pointed to the gun on the table.

'Could I ask what a vegan is doing with a rifle?'

'I use it to get our meat.'

Jared made a confused face.

Edward nodded.

'Seems like a contradiction, doesn't it?'

'You mean it's not?'

'There are lots of good reasons for being vegan. Ours include a reluctance to ingest the large amount of drugs and chemicals in farmed meat and dairy, the environmental impact of animal agriculture, and a refusal to be part of the exploitation and cruelty

244

involved in the industry. Unlike some we don't see it as unnatural or wrong to eat meat. It's an aspect of this Planet Earth experience that the various species eat each other for the energy needed to live. What we do see as unnatural is keeping animals captive and breeding them for the purposes of eating them and their babies, and taking the mother's milk for human consumption, and the sordid death animals go through.

'Many things that humans do are considered normal by virtue of the fact that they've been done for generations, when in actual fact they are anything but normal. Before farming, the human species found what it needed in terms of food in its environment; food was hunted and gathered. Such a habit meant that humans maintained close and respectful relationships with their environment and the others who shared it, recognising that they were all parts of an interconnected whole. The development of herding and farming changed that and shifted humans away from that relationship, and initiated a massive cycle of environmental destruction and horrendous cruelty toward animals. The move toward a male-dominated consciousness of exploitation then spread to the control and domination of other humans too.

'So our reasoning is political too. You see it's a mistake to see issues of human and animal exploitation as mutually exclusive. On the contrary, all exploitation is inextricably intertwined. Speciesism, racism, sexism, are all connected forms of exploitation. Deny one group their rights and any group can be denied their rights. As long as there's violence of any sort, there'll be violence of every sort. As long as there are slaughterhouses, there'll be battlefields.

'Humans are compassionate, empathetic beings. Eating farmed meat and dairy forces people to turn away from an essential part of being human. Compassion and empathy, two qualities essential for awareness of that interconnectedness, have to be switched off to take part in a system that inflicts so much violence and suffering on innocent beings.'

'We are what we eat. Observe one's fellow humans with that thought in mind and one can see the fearful, domesticated, sheep-like, and bovine. And the parallels don't stop there.

245

'Yet you still eat meat,' said Jared, jumping into the pause as Edward took a breath.

'Yes. As I said, I don't think it unnatural or wrong.'

'Eating meat that is,' added Lizzy, 'eating dairy is another matter. There are few things as obscene as the practise of repeatedly raping a captive female to keep her pregnant and lactating, stealing her newborn babies for slaughter or slavery, and using her breast milk. Talk about a lack of empathy. Granted, I haven't always been vegan, but when I was made aware of the details of the process I couldn't understand how I, a woman and mother, hadn't made the connection before when I'd known conceptually what was involved.'

'And there's the key,' said Edward, 'a simple question that can be, should be, applied to every action and interaction: how would I feel?

'I know how it feels to be shot,' said Jared.

Edward was silent momentarily and then nodded.

'I hear you. I hunt in the spirit of traditional societies worldwide, past and present, with much thought and respect, and only according to my needs. The death by my hand of my animal cousin is as swift and painless as I can make it, and I take responsibility for that. There are those who challenge our referring to ourselves as vegan because we eat meat, but it works from our frame of reference.'

The phone rang. Lizzy wiped her hands on her apron and answered it.

Jared picked up the coaster and examined it. It was clear resin threaded through with copper wire, iron filings, and what looked like spirals of fleece.

'That's not very Dickens.'

'Hm, what,' said Edward, whose attention had been on Lizzy.

Jared waved the coaster. 'Modern art?'

'Solid state technology.'

Jared held the question while Edward looked past him again, trying to catch Lizzy's eye. By the tone of her voice it was a child she was speaking with. Edward mouthed 'Friday afternoon' in her direction and then looked back to Jared, smiling.

246

'The granddaughter. Now she's something special, and I'm talking outside of my proud grandfather capacity. Smart like you've never seen, and so strong-willed, which is probably a bit of her grandmother in her. Give her a brand new concept though and she'll grasp the abstract and get to grips with the practical in double quick time, as long as she's interested that is. I call her Little Butterfly. Wears me out when she's here. Got a mind like a sponge, and gets like a little whirlwind. Infuriates her to stand in a queue. Her school has just recently labeled her ADD and recommended that she go on Ritalin. Mind-altering drugs for a ten year old, I ask you. Since when did a school start giving medical diagnoses?

'And the thing is even though ADD and ADHD are completely unproven and questionable diagnoses, when a child displays behaviour considered undesirable they're said to have a disease. Symptoms of this disease include fidgeting, daydreaming, problems doing boring tasks, and difficulty with rigid authority, normal child behaviour in my book. Been reading up on it since the school got on to my daughter and her husband telling them that Caja was disruptive,' he said, pronouncing the name Spanish-style.

He lifted a sheaf of papers and a thick book from the sideboard.

'You interested here, this fit in with your ad-libbing?'

'Yes on both counts.'

'Good. Cop a load o' this then, as they say.'

He perched a pair of wire-rimmed spectacles on his nose.

'Psychology professor Diane McGuinness: "Methodologically rigorous research indicates that ADHD and hyperactivity as 'syndromes' simply do not exist." The Australian National Association of Practicing Psychiatrists: "ADHD is not an inherited genetic disorder or organic disease" and "scientific evidence to support ADHD as a disorder is unproven". William B. Carey, of the Children's Hospital of Philadelphia: "What is now most often described as ADHD in the United States appears to be a set of normal behavioural variations. This discrepancy leaves the validity of the construct in doubt." Or how about this

247

one? Dr John Jureidini, head of the Department of Psychological Medicine at the Women's and Children's Hospital in Adelaide, in response to a question by a parliamentary commission: "There is monumental literature that takes as a given that ADHD is a neurobiological condition and starts from there to talk about different forms of treatment. Once you have many thousands of articles published about something, how can it possibly make sense for someone to stand up and say 'This is not an entity'? I want to emphasise that I quite clearly acknowledge that there are children who are very compromised because of difficulties with impulsiveness, attention and activity. I am not saying that these children are not suffering or are not worthy of attention. I am saying that, as a disorder, ADHD is a spurious entity."'

Edward waved the sheaf of papers.

'A phantom disease. Yet thousands of children are being drugged into compliance with very powerful and dangerous psycho-stimulant drugs. Stimulants like Ritalin and dexamphetamine are very similar to cocaine and both have grossly harmful impacts on the brain; they reduce overall blood flow, disturb glucose metabolism, and possibly cause permanent shrinkage of the brain…'

Lizzy leaned over as she walked past.

'Let me know when you're coming round next time and I'll hide his soap box.'

'This isn't just politics, it's our granddaughter we're talking about,' Edward's voice rose.

'I know it is, love,' said Lizzy gently, 'but Jared's got enough going on in his head without you adding to the weight. Have a care, eh.'

'That's okay, Lizzy. You're right, it's not exactly cheery, but I am interested.'

'On your head be it then. Just let me know when you need rescuing.'

Edward nodded to Jared and made a face at Lizzy.

'Developmental toxicology is the problem you see,' he continued, 'although not the only one. Children and adolescents are growing and developing not just physically but cognitively and emotionally. The drug-induced docile behaviour is caused by chemically blunting or subduing the child's higher brain function. They're being turned into zombies. Sensationalist? Listen to this. This one's talking about what's known as the 'zombie effect', a short-term calming effect which seems to relate more to a form of intense focusing on one thing, or no thing, as opposed to being aware of and involved in the various aspects of the child's environment. Quote, the amphetamine look, a pinched, somber expression, is harmless in itself but worrisome to parents...The behavioural equivalent, the 'zombie' constriction of affect and spontaneity, may respond to a reduction of dosage, but sometimes necessitates a change of drug, unquote. That's Arnold and Jenson in The Comprehensive Textbook of Psychiatry.

'And the diagnostic process beggars belief. There is no biological basis for diagnosis; in fact it relies entirely on behaviours. And every one of the eighteen symptoms of ADHD is qualified by the word "often". What constitutes often fidgeting, or often having difficulty organising tasks and activities? There are no objective guidelines. Even aside from "often", the rest of the definition is riddled with ambiguous and vague terminology. Which mistakes are careless ones? What is easily distracted, or when does a small movement qualify as a fidget or a squirm? Outrageous!

'And on that basis our young ones are being damaged and introduced to a life on drugs. Researchers at the University of California in Berkeley studied five hundred children over twenty six years and found that Ritalin is basically a gateway drug to other drugs, in particular cocaine. Lead researcher Nadine Lambert concluded that Ritalin makes the brain more susceptible to the addictive power of cocaine and doubles the risk of abuse. There's even account of an American media personality being treated for cocaine addiction crushing up her prescription Ritalin and snorting it. So what are they doing prescribing it to children?'

'You're not going to put your granddaughter on Ritalin then?' Jared asked, knowing he'd get a rise.

'Over my dead body, there's nothing wrong with her. Want to

know what the incident was that had the school phoning home?' Edward chuckled. 'I was so proud of her I can tell you. The army was in school giving human rights talks to the seniors. Blatant recruiting drive and PR exercise. It's not enough that we've got conscription back and Combined Cadet Forces in schools, they've got to brainwash them with human rights propaganda too. Well, little Caja, bless her, was booing the recruiting officers in the corridor and when told to explain herself did just that, at the top of her voice. Said the armed forces were just a big stick that the government used to bash people in other countries if they wouldn't do as they were told, that dropping bombs on women and children showed that they didn't care about human rights, and that children all over the world should refuse to go to school until all the killing stopped.'

Jared laughed. 'Sounds like a pretty switched on kid.'

'She is that. Special, like I say. She's got her work cut out for her though. The authorities don't want free thinkers, even at that age. Worrying thing is her little sermon will be logged, added to her databased file alongside her photo and biometric print. Goodness only knows who can access that information, or what it could be used for,' he shook his head. 'CCTV cameras, biometric register and library access, why? To stop bullying, truancy and book theft? Were things really that bad, and even if they were, is surveillance the best solution? Who's behind those cameras, watching our children? One presumes they're vetted, but are they, and if so by whom? Questions that need to be asked, especially as there's been council CCTV staff prosecuted for spying on naked and half-dressed women in their own homes, and police officers have been investigated for touting photographs of nude people taken with CCTV cameras. There's even a series of video's made from voyeuristic CCTV footage.

'I'm amazed and dismayed at the ease with which people acquiesce time and again to the invasion into their private lives by the State. Cards, chips, phones, radio frequency identification devices, cameras. The details of every phone call, car journey, swipe of a card and click of a mouse recorded and stored electronically, and available to anybody who knows how to get them. All the minutiae of a person's life easily summoned at the touch of a keypad. Did you know that Britain has the biggest spy base, the most surveillance cameras, and the largest DNA database anywhere in the world?'

Jared nodded.

'It's only a very elderly or foreign minority in this country that have come close to the kind of environment that these things are taking us to.'

Jared shook his head and smiled without humour. 'You really are cheery.'

'Real life, Jared. And informed is forearmed. We need to collect all the information we can and act on it as much as possible. Hard times are coming, no doubt about it. Global oil production peaked years ago and is now in decline. Modern civilisation is totally dependent on hydrocarbons. Rather than developing strategies to ease the transition into a post-petroleum world, trillions have been spent and millions of lives wasted in the military acquisition of the last of the oil stocks in the Middle East and the Caspian Basin, and the fundamental issue ignored or downplayed. On top of that the breakdown of the planet's essential ecosystems has also been ignored and downplayed.

'Because the problems result from the nature of capitalism we can't expect solutions from political leaders or corporations. Personally I wouldn't like to bet on which crisis is going to arrive first. The question should be though, where are you going to be and how are you prepared for it?

'We're as prepared as we can be here and we'd be okay for a while, depending on the nature of the breakdown of course. We already collect rainwater at two points from all roofs for drinking and cooking, and get all year round food from the garden. For meat I'll do what I do now and get it myself with the gun; for power there's the solar panels and the wind genny, and the Landy runs on veg oil, though I dare say that'll get scarce. Nowhere near as quickly as diesel will though. There's an emergency kit in the Landy too, in case we get caught away from home; spade, water, basic rations and a stove that'd keep us going for a few days.

251

'Y'see we can't depend on the government doing right by us. Even with the best intentions, emergency relief would be scarce and slow coming, as the people of New Orleans discovered a few years back. But they haven't got the best intentions now, and I don't expect them to have then. Towns and cities will be worst off. And don't depend on being able to leave the city when things get tough. They can annexe off cities or whole counties quicker than you can say 'be right back', and without an incident actually taking place too, just on the threat of say, chemical or biological incident. I try not to think about it too much, too depressing. Thought it through and prepared best we can.'

'You're well positioned out here though.'

'Yes and no really. Definitely better than being in a town or a city, but there's few places to hide when the government turns on you. Remember the big outbreak of Foot and Mouth a few years back? Leading up to it farming had turned into a huge government welfare programme, a mess of quotas and waste, and bureaucratic incompetence. During the epidemic the mass destruction of livestock was enforced right across the country. Tens of thousands of farm animals killed and bulldozed into enormous mass graves or burned on massive pyres that burned for weeks.

'Within a matter of months the government's troublesome subsidy burden was relieved, and more than one small concern had gone to the wall, consolidating agribusiness into even fewer hands. All for a disease that's not fatal to livestock, and is also not transferable to humans. Compare that to Mad Cows Disease that can kill the animal and is transferable and potentially fatal to humans, yet BSE infected meat is still legally reared and sold. Forgive the digression, but you see my point, you've got to be one step ahead, and prepared.

'There's also one or two people I've spoken to, and over a dozen more that I've heard of, have had dreams or premonitions of giant tidal waves or bits of the coastline falling into the sea. They didn't need convincing of the sense in preparing for crisis. And for those that haven't and come trying to steal what we've got, there's two hunting rifles, and Lizzy's as good with one as I am.'

Edward's continuing talk faded out. What he'd said had given form to the darkness in Jared's head, like dust blown at an invisible beast. It wasn't imaginary, it was there, menacing and threatening, crowding in on him stood with his back against the sea.

Edward's raised voice cut through his daze.

'Going to knit a cardigan?'

'Sorry Edward. Actually I'm half asleep, I didn't sleep too well last night.'

He excused himself and walked back to the caravan.

A wall of hot air met him as he stepped inside. He left the door open and walked around opening windows. It was too hot to sit inside, but being outside felt too open and exposed. He sat on the floor where it was cooler, and leaned his back against a cupboard. Edward's voice echoed in his head, spouting facts and statistics.

Even though he'd studied methods of control in the education system, he hadn't properly considered how much children were targeted. That they were, more than any other group in society, made total sense from a social control perspective. Children had the power to redirect the course of history; they were the next generation and held the fate of the future. The conditioning they received set the tone for what was to come, and was deliberately centred on the capitalist system of work and consumption. Schools were psychological laboratories where training in consumerism was the central activity; where children were 'human resources' moulded and shaped for the 'workplace'.

Naturally, teachers and administrators weren't let in on the plan; they didn't need to be. If they didn't conform to instructions passed down from increasingly centralised school offices, they didn't last long.

In an atmosphere of constant low-level stress and danger children were habituated into abandoning trust in their peers, and themselves, and familiarised into living in environments controlled by authority, represented by CCTV and ID cards and, in the case of their personal environment, pharmaceutical drugs.

The training produced dependable consumers and dependent citizens programmed to need and accept being told what to think and do by authority figures, whether in the flesh or on TV.

He shook his head to stop the spinning thoughts, but it didn't. He lay down on the hard carpet and drew his knees up to his chest. The position was oddly comforting.

The days led him deeper into depression. Idle lost its work-shy connotations and became a fitting label for the mode he was in, ticking over, but out of gear. Tired as he always seemed to be, sleep at night eluded him. A good nights sleep became three hours of tossing and turning, tormented by dreams of screeching tyres, sinking in quicksand, and an invisible presence, darkness itself coalesced, smothering him with a huge, suffocating hand. The day's fatigue mixed with his mood and dragged him down even further.

Lain in bed one morning sticky with sweat, the dream fading away like rolling thunder, his movement wafted his stale smell from under the blanket. It reminded him of Aled and Kay's cottage when his smell had forced him to go and have a bath. The parallel depressed him even more. Nothing had changed. His body still stank, still didn't work properly, and his mind was still fucked up. They'd broken him…and all the king's horses and all the king's men…

He snatched up a pillow and slung it across the caravan. It slid over the worktop, dragging stuff with it. Half empty cups, plates of uneaten food, and jars clattered to the floor.

He roared with frustration, and threw himself back on the bed. He felt like taking a baseball bat and smashing everything up. He kneeled up and stared at the wall, breathing heavily through his nose, trying to get a grip. He stayed there until the rage passed, then dropped back on the bed and stared at the ceiling. There was no point in getting up.

The overcast day slowly grew more overcast.

A suddenly urgent need to piss finally got him up. He stood in the little wardrobe of a toilet rubbing the ache in his back. He'd stopped doing the exercises Leon had given him, including the ones to strengthen his urinary system. The kidney pain had never completely gone away, even when he'd been doing the exercises.

He moved around slowly cleaning up the mess. All Edward and Lizzy's kindness and generosity and he repaid them by smashing things up. After he'd cleaned up he stood there, uncertain, not knowing what to do next. And that was the thing, there was no next, just the same round and round, hours, days, and months. Impotent, useless, crap.

He left the caravan before he broke anything else and stomped across the field. He left the path and made his way over the top of the cliffs and down out of sight of the path, within sight of the rock. A chewing gum grey sky pressed down over the slate grey sea. It felt like it was going to rain.

He sat hunched with his hands stuffed into the pockets of his jacket.

This was it. He wasn't going back. Enough was enough. It was his life.

His stomach creased and he swallowed against the trembling in his throat. His mouth was dry.

He stood up. No more fucking about.

This time he stood on the rock with both feet. The sea was calm and lapped around the rock below. If he aimed for the rock it would definitely be instant. He wasn't really into the thought of drowning. He wondered if he'd be able to let himself drown if the impact didn't kill him. Maybe he should come back another time with some rocks or chain to attach to his legs.

Maybe he should stop mincing about and just fucking do it. It wasn't even a jump, it was a step. Left or right, it didn't matter. One step and four seconds, then peace.

Tears blurred his vision. Why he was crying? He wasn't sad. He didn't feel upset at all, just resigned. He'd had enough. Who cared what waited on the other side, this side was a bag of shit. He wiped his eyes and wobbled dangerously. He took a deep breath.

A seagull rose up and around into his field of view about ten feet away and hung in front of him at eye-level; white, black-tipped wings making constant, tiny movements to maintain the stall. It fixed him with a small, bright eye, and gave a low 'hukukuk'.

He stared, open-mouthed. It couldn't be. It wasn't exactly a laugh, but it was close enough, and sounded too alike to be a coincidence.

The gull gave one more 'hukukuk' and swooped down out of sight.

He watched it fly down. The motioned teetered him forward. He thrust himself back and landed roughly in the heather, and grabbed it with both hands.

He looked at one hand and then the other, then let go and sat up.

He'd just nearly killed himself! That gull had Leon's laugh! He'd just nearly killed himself!

Tears spilled over and ran down his face. What the fuck was going on? He just wanted it to end. He didn't want any more; he'd had enough. There was no reason to carry on. It was all fucked; he was fucked.

That had been Leon's laugh.

He looked at the impressions on his hands made by the heather and looked back at the rock. Did he really want to end it now? Was it just some built in survival mechanism that had him grabbing the heather?

He tried to find the intensity and found only confusion. His indecision deepened his frustration and fuelled the feelings of inadequacy. Why didn't he just do it?

Maybe taking an overdose would be easier, less hectic... and let Edward or Lizzy find his decomposing body in the caravan. And anyway, what was so hard about jumping off a cliff?

He stared at the rock. All the pressure and darkness that seconds before had weighted the reasoning wasn't there anymore. Where had that gone? Where had it come from? Did he really want to die?

That had been Leon's laugh. Was it a coincidence? A message?

He stared out over the sea at the solid line of the horizon.

The knowledge that he wasn't going to jump presented itself, even though he'd made no decision.

9

Life ultimately means taking the responsibility to find the right answer to its problems and to fulfill the tasks which it constantly sets for each individual.
    —Viktor E. Frankl *Man's Search For Meaning*

It didn't matter how long he stared at the board, he couldn't see any way out. He'd lost too many key pieces and was hemmed in on all sides.

'Check.' Leon waved the piece in Jared's face.

Jared looked confused and frowned.

'You don't play Western chess.'

Leon grinned. 'And you're playing as if you lost your queen.'

'You do pull the maddest stunts though.'

'Got you all out of a pickle though didn't it? Anyway, listen to you, Mr cliff diver.'

'I'm dreaming.'

Leon threw the queen into the air. It arced slowly, then froze and winked out.

'Of course. Question is, which dream, the waking dream or the sleeping dream? Not that it matters for the purpose of this chat. And there is a purpose to it. You might think you've finished. You haven't. You still have a mission.'

'But how come we lost contact? How come we've got it now?'

'I've been right here. You've let grief and victimhood shut you down. It would've been frustrating had I been in a body. You've been so lost that you've been suppressing your subspace awareness. And on top of that you stopped your practise and now

257

your entrainment is faint.

'Anyway, we have a deal you don't remember making. I didn't choose my exit arbitrarily. I did what I came to do.

'Come on, stop wallowing in problems and create some solutions. Finish the mission. You're in the right place. Listen to Edward. He rambles on a bit, but he knows things.'

Jared felt a lump in his throat. 'So many questions.'

Leon smiled and rested his hand on Jared's shoulder. 'The answers are all within your reach. We'll catch up later, no worries.'

Jared opened his eyes to the dark and the feel of Leon's hand still on his shoulder. Tears welled up and ran down his face into his ears. He wiped his face on the pillow. It was a long time before he got back to sleep.

A screech jerked him awake. The beige ceiling stared back. Wind moaned softly and buffeting tremors reached him through the bed. The screech sounded again, this time joined by others, exultant and wild. He sighed, turned onto his belly and parted the curtains. The sudden gash of brilliant light resolved into an expanse of eye-blue sky, one corner resting on a swathe of steely sea, the other tabled with the green and purple tartan of the cliff. He opened to the scene, letting it pour in and swamp his already stirring monkey mind. The low moan of the wind reached in, harmonising with his melancholy. He lay his head on his arms and retreated back into sleep.

He woke later, sweating in a column of sunlight. It was gone noon by the look of the sun. He threw the covers back and lay luxuriating in the heat before getting up. He pulled on jeans and shirt and shuffled over to sit in the doorway.

But for the sound of the distant surf it was as though everything were in thrall, captured by the heat. The feeling suited him. He felt like a banded tree, severed and wrapped in iron. He stared at the grass at his feet, mind and gaze blank. He was unaware of Edward approaching until he spoke.

'I was hoping that you were studying ants rather than carrying the world on your shoulders, but by the look on your face I can see it's the latter.'

Jared sighed heavily. 'Don't mean to be rude Edward, but now is not the time for more negative news.'

'I'm sorry you feel that way, Jared. Brought it on myself, I'll admit. Today though I wanted to show you something, if you've a mind to see it that is. As it happens it's not a problem, it's a solution.'

The comment resonated like a struck bell and sent a shiver up Jared's spine. He sat up.

'Do you believe in life after death?'

'Scientific fact,' replied Edward offhandedly. 'Death is just our name for the transition of an individual's consciousness from one vibrational density to another, like a musical tone moving up an octave and out of our perceptual range. Because our ears can't pick up that frequency we say the tone has stopped, whilst dogs or bats know otherwise. Why do you ask?'

Jared stood. 'Let's see your solution first.'

'Actually, Nostradamus predicted that life after death would be validated by science by now,' Edward continued, as they walked down the track, 'and so it has, but the knowledge is being withheld, just like other discoveries he predicted which have been realised. Any discovery that threatens the grip of the powermongers in control just gets sat on and has for hundreds of years.'

They reached the big barn at the end of the yard and Edward unlocked the padlock and gestured Jared inside. Jared stepped into the dark interior and Edward clicked on the light. Sitting under moveable floodlights in the middle of the floor was a chair on a circular metal platform.

Jared looked at Edward. Edward just smiled and motioned him closer.

The platform measured about ten feet across and was made out of sheets of metal roughly welded together. The chair was a low-backed easy chair, ordinary except for the safety belt.

'Had to cobble the platform skin out of bits of moped body parts, but it works like a dream. Have a seat and I'll show you what it does.'

Nausea rose in Jared's stomach.

'How about you just show me, Edward, I have a thing about sitting in chairs in the middle of rooms.'

Edward looked at Jared for a moment.

'Trust me, Jared. You'll like this, I guarantee it.'

Jared hesitated and then walked slowly into the pool of light. He hesitated again.

'You have no idea how weird this is.'

Edward held up his hand.

'Jared, whatever happened to make you feel this way was in the past. This is the future.'

Jared stepped onto the platform. The chair was the low-backed easy chair variety. Nothing like the other chairs, he reminded himself, wiping his hands on his thighs.

'A low cockpit would've been more aesthetically pleasing,' Edward's voice echoed, 'but that's about as low as I can go without needing a winch to get me up again. The belt's there for your safety.'

The ordinariness of Edward's voice softened the dread. It was just a chair. He sat and fastened the belt.

Edward walked out of the shadows with what looked like a large gaming joystick in his hands. Jared felt a slight vibration through his feet and the platform rose several inches as if on hydraulic suspension. Edward walked backward into the shadows, smiling, and the platform followed him out of the circle of light.

Jared's stomach lurched and he gripped the chair arms as the platform took off obliquely over Edward's head and sped across the barn. It slowed rapidly as it neared the far wall, spinning a slow hundred and eighty degrees as it did, and hung motionless and silent about ten feet off the floor. The whole barn was silent.

'What do you think of that then?'

'I'm glad I fastened the belt,' replied Jared, still gripping the chair.

Edward chuckled again and the platform sank slowly to come to rest in front of him with a faint metallic thud. Jared unbuckled the belt and stepped off. Edward was smiling broadly.

'How?'

'A kind of Biefield-Brown effect, which I don't suppose means very much. Very basically by the interactions between the zero-point field of the quantum vacuum and electrical and magnetic fields.'

Jared arched an eyebrow.

'As it sounds, it's not that basic. The principle is though. Gravity is the result of spin. Because everything at a subatomic level is spinning in parallel, it falls into Earth's gravity well. Spin something and apply an electromagnetic field and you change the spin of it's subatomic elements. No longer parallel they are no longer influenced in the same way by gravity.

'NASA, Boeing, British Aerospace Engineering, Honda and others have been conducting research and development of exotic propulsion systems for years. Most of the known theories and designs are constructed around alternative energy systems.

'Most of the world's problems are the result of energy issues. Transport and industry the world over is dependant on the internal combustion engine model and the transverse wave electromagnetic system. Two extremely wasteful and flawed systems. Even the best engines waste around eighty percent of the energy produced in the process of gobbling up the planet's finite and rapidly dwindling resources. As a result the planet is plundered and poisoned, and its people displaced and bombed into oblivion.

'Transverse wave electromagnetic systems, batteries, only scratch the surface of the energy available, and over half of the energy that they do obtain is put to work actually destroying the inner workings of the system itself. Standard practise, accepted science, and complete and utter madness.

'The answer to the world's energy needs is to be found all around us. Empty space is anything but empty, it's literally seething with energy, and there is no problem at all extracting all the energy you could possibly want, any time, anywhere in the universe. All you need is a dipole. If you balance all the doping and the materials design, and correlate the switching, you can get all the free energy you wish. Properly utilised, a single car battery can be used to power an electric automobile

261

indefinitely. Or even to power a battleship. In the real world, of course, you will inevitably have a tiny bit of loss as you go, because there's a finite, though high, resistance between the two poles of your battery. Handling that is a piece of cake, as the man said. Simply run a separate little collection circuit to collect a little bit of trapped EM energy from the slowly leaking source, and every so often feed the collected energy back into the battery as power, to charge the battery and replace the small amount of the primary source's potential gradient that has been lost. The battery, load, and 'trickle charger' then become a closed circuit free-energy source that will last for years and years. Here, let me show you something else.'

He led Jared around the platform to a workbench against the wall. On one end of the bench was what looked like a series of magnets and coils connected to a small black box.

'Admittedly not as spectacular as the lifter, but it's applications and implications are far more wide-reaching. This is the Motionless Electromagnetic Generator, originally designed by Colonel Thomas Bearden and associates at Magnetic Energy Limited. This little beauty kicks out around three kilowatts, pollution-free, cost-free, potentially indefinitely given that there are no moving parts, and no limit to the energy itself. And if I want more power, I just connect another.'

'I never suspected you were such a boffin, Edward.'

Edward laughed. 'Me, I'm just a tinkerer, and I've taken advantage of nearly a hundred years of research by the likes of Tesla, Kron, and Bearden, to mention just three. As it is there's plenty of legitimate overunity electromagnetic energy systems patented by researchers in the U.S. alone. Luckily there are one or two scientists and researchers that have gone against the conspiracy of silence and made efforts, usually at great personal cost, to get the information out. As I'm sure you'll understand, access to an independent, plentiful and free source of energy isn't going to be initiated by government. Such a thing is a threat to them and other power structures because it would mean loss of economic control over people and countries. It's an exercise in imagining seeing how this would change the world, but it would, completely. What's not hard to see is why knowledge of extended electromagnetics has been suppressed right across the board.

'But people need to be made aware of this science so that they can use it for themselves, and steps need to be taken to make sure that it's used for humanity's benefit, and not it's detriment. Because there are other aspects to it that make scalar electromagnetics a very sharp double-edged blade.

'The Russians who for a long time were world leaders in this field categorised the science as energetics, bioenergetics, and psychoenergetics. Energetics covers the kind of applications we've mentioned thus far, actions on and in relation to inert matter. Bioenergetics covers all field and matter interactions in living matter such as the body, interactions that seem even more miraculous. But they only seem miraculous because our minds are conditioned and blinded by classical theory.

'As well as solving the energy crisis the world over, the engineering and application of longitudinal electromagnetic waves also has the capacity to neutralise radioactive waste in minutes, and to cure any disease, including cancer and HIV.

'In the nineteen sixties and seventies in France, Antoine Priore and a group of scientists used scalar electromagnetics in thousands of experiments to cure a whole range of infectious diseases, terminal cancers, and to restore damaged immune systems. The government withdrew his funding in nineteen seventy-four, and his work was suppressed.

'Becker proved conclusively that DC potentials with extremely weak currents can dedifferentiate cells, genetics and all, back into a previously healthy state. This is because unlike transverse waves that exist in what physicists call 3-space, the three-dimensional world we know, longitudinal waves exist in the vacuum, in 4-space or the fourth dimension of time. The diseased cells are time-reversed back to a healthy state. He demonstrated this on intractable bone fractures by making the red blood cell first dedifferentiate, time-reverse, by dropping its haemoglobin and growing a nucleus. Then that new cell redifferentiated, time-forwarded, into the type of cell that makes cartilage. That new type of cell redifferentiated into the type that makes bone and those cells were deposited in the fracture as new bone. Even though Becker was nominated for the Nobel Prize, he and his work got the same treatment as all the rest.

'HIV could be treated in the same way by dedifferentiating the HIV-infected cells, genetics and all, back into normal cells, restoring the suppressed immune system along the way. And all in a matter of minutes with weak, non-ionising electricity. Previously normal cells would just get a little younger.

'In the Soviet Union Koznacheyev showed how electromagnetic signals from damaged or diseased cells transported cellular death and disease patterns to healthy cells. His work too was suppressed and looks likely to have been used in the development of electromagnetic weapons that, rather than reversing the process, actually promote the development of disease or cellular degeneration in the target, as seems to have been the case with staff at the American Embassy in Moscow. And that's the problem –'

Jared held his hands up. 'Edward, no more, just for a minute.' He held his temples against a building pressure. 'Fuck, life is so mad, and this is the icing on the cake. Flying fucking saucers, 'scuse my language, reversed aging.' A wave of panic heaved slowly upward. ''Scuse me, I need some air.'

He stepped outside and leaned against the side of the barn with his hands on his knees. He shook his head and pushed all the colliding thoughts from his mind, and concentrated on his breathing. The focus gradually released him from the trapped, pressured sensations and slowly his breathing settled.

Edward came out of the barn. 'Alright there?'

Jared straightened up and nodded. 'Yes, thanks. My mind boggles easily these days.'

Edward gestured to the barn with his head. 'That's enough to boggle anyone's mind.'

He locked the door and beckoned Jared. They walked across to the farmhouse and around the back into the garden. High stonewalls created the perfect suntrap and the air was drowsy and still. The garden itself looked like an art installation. Curved, flowing lines moved the eye around banked tiers and mounds, raised beds and curious frameworks, all thick with lush and vibrant growth.

Edward led the way along slate and pebble paths around circular beds neatly and creatively set out with an array of herbs, vegetables and flowers. Red and yellow-tinted chard encircled kohl rabi. Onion and carrot leapfrogged lazy spirals. Purple broccoli watched over beetroot and radish and mooli. Bean canes arranged in cones hung with cucumbers, beans, and yellow courgettes. Interlacing the vegetables, alive with bees and other insects, lupin, marigold, marjoram, and lavender gave off heady scents that mixed with the heat and steady droning to give a timelessness to the oasis that settled a grounding calm over Jared. He was relieved when Edward suggested they sit on a bench. He commented on the hearty condition of all the growth.

Edward nodded. 'Spend a lot of time here I do.'

'It shows,' Jared replied.

'Oh I don't do much work besides planting out and pulling up. This is Nature's work. I just come here and sit and be. The vigour that you see here, and what you don't, is a result of another solution, literally. Ever hear of a Japanese scientist called Higa?'

Jared shook his head.

'Toward the end of last century there was an ecological revolution in Japan that came out of research and development by a horticultural professor called Dr Teruo Higa. For over a decade he'd been looking at microorganisms as a potential solution for soil depletion and crop yield problems. Ignoring disease, malnutrition as a result of low crop yield combined with dirty water kills millions every year in underdeveloped countries. Higa produced a synthesis of around eighty safe microorganisms he called Effective Microorganisms that regenerate soil and boost crop yields in record time. Crops grown with EM have less negative ions, which lowers pest and pathogen susceptibility, and have higher levels of vitamin C and carbohydrate.

'It produces what's known as zymogenic soil, which does away with chemicals and achieves better results right across the board. And it does this without harming Nature's balance. Quite the opposite in fact, it actually enhances ecological harmony by adapting to each circumstance rather than acting as an indiscriminate antibiotic, antifungal, herbicide or pesticide. Part of the reason it does this is a positive wave resonance it releases that promotes substance and energy field unity.

'But it doesn't stop there. EM is also an amazing chemical-free cleaner, compost accelerator, deodoriser, preservative and water purifier.

'It was used following the tsunami in Thailand years back, and in the aftermath of Hurricane Katrina to stop the spread of disease. It's used for the same reason in slums in Kenya to improve sanitation. The Japanese have been using it to recover polluted waterways in places like Ibaraki, Nagasaki, and Hiroshima. As a result they've seen an increase in notoriously sensitive wildlife such as octopus, shrimp, crab, and sea cucumber. It's used in Bangkok to reduce the foul odour and toxic water of shrimp farms. Germany used it to decontaminate waters after the Elbe River flood disaster, and it's used in Australia in sewage spill management.

'The list goes on and even extends to human health. A tonic made from EM contains eighteen amino acids, forty trace minerals, and dozens of antioxidant compounds and enzymes, and in studies in China and America have shown to be effective in treating, among other things, cancer and Parkinson's disease. And then there's the monoatomic element side of things, but that's a huge topic in itself.'

There was something deeply peaceful about the garden. The insect drone sounded like a just audible chant. Jared tried to gather his thoughts. Antigravity machines, free energy devices, magic microorganisms. Leon was right; he was in the right place. His mind went back to the talk in the barn.

'Part of me hesitates to ask, but in the barn you were about to tell me about the downside of scalar technology.'

'Hmm, yes, unfortunately there is a dark side to it. The same technology that can be used to provide free, unlimited energy, heal all known diseases and conditions, and neutralise radioactive waste can also be used as a weapon with a greater destructive

266

capacity than anything seen before, and I mean anything. Sadly, and typically, millions more have been put into research and development of the weapons than into the positive applications.

'Two linked scalar antennae form what's known as an interferometer, or "Tesla Howitzer", and can deliver a blast of energy anywhere in the world, above or below ground or sea, all from a computer. There's actually no delivery from anywhere to anywhere. Longitudinal waves don't travel through space. The energy of the blast is produced from the vacuum at the location of the target. Ripples and patterns in the fabric of spacetime are manipulated to interfere in and around the local spacetime of the target producing effects that exceed the destructive capability of nuclear weapons.

'Not only is the explosive capacity of that magnitude, it's also possible to destroy all electronics in any given area, missiles in flight, planes, submarines, power grids, anything, anywhere. Even a person can be killed if their exact position is known.

'Using one of these interferometers in what are called the endothermic and exothermic modes one can manipulate the weather as easily as pushing food around a plate; heat up the air over here, cool it down over there, whip up a tornado or a hurricane, create or suppress rain, whatever you like.

'There's been a number of incidents where this technology has been used; missiles rendered inoperable in their silos, planes shot down, weather manipulated to prevent rain, or create and steer tornados and hurricanes. Evidence also heavily implicates their use in bringing down the World Trade Towers Probably the only reason the technology hasn't been used wholesale, though I suspect there are psychopaths itching to, is that the potential for global disaster is so high on account of the earth and the sun being in a very delicately balanced scalar arrangement. A large scalar event on earth could easily alter that balance and precipitate a solar reaction that would wipe out life on the planet. The incidents I've just mentioned were probably low-level power posturing or warnings between the factions that possess the technology.

'Which is disturbing enough. Even more disturbing from my

subjective, organic perspective is the capacity to affect the electromagnetic mind-body connection. People, again anywhere on the planet, can be killed instantly, rendered unconscious, or have their minds entrained to a hypnogogic trance and any mind or body change whatsoever provoked, including strong emotion, intense pain, painful thoughts, images, memory changes, altered perceptions, or personality changes. The Soviets poured millions into psychotronic research, most of which disappeared into the hands of U.S. secret services after the fall of the Iron Curtain.'

Jared shook his head. 'I'm sorry I asked.'

'It's good you did. This information needs to be passed around. Everybody should know this. Knowledge is power. The withholding and suppression of knowledge facilitates the maintenance of the power structures we see in government and business, and makes it possible for a tiny minority to control an ignorant majority. Our ignorance is their bliss.'

Jared sat in silence and tried to digest some of the data and its implications. He thought about the neural security program and wondered whether the protection it gave included against scalar neural manipulation. He wished Leon were around to ask.

'Earlier you asked me if I believed in life after death,' said Edward, 'why?'

Jared told him about the dream and then, without initially intending to, the neural security program, the remote viewing and his out of body experience.

'Fascinating,' said Edward, 'and exciting. Quite exciting. All my independently thinking life, I've considered that the answer has to be accessible to everyone regardless of external circumstances. If you've got to eat it, drink it, or plug into it, it's not the real thing, however much value that thing may have in pointing one in the right direction.

'By the sound of it, the security program as you call it, was directed at the pineal gland which is situated between the two hemispheres of the brain. The most mysterious and undocumented organ in the body. About all that modern medicine knows about it is that it's connected to circadian rhythm and melatonin secretion. Ancient traditions the world over consider it to be the seat of the soul, and some modern researchers have located it as the source of ESP activity.

'One of my biggest concerns over the effects of mobile phones and pulse-modulated microwaves on the body are their effects on this organ, especially as it's so close to the transmitting device, and especially as that device can be used to cook eggs.

'As regards the frequency that can't be beat, I would guess it was the Schumann Resonance, Earth's background base frequency. The planet behaves like an enormous electrical circuit. Schumann Resonances are electromagnetic waves that exist in the cavity between the ground and the ionosphere and relate to electrical activity in the atmosphere and sunspot activity.

'Humans are complex electrodynamic beings, sensitive to natural and artificial electromagnetic fields. In fact, research points out that human evolutionary biology developed within an electromagnetic environment created by the Schumann Resonance frequencies. Particularly relevant when you consider the change to the electromagnetic environment caused by the various communications networks, especially in the long-term. It seems possible to the point of likely that it's going to cause genetic mutations in the collective human gene pool.

'Schumann Resonance frequencies coincide with brain waves. Influences in that geomagnetic field affect rhythms like hormonal secretions. Instabilities in certain rhythms produce a huge range of behavioural changes. Epilepsy is a well-known example. Then there's obsessive-compulsive disorder, aggressive behaviour, anorexia and bulimia, and panic attack; not the comprehensive list. More positively, the alpha rhythms produced in light meditation fall within the window frequency of the Schumann Resonance. When we intentionally generate alpha waves, say through visualisation and breathing, we resonate with that Earth frequency and naturally feel refreshed, in tune and in synch.

'I would say that the neural security program as you call it was a way of artificially inducing entrainment to those frequencies. Based on what I've read about the correlation between frequency and ESP, I'd also say that the ESP phenomena you and Sol describe are as much a result of that entrainment as any training you've done.

'Another interesting thing is that the Schumann Resonances seem to have been steadily rising. Without the deliberate pollution of our electromagnetic environment by communication and military microwaves, and the manipulation of the atmosphere with frequency weapons like HAARP, the development of those and other, what would be considered, extra sensory abilities could be expected in the whole population of the planet in response to that rising frequency.

'As for out of body experiences, now they've been an interest of mine for years, ever since an incident whilst I was working in the Health Service. A patient died on the operating table, clinically dead, flat-lined for several minutes. The team, including myself, eventually managed to resuscitate him. The next day a nurse took me aside and said that the man had some sort of a story about floating above his body in the operating theatre.

'When I got a chance I went and had a chat with him. He maintained that he remembered counting down after the anesthetic and getting to about seven. Next thing he remembers is floating above the operating table looking down on himself, watching the four of us frantically applying ER. On the second shock the vision blacked out and the next thing he's waking up out of the anaesthetic.

'I suggested that they were images generated by the brain, a kind of a dream sequence inserted by way of explanation for what had happened. Transparent I know, but I was the doctor, no hoodoo nonsense on my ward, thank you. But then he reminded me that he'd been clinically dead, so how could his brain have known what was happening? I mumbled something along the lines of "hmm, very interesting" and was already filing it away as just one of those things, when he said there was another thing. That on top of my head there was a birthmark, a burgundy, vaguely hourglass-shaped birthmark.'

He lowered his tonsure and showed Jared.

'He was delighted when he saw it again. Confirmed it for me too and set off a personal investigation into the phenomena that's still ongoing.

'There are more than enough documented instances to conclusively state that consciousness isn't confined to the body. Separation usually happens when a person is knocked out of their body as a result of some severe trauma like surgery, car accident, or what have you. It can, however, be made to happen consciously using certain techniques, not unlike the ones you described doing for remote viewing.

'Etheric matter is the life force generated by all living things. Scientific studies done on the phenomena have involved putting the beds of dying people on very sensitive scales whilst hooked up to EEG and ECG monitors. In all cases, at the exact moment of death a sudden weight loss of approximately a quarter of an ounce takes place. This is caused by a large amount of etheric matter being transferred to the astral body at the moment of physical death.

'This is what happens in a near death experience where the body, believing that it's dying, transfers etheric energy to its astral body. It also happens during sleep when the etheric sheath surrounding the body is put on charge. It expands and opens in order to pull in energy. During the recharging process the astral body separates and tunes into the astral dimension where it can create and experience dreams. If the separation is done consciously, it's possible to take control over it. It then becomes an out of body projection, an astral projection or a lucid dream.'

'What's the difference?' Jared asked, suddenly very interested.

'In an out of body experience you're aware of things happening in the real world in real-time, and people will often report conversations, or birthmarks, on regaining consciousness. An astral projection is different from a real-time out of body experience. The astral body is projected into the astral dimension where things are quite different from the real world. Time is distorted and reality is fluid and changeable. Lucid dreaming is where you become consciously aware during a dream and can take control over the dream or convert it to an astral projection. All three involve the astral body separating from the physical and experiencing reality separately from physical reality.'

271

'But how do you consciously separate from the physical body?'

'Well, various methods have been developed, but they all focus on the same things. The four things you need to do are relax a hundred percent whilst staying awake, concentrate a hundred percent on what you're doing, have enough energy available, and pressure the astral body to separate. Together these four things will produce a projection. Of the four, concentration is the trickiest. Lack of concentration is the single most common cause of projection failure.'

Jared listened with quietly growing excitement as Edward described the mechanisms of consciously phasing out of the physical body; visualising pulling energy through the feet into the various non-physical energy centres in the body with imaginary hands, and exteriorising the point of consciousness, again though through tactile imagery, to exert dynamic pressure on the astral body.

He left the farmhouse with a book and a file of papers on the subject having already decided to try that night. His excitement didn't stop him from falling asleep five minutes into the relaxation exercises.

The next day he began as soon as he'd finished breakfast. The relaxation was easy, but his concentration was shit. Even the remote viewing consciousness-settling procedure didn't produce the effect it once had. He sat on the bed and spent an hour counting his breaths whilst keeping his mind empty, trying to make it past ten breaths before a thought intruded. The focus gradually drew him into the stillness he sought.

He lay back on the bed and visualised his hands inside his body, reaching down through his feet. He breathed in and visualised drawing energy up into his body, a watery, mercurial band that his tactile imagination felt as pliable in his hands. With each in-breath he pulled the energy in and up to the energy centre in his groin area, and held it there on the out-breath. He repeated the movement for a few minutes, and then moved up to the next.

Several times he became aware of his body tensing in response to the visualisation, each time letting the tension go and refocusing on the mental action. After he'd worked his way through the major energy centres a few times he stopped. It didn't seem to be working. Even in his relaxed state he felt a rising impatience and frustration. He reminded himself that the paper had described some people not feeling anything during the first few attempts, but the reminder didn't calm him.

Eventually he gave up and picked up the book Edward had given him. It was dog-eared and nearly fifty years old, and described processes and experiences quite different from the ones in the research paper. The sincerity of the author and the puzzling aspects of the locales he reported held his attention into the afternoon.

He spent the rest of the day practising focusing his awareness exclusively on the impressions from his five senses, repeatedly cutting short any mental chatter. He walked around the field practising conscious awareness, taking in the details of the environment, the texture, smell, and direction of the breeze, the variety of greens, the sound of his feet in the grass, his breathing. After spending so much time in his head the focus was difficult at first, but eventually he managed to maintain a Zen-like state of being in the moment for longer periods.

That night he lay on his back on the bed, illuminated by moonlight streaming through the window, tensing and relaxing his muscles from his feet up through his body. When he reached his shoulders and neck he focused on his breathing and the slow rise and fall of his diaphragm. He visualised himself getting heavier with each out breath, as if he were falling in slow motion. His body willingly relaxed and submitted to its own weight, heavier and heavier.

He cleared his throat and began breathing rhythmically and dynamically through his nose. His belly rose and fell like bellows. Random thoughts rattled around his head threatening his concentration. He focused his attention on the undulation of his breathing between his belly and chest.

On each out breath he visualised energy flowing through his hands into the various energy centres. At each position physical sensations told of something happening: gurgles from his solar

273

plexus, an ache in his chest, a constricted feeling in his throat that made him swallow, and a sucking sensation in the middle of his forehead. Focusing the energy on his crown produced sensations similar to the ones when Sol had loaded the security program.

His hands and feet began to tingle.

Repeating the sequence from his pubis a cold began spreading from his toes. It rose up through his feet and into his legs. He calmed the spike of fear by reminding himself that Edward had described the sensations, and refocused on his breathing. The tingling in his hands deepened to a chilblain-like itch and a sweat broke out all over his body, combining uncomfortably with the cold sensation. His hands began to buzz and light trembling feelings rippled through his legs and groin.

The sensations got stronger and it became harder to concentrate. Every time his concentration lapsed it felt as if the energy went off in the direction of the thought. He remembered Leon saying that energy followed thought. The pang the thought of Leon produced was enough to make him totally lose concentration. He pushed the feeling aside and refocused on his breathing.

Slowly the buzzing slowly spread to all over his body. He lay fizzing all over, visualising sinking with each out breath to achieve a mental falling sensation. His body grew really heavy, a sign of his brain waves changing from Beta to Alpha.

Remaining totally relaxed he reached up with his imaginary hands and began pulling, hand over hand, on an imaginary rope hanging from the ceiling above him. A thick, coarse invisible rope up which he, hand over imaginary hand, was pulling himself out.

His body began to feel huge and swollen like an egg, another symptom, this time of the energy body expanding and loosening.

A slightly dizzy feeling in his torso grew into a mild vertigo as he continued pulling. He noted the combination of actions that produced the feeling as a reference for the next time, and then poured his concentration into climbing the rope, body totally relaxed, imaginary hand over hand.

He grew heavier, and realised he couldn't move, as if he was

274

completely paralysed. Paralysed and pulsating. The fizzing sensation had developed into a pulsing throbbing.

The throbbing turned into a low buzz. He focused all his concentration on the feel of the rope and the pull on his imaginary arms.

With a feeling of coming loose and a deep, protracted zipping he rose into the air and hovered above his body. The speed of the exit was breathtaking.

He looked down at his body lying on the bed, remembering what Edward had said about being a non-physical point of consciousness floating in space, unaffected by gravity and other laws of physics. It was just like in the cottage, only much less confusing now he knew the mechanics.

He reached upward in his mind and shifted through the ceiling out into moonlight. Pristine detail textured in violet-white surrounded him, land and sky, like the inside of a vast globe. Glittering stars packed the black expanse of sky, fading into the corona around the moon. Surf sighed in the distance.

He moved down to the bottom of the field feeling like an owl in flight. The feeling of freedom was like a lung full of fresh air to a free diver. The feelings he'd had of being trapped seemed like a dim, distant memory. Chains fell away from his mind as he passed silently over the tops of the trees.

He didn't know where he was going. He thought about the beach. He'd intended going at some point but, locked into his hermitage and avoiding people, he'd not made it. With the thought he was there, with no perception of movement in between.

The incoming tide drew a luminous line along the beach. He moved closer and saw that the surf was actually glowing. Millions of tiny plankton illuminated the foaming surf with green phosphorescence. He'd heard about it but never seen it, and just stared at the nature magic swirling and frothing in front of him.

He woke to a feeling that something had changed and lay on his back looking at the ceiling trying to work out what it was. He felt light and clean as if he'd just recovered from a long illness. The lead weight that had filled his veins was gone. His head felt

275

clear and an excitement had replaced the fatalism and dread that had begun his days. Maybe the energy exercises had displaced the depression. He wasn't even disappointed that he'd fallen asleep again before managing a projection. The buoyant feeling was so welcome after weeks of bleak heaviness.

He threw back the covers and without dressing went outside. The sun was already high and the grass warm under his feet. From somewhere close by came the call of a cuckoo. He laughed out loud. A cuckoo!

He ran a short way across the field, feeling light enough to fly. Everything seemed brand new, as if it had just sprung into existence overnight. All the colours were sharp and shining.

He couldn't stop laughing. The muscles on his face felt strange stretched into a big grin. He walked back to the caravan whistling the Cuckoo Waltz, the laughter and smiles making the action difficult. Even the rooks seemed to be laughing and making noises of amazement. The ridiculous thought made him laugh even more.

He was some kind of manic depressive. One day suicidal, the next ecstatic. Talk about all over the place.

He decided to go to the beach. It was crap he'd not been there yet, but he'd not felt like it before. Now though he felt like he could run the length of a beach and back again. He went into the caravan and pulled on some clothes, then set off over the field. At the edge of the field next to the stile, he stopped and smelled a thick cluster of gorse flowers and discovered the source of the delicate coconut smell in the air. Close up the smell was surprisingly strong and exotic.

He jogged along the cliff path feeling like he had springs in his legs. He couldn't remember the last time he'd felt so energetic. The exercises had worked a treat. Maybe that had been all he needed, like a smog-bound cityite nipping into an oxygen bar.

Heather rustled dryly as he brushed past and from somewhere came a strong, rich smell like fermenting figs. He looked around, but couldn't see anything it could have been.

A light tingling in his head made him stop. It was a similar sensation to the one he'd had after having the neural algorithm loaded. He walked on, wondering if the bioenergy technique had somehow stimulated the entrainment again. Maybe it was a way of stimulating the pineal gland anyway.

He was pleased to see only two cars in the beach car park. He liked the prospect of the beach to himself. He took off his boots and socks and walked down onto the beach. Two sets of footprints led away to the left. In the distance out beyond the breakers were two surfers. The beach was his. He ran along the sand with his boots in his hands.

Another song floated into his head and he walked along singing 'oh what a beautiful morning'. He finished the chorus and realised he didn't know any of the other words, laughed, and sang the chorus again.

He ran down to the water and along the shallows, splashing water and soaking his trousers. He wondered if the plankton were still in the surf, made invisible by the sun, or if they only glowed in the dark.

The thought stopped him in his tracks. Plankton? Still in the surf? The incoming tide swirled around him, loosening the sand under his feet. There'd been phosphorescence in the surf, he could picture it clearly, the dark beach traced with green glowing surf.

The image telescoped back to include the rest of the night's excursion. He had done it! He'd just not remembered it on waking.

He walked out of the water, sat down and stared at the white horses prancing in the frothing waves. He'd really done it. A feeling of lightness seemed to almost lift him off the sand. He lay back with his hands behind his head, eyes closed, smiling.

What Leon had said about the potential impact on society of the knowledge that consciousness wasn't confined to the body made more sense now. While remote viewing questioned spatial relativity and gave access to information from any point across the time-space continuum, it was only a fragment of his consciousness that did the investigation, during which he was aware of his body sitting at the desk. Consciously phasing out of his body went beyond that, he was all there.

Light tingling traces swept up and down his body. He tried to picture the movement of energy between the positive and negative electrical poles of his cells. A connection between the visualisation and what Edward had said about quantum potential presented itself. All that was needed to harness unlimited energy from the vacuum was a dipole, a positive and a negative. The body was bipolar, like a battery. Vague hints at the potential involved in the speculation glimmered enticingly, but remained out of reach.

He sat up and stared at the waves without seeing them. Thoughts, memories, and images replicated their motion in his mind.

Eventually he got up and walked back along the beach, and up the steep cliff path. He reached the top of the cliff and jogged along the path, getting pleasure from the exertion. It was no wonder he'd got so twisted, having had such little exercise. He reached the point on the path where he'd left it a couple of days before and stopped, remembering, unwilling for some reason to go down to the spot. Belligerence overcame hesitation and he left the path and made his way down to the lichen-covered rock. The difference was noticeable. The rocks and heather were the same, as was the heaving ocean, but something had changed. He was no longer stuffed against the end of a cul de sac.

He looked around. Tiny red and green clumps of samphire nestled in crevices around him. Red clover waved gently in the breeze; a warm breeze earthy with bracken musk that rolled off the land. He looked at the rock platform. The pressure had gone, but not the thought. He still wanted out. Like Leon had said though, they had a mission. And now he had another way out. He could go anywhere. He could even go to the moon. The thought made him smile. He stared at the foam-trail membrane on the glistening blue for a long time before getting up and heading back.

The hedgerows were wound with bramble and honeysuckle. He picked the grape-like berries and walked through sweet scented clouds. Back at the caravan he sat on the grass in front of it. The euphoria he'd felt earlier had condensed into a firm core, and he felt connected and poised. He wondered again whether the continuing expanded state of mind was a psychological shift resulting from the projection process, or whether the bioenergy generating procedure had restimulated the pineal gland's entrainment to the Schumann Resonances. He definitely felt more in synch than he had in a long time.

Out over the heat-hazy fields a buzzard corkscrewed slowly up the valley. Two crows sped up toward it and commenced dive-bombing the gliding bird. The buzzard's easy flight faltered as they took turns flashing past. The buzzard mantled, showing its pale yellow belly and claws, as one of the crows stooped on it, and the crow veered off. Undeterred by the size and power of their opponent, the crows kept at it, diving and scolding. The buzzard mantled again and then climbed with slow wing flaps. The crows continued to harass it as it veered off and away over the fields.

Jared smiled at the analogy.

His shadow moved around him as he sat thinking. It wasn't enough to leave people to their own devices. They weren't being left to their own devices. They were being bonsai'd; forced into constricting, restricting roles, wrapped in restraints to produce a twisted, stunted caricature of what could have been. Victims to the creative destruction that fed capitalism and infected and systematically degraded everything.

Throughout the undeveloped world, people were suffering from famine and disease. They had no major industries, no plentiful electrical power, little education, and poor medical treatment. They were born without hope; lived in misery and poverty, and died without dignity. Meanwhile, the factories, cities, and enclaves of the 'developed and developing' worlds polluted the planet with toxic fumes and poisonous wastes, and spewed forth weaponry that was used to arm the poorer nations, for use in destroying themselves and their impoverished neighbours.

All this despite the fact that they had the knowledge and technical capability to green deserts, provide the world with free and clean energy, and maintain balanced health in everybody, indefinitely. Paradise on Earth. But the changes to society, the removal of control and the emergence of that old and forgotten vision of a life freed from illness and wage slavery was suppressed and resisted every step of the way. Even more seriously, things were being done to prevent what was a natural evolutionary development, one that looked like the next major evolutionary advancement of the species.

Contemplating possible courses of action brought up feelings of powerlessness. The rot was so deep, the system sewn up. What could be done? Clear some space, the man said, but where to start?

The struggle wasn't just one against the external enemies in industry and government; it was equally an internal struggle of people against themselves, against the degrading effects of the capitalist system on their consciousness. The enemy was ultimately nothing but the product of people's own alienated activity. The leaders were such a tiny minority that they'd have been overwhelmed had they not managed to con a large portion of the population into identifying with them, or at least into taking their system for granted, and especially into becoming divided against each other.

If there was hope, it lay with the people. They needed to be made aware of their individual and collective power. The State's power was based on people's belief in their powerlessness to oppose it. As Leon had repeatedly said, the real strength in a pyramid was in its base.

Eventually a full bladder and a desire to see Edward moved him.

He found him in the garden stood under a trellis that supported an unlikely pumpkin vine, pendulous beige pods hanging around his head like Chinese lanterns. Edward looked over from winding the loose tendrils into the frame.

'Top o' the morning. You look like you had a good nights sleep.'

They sat down and Jared told Edward of his experience.

'Excellent,' said Edward when he'd finished, 'excellent. Well, happy travels, as they say.'

'Actually, I've been thinking of moving my body out of here too.'

Edward nodded. 'Remembered what you were doing did you?'

'Not so much what I was doing as much as that I was doing something. Doing nothing is a luxury my conscience won't allow.'

'What will you do, if you don't mind my asking?'

'Not sure really. Back into the fray.'

'Now there's a destructive mentality at work when we follow that old 'us' and 'them' routine,' said Edward. 'That dreary old us resisting them manipulating us conflict pattern. We're all in this together, the aggressors and the victims, to use two other questionable labels.'

Jared smiled. He was going to miss Edward's conversational style.

'How do you mean?'

'We're all in this together because were all suffering the effects of an undeveloped brain. It seems to me that as a species our evolution has slowed down enormously. Really, human development ground to a halt a long time ago. It's an accepted fact that we use less than ten percent of our total brain capacity. I think that the limits we've reached are determined by the fact that we've only climbed a few steps on that brain capacity ladder as it were. In many ways we've come a long way, but we've still got a way to go yet. At present we're like children playing with matches, denied the full awareness of our destructive and creative potential by our undeveloped brains. I think the growing up that we need to do as a species involves consciously accessing that other percentage of the brain.

'I believe that if we were to access some of that other percentage, the developments would mostly be seen and felt on a perceptual level, and in areas currently labelled non-physical. If you think about it humans have just about exploited the known physical universe. In fact, most recent recognised scientific discoveries have been of a theoretical nature, and about dimensions or realities that are out of our five-sensed perception.

'Environmental destruction, war, control and manipulation of the majority by an elite few, all the ugliness and suffering can only happen because our minds haven't evolved, we haven't grown up, individually and collectively.

'Around a hundred years ago it was proved by the likes of Einstein, Heisenberg, and Schrödinger that the observer of an experiment, far from being separate from it as had previously been thought, was actually part of the equation and altered the outcome of that experiment by the very act of observing. Everybody, every experiment. That discovery proved that reality was far more malleable than previously believed, and forced scientists to rework their model of it. It also placed humans firmly in the position of participator rather than observer stood at a distance behind a glass screen. Emoto's research into the effect of our mind on the molecular structure of water demonstrates the principle beautifully. One of the biggest scientific discoveries of last century. Also possibly the most downplayed and deliberately obfuscated.

'I'll be the first to admit that the concept can be a hard one to get your head around. But the level of difficulty depends entirely on your social and educational background. Try it out on an Amazonian jungle tribesperson, or a Zen or Taoist monk, and they'll laughingly congratulate you on finally realising something that's been observed and known for thousands of years in those and other traditional cultures. In fact, by the middle of last century scientists were having to use some very Taoist language to describe the sub-atomic phenomena that they were observing.

'Despite that there's still Newtonian physics being taught in school. Teach children a fixed and immutable reality and that's how they'll see the world as they grow up, which incidentally predisposes them to a mechanistic, hierarchical social order too. If in the future they get the chance and encouragement to reassess what they've been taught, which doesn't happen very often, they'll find the concept of a fluid reality very difficult to grasp, and that's just the concept, never mind the practical applications which are truly mind boggling. But it's the practical applications that they want to keep us away from. 'They' being those that use science and religion as social control mechanisms, and 'we' being the billions of other participants in this planet Earth experiment.

'Now there's a parallel here between modern science and the church of the fifth century. The church at that time rewrote the bible in Latin, a dead language that nobody understood, and then had their reps feed the population the watered down and heavily biased version. Both deceptions are for the same reason, to keep people away from information that would weaken the power base of those groups that control societies.

'In fact, I'd go one step further and say that they're actually utilising the principle for their own ends by encouraging a mindset based on ignorance and fear, which in turn is affecting this earthly experiment and producing the current reality.'

'So what's your answer?'

'Well, going back to what I said a minute ago, as a participant in this experiment, or reality, I can no longer consider my role to be a passive one. My attention, my presence and my thoughts affect the course and the outcome of the experiment, or reality. Remember, scientific fact. So in addition to being careful with my thoughts, very careful, I daily concentrate on and release the thought of everyone of my co-adventurers achieving a hundred percent brain capacity and accessing their full mental, emotional and spiritual potential.'

Jared said nothing.

Edward chuckled. 'Told you it was a difficult concept. Mull it over a while though and see what you think.'

'I think it's going to take you a while to get through to the billions of participants in this planet Earth experience.'

'Jared, don't get trapped by pessimism concerning human nature that's not balanced by an optimism concerning our divine nature. All journeys start with a single step. And I've got more science on my side. Ever hear of the Hundredth Monkey Principle?'

Jared shook his head.

'Basically it was a phenomenon observed by anthropologists

studying a particular species of monkey that inhabited a group of islands off Japan. One or several of these monkeys on one of the islands developed a new behaviour, rinsing tubers in seawater to remove the sand. This particular group learned the action until a hundred monkeys had adopted it. At that point all the other monkeys on the other islands got it, simultaneously. The conclusion was reached that the monkeys had access to a shared consciousness that was accessible beyond perceived constraints of space and time.

'The phenomenon is similar to shoals of fish being able to move in so synchronised a manner that they look like a single organism. Some birds, starlings for instance, have the same ability. I've seen huge flocks do it and it's uncannily beautiful.

'You're right, we have to face facts, the majority won't get it like that. But I don't have to wait for the entire population to get it in a drawn out linear fashion. I'm counting on a high-frequency minority stimulating a quantum reaction, a critical mass that'll catalyse the rest.'

'Meanwhile the war still goes on, the Third World gets slowly strangled with manufactured diseases and debt –'

'Jared, do you think there are answers that'll solve those problems any quicker?'

'Quicker than sitting in your armchair imagining a perfect world? Maybe.'

Edward sighed. 'Put it like that and it does sound like a cop out. But I've thought about this long and hard. I've been around long enough to see many things tried and fail. I've balloted and picketed and petitioned, I've marched and had to deal with being attacked by armoured police. Lizzy still carries a scar from being trampled by a riot armour-clad horse. I'm convinced now though that most methods tried thus far won't work in the long term, even if they seem to achieve success in the short term.

'By it's very definition, and in practise, a revolution brings you right back where you started. Any act of resistance just puts energy into the process, you're not fighting it, you're feeding it. I can't emphasise this enough, Jared. For any act of resistance to be effective it must be creative.

'Yes, it's dark and heavy, but it's also quite exciting. Connect with that excitement and naturally its vibration will energise your response and creativity. We're cresting the wave. The findings of scientists and researchers in a variety of disciplines indicate that we as a species are going through a paradigm shift.'

Jared said nothing. He didn't know what to say.

'But tell me,' Edward resumed after a moments pause, "where would you have us go? You seem to know what you're fighting against, but what are you fighting for? People want new cars, plasma screens, tropical fruit, and short-haul suntans.'

'But that materialism and consumerism are demands that are being generated by the suppliers.'

'What would you offer in their place though, Jared? That's the problem, you see. One person's utopia is another's nightmare.'

'I'm not offering anything in its place.'

'Oh?'

'No. All I'm thinking about is clearing a space to make room for change.'

Edward nodded. 'Which is needed, but I believe that it's also important to have a goal in mind. One never changes things by fighting the existing reality. To change something, we have to build a new model that makes the existing one obsolete. The map to a new world is in our imagination.'

'Which is my point,' replied Jared. 'How can we know what the possibilities are when we're surrounded by walls? Tear down the walls and whole worlds open up.'

'Agreed,' said Edward. 'The highest walls are in our heads though, Jared.'

The last phrase stayed with him, standing out among all the other data provided by Edward. It resonated with his image of his telepathic inability, and his awareness of the effect of the frequency fence on people's mind.

But there was all the other data too. Edward happily loaded him up with books and papers on the subjects he'd mentioned. Jared read them voraciously, the action as much of a buzz as the information itself.

Leon was right; the answers were within reach. There was the technology and the resources to solve all the major world problems of famine, disease, radioactive waste, and the energy problem itself. Individuals the world over could release themselves from the corporate stranglehold. Maybe if they explained how the nightmare worked, everyone would wake up. Or at least enough people to catalyse that Hundredth Monkey-like critical mass.

People also needed to be made aware of themselves as independent from the physical body and able to perceive and communicate with personalities that didn't have one. The impact of that would definitely be huge, personally and culturally. People could investigate things and discover answers for themselves instead of having to settle for the biased doctrines, false conclusions, and lies provided by society. Along with the knowledge that could be obtained, the removal of the fundamental psychological influence of the fear of death would further challenge the control of the authoritarian structures in society. The moves to suppress the development were predictable. The closed doors of state and religion couldn't withstand such accessibility and transparency.

The mission was to find ways to unlock the chains and remove the blindfold.

10

Civil disobedience on grounds of conscience is an honourable tradition in this country and those who take part in it may in the end be vindicated by history.
— Lord Justice Hoffman

The working masses of men and women, they and they alone, are responsible for everything that takes place, the good things and the bad things. True enough, they suffer most from a war, but it is their apathy, craving for authority, etc, that is most responsible for making wars possible. It follows of necessity from this responsibility that the working masses of men and women, they and they alone, are capable of establishing lasting peace.
— Wilhelm Reich, *The Mass Psychology of Fascism*

Strike against war, for without you no battles can be fought!
— Helen Keller

The line of marchers stretched back filling the road and out of sight round a distant corner. Banners and flags carried bobbing by the demonstrators flapped in the wind. Trade union banners, unseen in convoy for decades, straddled sections of the column. Homemade banners and placards weaved side to side and jiggled up and down – Bring The Boys Back Home – Not In My Name, Not With My Taxes – All We Are Saying Is Give Peace a Chance.

The Nixon-era phrase was echoed by the lyrics of the song being sung by the marchers, singing hand in hand across time with the bed-bound visionaries, all sharing a common dream.

The chant took on power and flowed over Dan like a canon; the waves of sound from the marchers ahead out of phase with the crowd behind, each part of the song being sung at the same time, though each singer sang it from beginning to end. It was good to be out in the open, moving with a unified mass. The perfect antidote to the head down existence demanded by society's boot. Democracy in action. They were the 'demos', and they were acting, finally.

The momentum had developed quicker than he'd expected, but then his faith in people hadn't been that strong. The PLO theory had been right, even though Sol admitted that it was an act of faith. Given all the information, the consequences for continuing on the same path, the promise of the alternatives, and the awareness of their individual and collective political power, people had embraced that power and grasped the vision.

Maybe the lies had worn so thin that the realities had become too noticeable to ignore, like the facts about who was behind the deliberate meltdown of the global financial system and why, and the facts about the grossly immoral U.S.-led world war. Or maybe the disaster capitalist's overused Shock Doctrine strategy had been used too often and become too obvious.

Whatever the reason, the campaigns had struck a chord. Despite the initial mainstream media suppression of the localised campaigns and prosecutions, the information spread rapidly.

The Conscience Campaign held that it was the individual's right, according to international law, to withhold from military service for reasons of conscience. The logical extension of that was that those so guided by their conscience should be able to withhold or redirect that percentage of their taxes that were used for military purposes.

So unjust laws existed. What was a person to do, obey them just because they were laws, or try to change them whilst obeying them until they succeeded, or disobey them? Everything that Hitler did in Germany was "legal", and everything the Hungarian freedom fighters did was "illegal". It was "illegal" to aid and comfort a Jew in Hitler's Germany.

Until now people had waited, willingly believing the façade of debate, the assurances and lies. Now the thousands who had, in opinion, been opposed to the war and sat with their hands in their pockets saying that nothing could be done had been shown that something could. And those who in the past had postured ineffectively had found a sharpener for their pitchforks. All that had been needed was for someone to show them the way.

With the simplicity of a lever, the withdrawal from financial co-partnership with the warmongering State signalled the end of that travesty of human existence and an end to the crime of complicity. It didn't fall to the individual to right the wrongs generated by their unscrupulous leaders. All they had to do was no longer support them. If all the good and moral souls out there were to not pay that percentage of their tax that went to the military, less violence and innocent bloodshed would be committed than if they'd paid them. The facts were as simple as that.

But the facts went further than that, and the flames of the 'Lawful Rebellion' sweeping through the land had been fanned by the disclosure through the Freedom Movement of the truth about people's indisputable rights according to the Law of the Land, which formed the basis of the Magna Carta and the U.S Constitution. Increased awareness of the facts of how their money was used to fund wars and how the tax and monetary system itself was used to create debt slavery throughout the population and shoulder the private liabilities of the rich had led to millions of people lawfully refusing to support the activities of the Criminals in power by refusing to pay their taxes.

The minority was powerless while it conformed to the majority, but irresistible when it came together.

The motion had been slow at first, isolated people whose principles were their politics. The early members of the Conscience Campaign were predictably seized as scapegoats and prosecuted. The scare tactic had backfired though with a rapidly growing popular support, recognised as the defendants were as the mouth of the nation's slowly wakening conscience, and outrage that someone taking a peaceful stand for peaceful solutions should be prosecuted. If that recourse wasn't open to them, then where did they stand in the democracy?

The fact that international laws drawn up in Nuremberg and Geneva were being broken meant that citizens possessed the basic duty and right under international law to engage in acts of civil resistance in order to prevent, impede, thwart, or terminate ongoing criminal activities perpetrated in the conducting of foreign affairs policies and military operations supposed to relate to defence and counter-terrorism.

Those like the majority of the population whose tax was automatically deducted found other ways of taking a stand. Letter writing, petitions, and appeals through MP's were a waste of time and easily ignored by the nation leaders. Direct action was the only way; you just took the initiative and did it yourself.

No large business was able to function without the spontaneous organisation of its workers, compensating for manager's mistakes, reacting to unforeseen problems, and a hundred other voluntary adjustments that kept things moving. 'Work-to-Rule' actions in the workplace meant that workers withdrew that voluntary extension of their activities and did no more than strictly follow their specific job descriptions. More active workers engaged in go-slows and sabotage. General Strike actions had increased, outpacing the dragging heels of the union bosses, and walkouts and sit-ins spiralled as workers came out in support of other workers and in support of the campaigns.

Once the machine began to grind to a halt, the cogs themselves began to wonder about their function. This had the unexpected effect of waking people up from the spell cast over them by the programmers. Realisations about who was behind the scenes and their agendas, and the intentional affect media advertising and various products and processes were having on their minds and bodies moved people to reassess their habits and choices. Large-scale consumer boycotts of products and services provided by companies with links to the military grew once people made the connection between their wallet and war.

Actions not seen since the 60's and 70's developed in college and university campuses all over the country in response to a growing realisation among the younger generation that the prospects for their inheritance were getting darker and smaller left in the hands of menopausal psychopaths.

Repressed for so many years, distracted with seductive and hypnotic media conditioning, students had rediscovered their political voice. It was their world too. Practical solutions were discussed at length in lively, emotional meetings where Marxist, Surrealist, Situationist, and Zapatista theory and history were brought out and aired. More than anyone, young people felt the disillusionment of the voting process. Government was so far away and concepts made too complex to consider except as an isolated curricular module. Now their investigations and actions put them in touch with sincere depths and creative, inspiring visions, which in turn resulted in some creative and inspiring action.

Typically, numerous potential abuses or disasters were evoked at the suggestion of a nonhierarchical society. People who accepted a system that condemned millions to death every year in wars and famines, and millions of others to prison and torture, suddenly let their imagination and their indignation run wild at the thought that in a self-managed society there might be some abuses, some violence or coercion or injustice, or even merely some temporary inconvenience.

Whatever the alternative, it was generally agreed that whichever system replaced the one they had, it didn't have to solve all the problems. It only had to deal with them better than the present system, which wasn't a very tall order. Also agreed was that the youth that refused military service were the pioneers of a warless world.

Peace Aid had been a natural, if unanticipated, sequence of events. The music and arts events pooled funds and distributed them into legal defence funds and financial support schemes for striking workers. Activities were creative, almost carnival, as people all over the country responded to the need for action in the call from their hearts. Peace Aid in the Park, a series of concerts and festival-style performances, catalysed a response when a bevy of mainstream music artists, emboldened by the strength of public feeling, rushed to show that they too cared and didn't want to be part of the slaughter.

The strike had been largely peaceful. Frictions between striker and scab couldn't breed in a climate of conscience and integrity. Violence was not only undesirable in itself, it generated panic and thus manipulability, and promoted militaristic, hierarchical organisation. Non-violence entailed more open and democratic organisation, and tended to foster the composure and compassion needed to break the cycle of hatred. An individual's choice to continue supporting the carnage was their right. They had to live with themselves.

Nearly ninety percent of the population had family consumed by the war. In that situation doubts were pushed into the background. You lived with the daily prayer that the stiff Ministry of Defence notification with its regrets and commiseration wouldn't fall on the mat, that they would come back alive. You had to believe it and believe in it. The moment doubts crept in about your loved ones coming back alive, or about the validity of the venture itself, they had to be shut out immediately, like a cartoon character building a wall in seconds; half-baked justifications and conformity the bricks and mortar in the wall. Receiving a flag-draped coffin or a shattered casualty sometimes resulted in cracks in the wall, but it rarely fell down. And no thought was ever given to the victims of their loved one's actions. The 'bring the boys back home' message of the campaign resonated with more than a few.

At some point the balance of public opinion had shifted. These weren't just issues of economics or politics, or any other grouping used to separate people from each other. Conscience and the desire and need for freedom were things everybody shared. Actions of conscience enlarged the world and links were made with struggles in other countries. Without all the constructed ideological and religious differences, people were the same, and setting aside the differences people had come together. They had a common enemy in what were ultimately the same financial and industrial groups.

But the beast was too big to confront head on. They had to lay siege to it, deprive it of oxygen, starve it of what it was taking from them.

The head of the march curved around the corner onto the long approach to the square. Dan felt a wave of uncertainty from the front at the same moment the chant faltered. Turning the corner himself, he saw the reason. At the far end of the road, stretching its width, the statues of the square rising behind it, was a steel barrier. Ranked behind it, filling one side of the street, waited double rows of riot vans. It looked like the march wasn't going to be allowed in the square.

He mentally slapped himself. What was he thinking, 'allowed' in the square? It was their right. Freedom of Assembly, Article 11. It was their city; they could assemble where they wanted.

Between the barrier and the march the pavements and roads were empty. The road signs on the exposed expanse of tarmac gave the impression of a runway.

Apprehension trembled in his guts.

The lead vehicle, an armoured personnel carrier redecorated in pink camouflage, sounded a blast of its air horn and the crowd responded with a single, cheering roar. The speakers atop the truck cut through the following lull with the voice of the dreamer himself, undimmed by time; determination, vision and purpose as fresh as the day when belief had shone like the sun on the seed of hope in people's heart. The voice of the crowd lifted in song. The sound filled the space between the buildings and flowed ahead of the chanting, clapping throng. Dan tilted his head back and sang louder.

The column advanced down the road. Apart from three or four regular uniformed police at the edges of the barrier, there were no others in sight. The show of force was ominous by its absence. Dan counted eighteen vans waiting, black grills poised in pre-joust position. He tried to imagine what the march looked like to the waiting occupants watching through the windows; the human tide flowing in lava-like slow motion down the road toward them, their single voice like a sonic snowplough. Did their guts cramp with fear and apprehension? Tooled up and organised they might have been, but they were still a handful compared to what they faced.

Realism prevailed and enlarged the equation with unseen ranks waiting in the wings. Highly strung choreographed players in game plans drawn up by crowd control experts who devised methods for their masters, thinking themselves strategists against the civilian enemy without realising that they too were

293

controlled; minds infected with venom that had already begun the process of digestion, sucking the empathy and humanity out of their marrow, leaving them empty and brittle.

Well, the people had their strategies too, even if they didn't have the organisation of the civil hive mind. History had seen this drama played out again and again. The faces had changed, but the struggle was the same.

Riot police began spilling out of the vans. The area behind the barrier filled with black, shiny, armour-clad TETRA troops. Sunlight reflected off the jointed carapaces.

Passing side streets about five hundred yards away from the barrier, Dan spied serried lines of riot vans and began to regret his decision not to carry a helmet. He still thought it attracted harsher treatment from the men in black, but it would have been reassuring to have had one when things got hectic, which it looked like things were going to.

The Ya Basta and Womble crews at the front of the march had the right idea. Sections of inflated inner tube stuck together, painted white, worn over white overalls was their protection. The sausage-shaped, party balloon-ridiculousness removed the psychologically hardcore visual aspect of protective clothing like leather jackets and helmets, but still provided effective, air-cushioned protection.

Riot police began pouring around the sides of the barrier and formed lines of anonymous shields and batons in front of it. The scene reminded Dan of pictures of Roman legion phalanxes.

This was a peaceful march though. Conscientious citizens making their voice heard. Although it wasn't just their voice that was being heard. If that had been the case then the demonstration would have been allowed. The government could accommodate a million plus people marching, waving placards and letting off steam, smug with the knowledge that when the day was done the placard wavers would return to their homes and reposition themselves in front of their televisions, and then go back to work, self-satisfied and self-deluded. The wheels kept turning and the money kept rolling in.

Now though the money wasn't rolling in and the once well

greased wheels had begun to seize up. Furious at the people's disobedience, and the drying up of their war funds, government's big stick had come down.

The pink camo' truck stopped just short of the shield-line.

Dan had a fleeting image of the scene from above where doubtless surveillance drone planes circled; the multicoloured wave fringed with the white buffer zone of the Ya Basta and Womble crews, the pink truck, and the deep flange of black, like a leather strap that had no intention of spoiling the child.

He tried to remember the answer to the conundrum what happened when an irresistible force met an immovable object.

Wave upon wave of voices flowed out from the standing crowd, all but drowning out the metallic voice of a police loudspeaker.

'THIS IS AN ILLEGAL ASSEMBLY. DISPERSE OR OFFICERS WILL BE SENT AMONG YOU TO MAKE ARRESTS.'

The chanting changed to booing.

'…SENT AMONG YOU TO MAKE ARRESTS.'

The loudspeaker on the pink truck crackled into life with a brief whine of feedback.

'This is a peaceful gathering, our right as expressed by the European Convention. Whoever acts against that, acts against international law. And it's lawbreakers that have put you police between our destination and us. They've set you on us because we've chosen not to cooperate with them. We won't do as we're told just because we're told, especially if it goes against our humanity. We're not going to let them take our humanity. And you have the same choice here today. Don't let them take your humanity. It's the simplest thing in the world to do, just say no.'

The line crept forward pushed by the pressure of the numbers packing the street.

'There's thousands and thousands of us and we are going to gather peacefully in the square. Question is, are you going to stand aside, or do we have to climb over you. Of course there's a third option, you can join us. After all, we're on the same side. This isn't politics, this is humanity. All we're saying is give

295

peace a chance.'

The crowd cheered.

CS gas canisters arced through the air spitting sparks and gouting white clouds of gas. They hit the road beside the truck and skittered toward the marchers. Figures ran forward, snatched them up and threw them back. More canisters rattled in, were picked up and thrown back. Clouds of gas hung in the air, slow to disperse. People covered their faces with clothing, and already many were coughing and choking, tears streaming down their faces.

The lines of riot cops ran forward, shields and batons raised. The white arm-linked buffer met the black line and bent their heads against the attack. Batons bounced off the air-cushioned marchers. The line broke quickly and pandemonium broke out. People were knocked to the ground and beaten repeatedly, batons rising and falling like some mediaeval threshing device. Those going to their aid were cudgelled and dragged by hair, arms, or legs as the police "moved among them and made arrests".

There was nowhere to go but forward. Dan moved to the edge of the crowd to avoid being trapped in the middle. From behind him came sudden screaming and shouting. People fell over each other and scrambled out of the way to avoid being run over as a water cannon shot out of a side street.

A thigh-thick jet of water hit a woman in the chest, sending her tumbling backward head over heels. The water cannon's tyres screeched as it drove in a wide circle, blasting people off their feet. It continued it's circling, hosing the area in front of the barrier free of people. People ran for shelter wherever they could find it, behind phone boxes or bus shelters, or in shop doorways. A knot of people sheltered behind the pink personnel pod.

The water cannon turned and retreated. More riot police rushed out of the side street with batons raised. Hissing canisters fell into the crowd itself. The head of the march broke up as people tried to escape the gas and the baton charges.

Two cops dragged a frantically struggling youth back toward the barrier. One of the cops had a gloved hand clamped over the youth's nose and mouth. Somebody grabbed the youth's arm and was slammed in the face with a shield.

The loudspeaker on the pink personnel pod cut through the shouts and screaming.

'This is a peaceful gathering. You police, we're the people you're sworn to protect. Don't let the parliamentary criminals use you.'

Riot cops surrounded the pod and began pulling at the doors and pounding the windows with their batons. The glass was obviously toughened and remained unmarked. A face appeared at a side window and flashed a peace sign. A microphone went up to his mouth.

'Forward, united, we'll never be defeated!'

The crowd caught the chant, and the chant caught the crowd. The frontline solidified and moved forward.

The riot police regrouped into lines and began banging their batons against the backs of their shields.

The reply to the cohesion of the chanting crowd, for that it obviously was, seemed to Dan a crude and sad gesture. The speaker was right; it was about humanity. Faced with a vocalised community and the basic harmonies of united voices, the sound of batons bashing against plastic seemed Neanderthal and lacking in humanity.

Again the police charged and again from the sides, nipping off the head of the snake. The street filled with coughing, retching, and bleeding people, supporting each other or being supported.

Dan saw two cops dragging a man off by his legs. The man's head and face bounced on the concrete as he flailed around trying to grab onto something. Without thinking Dan shoved his way through the crowd and ran after them. He caught up and grabbed the man's arm. Immediately the man gripped Dan's arm and began pulling desperately. His body lifted off the ground and Dan staggered with the combined weight and pull of three people.

One of the cops let go and took a step toward Dan, raising his baton.

Dan pulled back in an effort to stand upright against the weight that was pulling him forward and down, trying unsuccessfully to prise his arm out of the man's grip to ward off the blow.

A figure in white shouldered past him and took the falling baton on a tube-strapped arm. Another figure came round the other side and pushed against the cop still holding a leg. The cop dropped the leg and brought his baton round.

Dan helped the man scramble to his feet. His face was scraped raw in patches and blood ran from gashes above his eyes and a ripped ear. He clapped Dan's shoulder.

The riot cops hacked at the marshmallow men as they backed away, their mission accomplished.

'Forward, united, we'll never be defeated!' bellowed the liberated man through cupped hands.

Dan looked back along the choked thoroughfare. It seemed ludicrous that they could be stopped. Corralled like that though, the police only had to take on the front lines of marchers. There had to be some way to get past the barrier. Even if they managed to climb over it though, the waiting cops would pick them off easily. Maybe Sol had been right. There was no point. The police were just too good at manipulating crowds.

The severed neck of the snake grew another head. The front lines linked arms and moved forward, singing. Again the police responded with baton charges from the front and sides.

A man in a blue boiler suit waving a placard with the words War Is Peace took on two baton-wielding cops with such virtuoso two-handed 'swordsmanship' that people stopped and stared.

The most striking thing was the fact that the man was clearly not trying to hurt the cops. They were so armoured that even had he tried he would have been unable to. Instead as well as successfully and stylishly dodging and parrying their blows, the man was providing an exhibition of making mock tapping contact at various armoured points. The performance ended abruptly with two more cops joining in and the four descending en masse. After clubbing him to the floor they carried him off, one on each arm and leg. Another marcher retrieved the fallen placard and took up the chant.

The air-horn of the pink personnel pod trumpeted, its wheels spun and it leapt forward and smashed into the barrier. It backed up again. Riot police rushed to make lines in front of it. The pod revved its engines, but didn't move.

The front lines of the column ran forward, flowing either side of the pod and filled the gap in between, ten or twenty deep to the police two. There was a commotion in the centre of the line parallel with the pod as marchers at that point engaged the police. The rest of the lines stood still. Without room to manoeuvre or reinforce the police line broke in the middle. Immediately a shout went up and a wedge surged into the gap. People linked arms and began forcing their way outward. More marchers ran into the gap and joined the lines.

An avenue opened in front of the pod. It let out a blast of its air horn and screeched forward. It hit the barrier with a high-pitched smash and the rear end went up in the air. The crowd cheered. The pod screeched back and then forward again. The barrier buckled, but held.

The riot police looking on beyond the lines of marchers suddenly retreated behind the barrier and lined up. The pod backed up further than before and then screeched forward again. It hit the barrier and again the rear end rose. It continued its momentum and burst through the overlapped barrier with a rending shriek. The police line scattered.

A roaring cheer went up from the crowd and the column surged forward like water breeching a dam. Dan dived into the crowd and hurried past the twisted barriers and staring police. The pod's speakers crackled into life, and thousands of voices filled the air as the march followed it.

Dan walked backward, watching the riot cops withdraw back into the vans, some shoving their way through the march to reach them.

The column reached the square. The slow, steady chant grew in strength and intensity as more and more people filed in.

Dan climbed onto the plinth of a statue of a soldier. An uneasy feeling foreshadowed the sense of achievement at having reached the square. Although there was nothing they could have done, the police had given way. Control had been wrested out of the hands of the State. Would it just stand back, or would it feel forced to reassert its authority?

He scanned the square in an attempt to estimate numbers. The crowd heaved and swirled like a shifting, multicoloured mosaic, elementary particles unpredictable beyond anything but possibilities and probabilities. He gave up counting and wondered instead on the financial impact of the ongoing collective action on the State's coffers. If just half the people in the march were withholding the percentage of their taxes that funded the war, that was a sizeable amount of money. The government was going to have to do something, that was for sure.

He thought about Jared and wondered where he was. Several times that day he'd had the sensation that Jared was next to him, or thinking about him. He wondered if he'd ever see him again. It didn't seem likely. Jared had grown more out of reach than ever. Initially he'd had put the distance between them down to Jared joining the PLO. Now though he suspected otherwise. What had happened to Jared had changed him. Violence followed him; it's mark on him and in him. It seemed likely that, having taken up armed resistance, his death would be violent too.

There was a whine of feedback from the PA set up around the pink personnel pod. The crowd cheered. A woman on top of the pod took the microphone.

'Hello everybody!'

The crowd cheered some more.

'Anyone needing medical attention will find paramedics set up underneath the green helium balloons to the left of here, and a meeting place is over there under the red balloons.

'According to the authorities this is an illegal demonstration. But this isn't a demonstration. We've already demonstrated how we will no longer be part of the dehumanisation of our species. We've demonstrated that we'll no longer be manipulated by their media, nor moved by their lies, and today we've shown that neither will we be intimidated by their heavy-handed police.'

The crowd cheered and whistled.

300

'We're here to show our support for life and liberty, and our opposition to tyranny and oppression. If this is a demonstration, it's a demonstration of the community that we're all part of. A sane, high-principled, and growing community. All over the country marches like this are taking place. The government has to listen to us. Their insane craving for power and control may have silenced their consciences, but we are the conscience of the nation and we will be heard!'

The crowd cheered wildly.

'We speak for those whose land is being laid waste, whose homes are being destroyed, whose culture is being subverted. We speak as citizens of the world, for the world as it stands aghast at the path we've taken. We must find new ways to speak for peace and justice. Somehow this madness must cease. War is not the answer. We still have a choice today, nonviolent coexistence or violent co-annihilation.'

Microphone in hand, Dylan spoke to the camera.

'Despite clashes with the police, marchers are now gathered in the square. We're waiting for official attendance figures from both organisers and police, but by the looks of it the numbers here today exceed that of any demonstration in this country to date, which shows the extent of what has become a momentous movement for social change.'

The camerawoman lowered the camera and Dylan dropped his roving reporter face.

'Let's give it twenty minutes. I could do with sitting down.'

He sat on the wall and sighed with the instant relief in his back and legs. He'd walked further than he had in years. He chided himself for slothfulness and gave the cigarette he'd just pulled out a glum and resigned pause before lighting it. Maybe it was time to stop that too. Throw it on the wagon with all the other stuff he'd hauled up there, the job, the booze, the phone, everything that didn't fit his recently revised code of conduct. If it didn't make sense, bin it and replace it with something that did. Live life as if there were a point to it other than just lining somebody else's pockets and keeping your head above water.

And as Alex had pointed out, one of the biggest tobacco companies was a subsidiary of one of the biggest war-profiteers, who'd constructed the concentration camp prisons that were being used to silence opposition.

Alex's death had really shaken him up and jerked him out of a rut. That and what they'd talked about. Trawling the Internet to look into what Alex had said had been a waste of time. Traffic no longer moved unimpeded along the Information Superhighway, comprised as it now was of barricades, tollbooths, slip roads that led to dead ends, choke points, and security checks. Doing the searches he'd also been uncomfortably aware of the fact and details of his searches being recorded.

It took cashing in an IOU from a private investigator in 'The Circuit', a shadowy network of former MI5, Special Branch, Military Intelligence officers, and journalists in the private investigation and security business, to access the data. The obese slug of a man had been amused by Dylan's data requirements, after he'd kept him waiting for nearly an hour. Dylan knew his line of work tended more toward physical and technological surveillance, and commercial intelligence, but he had connections. He also knew that, despite the man's arrogance, most of the work was sub-contracted out to cutting edge geeks who knew the routes, codes and jargon to be able to rapidly access and extract a substantial dossier of personal information on anyone. Virtually any data held in a system was accessible including, within forty-eight hours, everything that Dylan had listed.

Page after page of research and investigations prised the lid off his denial and ignorance and opened his eyes to a totally different world. A world whose populations and resources were pieces in a game of world domination. The phrase 'full spectrum dominance' took on a whole new dimension.

His priorities had shifted, habits questioned and discarded. Triviality fell away or was avoided as a waste of valuable time and space. Leaving it until mañana was a blind bend to tragedy, and seizing the day the best generalised strategy. He'd bid a fond fuck you to Fleet Street and taken on three days a week in a small press. After twenty-years in the media environment it was the devil he knew and it left time for independent investigative reporting for alternative media outlets, which fed the incurable reporter in him. Knowledge was power. The suppression of information was essential to those groups that had control agendas. Working to make information public through alternative media outlets was a way of giving back, a way of being part of the solution rather than part of the problem.

Although he'd taken what Alex had said on board, he hadn't fully appreciated the drain on his soul until he'd unhooked from the machine. He got less money from the new job, a lot less, but he had more life and energy to enjoy it, and he liked himself more; he could look at himself in the mirror. Accommodating the reduction in income had stimulated an appreciation of the simpler things in life.

He thought of Alex and how his eyes had lit up when he'd talked about giving something back. His death just when he'd found a real way of living was one of life's cruel jokes.

It was obvious to Dylan that he hadn't taken his own life, even before he'd made enquiries. What he'd found out though confirmed what he already instinctively knew.

There had been more than a therapeutic dose of painkillers in his blood but, according to the forensic toxicologist, nowhere near enough to kill him. According to blood tests the amount in his blood was a quarter to a third of what was normally a fatal amount.

There was nothing he could do about it though. The case was closed. And as for picking up the baton and finishing the race as the bloke at the soup van had described it, there was nothing politically sensitive among the effects delivered to his wife. No baton, race over.

His decision to really live his life was as much out of respect for Alex's sacrifice as gratitude for the gift Alex had given him.

***

Jared watched the dry-stone walls and green expanse of the moor out of the car window. Dour grey farms dotted the landscape surrounded by sheep. Once he would have enjoyed the scene, but the knowledge of what was going on behind the scenes robbed him of even that small pleasure. Despite appearances, things were anything but idyllic.

Doing something felt good though. Even though he'd been busy since leaving Edward's, it had been cerebral work. Cooped up in a room in a safehouse, poring over books and technical papers as if he was cramming for an exam. This was possibly the biggest test of his life though, and so much more depended on it than an academic pass or fail.

Day after day photoreading and processing more data than he'd ever done. Eventually he'd reached a point where his check rate hovered around ninety five percent and he could talk the talk of an experienced systems technician. Both he and Sol spent hours creating and solving complex technical problems for each other as part of the training. It had been like learning a new language and a new world had opened up to him, an unimaginable world of cutting edge microprocessing and computing.

The founder of Intel, Gordon Moore, predicted that microprocessors would double in complexity every two years. For over forty years since that statement the number of electronic devices in a microprocessor had doubled every eighteen months to a point where single DSP chips could perform around ten billion operations a second. Clustered DSP's working in parallel, fed data through solid-state disk technology, could perform around two hundred billion operations a second. Clustering the clusters produced performances in the range of one terra flop, one trillion floating point operations a second.

Moore's Law, as it was known, had reached a limit based on the speed and miniaturisation limits of silicone. The search for an alternative to silicone had 'naturally' focused on the most complex computer known, the human brain. DNA processed data at speeds well in excess of the world's fastest silicone-based supercomputer and stored much more information in a much smaller space. A pound of DNA had more information storage capability than all the electronic computers ever built.

Brain tissue cultured on semiconductors allowed incredible sensory transistor density, around twenty thousand transistors to a square millimetre, and speeds of over three hundred trillion operations per second. Because DNA worked in parallel it provided the best model for topic analysis and fuzzy logic computation methods needed by facilities that processed large volumes of data. Hybrid systems had developed, silicone-based with DNA co-processors.

He turned to Sol who was driving.

'An alternative just occurred to me that might have got this done quicker.'

'Go on then,' said Sol without looking away from the road.

'Extrapolate and record the frequency for necrotising fasciitis or some other tissue wasting disease, digitise it and transmit it on a known compromised channel. The signals get picked up and filtered through the system and infect the DNA interface on the biochips.'

Sol was silent for a moment and then raised his eyebrows.

'Sounds far out, but no further out than some of the stuff we've been reading. You should've thought about it before, you might have saved us a trip.'

'No,' said Jared, 'this way was meant to be.'

Around the time he'd re-established contact with Sol, contact had been made through the underground network with a U.S. SIGINT specialist sympathetic to the cause. Sympathetic wasn't an accurate description though, the man was on a revenge mission.

During his third deployment, the man's wife had given birth to their first child. The baby was born with severe congenital defects: fused fingers, no eyes, and missing organs. Mercifully it only lived a short time. Compassionate leave was denied the man on the grounds of maintaining his unit's combat readiness.

A month later he lost both legs in an IED explosion. He was shipped out and sent home a war hero. Already traumatised by the birth and death of her child, the man's wife couldn't deal with his injuries as well and committed suicide less than a week later. The man had needed heavy sedation, restraint, and twenty-four hour care to prevent him killing himself.

After a period he reapplied for military service and literally begged the army to take him back. A number of his former officers lobbied on his behalf and succeeded in having him reassigned to the Signals Intelligence Corps. As everybody said, including the man himself, even without legs he could still work a computer and, after what had happened, the army was the only thing left of his former life.

Unspoken, but carried like a gelignite vest, was his promise to himself to make the military pay for ruining the lives of him and his family, a promise that was his sole reason for living. And now Jared and Sol had become agents of that promise. They were his legs and they were going to kick ass.

Jared wasn't comfortable being unarmed. He knew there was no way they could have done it armed, but he still felt naked. Which made what they were doing good in more ways than one. Within a really short time he'd become psychologically dependent on a gun. He understood why he'd adopted the strategy, but he also saw that in a way he was holding onto the possibility of needing it and in doing so potentially generating situations where he would.

But guns, like war, were backward, not the way forward. A sad yesterday, not a bright tomorrow. What they were doing represented the way forward, using their intellect, imagination and integrity. Walking the talk. Even if it meant their death, the energy would propagate out. Exactly what it would stimulate was anybody's guess, but it was more likely to be creative than destructive. The end didn't justify the means; the means coloured and influenced the end in ways both obvious and subtle. As Edward had pointed out, it was scientific fact.

Also fact was that he wasn't his body. Death was okay. A bit of a drama maybe, but a door out of there. He wouldn't be sad to leave, drop his genetic spacesuit and move on to something different.

They passed the service station where, after completing the

mission, they were to rendezvous with Nicole. He felt a thrill of nervous excitement at the prospect of seeing her again. She'd dropped out soon after what he'd come to think of as Bloody Wednesday and his disappointment had bordered on frustration. Memories of the feel of her lips and hard body against his in the tunnel had constantly distracted him while he was studying.

Shapes appearing on the horizon pulled him from his reverie.

The Boyswith Mound base was a five hundred and sixty acre blot on the landscape. The moor looked afflicted with a weird skin disease; a localised eruption of boils on the site of an infection. Radomes, huge white balls, grouped around the site with HFDF aerial collections and arrays of satellite dishes, surrounding blocks that housed the innards of the machine, including the two thousand staff that lived and worked in social and diplomatic isolation; beyond the reach of investigation or legislation, and answerable to no one but their transatlantic handlers.

It was the biggest spy base in the world, one of several hubs in a vast network of hundreds of nexus that stretched around the planet and out into space. Designed and coordinated by the U.S. National Security Agency, one of five major players in the global surveillance business, along with Britain's GCHQ, New Zealand's GCSB, Canada's CSE, and Australia's DSD. Lesser players included Germany, Denmark, Norway, Turkey, Japan, and China.

A multi-armed beast conceived long ago and spawned during WWII, the largest and most important form of wartime intelligence, signals intelligence. Once the European war theatre bowl ran dry it had turned its jaws on the communist states. Forty years of goaded paranoia fattened its tentacles and stretched them further and deeper before that trough too dried up. So, casting around its influence, it widened its scope again and became a reassuring weapon in the War on Terror.

One disturbing thing about that was that where once war had been defined as conflict between nations, now, with no Berlin or Tokyo to liberate and no possible victory, it had become a sustained, open-ended and never-ending form of 'business as usual'. And healthy business it was too, making year on year growth and profit, continually developing its market and widening operations into all economic, corporate, and individual areas. Allegedly protecting the world from organised crime, terrorists, drug traffickers and arms dealers, the reality behind the sound-bite bullshit was that the justifications were running the show.

In secrecy the beast called Echelon bloated like fungus in the dark, its mycelium silently invading, penetrating every cellular and satellite nook and fibre-optic cranny. Top-secret geosynchronous satellites and a network of land-based intercept stations and intelligence ships meant that precious few signals escaped its electronic net. Like a giant electronic vacuum cleaner it sucked everything in.

At Boyswith those signals were then fed through a complex of around thirty receiving stations, each with its own Vax or Cray supercomputer system, and filtered at inconceivable speeds by advanced voice and optical character recognition software for keywords or code words from constantly updated 'dictionaries'. Any recognised was flagged as data for further analysis. The captured conversations, documents or images were then sent to the respective UKUSA agencies that requested the intercepts. Intercepts ranged from political to commercial and personal. The extreme processing capacity meant that the filtration range was extensive and inescapably thorough. Which was invasive and intrusive enough. But receiving wasn't their only activity. Here an even darker menace lurked. The UK link in the fence.

A soldier stepped out of the booth as they pulled up to the gates.

Sol lowered the window. 'Morning.' He handed the authorisation papers over.

'Could I have your ID too please, sir,' said the guard.

Sol passed the ID cards over.

The soldier looked at the cards and then at Jared and Sol, and then walked back to the booth and handed the papers to someone else. He stood looking at the car through the tinted window.

Okay Specialist, thought Jared looking at the booth, this is for the daughter you'll never hold and the dance you'll never have.

The soldier came back out of the booth and walked to the car.

'Your laminates and papers, sir. The laminates will need to be worn from here on in. Proceed and left at the second intersection.'

Sol took the papers. 'Thanks, have a nice day.'

'Thank you, sir, you have a nice day too.'

The barrier rose and they drove through.

'Thank you, sir, you have a nice day too,' mimicked Jared after they'd gone a little way. His laughter sounded strained, and did nothing to ease his tension.

He looked around at the approaching complex. Closer up the radomes looked even more like giant spoor; squat fat bases and huge bulbous bodies latticed in geodesic diamonds. They drove past a forest of huffduff aerials and satellite dishes. The roads were empty and the only people in sight were solitary figures near buildings.

Jared's stomach clenched with the thought of going inside. The thought of being enclosed and restricted made him feel trapped. As if he wasn't already in the lion's den. He pulled at the collar of his shirt. Sol reached over, pushed his hand away and wagged one finger from side to side.

'You're right,' said Jared. 'I've just got to keep my eye on that bonus carrot they're dangling to get me to fix their incompetent mess. Can't wait for the weekend.'

The office worker role-play training had included emphasis on how body language had to communicate familiarity with the unfamiliar clothes. It also included current topics mentioned in various IT magazines both as a way of strengthening their role and as a cover for the surveillance that could be expected in that environment. Given the nature of the facility, it was likely that the staff were under constant audio-visual surveillance. Thieves trusted no one.

They pulled into a car park in front of a three-storey block. There was a palpable background hum in the air as they walked toward the building. The bright concrete reflected radiant heat.

'Fifteen percent?'

The question took Jared by surprise. He'd been trying to visualise the inside of the building and anticipate what they were going to meet, and forgotten about the role-play.

'Yeah,' he replied, 'but only if I signed a two year contract with more clauses than Sylvester the cat.'

A laser mounted above the tinted glass doors scanned the laminates around their necks and the doors slid open. A refrigerated air-conditioned chill wrapped around Jared and slipped menthol-like into his lungs. The reception was airport lounge style, complete with check-in desk and walk-through scanner. They approached the desk.

'Morning sir, welcome to Magistrand.'

Cold sweat trickled down Jared's sides as the guard checked their authorisation on the computer. He tried to keep his breathing slow and easy and a relaxed semi-smile on his face.

The guard passed the papers back and motioned to the waiting scanner.

Sol emptied his pockets into a tray and walked through. Jared put the briefcase onto the bag scanner, emptied his pockets and then walked through the scanner.

The alarm went off. Instantly all eyes were on Jared.

A guard walked toward him. Jared smiled and raised his arms.

The guard felt around his collar and shoulders and briskly but thoroughly down his body, checking all hems and flaps and the bottoms of his shoes. He unhooked a scanner from his belt.

Jared's mind flashed and the scanner became an electroshock baton. He managed to stifle his scream, but not without contorting his face and stepping back. The guard froze and narrowed his eyes.

Jared felt everybody around him tense. His mind raced. What was he doing? What was he going to do now? Panic must have been written all over his face.

He held a hand up to his face and one out in front. He looked down and reached into his jacket and brought out a handkerchief. He blew his nose loudly, then looked up at the guard and raised his eyebrows. He returned the handkerchief and raised his arms.

'You nearly got it down your front.'

The guard smiled without humour and started scanning.

Jared looked over at Sol and raised his eyebrows.

The scanner beeped at his belt buckle and the guard examined it closer before moving on. He finished the scan, straightened up and nodded. Jared joined Sol and they set off down the corridor.

He swallowed against a rising nausea and realised his fists were clenched. He opened them quickly and took a deep breath.

'Bet you won't wear that belt to work again,' said Sol, passing him the briefcase.

Jared stopped fighting the feelings and picked up the role-play again. He was here on a mission. The angst subsided as he concentrated on the banter of imaginary office politics and new products. Fields of heads and monitors filled open offices off the corridor as they walked deeper into the complex.

'Next left,' said Sol finally.

It was a semi open-plan space arranged with basic workstations positioned so that none overlooked another, with banks of receivers against one wall. Eyes glanced up from monitors and then back down again. They approached the technician desk.

'Help ya gents?'

'Morning, were from Lockheed.'

'Okay. Saw you on the schedule this morning, what's on, we got no hitches?'

'Glad to hear it,' said Jared. 'We got a call in the middle of the night from ASCIET in Georgia questioning the integrity of the DSP's on the SS2. Sounds like the SNR calculations from their SS2 SPAT weren't calibrating across the full range of DSR. So we're checking the shortfall, if any, and if there is recalibrating the config'.'

'Takes two?'

Jared nodded. 'Cutbacks. They breed us with only a half brain these days.'

The man chuckled and gestured with his head. 'Step this way.'

He led them past a bank of FSS receivers to an empty workstation. Jared put the briefcase on the table and sat down. He opened the case, took out a laptop and booted it up. The

311

Lockheed logo appeared and was replaced by a systems analyst desktop. He took off his laminate and loaded it into the drive of the workstation. He looked up at the watching technician.

The technician straightened up and nodded. 'Leave ya to it then.'

Jared waited until he'd walked away then keyed the password into the login window. A systems operation terminal appeared. He went through the system as if following a problem solving procedure, mumbling jargon-laden obscurities to Sol.

The familiarity of the system felt strange and the thought occurred to him again that he'd have no problem getting a job in that sector. He noted the thought as positive and concentrated on what he was doing.

He reached two disks out of the case. One was authentic Lockheed software, the other the result of months of painstaking work by the specialist. Externally hacking the system wasn't an option because of its baked-in security. The stealth virus he held was a polymorphic macro Trojan. Its tunnelling properties were specifically designed to bury it beneath the detection software of the Echelon system. The system itself was tricked into self-transmission by identification tags based on Dictionary terms. Each transmitted virus would then morph into another variant with a different signature, which the system would then transmit again. The whole thing was armoured to prevent detection on insertion. Timed activation would result in system-wide corruption involving mass file deletion, drive damage and back door installation. A battery of Resistance hackers waited for the opening of the back door.

He loaded the latter into the drive. A disk icon appeared with the word SPOKESHAVE.

So far, so good.

Accessing the network was easy, streamlined by the software designers for rapid human interfacing. He found what he was looking for quickly, PLATFORM, the global nervous system of the UKUSA stations and agencies. It was this system that transmitted the analysis transcripts and messages to the various agencies and countries.

He opened a transmission window and entered – ALPHA-ALPHA, ECHO-ECHO, INDIA-INDIA, UNIFORM-UNIFORM, OSCAR-OSCAR.

Britain, Australia, New Zealand, Canada, and America, all got a slice of this pie. Which was only fair, they all had their thieving fingers in pies everywhere.

He hit Return and held his breath. Would an upload trip the alarm?

The word COMPLETED appeared.

He gritted his teeth to hold back a relieved and jubilant smile and kept his face expressionless. He repeated the process, this time to SILKWORTH, their state-of-the-art soon to be junk.

Once done he retrieved the disk with a trembling hand, closed the transmissions window and logged out. He shut down the laptop and closed the case.

Walking back through the office he could feel the wet sides of his shirt sticking to him.

'All done,' he said when they got to the technician.

'That was quick enough,' said the man.

'No problem here, everything's tight. So now we've got time for a nice slow pub lunch.'

'Well, enjoy it.'

'Will do, cheers.'

Walking down the corridor, Jared's tongue stuck to the roof of his mouth. He breathed through his nose and tried to think of lemons. Visions of what he'd just done showing up on the security system bringing armed guards after them made him wish he was armed.

He stopped at a water dispenser and drank two cups of frigid water. He looked across at Sol stood with both hands clasped in front of him. He really did look like an office wallah.

Jared attempted a smile. 'Can't wait for the weekend.'

They retraced their route, passing more staff than before. Jared's stomach rumbled.

'Lunch time,' said Sol jovially.

Struggling with mounting nausea and panic, Jared said nothing. He forced long, slow breaths in and out.

The briefcase handle grew slippery in his hand.

The corridor stretched on and seemed much longer than on the way in. He swallowed with difficulty and glanced to the side. Sol met the look and smiled. The smile was stiff and Jared saw concern in his eyes.

He saw himself through Sol's eyes and knew he'd be worried too in Sol's shoes. He had to get a grip. He was jeopardising them both.

He put his tongue between his teeth and bit down slowly. Saliva flooded his mouth. Pain commandeered his focus, too real to barge past with some fearful imagining.

The reception area came into view. The walk-through scanner looked like a waiting guillotine.

The muscles in his legs suddenly turned to water and drained through his feet. Helpless panic hit him.

Sol's voice startled him.

'The French called her Madame Guillotine. Kind of poetic in a way, entering and exiting life through a woman.'

At the mention of a woman, Jared's mind immediately went to Nicole…and found her, felt her waiting, wanting too. Warmth spread through him, evaporating the fear, firming his legs and loosening his hips. His shoulders relaxed and he lifted his head.

He was smiling when they reached the desk and handed over the laminates.

Walking toward the door he looked at Sol. 'Good comment that.'

Sol just smiled.

The double doors slid back and they stepped out into the light.

Appendix I
(Updated and additional information, links, and streaming video can be found at **www.centreofthepsyclone.com**)

The main purpose of Psyclone is to inform, not entertain. The sole reason for writing Psyclone was to connect people with data expanded on in this section. Woven within the narrative is a blueprint with the potential to transform our world, literally. Every piece of information and fact conveyed through internal and external dialogue in the novel with one exception is based on facts and information expanded on and linked to in this section. The exception is the story of 'the Specialist' in C10, which is to my knowledge wholly fictional. The fact that the U.S. government is maiming its troops and their future families with nuclear weapons brings the fiction disturbingly close to the truth (see the statements in C6 and entries in this appendix for facts about post-Gulf War I (Desert Storm) troop death and disability, and birth defects among their later offspring).

There is too much data involved and available concerning the things in the novel to include in it, hence this appendix. The following pages contain and link to more information than could be contained in fifty books. <u>I consider this to be the most important section in the book</u>. This is the access point for information that the powers-that-be would rather was kept away from people. Taking in and acting on this information can free you from the control of energy and drug companies, politicians, and religions.

I apologise if the length of this appendix seems daunting. The number of entries is not gratuitous, and presents just a fraction of the information available. They have been condensed from at least three times their number to include the most balanced and informative on the subjects covered. Their breadth demonstrates the wholesale suppression of information, censoring, by those who control society. This is information you won't find in the mainstream.

1

(An asterix * identifies specific entries that need to be read, viewed and shared, which contain fundamentally important, potentially life-changing information. To make your online investigation easier, a (free) PDF version of Psyclone containing active hyperlinks is available on the Psyclone website.)

We are in a special, privileged, "information rich" position with access to more information via the Internet than it's possible to read or digest in a single human lifetime. There is no reason why we can't understand who we truly are and where we are going. There is no reason why the average individual can't be fully empowered. We can accelerate the transition of our species out of the "era of slavery" into the era of physical and spiritual freedom if we study, analyse, question and act on this information.

Knowledge is power. The simplicity of the statement conceals its implications. Basically, the more you know, the bigger your advantage; the less you know, the bigger your disadvantage. For that reason restriction and suppression of information is a very basic social control technique. Very basic and very easy given that control of the media has been consolidated into such few hands. Failing to consider the aims and effects of the overall media output, as well as its detail, is dangerously naïve. Even a cursory glance at facts reveals mainstream media's worrying links, policies and agendas. Whatever you see on television, hear on the radio, or read in the newspapers has been, at the very least, allowed. More often than not though, it has been meticulously designed using principles of behavioural psychology and linguistics toward very specific aims, (as the video **The Century of the Self** listed in **DVD/Films** reveals). Put another way, if your channels of information are confined to those listed above, then your awareness, your reality, is being manipulated and compromised.

Much of the information in this appendix may be new to you, and might challenge previously held beliefs, giving rise to reactions described in **Appendix II – A Word on Cognitive Dissonance**. It is crucially important for you and those you care about that you consider the information with an open and inquiring mind before forming opinions and conclusions.

2

A little scepticism is healthy, but only when it moves one to investigate further before arriving at a judgement (see the Want To Know statement on p68). The Internet contains year's worth of research by some very dedicated and professional people. Keep your eyes open. The validity or authenticity of the information can be checked by following the data-source trail back. No cross-references or source listing suggests a certain lack of substance in most, but not necessarily all, instances. Be discerning.

Entries in **Section 1** refer directly to information communicated throughout the novel, and provide Internet links to sources of that information and other related research sources. The **Online Articles** in **Section 2** are additional perspectives, sometimes more detailed, on the subjects covered in the previous section. Some material was written up to three years ago, and is included for its enduring relevance. Given that the research, investigations and comments have been validated repeatedly, and that many of the projections have been near prophetic in their accuracy, they also serve as examples to those pathological sceptics who dismissed them, and continue to dismiss other research as empty theorising. **DVD/Films** is a collection of media-rich film and documentary from producers dedicated to getting the messages out, most entries are viewable online.

Looking into some of this information could produce discomforting effects, presuming of course the facts manage to penetrate the filters of cognitive dissonance and denial (see **Appendix II**). Educate yourself on the situation and potential developments, but also more importantly on your strategy options, for therein lies much hope and exciting potential. Models, data and information contained and linked to within this book can be applied not only to solve problems on a variety of individual and socio-political levels, but also to 'quantum-jump' an evolutionary advancement in ourselves as individuals and collectively as a species.

Discovering and developing our potential is the solution. You are so much more powerful than you know, politically and 'spiritually'. Reclaiming and developing that power can create new worlds, <u>literally</u>. Which may sound 'New Agey', but is

3

actually scientific fact. With that in mind some of the entries connect you with the leading edge work of some of the most advanced minds in the fields of science and human potential.

Regarding the links, do it soon before Internet Service Providers and search engines bow to pressure to exclude politically sensitive sites from their search options, as has been the case with Google and the Chinese government (see **Internet Threats**). That said, ways of getting around censorware blocking or filtering are also linked to in the same section. Because of Google's practise of collecting and trading user's personal data which has increased after a merger with Doubleclick, much recommended is a search facility called Scroogle (**www.scroogle.org**), an ad-free scraper of Google's main search results that serves as a proxy to protect your privacy on the Web. Scroogle addresses the privacy issue, but not the censoring. Google isn't the only search engine. There are plenty of others that do the job, and have been doing longer than Google. Shop around. Diversifying one's habits is one way of resisting the process of unhealthy consolidation and homogenisation.

Google, however, are not alone in collecting and trading personal data. Personal and behavioural data is an essential tool for corporate and governmental manipulation of the population.

Online surveillance and tracking (Dataveillance) are so much easier than traditional forms. Because of this also advisable is looking into ways of anonymising one's Internet activities such as Tor, a software project that helps defend against network surveillance. More details can be found in **Links.** (Updated information can be found on the Psyclone website.)

History does repeat itself; a statement can be looked on fatalistically or as a source of inspiration. Empires come and go. Aside from their moral bankruptcy, it's been the combined actions of little people that have brought them crashing down, like termites undermining the foundations of a building.

More creatively than that though, I'm counting on a high-frequency minority catalysing a quantum jump throughout the rest; a jump out of the swamp of obsolete thought and action into a future more amazing than anything yet experienced.

Section 1

The depictions of torture in C1 and C2 are based on real actions perpetrated in U.S. institutions around the world from U.S. prisons to camps like the now infamous Abu Ghraib internment camp. The article 'Torture Inc. Americas Brutal Prisons' by Channel 4 Dispatches reporter Deborah Davies asks the question 'Savaged by dogs, electrocuted with cattle prods, burned by toxic chemicals, does such barbaric abuse inside U.S. jails explain the horrors that are committed in Iraq?'(Includes potentially distressing video footage) 'U.S. Torture and Abuse of Detainees' from Human Rights Watch investigates the issue further. The UN Convention against Torture and Other Cruel, Inhuman or Degrading Treatment or Punishment provides international legal definitions and guidelines.
www.informationclearinghouse.info/article8451.htm
www.hrw.org/campaigns/torture.htm
www.hrweb.org/legal/cat.html

The well thought out and researched article Countershock: Mobilizing Resistance to Electroshock Weapons by Brian Martin and Steve Wright covers electroshock weapon technology, (batons, stun guns, tasers, etc), corporate and government policies and practises, and non-violent ways of combating them.
www.uow.edu.au/arts/sts/bmartin/pubs/03mcs.html

The statistic quoted in C3 about U.S. involvement in the overthrow, or attempted overthrow, of numerous governments was taken from, 'Overthrowing other people's governments – The Master List' by William Blum. See also 'Freeing the World to Death – Essays on the American Empire', which include 'Hiroshima – Last military act of World War II or first act of the Cold War', and 'United States bombing of other countries – The Master List'. Also the excellently researched and written 'Rogue State – a guide to the world's only superpower', sample chapters of which can be found on Blum's website **www.killinghope.org** and **http://thirdworldtraveler.com/Blum/William_Blum.html**

Phil mentioned in C3 ('...or like Phil come out in a couple of months not being able to write his own name or hold a spoon...') is Phil Russell, also known as Wally Hope, the inspiration behind the Stonehenge People's Free Festival. The Last Of The Hippies-An Hysterical Romance, the account of his demise at the hands of the authorities told by Penny Rimbaud of the band Crass, can be found at **www.spunk.org/texts/places/britain/sp001297.txt**

The socio-political description in C3 ('It took an acute perception to see the gradual habituation...unpatriotic or sympathetic with the enemy') is from the book 'They Thought They Were Free: The Germans 1933-1945' by Milton Mayer (University of Chicago Press). An American Jew of German ancestry Mayer went to Germany seven years after Hitler's fall and befriended ten Nazis. The book is, in large part, a story of that experience. Reflected in the book is his fear that what happened there could happen anywhere. An excerpt of the book can be found at **www.thirdreich.net/They_Thought_They_Were_Free_nn4.html**

See also Thom Hartmann's review of the book at **www.thomhartmann.com**

*More information on the use of microchips (RFID's and otherwise) can be found at the website of CASPIAN (Consumers Against Supermarket Privacy Invasion and Numbering) **www.nocards.org** and **www.spychips.com** (contains IBM's patent application 'Identification and Tracking of Persons Using RFID-Tagged Items'). A related and slightly disturbing fact is that according to public record IBM's New York office supplied the German Nazi's with the technology and equipment that allowed Hitler to number and track concentration camp prisoners. ("How IBM Helped Automate the Nazi Death Machine In Poland," E. Black, Village Voice.com 3-27-02.) See also the Guerrilla News Network video 'IBM and the Holocaust'. **http://gnn.tv/videos/10/IBM_and_the_Holocaust**

For a balanced and detailed overall view of possible futures indicated by the rapid development of multiple surveillance technologies read A Report on the Surveillance Society (2006) compiled by the Surveillance Studies Network on the orders of the Information Commissioner Richard Thomas. The report provides details on the workings and implications of CCTV, Automated Number Plate Recognition, Universal Facial Recognition, Biometrics, ID cards and chips, and Radio Frequency Identification Devices (traceable, transmitting microchips in the products you buy), as well as scenarios based on trends and intentions discovered by the group. Worrying to note is that the authors point out that their projection is "fairly conservative. The future spelled out in the report is nowhere near as dystopian and authoritarian as it could be."
www.libertysecurity.org/article1194.html

(Links to information about technology listed above can be found at **www.centreofthepsyclone.com**)

For a list of links to information about the uses, development, and planned future of microchips see
www.prisonplanet.com/archive_big_brother.html

See also 'Microchip Implants, Mind Control & Cybernetics' by Rauni Kilde, MD, former Chief Medical Officer of Finland.
http://educate-yourself.org/mc/
implantmcandcybernetics06dec00.shtml

The PDF of the article by Dr Kilde originally published in the Finnish-language journal, SPEKULA, (mailed to all medical students of Finland and all Northern Finland medical doctors, circulation 6500) is also available online. Dr Kilde is also quoted in Canada's national newspaper regarding plans to microchip newborn children in the U.S. and Europe. She also mentions the technology described in the entry below.
www.agoracosmopolitan.com/home/Frontpage/2007/01/08/
01290.html

Those with lingering doubts about the capability and potential of microchip technology should also consider the 'Soul Catcher 2025' being developed by British Telecom's Futures Division, described in (among other places) the article 'The End of Death: 'Soul Catcher' Computer Chip Due...' by Robert Uhlig. **www.geocities.com/Area51/Shadowlands/6583/project108. html**

*Silver is a natural antibiotic and one of the oldest remedies in the world. It is non-toxic, non-addictive, free of 'side effects', and doesn't damage the immune system. In its colloidal form (micro particles held in suspension by electrostatic charge in purified water) it kills over 600 organisms as compared to the 6 or 7 of conventional antibiotics. In addition to that, bacteria are unable to develop a resistance to it, unlike conventional antibiotics. As well as dealing with infection, silver helps human tissue regrow when used in burn therapy. It also stimulates bone-forming cells. Colloidal silver is not a controlled drug and is classified as a food supplement, and is therefore not part of Big Pharma's monopoly. Indeed, it poses a threat to their lucrative trade. Unsurprisingly then it's generally labelled a poison by mainstream medicine and demonised whenever possible, as are most other effective alternative medicines and therapies. UK Colloidal Silver has one of the most balanced and informative colloidal silver sites on the Web (see their Research and FAQs sections) and produces one of the best colloids on the market. **www.ukcolloidalsilver.co.uk**

Those considering making it themselves should read 'A Closer Look At Colloidal Silver' by Peter A. Lindemann, developer of the CS-300C and CS-300D Colloidal Silver Generators at **www.elixa.com/silver/lindmn.htm**

Regarding the statement in C4 about fluoride/aluminium compounds in public water supplies, the following is a statement contained in an 'Address in Reply to the Government's Speech to Parliament', as recorded in Victorian Hansard of 12 August 1987, by Mr Harley Rivers Dickinson, Liberal Party Member of the Victorian Parliament for South Barwon, taken from the thesis 'The Dickinson Statement: A Mind-Boggling Thesis' by Ian E. Stephens. The abstract reads as follows:

"At the end of the Second World War, the United States Government sent Charles Eliot Perkins, a research worker in chemistry, biochemistry, physiology and pathology, to take charge of the vast Farben chemical plants in Germany.

"While there he was told by the German chemists of a scheme which had been worked out by them during the war and adopted by the German General Staff.

"This was to control the population in any given area through mass medication of drinking water. In this scheme, sodium fluoride occupied a prominent place.

"Repeated doses of infinitesimal amounts of fluoride will in time reduce an individual's power to resist domination by slowly poisoning and narcotising a certain area of the brain and will thus make him submissive to the will of those who wish to govern him.

"Both the Germans and the Russians added sodium fluoride to the drinking water of prisoners of war to make them stupid and docile."

Extracted from thesis is the article Fluoridation – Mind Control of the Masses listed in **Online Articles**.

For background to the statements in C4 concerning the factions behind Hitler see **Wall St and the Rise of Hitler** and **How the Allied multinationals supplied Nazi Germany throughout World War II** in **Online Articles**.

The statement in C4 that schools are factories "in which raw products, children, are to be shaped and formed into products...manufactured like nails..." is taken from the dissertation for Columbia Teachers College written by the Dean of Education at Stanford (see the article 'The Educational System Was Designed to Keep Us Uneducated and Docile' in **Online Articles**)

9

For detailed research of the history of the education system and its real purpose read the book 'The Underground History of American Education' by John Gatto listed in **Online Articles**. Gatto, named as New York State Teacher of the Year on three occasions, quit teaching claiming he was no longer willing to hurt children, and is now active in the area of school reform.

See also 'The Deliberate Dumbing Down of America', the result of over twenty years of research by former Senior Policy Advisor in the Office of Educational Research and Improvement (OERI), U.S. Department of Education, Charlotte Iserbyt. Available as a free PDF from
www.deliberatedumbingdown.com

(Although the above works focus on American education methods, similar and sometimes identical policies and trends can be found in the UK)

Information about Operation Paperclip can be found at, among other places, **www.thirdworldtraveler.com/Fascism/ Operation_Paperclip_file.html**

An article which describes a new generation of sophisticated electromagnetic weapons that the U.S. and Russia have developed to manipulate the climate for military use is 'Weather Warfare: Beware the US military's experiments with climatic warfare' by Prof. Michel Chossudovsky.
www.globalresearch.ca/index.php?context=va&aid=7561

For the latest HAARP (High Frequency Active Auroral Research Program) information see
www.earthpulse.com/src/category.asp?catid=1

The statement, also in C4, beginning 'The People versus the Powerful...' is quoted from William Rivers Pitt. Pitt is a New York Times bestselling author of two books - War On Iraq (with Scott Ritter) and The Greatest Sedition is Silence.

John C. Lilly, quoted in the heading of C5, was a physician, biophysicist, neuroscientist, and inventor who specialised in the study of consciousness. An unparalleled scientific visionary he made significant contributions to psychology, brain research, biophysics, neurophysiology, neuroanatomy, computer theory, medicine, ethics, and interspecies communication. Lilly founded the Communications Research Institute in the Virgin Islands and served as its director from 1959 until 1968. There he worked with dolphins exploring dolphin intelligence and human-dolphin communication. As well as initiating worldwide efforts at interspecies communications with dolphins, he sowed the seeds of several scientific revolutions, including the theory of internal realities, the hardware/software model of the human brain/ mind, and as the inventor of the isolation tank pioneered research in sensory deprivation. Details of his work can be found at **www.johnclilly.com**

Details of the psychological experiments conducted by Milgram and Zimbardo can be found at
http://alevelpsychology.co.uk/social-psychology/social-influence/milgram-study.html
www.prisonexp.org

'Jerry Floyd and his cameraman Ted' mentioned in C5, refers to ITN reporter Terry Lloyd and cameraman Fred Nerac. The two and their local translator Hussein Othman were killed by some very unfriendly 'friendly fire', essentially because they weren't part of a military organisation.

An excellent documentary revealing the media's true role in war reporting is **WMD-Weapons of Mass Deception**, details of which can be found in **DVD's/Films**. Also see the article Manufacturing Consent – A Propaganda Model in **Online Articles**, which describes the propaganda methods used by the mainstream media.

Those wanting to read and view balanced, unbiased international news and current affairs commentary will find such

11

in one of the last voices of integrity in British mainstream journalism, the foreign correspondent, John Pilger.
www.john-pilger.com
www.thirdworldtraveler.com/Pilger_John/John_Pilger_page. html

Mumia is Mumia Abu Jamal, a Philadelphia journalist framed for murder who has spent most of his life on Death Row, (1981 to date) despite the seriously flawed and biased prosecution. The Free Mumia campaign can be found at **www.freemumia.com** Radio broadcasts featuring Mumia can be heard at **www.prisonradio.org**

One subject that Mumia as an independent journalist was very vocal about (which some consider instrumental in his subsequently being framed and imprisoned) was the persecution of the MOVE organisation by the U.S. authorities, which included the bombing of a MOVE house and the murder of six adults and five children, and which persists today in the form of the unfair incarceration nearly thirty years later of nine MOVE members. Details of the atrocities and miscarriages of justice can be found at **www.centreofthepsyclone.com/mumia&move**

The 'buried report' mentioned in C5 refers to a paper by Chris Busby & Saoirse Morgan titled 'Did the use of Uranium weapons in Gulf War II result in contamination of Europe? Evidence from the measurements of the Atomic Weapons Establishment, Aldermaston, Berkshire, UK.'
www.greenaudit.org/new_page_31.htm

See also 'The Queen's Death Star - Depleted Uranium Measured in British Atmosphere from Battlefields in the Middle East' by Leuren Moret.
www.globalresearch.ca/index.php?context=va&aid=2058
www.indymedia.org.uk/en/2006/02/334667.html

Images (of a distressing nature) of the effects of white phosphorus on civilians can be found at **http://mindprod.com/**

politics/iraqwarpix.html

*The Nuremberg Principles, a set of international guidelines that constitute what a war crime is, were compiled during the Nuremberg Trials of Nazi Party members after the Second World War. They are reproduced on the Psyclone website to demonstrate clearly how Britain, Israel and the U.S. are breaking international law and committing war crimes. People's duty in response to those crimes is also made clear. As Justice Robert Jackson, chief prosecutor at the Nuremberg trials, said, *"The very essence of the Nuremberg charter is that individuals have international duties which transcend national obligations of obedience imposed by the state."*
www.centreofthepsyclone.com/nuremberg

The description of facts surrounding Alex's death in C10 is based on the forensic toxicologist's report to the Hutton Inquiry in the case of the death of Dr David Kelly. One-time Senior Advisor on Biological Weapons to UNSCOM, Dr Kelly was one of the most senior and highly respected weapons inspectors involved in the investigation of Iraq's alleged WMD. It was Dr Kelly who leaked information to the Observer that the mobile laboratories found in Iraq were not for WMD. More information can be found in articles by Rowena Thursby of the Kelly Investigation Group on the website for the Centre for Research on Globalization at **www.globalresearch.ca/articles/ THU409A.html**

See also the two-part article 'The Murder of David Kelly' by Jim Rarey at **www.fromthewilderness.com/free/ww3/ 101403_kelly_1.html**

Mysterious 'suicides', smear campaigns, and wrongful imprisonment are some of the disturbingly often results of an individual's decision to maintain their integrity and honesty in opposition to the State.

'If Mobile Phones Were a Type of Food, They Simply Would Not be Licensed' by Dr Gerald Hyland, (originally published in The Lancet), covers the mechanisms by which mobile phones can cause adverse affects in people and animals and can be found at, among other places, **www.cancer-health.org**

*The section Wireless Dangers on the Psyclone website covers the biological effects of RFID, mobile phone, and wireless technology, and their covert uses. <u>The information in this section needs to be read by everybody</u>.
www.centreofthepsyclone.com/wirelessdangers

The one of the most recent demonstration of the fact that mobile phones emit sufficient microwaves to cook an egg was by conducted by two Pravda journalists, Lagovski and Moiseynko. **www.rense.com/general72/cellcook.htm**

(For a selection of video links exposing the dangers of mobile phones and wireless technology see **DVD/Films** and **www.centreofthepsyclone.com**)

A revealing article 'High-Tech Genocide in Congo' compiled from several sources including The Taylor Report, Earth First! Journal, and Z Magazine, exposes one of the real reasons behind the death of over seven million people in the Congo, (Rwanda and Uganda) over the last decade. Cobalt, Coltan, and Niobium are minerals essential for the production of mobile phones. Foreign governments and multinational mining companies have been funding the internecine warfare in the region as part of a concerted policy of destabilisation and mineral expropriation. **www.projectcensored.org/censored_2007/index.htm**

C4ISR stands for Command & Control, Communications, Computing, Intelligence, Surveillance and Reconnaissance, an aspect of the new 'Network-centric' warfare (NCW).

The article **FBI taps cell phone mic as eavesdropping tool** by Declan McCullagh, provides details of the U.S. vs. Ardito

14

federal case mentioned in C5, and the ways in which mobile phones can be used for surveillance. **http://www.news.com/FBI-taps-cell-phone-mic-as-eavesdropping-tool/2100-1029_3-6140191.html**

Descriptions of the Celldar system can be found in Roke Manor's own press release and this 2002 article in The Observer. **www.roke.co.uk/press/38.php**
www.guardian.co.uk/uk/2002/oct/13/humanrights.mobilephones

For a report on how British councils are recruiting children as young as eight with cash incentives to act as surveillance operatives ('Junior Streetwatchers') see
http://www.dailymail.co.uk/news/article-1052962/Schoolchildren-recruited-councils-spy-neighbours-drop-litter.html

The following three papers deal with the Echelon global surveillance system:
- ECHELON: America's Secret Global Surveillance Network by Patrick S. Poole
- ECHELON by the Federation of American Scientists
- Leading Surveillance Societies in the EU and the World 2007 by Privacy International

http://home.hiwaay.net/~pspoole/echelon.html
www.fas.org/irp/program/process/echelon.htm
www.privacyinternational.org/article.shtml?cmd[347]=x-347-559597

See also the Developments in Surveillance Technology section of the Omega Foundation Report For The European Parliament – An Appraisal of the Technologies of Political Control. **www.statewatch.org/news/2005/may/steve-wright-stoa-rep.pdf**

Three years ago discussions of Federal concentration camps moved out of the realm of 'paranoid' speculation and into mainstream news. In January 2006 Kellogg, Brown and Root (KBR), a subsidiary of Halliburton was awarded a $385 million contract by the Department of Homeland Security to build detention centres in the U.S. These are to provide "temporary detention and processing capabilities" in preparation for "an emergency influx of immigrants, or to support the rapid development of new programs" in the event of other emergencies, such as "a natural disaster". Halliburton is the company that built the Guantanamo Bay 'temporary' detention centre where prisoners are held incommunicado indefinitely without access to attorneys, chaplains, translators, the media, or human rights organisations. The implications of this and other, seemingly at first, disconnected developments should not be underestimated. The article Red Alert: FEMA Camps, Martial Law and Indefinite Detention Without Trial covers aspects such as martial law training among the U.S. police force and army, the designation of dissenters as 'enemy combatants', the establishment of a civilian inmate labour program under development by the Department of the Army, and the alarming historical parallels of Nazi Germany.

www.oilempire.us/redalert.html

The Grand Chessboard mentioned in C6 is from the title of a book by Zbigniew Brzezinksi 'The Grand Chessboard – American Primacy And It's Geostrategic Imperatives'. The contents are evidence that what the world is witnessing is a cold and calculated war plan, and that, from reading Brzezinski's own words about Pearl Harbour, the World Trade Centre attacks were just the trigger needed to set the final conquest in motion. More information can be found at

www.fromthewilderness.com/free/ww3/zbig.html
www.wanttoknow.info/brzezinskigrandchessboard

Written in 2006 by Zoltan Grossman, New U.S. Military Bases: Side Effects or Causes of War? provides a perceptive overview of worldwide U.S military expansion, and demonstrates how events since were predictable.

www.counterpunch.org/zoltanbases.html

16

Ex-British Environment Minister Michael Meacher MP gives an alternative perspective on U.S. President George Bush and his administration's attempt to manipulate the events of Sept 11, 2001 to create justification for his incursions into Afghanistan, and Iraq (and other dominoes to come). Much of the information discussed is completely available in the public domain, but Mr. Meacher does an excellent job of putting everything into context in his article entitled 'This War on Terrorism is Bogus'.
www.guardian.co.uk/politics/2003/sep/06/september11.iraq
www.commondreams.org/views03/0906-01.htm

Evidence revealing the concealed motivations behind current global military situations can be found in the series of entries in **Online Articles** beginning with Professor P.D. Scott's **Afghanistan, Columbia, Vietnam: The Deep Politics of Drugs and Oil**, and **The Global Drug Meta-Group: Drugs, Managed Violence, and the Russian 9/11**.

The incident described in C6 at the checkpoint and the recounted 'hit on the 82nd' were reported by service personnel eyewitnesses in the publication GI Special produced by GI's in the spirit of Veterans For Peace. The driver's sister and cousin, and the unborn child died. The life lost during the 'hit' was lost for the reason mentioned, a carpet. [Editor's Note: The character narrating the account in the novel in no way represents the eyewitnesses who originally related the incidents.] Other things like helicopters being shot down due to being inadequately equipped because of budget skimming, a wedding party being shot by a patrol, a family being run over by a tank, and widespread drug abuse are all reported in issues of the same publication. **www.militaryproject.org**

An article dealing with the numerous 'enduring' (military euphemism for permanent) bases, particularly in Iraq, and the objectives being pursued is 'Plan Iraq – Permanent Occupation' by Stephen Lendman.
www.populistamerica.com/plan_iraq_permanent_occupation

An article regarding 'Baghdad Boils' entitled 'Iraq: Depleted Uranium aka Baghdad Boils' can be found at
http://uruknet.info/?p=18948&hd0&size=1&l=x

*The videos **Afghanistan AC-130 gunship** and **Take 'em Out** show cockpit footage showing how unarmed civilians are being massacred in Afghanistan and Iraq. For the links see the entry in **DVD/Films**.

*Those 'with eyes to see', and with the integrity and humanity to face facts should look at the entries below to see the result of U.S. nuclear weapons. The entry 'Your Tax Dollars in Action' is from Dr Miraki, the author of the book Afghanistan After Democracy, published to highlight the effects of the U.S. genocide in Afghanistan and Iraq (see the entry in **Links**), and to purchase land on which to build a hospital specifically to deal with the massive rise in chronic birth defects and congenital deformities resulting from the thousands of tonnes of depleted uranium used against the people in those areas.
www.rense.com/general74/afgg.htm

*It is for reasons such as those in the abovementioned entries that the Peace Tax Seven have taken the stand of legally withholding that portion of their tax that is put to military uses, and currently faces the government in the European court. Unsurprisingly the Conscience Campaign is suffering a mainstream media blackout. This is definitely a response that governments are keen to suppress.
www.peacetaxseven.com
www.conscienceonline.org.uk

*Those doubting the existence of a policy of selective information suppression in the mainstream media should consider the account of what police called "the largest amount of chemical explosives of this type [bomb making] ever found in this country [Britain]" in September 2006. Very few people heard about it because of suppression by the mainstream media. Find out more in the articles 'The terror plot that didn't fit' and

'The racist 'War on Terror'' on the UK Indymedia website.
www.indymedia.org.uk/en/2006/10/353373.html
www.indymedia.org.uk/en/2006/10/353458.html

*Questions about the validity of the official account of the bombing incidents in London on the 7th July 2005 are raised in the article 'The Magic Bomb Theory' at
www.indymedia.org.uk/ennull319361.shtml

The newspaper article mentioned in 'The Magic Bomb Theory', entitled 'I was in tube bomb carriage – and survived' is (or was) available from the Cambridge Evening News website in PDF format.

*Another near completely suppressed aspect of that day's incidents, an eyewitness account from a passenger aboard the No.30 bus that exploded in Tavistock Square, needs to be made public, and questions like 'why was the bus stopped, held, and then redirected along a different route by unidentified persons in two black Mercedes immediately prior to the explosion?' answered. Examine the evidence for yourself at
www.the4thbomb.com

Those ignorant of the history, capability, and uses of 'PsyOps' and 'PsyWar' techniques should peruse the site Psywarrior run by Major Ed Rouse (Ret). Mr Rouse, an active proponent of Psychological Operations/Warfare, presents volumes of information on the above aspects of what he calls 'truly, a humane weapon'. Defined on the website as **'the planned use of communications to influence human attitudes and behaviour ... to create in target groups behaviour, emotions, and attitudes that support the attainment of national objectives...disseminated by face-to-face communication, television, radio or loudspeaker, newspapers, books, magazines and/or posters'**. Over 200 links to articles concerning its current and historical uses.
www.psywarrior.com

(See also the Information Operations Roadmap listed in **Internet Threats**)

A classic example of a recent PsyOps program is the 'Zarqawi Legend' fabricated by the Pentagon and disseminated by the mainstream media. Zarqawi was allegedly the 'terrorist' mastermind behind the 'insurgency' in Iraq, a story designed to undermine the public's perception of the legitimate resistance against the illegal U.S. invasion. The article 'Who is behind "Al Qaeda in Iraq"? Pentagon acknowledges fabricating a "Zarqawi" Legend' reveals the details of that program.
www.globalresearch.ca/index.php?context=va&aid=2275

*The description in the previous article of how disinformation is fed into the news chain by 'official sources' is elaborated on in a three-part article from Media Lens entitled 'Intellectual Cleansing', which includes Jonathan Cook's excellent analysis.
www.medialens.org/alerts/08/081002_intellectual_cleansing_part1.php

A revealing description of The Project for the New American Century (PNAC) and its White Paper 'Rebuilding America's Defenses: Strategy, Forces and Resources for a New Century' can be found on the website of the Information Clearing House. The personalities behind the recently disbanded (2008) PNAC, (ICH list Vice President Dick Cheney as a founding member of PNAC, along with Defense Secretary Donald Rumsfeld and Defense Policy Board chairman Richard Perle. Deputy Defense Secretary Paul Wolfowitz is the ideological father of the group. Bruce Jackson, a PNAC director, served as a Pentagon official for Ronald Reagan before leaving government service to take a leading position with the weapons manufacturer Lockheed Martin), and the aims set out in the paper leave no doubt as to what is happening regarding U.S. expansionism. A must read.
www.informationclearinghouse.info/article1665.htm

Phil Schneider was a geologist and ex-government engineer who was involved in building underground facilities. Until his death under mysterious circumstances in January 1996, Schneider went public with what he had discovered during his career. His memorial website contains videos, documents and more on a variety of subjects including deep underground bases. **www.philschneider.org**

An intriguing, and disturbing, example of a deep underground base is the new Denver International Airport. This site contains some of the most comprehensively researched information I've found, including photographic evidence of something very bizarre, and quite sinister, going on.
www.anomalies-unlimited.com/Denver_Airport.html

The issue touched on in C7 of drugs being used as a social control mechanism is discussed in more detail at **www.centreofthepsyclone.com/thoughtsforsmokers**

The perceptive and well-referenced 'Mind-Forged Manacles' by George Monbiot reveals how, despite the crime levels falling, the UK prison population is rising. **http://rinf.com/alt-news/ politics/mind-forged-manacles/3960/**

The quote from Pastor Niemoeller, the anti-Nazi resistance activist, describing the German people's inactivity following the Nazi rise to power, and the Nazi's selective persecution is reproduced at **www.centreofthepsyclone.com**

The sociopolitical commentary in C7 and elsewhere is taken from 'The Joy of Revolution' produced by the Bureau Of Public Secrets. **www.bopsecrets.org/PS/joyrev.htm**

The description of urban guerrilla techniques in C7 is taken from the Minimanual of the Urban Guerrilla by Carlos Marighella; a highly informative (if a little dated) document that presents the perspective of the urban guerrilla (resistance/freedom fighter) of the late 1960's.
www.marxists.org/archive/marighella-carlos/1969/06/ minimanual-urban-guerrilla/index.htm

Relevant within this context are the writings of other historical revolutionary libertarian groups ('terrorists' in media parlance) who focused their attention on the 'imperialist State'. Two communiqués that reveal the reasoning behind the actions of two particular groups are: The Urban Guerilla Concept – April 1971 by the Red Army Faction (also known as the Baader-Mienhof Gang), and The Struggle Continues by the Angry Brigade.

www.germanguerilla.com/red-army-faction/documents/ 71_04.html

www.spunk.org/cat-us/agb.html

For example, consider this insight found within the Red Army Faction Strategy Paper dated May 1982 entitled The Guerilla, the Resistance and the Anti-Imperialist Front:

"*Imperialism is militarily and politically aggressive, overdeveloped in technologies and the techniques of production and organization. Its goal is to once again be the sole world power, whether this means militarily defeating the Soviets and the socialist States, which wish to remain an equal power, or whether this means politically defeating the consciousness of the peoples of Africa, Latin America and Asia. It will surely fail, but it is politically, militarily and economically powerful enough to block those countries that have realized their national liberation by dictating to them the conditions of their development. It may also be powerful enough to impose an arms race, and to use the world market in order to unsettle the economy of the socialist countries. In the metropole, where the State never stops trying to carry imperialist power to hegemony by exploitation, police state tactics, and crisis management, it will stamp out a decaying society.*" It shouldn't need pointing out that every aspect of the described strategy can currently be seen on operation in the places mentioned.

There are a number of websites related to the people-led revolutionary movement in Chiapas, Mexico. The Zapatista Army of National Liberation (EZLN in its Spanish initials) has been fighting against the U.S.-backed Mexican government's oppression and persecution of the indigenous people of the area

22

for nearly twenty years. Their aims are simple, to live with dignity, liberty, equality, and true democracy. 'The Mysterious Silence of the Mexican Zapatistas' gives a view of the movement from the perspective of a reporter travelling with them. **www.narconews.com/Issue33/article970.html**.

'Zapatistas smell war in the air of Chiapas' describes the serious and worsening situation in Mexico (written Jan 2008) **www.infoshop.org/inews/article.php?story=200801021748197 93**

For links to a variety of sites devoted to the cause see the links section of **www.zapatista.org**

Lawyer and novelist Blake Bailey, recently selected for and interviewed on 'America's Premier Lawyers' has written a brilliant (downloadable) story, Zapatista, that describes the people and spirit of the revolution, and its cultural and physical environment. **www.zapatistarevolution.com**

*An excellent overview of the basis of Lawful Rebellion is, 'My Personal Journey Into Lawful Rebellion' by Justin of the Walker family: Freeman-on-the-land.
www.davidicke.com/content/view/23081/48/

*Reclaiming our freedom now is possible using non-violent, positive, and lawful means. Details of the concepts and lawful basis of the Freedom Movement should be read at **www.tpuc.org** and **www.fmotl.com**

The vision and suggestions put forward by Sanderson Beck are some of the most direct, straightforward, and practical individual and collective responses to the current world situation I've come across. Beck's impressive output of writings on non-violence (some written whilst incarcerated for his non-violently protesting against the illegal invasion of Iraq) reflect the depth and power of those of Gandhi and King, and like those have the potential to change society and the world for the better. As well

23

as his own work, the website also contains a huge array of traditional and contemporary works in the fields of ethics, philosophy, spirituality, and politics. Three recommended books are listed in **Books**. **www.san.beck.org/index.html**

The following articles cover the Active Denial System (ADS) mentioned in C7. Note that the New Scientist article is dated over two years ago, and consider how things might have progressed since, especially with the amount of money poured into its R&D during that time. The second article covers one such development. The third article, and the next entry, is for those who believed the transparent official statement that uses would be to keep attackers from approaching military installations or navy ships in dock.
www.newscientist.com/article.ns?id=mg18725095.600
www.strategypage.com/htmw/htweap/articles/20071217.aspx
www.azstarnet.com/business/215372

Currently being used in the Middle East by the U.S. and its allies, Active Denial Technology does more than the press releases mention. 'Bio-electromagnetic Weapons: The ultimate weapon' by Institute of Science in Society reveals some of its covert uses. **www.globalresearch.ca/index.php?context=va& aid=5797**

*The article **'Suicide Bombers' and the Promise of Heaven?** examines the issue of suicide attacks from a variety of angles, and links to some little-known (suppressed) facts.
www.centreofthepsyclone.com/suicidebombers

Mentioned in the previous article is an incident in 2005 in which two British SAS soldiers disguised as Arabs, driving an explosive-laden booby-trapped car heading for the centre of Basra opened fire when stopped by Iraqi police. The men were detained by the police and refused to say what their mission was. British forces then used up to 10 tanks, supported by helicopters, to smash through the walls of the jail and free the servicemen. **www.globalresearch.ca/index.php?context=viewarticle&code**

24

=20050920&articleId=972

Information on the hundreds of addictive and carcinogenic additives in cigarette tobacco is contained in the section **Some Thoughts for Smokers (and other 'recreational' drug users)** on the Psyclone website. The section links to another article covering the disturbing socio-political implications of current anti-smoking trends and developments.
www.centreofthepsyclone.com/thoughtsforsmokers

Edward's reference to Jared as 'friend' echoes a traditional habit of the Quakers, a Christian sect whose members have historically engaged in conscience-based activities. Such conscience-based activities could be the reason why groups like Christian Aid are targeted for surveillance by U.S. authorities.
http://home.hiwaay.net/~pspoole/echelon.html

*The description of the vaccination concept in C8 is from an article entitled 'Genuine Immunity Versus Vaccine Immunity' by Dr. Richard Moskowitz, M.D. This and other related articles can be found at **www.consumerhealth.org/articles**

A comprehensive, link-laden article 'The Vaccination Hoax and Holocaust' which covers the little-known history and methods of the vaccination industry can be found at
www.whale.to/b/hoax1.html

See also the study 'Vaccination-Assault on the Species' by P Rattigan ND at **www.ivanfraser.com/articles/health/vaccination.html**

Related are the articles 'Cancer Causing Vaccines, Polio, AIDS & Monkey Business' and 'The Manmade Origin Of AIDS' by Alan Cantwell, MD at
www.newdawnmagazine.com/Articles/Cancer_Causing_Vaccines.html
http://heyokamagazine.com/HEYOKA.7.HEALTH.AlanCantwell.MD.htm

See the video **Merck Vaccine Chief Brings HIV/AIDS to America** in **DVD/Films**

Regarding a policy of population reduction, the article Eugenics and Environmentalism: From Quality Control to Quantity Control exposes the continued practise of eugenics in its modern form by the same families and connected factions that funded and promoted the practise prior to WWII.
www.oldthinkernews.com/Articles/oldthinker%20news/ eugenics_and_environmentalism.htm

The National Security Memo 200 (a directive issued by the Assistant for National Security Affairs, Henry A. Kissinger), mentioned in the above article, dated April 24, 1974, titled Implications of World Wide Population Growth for U.S. Security & Overseas Interests, states: *"...the U.S. economy will require large and increasing amounts of minerals from abroad, especially from less-developed countries. That fact gives the U.S. enhanced interest in the political, economic, and social stability of the supplying countries. Wherever a lessening of population can increase the prospects for such stability, population policy becomes relevant to resources, supplies and to the economic interests of U.S....world population growth is widely recognized within the government as a current danger of the highest magnitude calling for urgent measures...Attainment of this goal will require greatly intensified population programs...We cannot wait for overall modernization and development to produce lower fertility rates naturally since this will undoubtedly take many decades in most developing countries..."*
www.whale.to/v/memorandum.html

The evidence of 'Third World' vaccinations being contaminated with sterility agents moves one to consider reports such as the following in a different light.
www.alertnet.org/thenews/newsdesk/IRIN/f3ae75c8932d0130 132b9a8f47a83ee5.htm

Another very thought-provoking report concerning a covert global depopulation policy comes from the former Asia-Pacific Bureau chief for Forbes magazine, Benjamin Fulford. In the course of his investigations into artificially created pandemics that targeted Asians (SARS/Avian Flu), Fulford was tasked to act as a spokesperson for "a powerful organisation with deeply embedded networks in Japanese society". Through him a very clear warning has been sent out to European and North American factions "intent on a radical global depopulation plan through a contrived war on terror, artificially created pandemics, and environmental disasters produced through advanced eco-weapons."

http://exopolitics.org/Exo-Comment-54.htm
http://rense.com/general77/fulf.htm

(For more information on the 'advanced eco-weapons' mentioned see the Scalar technology entries in this appendix)

Regarding the dangers of SSRI psychiatric drugs (Prozac, Ritalin, etc) see the site of Dr. Peter Breggin MD. Eminently qualified, Dr Breggin has been advising the professions, media, and public about the dangers of psychiatric drugs and other aspects of psychiatric medicine for over three decades.
www.breggin.com

See also the interview between Dr. F Baughman and Mike Adams on the 'ADHD fraud and the chemical holocaust against a generation of children'. A PDF of the interview is available from Dr Baughman's website at **www.adhdfraud.org** and **http://downloads.truthpublishing.com/LivewithFredBaughman.pdf**

*The detailed discourses on scalar electromagnetism and free energy are the words of Col T Bearden. I would encourage the examination of the concepts and practicalities within their own environment in the Cheniere website. Col Bearden provides clear and comprehensive explanations of the concept and applications of scalar electromagnetism. The possibilities for good and ill

27

mentioned in the novel are real and are covered in greater detail on the website. The paper 'The Solution to the World's Energy Crisis' presents a working model based on the patented Motionless Electromagnetic Generator. This scientifically tried and tested (obviously to have been patented) device provides <u>unlimited, non-polluting energy, free, indefinitely</u>. Special attention should be given to the paper 'The Final Secret of Free Energy', the results of 30 years research by Bearden and his associates. Although a technical paper the objective is for the moderately technical reader to understand the principles and mechanisms involved in different kinds of free energy devices, and their construction. As the expected production of the Motionless Electromagnetic Generator looks to have been suppressed by vested industrial-political interests, DIY may be the only way anybody will get one.

Cheniere also provides a platform for the amazing, and typically, tragically suppressed work of Antoine Priore, who up until the mid 1970's was funded by the French government. **www.cheniere.org**

A kind of 'beginner's guide' to the concepts and applications of the science entitled 'The Brave New World of Scalar Electromagnetics' by Bill Morgan can be found at **www.prahlad.org/pub/bearden/scalar_wars.htm**

The evidence mentioned that 'heavily implicates' the use of weaponised scalar technology should be reviewed on the website of Dr Judy Wood. "The importance of the evidence that Dr. Wood has uncovered, when put in context, cannot be overstated – it forms a nexus point – joining several areas of research and crystallizing an overall picture to a level of clarity never before realised." **www.drjudywood.com**

Independent scientist and former university professor James DeMeo has, along with others in over 25 years of field research, verified the science and technology originally developed by Wilhelm Reich. Read the Research Summary and Interview on a

'New' Method for Drought-Abatement and Desert-Greening: Cloudbusting at **www.orgonelab.org/ResearchSummary2.htm**

*Continuing on the theme of free energy, albeit in a different form, variously described as Bioenergy, Dark Matter, and Zero Point Energy (among other names), the website of Jon Logan's R&D group contains extensive information on the energy itself and the Solid State Quantum Flux Technology instruments and devices (such as the 'coaster' examined by Jared, and the 'Tower Buster wrapped in a toroidal coil' found by Leon) used for working with it. Provides comprehensive instructions on their construction and use, and links to companies manufacturing and retailing the technology. For a general, but detailed overview see the article 'How to beat problem energy', available as a downloadable PDF. **www.littlemountainsmudge.com**

*Those looking to develop the bioenergy generating and out-of-body projection processes described are advised to read up on the research of Robert Bruce, whose Treatise on Astral Projection was the template used in the novel. Bruce's bioenergetic development system can be used to enhance any form of spiritual or psychic healing, and empower any type of psychic ability. Any ability (natural or developed) requiring personal energy usage can be enhanced, e.g. boosting the immune system for self-healing, enhancing athletic performance, and speeding the healing of physical injuries. The Complete Online Works contain both of the above and can be freely downloaded from **www.astraldynamics.com**

*The energy generating method described utilising the dynamic breathing technique is explained in more detail at **www.centreofthepsyclone.com/bioenergetics**

(I have attempted to outline within the novel as complete a methodology (for two methods) as possible within a fictional framework for remote viewing and out-of-body projection, to enable investigation by those without access to additional information. The one thing not depicted or emphasised is the amount of perseverance necessary.)

*The remote viewing protocols described in the novel are based on the Scientific Remote Viewing (SRV) protocols developed by, and downloadable from, the Farsight Institute. I highly recommended that you get together with a few friends and, using these protocols, join the leading edge of human development. **www.farsight.org**

Ingo Swann is an often-heard name in the field of Remote Viewing (RV). One-time U.S. government consultant and CIA-sponsored researcher with top secret clearance, he was employed by the CIA, DIA, DOD, and INSCOM for a variety of tasks including 'psychic' spying and the training of government personnel in Remote Viewing, what the Defense Intelligence Agency refers to as "Anomalous Mental Phenomena (AMP)". He was also involved in RV experimentation and testing with the Sanford Research Institute. Gary S. Bekkum's article To the Moon and Back, With Love describes Swann's testimony, supported by declassified documents from the STAR GATE program, of his involvement in remote surveillance of the moon, and what he encountered.
www.americanchronicle.com/articles/12104

*Those interested in out-of-body phenomena should read the article 'Out-of-Body Experience – A Powerful Tool for Self-Research' by Sandie Gustus, Director of the International Academy of Consciousness, a non-profit scientific and educational organisation dedicated to consciousness studies and research. **www.iacworld.org**
The article also features in Vol 11 No.3 of Nexus magazine. **www.nexusmagazine.com/articles/oobe.html**

Related is William Buhlman's article on the researched evidence of the life changing benefits of out-of-body-experiences at **www.astralinfo.org** and **www.lightworks.com/Monthly Aspectarian/2005/September/feature1.html**

The unnamed book read by Jared in C9 refers to Journeys out of Body by Robert A. Monroe. First published in 1972, it's considered a classic in the field and provides a different projection methodology to that of Robert Bruce. Robert Monroe went on to found the Monroe Institute, which is still involved in Research & Development in the field of consciousness studies. **www.monroeinstitute.com**

Johnjoe Mcfadden at the University of Surrey, UK has conducted further scientific research into Conscious Electromagnetic Field Theory (CEMI). An overview and PDF versions of the studies 'Synchronous Firing and Its Influence on the Brain's Electromagnetic Field – Evidence for an Electromagnetic Field Theory of Consciousness' and 'The Conscious Electromagnetic Information (Cemi) Field Theory – The Hard Problem Made Easy?' can be found at **www.surrey.ac.uk/qe/cemi.htm**

*Dr Rupert Sheldrake pioneered research into morphogenetic fields. His study paper 'The Sense of Being Stared At', details his findings regarding the processes involved in telepathic communication; the series of essays 'Mind, Memory, and Archetype: Morphic Resonance and the Collective Unconscious' presents the perspective of a paradigm shift taking place in science: the shift from the mechanistic to an evolutionary and holistic world view; the related 'Prayer: A Challenge for Science' seriously questions science's underlying assumptions about the nature of causality. Much recommended are the series of 'Seven Experiments that Could Change the World', which anybody can conduct in order to demonstrate and develop the processes.
www.sheldrake.org/Articles&Papers/papers/staring
www.sheldrake.org/articles/pdf/44.pdf
www.sheldrake.org/experiment
www.sheldrake.org/articles/pdf/50.pdf

Quantum physicist and author of a number of widely cited physics papers, Fred Thaheld's study "A New Empirical Approach to the Search for Extraterrestrial Intelligence:

Astrobiological nonlocality at the Cosmological Level", proposes the use of telepathy (which he terms Controlled Superliminal Communication) as a more feasible form of communication than the radio frequencies currently used by SETI in their attempts to contact extraterrestrial intelligences.
http://xxx.lanl.gov/ftp/physics/papers/0608/0608285.pdf

Michael E. Salla, Ph.D reviews the study at
www.exopolitics.org/Exo-Comment-48.htm

A fairly technical commentary from a quantum physics perspective on how thoughts affect matter, 'How Thoughts Shape Matter' by Jack Sarfatti, one of the foremost scientific thinkers of the day, can be found at the Internet Science Education Project at
www.stardrive.org/bohm.html

(Also see the entries for **Living the Field** and **The Field** in **Links** and **Books** and on the Psyclone website.)

Positive self-control of one's mind can be developed through techniques set out in the José Silva method. Several military remote viewers have commented how their early training in the Silva method primed them for later psionic development.
www.silvamethod.com

*A major paradigm shift in the science of the mind in the form of Mimetics (mind viruses) can be examined at Meme Central. Essential for those wishing to 'disinfect' their mind.
www.memecentral.com

Information on, and resources for, the accelerated learning technique described in C4 can be found at
www.photoreading.com

*Regarding the concept of life after death read 'The Scientific Proof of Survival After Death' by Michael Roll, a work censored in the UK. That and other excellent work and research from a variety of suppressed sources (some of it censored in its country of origin) that link survival after death with sub-atomic physics can be found at the website of the Campaign for Philosophical Freedom. **www.cfpf.org.uk**

Related is the article regarding Induced After-Death Communication (IADC) by Michael E. Tymn, about a processing technique developed by clinical psychologist Dr. Allan Botkin, which allows people to deal with grief by communicating telepathically with departed souls.
www.nexusmagazine.com/articles/IADC.html

Dr Botkin's website **http://induced-adc.com**

Further information on IADCs can be found on Dr Craig Hogan's website. **http://mindstudies.com**

Scientist and researcher Vinny Pinto has an excellent website devoted to disseminating comprehensive and balanced information about Effective Microorganisms (EM) and its various applications, including its Ormus elements (ORME) aspect. **www.eminfo.info/moreem1.html**

For an overview of the subject of ORMEs/Ormus see the article 'The Magic and Mystery of ORMUS Elements' by Roger Taylor, PhD, BVSc in Nexus magazine Vol 14, No2.
www.nexusmagazine.com/articles/Ormus.html

The method for making the compound referred to as 'white powder gold' is prohibitively complex, beginning with the prohibitively expensive hard stuff. A 'Simple Ormus-Making Recipe' is offered (for research purposes) by Anne Beversdorf, which uses sea salt as the source for the needed elements. **www.quantumbalancing.com/make_ormus.htm**

One of the best sources of information, data, and links concerning the group of monoatomic elements labelled Orbitally Rearranged Molecular Elements is
www.subtleenergies.com/ormus/whatisit.htm

*Emoto mentioned in C9 refers to the Japanese researcher Masaru Emoto. If you are unaware, or have any doubt, that our thoughts affect everything in and around us, the findings of his team's research into water will change your mind and alter your beliefs, profoundly. Mr Emoto has provided scientific factual evidence that water is alive and highly responsive to our thoughts and emotions, and that our thoughts and words affect its molecular structure. When one considers that water comprises over seventy percent of the human body, and covers roughly the same amount of the planet, one gets a glimpse of how potentially Earth-changing these discoveries are. The research proves that we can positively heal and change our planet and ourselves by the thoughts we choose to think. Read how fundamental, powerful, and immediate the change can be, and see some of the photographic evidence at
www.masaru-emoto.net/english/entop.html

For more information on Kvass, also known as Kombucha, see the article Kombucha – Green Tea Symbiont: A Scientific Health Literature Review by Stuart Thomson, Director at Gaia Research. **www.gaiaresearch.co.za/kombucha.html**

Two other substances not mentioned in the novel, but worthy of mention here in the context of personal health strategies, are Bentonite Clay and Chlorella. As well as a nutritional and physiological value that has to be reviewed to be appreciated, Chlorella, one of the most scientifically researched foods ever, also binds to environmental toxins (poisons) such as mercury, lead, cadmium as well as hydrocarbon pesticides like DDT and PCB's. Bentonite also known as Montmorillonite, it is one of the best removers of heavy metals from the body. For more information on its properties see **www.alternativemedicine.com**

The website **www.evenbetterhealth.com** contains useful information and indications of the potential range of Bentonite's uses in its endorsement of a specific product.

The body's own immune system, if sufficiently strengthened and boosted by natural means, can resist or surmount an attack against any natural biological organism. For information on boosting immune system efficiency see
http://educate-yourself.org/immunboosting

Shock Doctrine, as defined by Naomi Kline in her book The Shock Doctrine: The Rise of Disaster Capitalism (see **Books**), is the use of an event, terrorist attack or economic meltdown for instance, that creates a period of confusion, dislocation, and regression after which the politicians use that period of dislocation to push through policies in a state of emergency that they wouldn't be able to do otherwise.

An image of the street barrier described in C10 can be found at **www.indymedia.org.uk/en/2005/07/316897.html**

Images relating to the description of riot police actions in C10 can be found at **http://codshit.blogspot.com/2002_08_01_ codshit_archive.html** (entry entitled We Are Not The Enemy!), and in the **Image Gallery** section of the Psyclone website.

Section 2: Recommended Reading – Online Articles

*Blueprint For a Prison Planet by Nick Sandberg. In his own opening words: *"The purpose of this piece is to introduce the reader to the possibility that much of what we typically believe about our world, notably its history and its political structure, may be some distance from the truth."* Excellently written, balanced, and insightful. **www.nick2211.yage.net/chips.htm**

Wall St and the Rise of Hitler by Anthony C. Sutton.
An incredibly detailed work (a 12-chapter book) that reveals American and British political and financial involvement in the deliberate manufacture of the Second World War. The strategies used by politicians and bankers (often the same factions and families) can still be seen in current use. An extensive study of the rise of modern socialism and the corporate socialists. **www.reformed-theology.org/html/books/wall_street/index. html**

How the Allied multinationals supplied Nazi Germany throughout World War II by Ret Marut. In depth article documenting how behind the patriotic propaganda that encouraged the working class to slaughter each other in the interests of competing national interests, international capital quietly kept the commodity circuits flowing and profits growing across all borders. With excerpts from Trading With the Enemy: An Exposé of The Nazi-American Money-Plot 1933-1949 by Charles Higham; and The Coca Cola Company under the Nazis by Eleanor Jones and Florian Ritzmann.
http://libcom.org/library/allied-multinationals-supply-nazi-germany-world-war-2

The 14 Defining Characteristics Of Fascism demonstrated throughout a variety of fascist regimes examined by Dr. Lawrence Britt. **www.rense.com/general37/fascism.htm**

Achtung! Are We The New Nazis? by Douglas Herman. Covers the disturbing similarities in policy and practice between Hitler's Nazis and the U.S. administration. See also **Achtung, Nazi! One Year Later**.
www.striketheroot.com/3/herman/herman3.html

A Nazi in the (pocket) is worth four in the Bush (family) and **The Bush-Carlyle Connection** by William Bowles. The links with the U.S. administration, notably the Bush family, and fascism are alarming to say the least. The above articles have described in detail how money was funnelled from America to Nazi Germany by American banks and businesses, primarily through I.G. Farben. The Carlyle Group is one of the largest defence contractors in the world. Its directors include ex-presidents, ex-prime ministers and Saudi aristocracy. The parallels with the military-industrial manipulations of I.G. Farben need examination, especially in view of the fact that American and British soldiers are dying in manufactured conflicts in exactly the same way as in the Second World War. The extensively researched and hyperlinked articles detail the criminal activities of the Bush family and the Carlyle Group from supporting fascism, laundering Nazi money, selling weapons to the mullahs of Iran, trading guns for drugs, doing business deals with Osama bin Laden, and supporting the Eugenics movement (or racial purity, to give it its real name).
www.informationclearinghouse.info/article3255.htm
www.informationclearinghouse.info/article3309.htm

(Also see the documentary **Exposed: The Carlyle Group** in **DVD's/Films**)

Not See's and Nazis: Denial about 9/11, Empire, Peak Oil, and the Nazi Holocaust. In 1941, the Nazis invaded Lithuania, imprisoned the Jews of Vilna into a ghetto, and started killing thousands of them in a pit outside of the town. After a while, a woman managed to stagger back to the ghetto after only being wounded at the shooting pits. The doctor who treated her became convinced she was telling the truth, and tried to warn the rest of

37

the community about the fate the Nazis had in store for them. He found it extremely difficult to persuade people - not because they'd done any research of their own to discredit the story - but because psychologically it was too difficult to cope with, and therefore denial was used instead to get through the misery of their daily lives. Needless to say, everyone was eventually killed save those who hid or fled to the forests. The modern day parallels shouldn't need pointing out.
www.oilempire.us/denial.html

Afghan massacre haunts Pentagon is a Guardian newspaper report of how thousands of Afghan prisoners were killed while travelling in sealed containers on their way from Konduz to a prison at Sheberghan. The bodies of the dead and some who survived were then buried in a mass grave at nearby Dasht Leile. U.S. Special Forces were closely involved and in charge at the time. **www.guardian.co.uk/international/story/ 0,3604,791840,00.html**

(Also see the documentary **Afghan Massacre – The Convoy of Death** in **DVD/Films**)

*Creeping Fascism: History's Lessons by Ray McGovern. Retired army and CIA officer McGovern comments on the book Defying Hitler by Sebastian Haffner. Haffner, a young lawyer in Berlin during the 1930's, wrote an account of the Nazi takeover. His description of the attitudes and inactivity displayed by the German people and their politicians parallels disturbingly with current times. The article is featured on the website of the Muslim-Jewish-Christian Alliance for 9/11 Truth. **http://mujca.com/mcgovern.htm**

The Company That Runs the Empire - Lockheed and Loaded By Jeffery St. Clair.
www.counterpunch.org/stclair01222005.html

From They Rule to We Rule: Art and Activism by Josh On. Comprehensive commentary on the reasoning behind the

excellent corporate research tool They Rule (see entry in **Links**)
www.aec.at/en/archives/festival_archive/festival_catalogs/
festival_artikel.asp?iProjectID=11803

The Inexplicable Enrichment of Bush Cronies – The Iraq Money Trail by Evelyn Pringle. The only people who are benefiting from the war on terror are members of the Military-Industrial Complex. An investigative work guaranteed to outrage. **www.informationclearinghouse.info/article17547.htm**

(*Important information on the continuation of military-industrial-congressional structures and policies within the Obama administration, and the dangers they present to the world should be viewed on the Psyclone website.)

Afghanistan, Columbia, Vietnam: The Deep Politics of Drugs and Oil by Peter Dale Scott reveals the connections between CIA and U.S. military activities of the last 60 years and the petrochemical industry, international money laundering, and international drug trafficking. **http://www.peterdalescott.net/**

The Global Drug Meta-Group: Drugs, Managed Violence, and the Russian 9/11 by Peter Dale Scott. In depth and extensively referenced article that reveals very different and disturbing reasons behind political and military actions in Afghanistan and Russia, and their connections with the ever-increasing international drug trade. For example, this statement from an article in the Asia Times: *'Tajik authorities have claimed repeatedly that neither the US nor NATO exerts any pressure on the drug warlords inside Afghanistan. "There's absolutely no threat to the labs inside Afghanistan", said Avaz Yuldashov of the Tajikistan Drug Control Agency. "Our intelligence shows there are 400 labs making heroin there, and 80 of them are situated right along our border...Drug trafficking from Afghanistan is the main source of support for international terrorism now", Yuldashov pointed out last year.'*
www.lobster-magazine.co.uk/articles/global-drug.htm

State-Organized Crime as a Case Study Of Criminal Policy is a Kentucky University Criminal Justice and Police Studies Department module that observes the following regarding the business dealings described in the above article: *"The close relationship between the U.S. government, the financial community, and organized crime is nowhere clearer than in the activities of the Bank of Credit and Commerce International (BCCI) (Kappeler, Blumberg, and Potter, 1993: 237-238). BCCI was the seventh-largest privately owned bank in the world...Among its many criminal activities was the laundering of at least $14 billion for the Colombian cocaine cartels; the facilitating of financial transactions for Panamanian president Manuel Noriega and international arms merchant Adnan Khashoggi; the funneling of cash to the contras for illegal arms deals and contra-backed drug trafficking.... Despite the enormity of BCCC's crimes and its vital role in drug trafficking, the U.S. Justice Department was more than reluctant to investigate. In fact, the Justice Department had complete information on BCCI's drug and arms operations and its illegal holdings in the United States for over three years before it even initiated an inquiry. Perhaps the reluctance of American law enforcement to interfere with such a major organized crime entity can be explained by the proliferation of what some have perceived as BCCI's 'friends' in the U.S. government holding high office."*
www.policestudies.eku.edu/POTTER/Module9.htm
www.btinternet.com/~nlpwessex/Documents/Kentuckystatecr ime.htm

The Ballad of Drugs and 9/11 is an excellently researched and composed verse by Peter Dale Scott. It radically reveals and informs with content, notes, and bibliography the actions and manoeuvres of political and international banking personalities within the global drug trafficking and money laundering industries. **www.lobster-magazine.co.uk/articles/liberation. htm**

Peter Dale Scott is a former Canadian diplomat and Professor of English at UC Berkeley. A comprehensive list of his articles, books, lectures, and videos, and those of others should be viewed at **www.peterdalescott.net/**

The Bush-Cheney Drug Empire. Article based on testimony written by ex-LAPD Narcotics Officer turned whistle-blower, Michael C. Ruppert, for the Senate Select Committee on Intelligence. Details U.S. administration connections with international drug trafficking, and the role played by Halliburton subsidiary Kellogg, Brown and Root. Also relates Ruppert's personal account of why he turned whistle-blower and political investigator. **www.fromthewilderness.com/free/ciadrugs/ bush-cheney-drugs.html**

The Lies About Taliban Heroin – Russia and Oil the Real Objectives With Heroin As A Weapon of War by Michael C. Ruppert. Investigator par excellence, Ruppert, shreds the veil of lies and propaganda thrown up by the media and exposes the real story, and in doing so provides a different perspective on political and military developments in places like Chechnya, Uzbekistan and Tajikistan. **www.copvcia.com/stories/oct_2001/heroin.html**

Drugs and the Financing of U.S. Sponsored Conflict is a collection of reports from a wide variety of mainstream media sources related to CIA/U.S. involvement in the international drug trade. **www.btinternet.com/~nlpwessex/Documents/drugs.htm**

CIA Covert Actions & Drug Trafficking by Alfred McCoy Professor of Southeast and Asian History at the University of Wisconsin, Director of the Center for Southeast Asian Studies and author of The Politics of Heroin: CIA Complicity in the Global Drug Trade. The article is extracted from testimony before the Special Seminar focusing on allegations linking CIA secret operations and drug trafficking, and details activities in South America and Afghanistan.
http://sonic.net/~doretk/Issues/97-06%20JUN/ciacovert.html

Dark Alliance by Gary Webb. Webb was the Pulitzer Prize winning reporter who first exposed direct CIA involvement with international drug trafficking and the crack epidemic of the 1980s that decimated communities across America. Following his Dark Alliance exposé in the San José Mercury News in 1996 his 25-year journalist career was destroyed by an attack from the national media who were as another journalist put it 'unaccustomed to seeing their role as gatekeepers diminished by the emerging medium known as the WorldWideWeb'. Months later Gary Webb was dead, verdict 'suicide' (two gunshot wounds to the head), a death not unlike at least two other investigators who got too close to the same people. The following links are for the transcripts of the Dark Alliance and a multi-contributor memorial tribute from From The Wilderness entitled A Giant Falls. **www.mega.nu:8080/ampp/webb.html www.fromthewilderness.com/free/ww3/121304_gary_webb.sh tml**

(See the video interview **Gary Webb: In his own words** in **DVD/Videos**)

CIA/U.S. involvement in international drug trafficking is nothing new. There is extensively documented evidence of the same parties being involved in trafficking heroin from South-East Asia during the Vietnam War. **Heroin Smuggled in Body Bags of GIs Reported by Military Eye Witness** is retired USAF Chief Master Sergeant Bob Kirkconnell's testimony regarding U.S. drug trafficking activities.
www.wanttoknow.info/militarysmuggledheroin

The Middle East Cauldron Will Scald Us All - Islam's Resistance Movement by Georges Corm
http://mondediplo.com/2006/03/02islam

Enraging 1.4 Billion Worldwide Muslims – "Blood in the Streets" Strategy – Part 1-Sexual Abuse and Specific Humiliation of Iraqi Prisoners. Subtitle: *When American and British forces sexually abused Iraqi prisoners of war, they were directly targeting one of the most sensitive areas of Islamic religion. The manner in which our sexual abuse and humiliation*

occurred was even more important than the fact that sexual abuse did occur. Evidence collected by the Cutting Edge Ministry presents a compelling theory regarding motivations behind atrocities in the Middle East.
www.cuttingedge.org/news/n1631.cfm

How We Would Fight China. A Global Policy Forum article by Robert D. Kaplan. *"The Middle East is just a blip. The American military contest with China in the Pacific will define the twenty-first century. And China will be a more formidable adversary than Russia ever was."* An informative overview of military projections for the coming years, and an insight into the martial mentality.**www.globalpolicy.org/empire/challenges/competitors/2005/june05fightchina.htm**

*The facts referred to in C10 "about who was behind the deliberate meltdown of the global financial system and why" can be found in the following articles from a variety of credentialed sources originally posted on the website of the Center for Research on Globalization. Given the Psychological Operations propaganda campaign throughout the mainstream media that effectively hid the facts, most people are completely unaware of what's really going on. These are research works that everyone needs to read.

Behind the Panic: Financial Warfare and the Future of Global Banking
"There is serious ground to believe that US Goldman Sachs ex CEO Henry Paulson, as Treasury Secretary, is not stupid. There is also serious ground to believe that he is actually moving according to a well-thought-out long-term strategy. Events as they are now unfolding in the EU tend to confirm that. As one senior European banker put it to me in private discussion, 'There is an all-out war going on between the United States and the EU to define the future face of European banking.'"
www.globalresearch.ca/index.php?context=va&aid=10495

Global Financial Meltdown

*"What we are dealing with is a clash between a handful of major financial institutions, which have developed through mergers and acquisitions into Worldwide financial giants...The financial meltdown on Wall Street largely benefits **Bank of America** and **JP Morgan Chase**, which is part of the Rockefeller empire, at the expense of Lehman Brothers, Merrill Lynch, Goldman Sachs and Morgan Stanley."*

www.globalresearch.ca/index.php?context=va&aid=10268

"Grand Larceny" on a Monumental Scale- Does the Bailout Bill Mark the End of America as We Know It?

"What is happening is that the Bush administration is engineering a massive raid on the Federal treasury to pay off the people within the financial industry who have been operating the housing scam because the politicians told them to do it. This is hush money... A long-term recession and depression are inevitable, and they are expected by those in the know. In fact, there has been a plan in the works for a very long time to bring down the U.S. economy, and it will be happening over the coming months. This is why the government is also preparing to implement martial law, or something close to it, in case public unrest breaks out. We will likely also see a clampdown on free speech, the right to protest, and use of the Internet. Federal facilities are being prepared all around the country to backstop state prisons and local jails that are already bursting at the seams."

www.globalresearch.ca/index.php?context=va&aid=10413

It's Official: The Crash of the U.S. Economy has begun.

"Among those poised to profit from the crash is the Carlyle Group, the equity fund that includes the Bush family and other high-profile investors with insider government connections. A January 2007 memorandum to company managers from founding partner William E. Conway, Jr., recently appeared which stated that, when the current "liquidity environment"—i.e., cheap credit— "ends, the buying opportunity will be a once in a lifetime chance."

www.globalresearch.ca/index.php?context=va&aid=5964

Who is Behind The Financial Meltdown?

"The winners of financial warfare are JP Morgan Chase and Bank America. Both banking institutions have consolidated their control over the US banking landscape. They have used the financial crisis to displace and/or take over rival financial institutions. The concentration of wealth and the centralization of financial power resulting from market manipulation is unprecedented."

www.globalresearch.ca/index.php?context=va&aid=10529

Banks Dictate Conditions of U.S. Financial Bailout

"The 936 point rise on the US stock market yesterday was the American ruling elite's initial verdict on the extraordinarily favorable terms the government is granting to financial firms in the $700 billion bailout passed by Congress on October 3. Far from heralding improving economic conditions for working people, the Wall Street surge reflects the financial establishment's success in extorting massive sums of money from taxpayers... The stock market's rise today is not the advent of a new era of prosperity for the American people. Rather, the bourgeoisie is celebrating the Great Heist of 2008."

www.globalresearch.ca/index.php?context=va&aid=10557

Deconstructing The Power of the Global Elite: Brute Force, The Power to Hurt, and Psychological Control

"In the aftermath of Congressional approval of bailout legislation granting sweeping powers to the financial elite, the body politic appears to be helplessly mired in the relentless unfolding of classical fascism before its very eyes. Coming to terms with this terrifying predicament can benefit from a primer that renders naked the forms of raw power used by the global elite in advancing its agenda for full spectrum dominance. This will enable us to determine if we are in fact helpless and to use care and deliberation in finding the means to take our power back."

www.globalresearch.ca/index.php?context=va&aid=10493

45

For more revealing articles regarding behind the scenes activities in war and global finance see Global Research's list of Top 100 Stories.
www.globalresearch.ca/index.php?context=va&aid=10448

Safe in Our Cages by AC Grayling.
"Not even George Orwell in his most febrile moments could have envisaged a world in which every citizen could be so thoroughly monitored every moment of the day, spied upon, eavesdropped, watched, tracked, followed by CCTV cameras, recorded and scrutinised." **www.guardian.co.uk/commentisfree/2008/aug/26/civilliberties.labour**

How Big Brother Watches Your Every Move
In one week, the average person living in Britain has 3,254 pieces of personal information stored about her or him, most of which is kept in databases for years and in some cases indefinitely. The data include details about shopping habits, mobile phone use, emails, locations during the day, journeys and internet searches. Every telephone call, swipe of a card and click of a mouse, information is being recorded, compiled and stored about Britain's citizens. All this personal information can be accessed by a disturbing and increasing amount of people, security and law enforcement agencies, local councils, and "other public bodies". For example, phone companies retain data about their customers and give it to 650 public bodies on request.
www.telegraph.co.uk/news/uknews/2571041/How-Big-Brother-watches-your-every-move.html

Total Information Awareness One of the extensive governmental databasing and data mining projects (like Novel Intelligence from Massive Data), which compile data on the day-to-day activity of individuals and checks for 'terrorist-related activity'. See the Electronic Privacy Information Center.
www.epic.org/privacy/profiling/tia

Shouting Telescreens Announce United Kingdom Of Fascism.
Did Orwell see it coming or have they copied his ideas?

www.prisonplanet.com/301003shoutingtelescreens.html

For a list of links to examinations of the worrying development and the extent of surveillance in its various forms (including implantable microchips) see
www.prisonplanet.com/archive_big_brother.html

Fluoridation – Mind Control of the Masses by Ian E. Stephen. Extracted from the book 'The Dickinson Statement: A Mind-Boggling Thesis'. Covers the practise of fluoride mass medication, its effects, and the agencies involved. Outstanding research. www.ivanfraser.com/articles/health/fluoride.html

*Mammograms cause breast cancer (and other cancer facts you probably never knew) by Dawn Prate. Fact-filled article with comments from over 20 experts.
www.newstarget.com/010886.html

(See **www.centreofthepsyclone.com** for additional information and links on the above subject.)

*How Television Fuels the Class War by Ron Kaufman. Whether we like it or not the medium of television has the capacity to shape society. Unfortunately, like so much technology that could be used for the advancement of society, this 'tool of the rich' is used to further their own agendas, to keep people divided and deceived. Site contains scientific research from a variety of sources regarding the effects of television on the mind and body. **www.turnoffyourtv.com/commentary/classwar/classwar.htm**

*Manufacturing Consent – A Propaganda Model. An overview of the Propaganda Model of the media as described by Edward Herman and Noam Chomsky in the book 'Manufacturing Consent - The Political Economy of the Mass Media.
www.thirdworldtraveler.com/Herman%20/Manufac_Consent_Prop_Model.html

47

The Neurobiology of Mass Delusion by Jason Bradford. www.globalpublicmedia.com/the_neurobiology_of_mass_del usion

*Information Control For Social Manipulation by David B. Deserano, MS. A comprehensively researched work (originally a Masters thesis) on how people's thoughts and opinions are shaped, not just by media and entertainment corporations, but also by governments, their agencies and the military-industrial complex.
www.nexusmagazine.com/articles/InformationControl.html

(See also **The Century of the Self** listed in **DVD/Films**.)

Additional information about how the media controls people's minds using subliminals and symbology can be found at **www.prisonplanet.tv/articles/july2004/120704 subliminaladvertising.htm** and **www.taroscopes.com/highwindowsarticles/symbol_literacy_1. html**

*The Cause of Internet and TV Addiction by Christopher McPeck. Information from, and links to, research into the physiological and neurological effects of TV and Internet. Puts data from the previous two entries into an even more disturbing context. **www.causeof.org**

*Disturbing information on the potential dangers of digital TV can be found **at www.centreofthepsyclone.com/digitaldangers**

It's Capitalism or a Habitable Planet: You Can't Have Both by Robert Newman / Guardian (UK) 2 Feb 2006. **www.guardian.co.uk/environment/2006/feb/02/ energy.comment**

On the Possible Effects of Changes in Schumann's Resonances on Human Psychobiology by Miller and Miller. **www.nwbotanicals.org**

The Microwave Syndrome: An International Epidemic by Dr. Carlos Sosa M.D. In describing his problem with electrosensitivity Dr. Sosa provides some interesting information on the players in the microwave communications arena. The article includes over twenty links to related websites. **www.Mast-Victims.org** (See also **www.mastsanity.org**)

Related is Barry Trower's confidential report for the Police Federation of England and Wales on the TETRA communication system adopted by the police. The research paper includes the findings of several other peer reviewed research papers, and explains in detail the effects of low-level electromagnetic radiation on the body and mind.
www.planningsanity.co.uk/reports/trower.htm

The dangers of EMF pollution and what we can do to improve our health in today's polluted world by Steve Gamble. Well-referenced paper on the effects of electromagnetic radiation (EMF/ELF/VLF), and strategies for reducing them.
www.equilibra.uk.com/emfsbio.shtml

Synthetic Telepathy and the Early Mind Wars by Richard Alan Miller. **www.nwbotanicals.org**

On The Possibility of Directly Accessing Every Human Brain by Electromagnetic Induction of Fundamental Algorithms by M.A. Persinger /Laurentian University
This statement by the author of the paper (published in 1995) says it all: *"Within the last two decades (Persinger, Ludwig, & Ossenkopp, 1973) a potential has emerged which was improbable but which is now marginally feasible. This potential is the technical capability to influence directly the major portion of the approximately six billion brains of the human species without mediation through classical sensory modalities by generating neural information within a physical medium within which all members of the species are immersed."* (The medium he is referring to is the atmosphere of this planet.)
www.rumormillnews.com/cgi-bin/archive.cgi?read=2929

For another list of articles and papers on the subject of neurological manipulation (mind control), many from within the Defense Intelligence Agency see
www.earthpulse.com/src/category.asp?catid=12

For a list of U.S. patents for mind control and behaviour modification technology see
www.surfingtheapocalypse.com/intelligence2.html

*Seven Warning Signs of Bogus Skepticism. Unfortunately, much of what comes out of the "skeptical" community these days is not proper skepticism, but all-out, fundamentalist disbelief. Such skepticism can be called pseudo-skepticism, pathological skepticism or bogus skepticism.
www.suppressedscience.net/sevenwarningsigns.html

The Limits of Liberty-We're all suspects now by Henry Porter.
www.ministryoftruth.org.uk/the-limits-of-liberty-were-all-suspects-now-henry-porter

The Register Idiot's Guide to the UK ID Card. IT experts at The Register provide a detailed projection (dated 2004) of the process by which biometric ID cards will be introduced 'by stealth' and how they will work and affect our lives.
www.theregister.co.uk/2004/05/05/complete_idcard_guide

Boycotting the Hegemony by Gerard Donnelly Smith. Shows the connection between your wallet and the war.
www.swans.com/library/art11/gsmith36.html

The Underground History of American Education: An Intimate Investigation into the Problem of Modern Schooling by John Taylor Gatto. **www.johntaylorgatto.com**

The Educational System Was Designed to Keep Us Uneducated and Docile
http://thememoryhole.com/edu/school-mission.htm

Twilight of the Psychopaths by Dr Kevin Barrett. *"Civilization, as we know it, is largely the creation of psychopaths. All civilizations, our own included, have been based on slavery and "warfare." Incidentally, the latter term is a euphemism for mass murder."* An informative and heartening article that ends, *"Truly, we are witnessing the twilight of the psychopaths. Whether in their death throes they succeed in pulling down the curtain of eternal night on all of us, or whether we resist them and survive to see the dawn of a civilization worthy of the name, is the great decision in which all of us others, however humbly, are now participating."* **www.agoracosmopolitan.com/home/ Frontpage/2008/01/02/02073.html**

*Free or Slaves? Dr. Nick Begich. A thought-provoking essay on modern economics. Written from an American perspective, but relevant to all modern societies. **www.earthpulse.com/src/ subcategory.asp?catid=8&subcatid=1**

Internet Threats

In this technological age 'knowledge is power' also translates as 'information is power'. An unrestricted flow of uncensored information is a threat to authoritarian control structures of all kinds. It's for that reason that the Information Superhighway is under attack. The following articles describe how the Internet has already been compromised and details plans afoot to 'pull its teeth'.

Google's Gag Order: An Internet Giant Threatens Free Speech
www.perrspectives.com/articles/art_gagorder01.htm

Google Censors Another 9/11 Documentary
www.infowars.net/articles/august2007/290807Google.htm

Microsoft helps China censor blogs
http://english.aljazeera.net/English/archive/archive?ArchiveI d=12946

51

Google may use games to analyse net users
**www.infowars.com/articles/bb/google_may_use_games_to_an
alyse_net_users.htm**

Google Censorship - How It Works
Contrary to earlier utopian theories of the Internet, it takes very little effort for governments to cause certain information simply to vanish for a huge number of people. This report describes the system by which results in the Google search engine are suppressed. **www.sethf.com/anticensorware/general/
google-censorship.php**

"Smart-Mob" Censorship at Google and YouTube
Explains the mechanism by which video content is censored by faceless and unaccountable 'censors' resulting in the curtailing of free speech.**www.opednews.com/articles/genera_marc_bab_
070621__22smart_mob_22_censorsh.htm**

MySpace Is The Trojan Horse Of Internet Censorship
"MySpace isn't cool, it isn't hip and it isn't trendy. It represents a cyber Trojan horse and the media elite's last gasp effort to reclaim control of the Internet and sink it with a stranglehold of regulation, control and censorship."
**www.prisonplanet.com/articles/march2006/160306myspace.h
tm**

The Digital Imprimatur by John Walker. How Big Brother and Big Media can put the Internet genie back in the bottle. (Dated but still relevant) **www.eff.org/deeplinks/archives/001379.php**

Pentagon sets its sights on social networking websites by Paul Marks.
**http://technology.newscientist.com/channel/tech/mg19025556.
200-pentagon-setsits-sights-on-social-networking-websites
.html**

Choking the Internet: How much longer will your favorite sites be on line? By Wayne Madsen.

www.waynemadsenreport.com

U.S. plans to 'fight the net' revealed by Adam Brookes, BBC Pentagon correspondent.
http://news.bbc.co.uk/1/hi/world/americas/4655196.stm

The declassified 78-page U.S. military document mentioned in the previous report titled 'Information Operations Roadmap' (parts are redacted) can be downloaded from
http://news.bbc.co.uk/1/shared/bsp/hi/pdfs/27_01_06_psyops. pdf

Our Web, Not Theirs. In Who's Interest is the Internet Being Shaped? The question considered by a revealing video from the Guerrilla News Network. **http://gnn.tv/videos/84/ Our_Web_Not_Theirs**

Read the Currents Of Awareness article of the above title at
http://coanews.org/article/2007/our-web-not-theirs

Internet Has 3 Years Before Facing Assimilation. Dated article by Kurt Nimmo that describes corporate plans to control the Internet. **www.truthnews.us/?p=2173**

Solutions to some of the problems described in the previous entries, other information on security issues in modern communications networks, and methods of protection can be found in **Links**. Updated information on the issue can be found at **www.centreofthepsyclone.com**.

———

My Heroes Have Always Killed Cowboys/Black Autonomy/War is the Health of the State Three articles taken from Do or Die, a journal published in the UK from 1992-2003, which featured reports and analysis from social and ecological frontlines around the world. Two are interviews with members of international social and ecological movements, which give a fresh perspective on the actions and principles of two much media-maligned groups, as well as the authorities actions against them. The other is a commentary by the Brighton and Hove Stop the War Committee on the war in Kosovo that, again, gives new perspective on another misrepresented and largely forgotten time. The site is an archive of the journal. **www.eco-action.org/dod**

*One of the clearest insights of anarchist principles in action in a modern business, and a window into a society run on those principles is the description of the workings of AK Press. **www.akpress.org/.aboutakpress**

Psychological Freedom – Do It Yourself Now And Increase Your Liberty. A brief anarchist critique of the capitalist order that outlines some anarchist thinking, and the fallacies and contradictions in the class system. Hosted on the Pierre J. Proudhon Memorial Computer.
http://flag.blackened.net/ishalif/anarchy.html

What Would an Anarchist Society Look Like? Anarchism is essentially a constructive theory, despite the picture usually painted of it as chaotic or mindlessly destructive. Over 70 articles explain the theoretical facets of a free society.
www.geocities.com/CapitolHill/1931/secIcon.html

*Specific Suggestion: General Strike** by Garret Keizer in Harpers Magazine. Describes valid strategies for the U.S. that are equally as valid and applicable in the UK, or anywhere for that matter. **http://harpers.org/archive/2007/10/0081720**

*Disobey** by John Pilger. A five-year old message that has yet to be properly heard. "*There is only one form of opposition now: it is civil disobedience leading to what the police call civil unrest. The latter is feared by undemocratic governments of all stripes.*" (Ed's note: Regarding a reaction to that fear see the entry in **Section 1** regarding U.S. concentration camps)
www.thirdworldtraveler.com/Pilger_John/Disobey.html

Peak Oil and the Working Class by Dale Allen Pfeiffer. Revolutionary views on how the working classes are being exploited, and will continue to be exploited during the developing crisis caused by rapidly dwindling oil reserves, and what they can do about it. Again written from an American perspective, but relevant everywhere.
www.mountainsentinel.com/content/peakoilworkingclass.pdf

*The Unnecessary Energy Crisis: How to Solve It Quickly by T. E. Bearden. The perceptive and practical vision of the inventor of the tragically 'buried' Motionless Electromagnetic Generator. A 'must read'. **www.cheniere.org**

Where in the World is all the Free Energy? by Peter Lindemann, DSc. Since the late 1800s multiple methods for producing vast amounts of energy at extremely low cost have been developed. None of these technologies has made it to the 'open' consumer market as an article of commerce.
www.nexusmagazine.com/articles/freeenergy.html
www.free-energy.cc

Breaking the "Political Consensus" The Science of Climate Change: What does it Really Tell Us? Andrew G. Marshall. The purpose of this report is to examine the science behind climate change so as to better understand the issue at hand, and thus, to be able to make an informed decision on how to handle the issue. The primary aim is to examine climate change from a perspective not often heard in media or government channels; that of climate change being a natural phenomenon, not the result of man-made carbon emissions.
www.globalresearch.ca/index.php?context=va&aid=9763

Interplanetary 'Day After Tomorrow' by Richard Hoagland and David Wilcox.
"The entire solar system, not just our one small planet, is currently undergoing profound, never-before-seen physical changes. This paper will address and scientifically document a wide variety of significant examples, drawing from a host of

55

published mainstream sources. This Report's scientific data, from a variety of highly credible institutions (including NASA itself), reveals that startling "climate change" phenomena are occurring, not just here on Earth, but, in fact -- throughout the entire solar system."
www.enterprisemission.com/_articles/05-14-2004_Interplanetary_Part_1/Interplanetary_1.htm

Author of the above article, Richard Hoagland, served as a Curator of Astronomy & Space Science at the Springfield Museum of Science, and as a science adviser to Walter Cronkite and CBS News during the Apollo program. He has also been a consultant to NASA. Together with Mike Bara he authored the New York Times bestseller Dark Mission listed in **Books**.

Finding The Strength To Love And Dream by Robin D.G. Kelley. An inspiring and thought-provoking essay from Kelley's book Freedom Dreams: The Black Radical Imagination. **www.swans.com/library/art8/zig076.html**

A Prescription for Peace by Doug Soderstrom. Practical philosophical methods for each of us to adopt to develop an organic process of peace.
www.informationclearinghouse.info/article15691.htm

The Imaginal Energy of Earth by Joanne H. Stroud, Ph.D. The transcript of a talk at the Dallas Institute of Humanities and Culture, which includes the findings of various theoretical scientists in a discussion of the necessity of replacing the mechanistic model with that of Earth as a self-regulating organism, and the true position of the human species in relation to it.**www.dallasinstitute.org/Programs/Previous/Fall% 202001/talks/jstroudimageearth.htm**

*Hope, Delusion and Evolution - how the desire hope has been used as a weapon. A collection of articles by noted authors. *"Only when you have reached that deep level of hopelessness, where you see no avenue of escape, can you clear* *your mind enough to begin to see where the real problem lies. The real problem lies, my friends, in the fact that you and I have nothing to say about how our societies are run. Any one of us has more sense than the people who are running things, and we certainly have our fellow beings more at heart. Our problem lies in our own powerlessness, leaving power in the hands of those who always abuse it, in one way or another, in one age after another"* – From The Post-Bush Regime: A Prognosis by Richard K. Moore. **www.oilempire.us/hope.html**

*Fluid Intelligence explains how our deepest beliefs and conceptions about life and the world are to a large degree conditioned by our childhood experiences, our education, the mass media, and various other external influences. An individual's level of fluid intelligence can be determined based on the degree to which s/he is able to let go of previously held conceptions on encountering reliable information or experiences which show these conceptions to be mistaken or overly simplistic. **www.wanttoknow.info/fluidintelligence**

*Following advice to focus on what's breaking through, not what's breaking down, see the inspiring and very informative transcripts from the U.S. TV series Thinking Allowed, Conversations On the Leading Edge of Knowledge and Discovery, between psychologist and President of the Intuition Network, Dr Jeffrey Mishlove, and personalities from the cutting edge of science and philosophy. Current research indicates a paradigm shift developing throughout the human species, an evolutionary development that has the potential to lift us out of the swamp caused by outmoded thinking and behaviour. The following is a related list:

A Manifesto for Psychic Liberation – J Mishlove, Ph.D.
The Psychodynamics of Liberation - Kathleen Speeth, Ph.D.
The Emerging New Culture - Fritjof Capra, Ph.D.
Global Mind Changes - Willis Harman, Ph.D.
Brain, Mind and Society - Marilyn Ferguson
www.intuition.org/idxtran.htm

Other 'free society' models can be found at
www.geocities.com/CapitolHill/1931/secIcon.html

DVD's/Films
(Viewable online with three exceptions)

*WMD-Weapons of Mass Deception
'A comprehensive and devastating critique of the TV news networks' complacency and complicity in the war on Iraq...brilliantly argued and scrupulously documented... a must see' (Chicago Reader). A Globalvision documentary by Danny Schechter that demonstrates how the media are the biggest WMD (Weapon of Mass Deception) being used in the Middle East.
www.wmdthefilm.com/mambo/index.php

*Loose Change
Exceptional documentary showing evidence that the U.S. government was, at the very least, criminally negligent regarding the attacks of September 11th, 2001. A deeper look at the evidence, however, presents the conclusion that elements within government may have been directly responsible for the attack themselves.
www.loosechange911.com
http://video.google.com/videoplay?docid=78669294481927535 01&q=loose+change+recut
http://stage6.divx.com/Louder-Than-Words/video/1005782/ Loose-Change

Terrorstorm
'The DVD of the Resistance'. Excellent, graphic documentary that puts Middle East and 'terrorist' activities in perspective. See it at Google Video (unless by the time of reading Google has censored this too!), and read about it/buy it at Prison Planet, the website run by the film's maker, Alex Jones.
http://video.google.com/videoplay?docid=-594826360757 9389947
www.prisonplanet.com/articles/august2006/110806terrorstor m.htm

*The Power of Nightmares
This eye-opening BBC documentary shows that, especially after the events of the 11th of September, 2001, fear has been used widely in the media to manipulate the public into giving up civil liberties and turning over power to elite groups with their own hidden agendas. It presents highly informative interviews with experts and top officials in combating terrorism that raise serious questions about who is behind all of the fear mongering. These experts and riveting footage also show how the media have been manipulated to support secret power agendas. *The Power of Nightmares* clearly demonstrates that the nightmare vision of a powerful, united terrorist organization waiting to strike our societies is largely an illusion. Wherever the BBC team looked for al-Qaeda, from the mountains of Afghanistan to the sleeper cells in America, they found that we are chasing a phantom enemy. For all citizens who care about the future of our world, this is a must-watch video.
http://video.google.com/videosearch?q=%22power+of+night mares%22&hl=en
www.archive.org/details/ThePowerOfNightmares
www.dkosopedia.com/index.php/The_Power_of_Nightmares:
_The_Rise_of_the_Politics_of_Fear

(See ex-U.S. presidential interpreter Fred Burk's entry at
www.wanttoknow.info/powerofnightmares)

*The Century of the Self - The Untold History of Controlling the Masses Through the Manipulation of Unconscious Desires. Adam Curtis' acclaimed series tells the untold and sometimes controversial story of the growth of the mass-consumer society in Britain and the United States. In the words of Edward Bernays, the 'father of PR (spin)', nephew of Sigmund Freud, who was instrumental in the creation and development of the process: *"The conscious and intelligent manipulation of the organized habits and opinions of the masses is an important element in democratic society. Those who manipulate this unseen mechanism of society constitute an invisible government which is the true ruling power of our* *country.*

We are governed, our minds are moulded, our tastes formed our ideas suggested, largely by men we have never heard of. This is a logical result of the way in which our democratic society is organized."

Downloadable in four-parts from
www.informationliberation.com/?id=8339

Sir! No Sir!

The suppressed story of the movement that rocked the world, the GI movement against the Vietnam War. The film brings to life the history of the GI movement through the stories of those who were part of it; Reveals the explosion of defiance that the movement gave birth to with never-before-seen archival material; Explores the profound impact that movement had on the military and the war itself; and tells the story of how and why the GI Movement has been erased from the public memory.
www.sirnosir.com

Beyond the Green Zone

Unembedded Journalist, Dahr Jamail talks about his experiences reporting the Iraqi side of the war. Torture, white phosphorus and deadly attacks unfold in graphic stories of the American occupation.
www.informationclearinghouse.info/article19406.htm

Paying The Price: Killing The Children Of Iraq

A documentary film by John Pilger.
Sanctions enforced by the UN on Iraq since the Gulf War have killed more people than the two atomic bombs dropped on Japan in 1945, including over half a million children - many of whom weren't even born when the Gulf War began.
http://informationclearinghouse.info/article15385.htm

Iraq: The Hidden War

The film shows the footage used by TV news broadcasts, and compares it with the devastatingly powerful uncensored footage of the aftermath of the carnage that is becoming a part of the

fabric of life in Iraq. Images of Iraq dominate our TV news bulletins every night but in this film, Channel 4 news presenter Jon Snow, questions whether these reports are sugarcoating the bloody reality of war under the U.S.-led occupation.
www.informationclearinghouse.info/article13420.htm

*Everyone who uses a mobile phone and/or whose children use a mobile phone, needs to view the following list of videos, which expose the life-threatening dangers of mobile and wireless technology and the moves made by the phone and wireless companies and the media to keep the information from the public.

Public Exposure: DNA, Democracy and the Wireless Revolution
www.youtube.com/watch?v=VGnLT5U75rQ

Skull Penetration of Cell Phone Radiation in Children
www.youtube.com/watch?v=lwmpdFJijn8&mode=related&search=

Cell Phone War
www.youtube.com/watch?v=sEqCkwPmQ_w&feature=related

Invisible cell phone dangers Part 1
www.youtube.com/watch?v=MSPb-8XtdzI&mode=related&search=

Public Exposure part1
http://video.google.com/videoplay?docid=6518153738782954894&hl=en

(*More information on the dangers of wireless technology can be examined at **www.centreofthepsyclone.com/wirelessdangers**)

Merck Vaccine Chief Brings HIV/AIDS to America
A section of the documentary **In Lies We Trust – CIA, Hollywood, and Bioterrorism** by Leonard Horovitch, showing

an interview of Maurice Hillerman, then Vaccine Division Chief of pharmaceutical giant, Merck. Hillerman casually, and laughingly at times, describes how AIDS was knowingly introduced into America.
http://ca.youtube.com/watch?v=edikv0zbAlU

*Afghanistan AC-130 gunship
*Take 'em Out
Two pieces of cockpit video footage showing how unarmed civilians are being massacred in Afghanistan.
http://hk.youtube.com/watch?v=F6i3Pdm0jP4
www.informationclearinghouse.info/video1011.htm

*Afghan Massacre – Convoy of Death
This film tells the story of thousands of prisoners who surrendered to the U.S. military's Afghan allies after the siege of Kunduz. According to eyewitnesses, some three thousand of the prisoners were forced into sealed containers and loaded onto trucks for transport to Sheberghan prison. Eyewitnesses say when the prisoners began shouting for air, U.S.-allied Afghan soldiers fired directly into the truck, killing many of them. These witnesses say U.S. Special Forces redirected the containers carrying the living and dead into the desert and stood by as survivors of the ordeal were shot and buried. Now, up to three thousand bodies lie buried in a mass grave. Afghan Massacre has outraged human rights groups and international human rights lawyers, who are calling for investigation into whether U.S. Special Forces are guilty of war crimes.
www.informationclearinghouse.info/article3267.htm
www.youtube.com/watch?v=A-NpdoGkaEc

*Gaza's Reality
Footage from one of the many camps in Gaza for Palestinians displaced by the Israeli occupation, presented with the question 'Could you live like this?' Desperate conditions lead to desperate acts. **www.informationclearinghouse.info/article15693.htm**

The Shock Doctrine: The Rise of Disaster Capitalism
In this short interview Naomi Klein discusses her book The Shock Doctrine: The Rise of Disaster Capitalism and how disaster capitalism has worked in Iraq, post-Katrina New Orleans, and past military coups to push through extreme economic practices which privatise everything and gut social programs and government agencies against the will of the general populations of the countries in which the disasters occur. **www.alternet.org/blogs/video/69481/**

Exposed: The Carlyle Group
This highly informative documentary film uncovers the subversion of what's left of democracy in America. (See the entry in **Online Articles**)
www.informationclearinghouse.info/article3995.htm

Gary Webb – In His Own Words
Gary Webb is the Pulitzer prize-winning reporter who broke the story of the CIA's involvement in the importation of cocaine into the U.S. His death in 2004 was reported to be a suicide (two gunshots to the head). In this interview Webb discusses the media battle that erupted in the aftermath of his groundbreaking 1996 investigation into the CIA's drug dealing operations during the 1980s. Page includes eleven links to tributes from other journalists. **www.gnn.tv/videos/video.php?id=30**

(The above video is one of 397 hosted by You Tube under the search 'CIA cocaine'.)

*U.S. vs. John Lennon
A moving and inspiring documentary by the team behind Fahrenheit 9/11, which provides insights about the man himself, Yoko Ono Lennon, and other revolutionary individuals and members of the anti-war/peace movement. Includes footage of and interviews with members of the Black Panthers/Black Power movement; and the devious, scheming activities of, and characters in, the U.S. administration of the 60's and 70's when the U.S. was waging an eerily similar war in Vietnam,

Cambodia, and Laos. As the filmmakers say, the movie "will also show that this was not just an isolated episode in American history, but that the issues and struggles of that era remain relevant today".

www.theusversusjohnlennon.com
**http://video.google.com/videoplay?docid=77704669923438999
6**

*V for Vendetta
A film based on the graphic novel by Alan Moore and David Lloyd. Screenplay by the Wachowskis, the creators of Matrix. A perceptive, powerful, and inspiring (and suspiciously under-marketed!) tale of anarchist response to fascism. As Moore commented about the catalytic character, V, *"...the central question is, is this guy right? Or is he mad? What do you, the reader* [of the graphic novel]*, think about this? Which struck me as a properly anarchist solution. I didn't want to tell people what to think, I just wanted to tell people to think and consider some of these admittedly extreme little elements, which nevertheless do recur fairly regularly throughout human history."*
http://vforvendetta.warnerbros.com

(The message of Guy Fawkes, on whom the main character of the film bases his identity, has been the subject of a psychological operations (PsyOps) campaign aimed at the British public for the past few years. See the extended commentary on the Psyclone website.)

65

Links

http://www.google-watch.org
Public Information Research watchdog concerned with Google's monopoly, algorithms and privacy policies.

http://www.wikipedia-watch.org
*Considered by some to be "almost as accurate as the oldest continuously published reference work in the English language" the Encyclopaedia Britannica, the reality is that because of its editorial and administrative policies and practises, Wikipedia is a website perfectly suited to the distribution of misleading and inaccurate information. Founding member of the Committee of Concerned Journalists, John Siegenthaler, called it a "flawed and irresponsible research tool" after becoming the victim of malicious character assassination through Wikipedia (Siegenthaler has posted a balanced and very informative response on Wikipedia Watch). What prompted my discovery of this site was finding subtle biases and inaccuracies when using Wikipedia for my own research, (see the article **'Suicide Bombers' and the Promise of Heaven?** on the Psyclone website). The fact that such disinformation exists on a site used by millions for research purposes has some quite disturbing implications. Even more disturbing is evidence that suggests input from at least one intelligence agency.

http://wikiscanner.virgil.gr
Wikiscanner is an investigative site that uncovers and lists Wikipedia edits carried out by vested political and corporate interests.

https://ssd.eff.org/
The Electronic Frontier Foundation provides some of the best advice for security in communications networks (Internet, Wi-Fi, mobile phone) through their Surveillance Self-Defense Project. Essential reading for anyone who uses the networks listed.

http://sethf.com/anticensorware/
Electronic Frontier Foundation Pioneer Award winner, anticensorship activist and programmer Seth Finklestein's Anticensorware Investigation. Contains reports such as Searching Through The Great Wall Of China which describes a simple technique that can be used with some search engines to bypass censorware bans when searching for forbidden words.

http://www.peacefire.org/
Anticensorship website that provides (among other things) access to the Circumventor, a program which gets around blocking (filtering) software.

http://www.internetrights.org.uk
Home of the Civil Society Internet Rights (CSIR) Project, a GreenNet sponsored initiative to provide knowledge, resources and tools for civil society organisations to safely and productively use the Internet as a means of increasing democracy and to campaign on social justice issues. Excellent source of up to date information and advice on subjects such as civil rights and Internet regulation, communications data protection and retention, privacy, surveillance, and encryption.

http://www.riseup.net
The Riseup Collective provides web hosting and services for those working on liberatory social change. Included less from experience of their service than for the spirit of their political principles, which are an inspiration to read.

http://www.privacyinternational.org
International human rights watchdog concerned with surveillance and other privacy threats.

http://tor.eff.org
Tor is a software project that helps you defend against traffic analysis, a form of network surveillance that threatens personal freedom and privacy, confidential business activities and relationships, and state security. Tor protects you by bouncing

your communications around a distributed network of relays run by volunteers all around the world: it prevents somebody watching your Internet connection from learning what sites you visit, and it prevents the sites you visit from learning your physical location. Tor works with many of your existing applications, including web browsers, instant messaging clients, remote login, and other applications based on the TCP protocol.

http://www.fromthewilderness.com
Mike Ruppert, ex-LAPD investigator and whistleblower, has been working to expose secret dealings of the U.S. government and Secret Services for nearly thirty years, and publishing the evidence in From The Wilderness. Recent incidents have resulted in the closure of FTW and Ruppert taking exile in Venezuela. FTW is being maintained online for archive purposes. Excellent, sadly archival only, investigative journalism. (Read the sections 'Evolution' and 'A Personal Message From Michael C. Ruppert…' to get a feel of the man's ethos)

http://www.indymedia.org
"*A network of individuals, independent and alternative media activists and organisations, offering grassroots, non-corporate, non-commercial coverage of important social and political issues.*" Global independent media with nodes in every country.

http://www.wanttoknow.info
"If the facts presented here were reported in headline news where they belong, concerned citizens would be astounded and demand to know more. This has not happened, which is why we felt compelled to create this website. **The verifiable information presented here may at first disturb you. It may even change the way you look at the world. Yet we invite you to see this as a powerful opportunity for building a brighter future. By sharing this vital information with your friends and colleagues, you can play a key role in restoring a true democracy of the people, by the people, and for the people… We encourage you to be skeptical in exploring this information. Some of what you read may at first seem quite unbelievable. Yet we also encourage you*

68

to do a little research using the links to the reliable sources provided and determine for yourself whether there is truth to the information provided."

http://www.zmag.org
"I hesitate to call ZCom the leading samizdat of our age, because it is also one of the great newspapers of the Internet, print, and video. You get more in one visit than hours of thumbing through voluminous newspaper voices of rapacious power. The range of good journalism, writing and scholarship on ZCom is astonishing: from the pen of the well-known to eyewitness reporting of 'citizen journalists'." John Pilger

http://www.medialens.org
Independent media whose aim is *"to encourage the general population to challenge media managers, editors and journalists who set news agendas that traditionally reflect establishment/elite interests. We hope to raise public awareness of the underlying systemic failings of the corporate media to report the world around us honestly, fairly and accurately... to highlight significant examples of the systemic media distortion that is facilitating appalling crimes against humanity..."*

http://www.propagandacritic.com
*Website devoted to the analysis of propaganda techniques used by politicians and media.

http://www.infowars.net
Alternative media website of the maker of the documentary TerrorStorm, Alex Jones. Of particular relevance is its coverage of the preparations going on in the U.S. to move it into military rule.

http://globalresearch.ca
The Centre for Research on Globalisation. Wide-ranging and in depth studies. Excellent audio and video section.

69

http://www.informationliberation.com
Alternative media that brings you 'the news you're not supposed to know'.

http://www.projectcensored.org
Project Censored is a media research group out of Sonoma State University that tracks the news published in independent journals and newsletters. From these, Project Censored compiles an annual list of 25 news stories of social significance that have been overlooked, under-reported or self-censored by major national news media in the U.S.

http://www.theyrule.net/html/index.php
A few companies control much of the economy and oligopolies exert control in nearly every sector of the economy. The people who head up these companies swap on and off the boards from one company to another, and in and out of government committees and positions. These people run the most powerful institutions on the planet. This is not a conspiracy. They are proud to rule. And yet these connections of power are not always visible to the public eye. They Rule is a starting point for research about these powerful individuals and corporations. (See also the article **From They Rule to We Rule: Art and Activism** in **Online Articles**)

http://www.afghanistanafterdemocracy.com
The website for the book of the same name. The untold story through photographic images. Proceeds from the book go toward the building of a hospital to deal with the huge increase in severe congenital defects resulting from U.S. short and long term genocide using weapons of mass destruction (see the article 'Your Tax Dollars in Action' at **www.rense.com/general74/ afgg.htm**)

http://www.iraqbodycount.org
Iraq Body Count is an ongoing human security project that maintains and updates the world's largest public database of violent civilian (non-combatant) deaths during and since the

2003 invasion. Data is drawn from crosschecked media reports, hospital, morgue, NGO and official figures to produce a credible record of known deaths and incidents.

http://avmp.info
The Afghan Victim Memorial Project is an online memorial for some of the over a million civilians who have died at the hands of the U.S. in Afghanistan. The Afghan Victim Memorial was created to pay tribute to these victims and create an accurate database resource for the future.

http://www.militaryproject.org
Website of the publication GI Special. Produced by GI's 'on the ground'. Read how the words of those who are there differ greatly with those (politicians and media) who aren't. It's sister publication Traveling Soldier can be found at
http://www.traveling-soldier.org

http://stopthewall.org
*Website of the Grassroots Palestinian Anti-Apartheid Wall Campaign. See how, with the backing of the U.S. administration, the Israeli regime is turning back the clock with its illegal and brutal occupation. (A portion of the proceeds from Psyclone goes toward helping children in Palestine affected by the Israeli apartheid)

http://www.safeminds.org
Website of the Coalition for SafeMinds (Sensible Action For Ending Mercury-Induced Neurological Disorders), a non-profit organisation dedicated to investigating the risks of exposure to mercury from medical products, particularly vaccinations. Research shows disturbing similarities between symptoms of mercury poisoning and symptoms of autism, described as virtually identical in young children.

http://www.brojon.org
The Brother Jonathan Gazette. Comprehensive news and media, updated hourly. Contains a three-chapter excerpt from the book

Black Gold Hot Gold - The Rise of Fascism in the American Energy Business by Marshall Douglas Smith.

http://www.mediafilter.org/caq
Website of the Institute for Media Analysis. Source for Covert Action Quarterly.

http://www.akuk.com
International radical press and distributor. Comprehensive list of titles in book, magazine and periodical, and audio-visual formats. Exceptional source for radical and underground publications not found in mainstream bookshops.

http://www.gnn.tv
*Guerrilla News Network is an independent news organization whose mission is to expose people to important global issues through cross-platform guerrilla programming. Contains volumes of outstanding content from a wide variety of digital media guerrillas.

http://www.undercurrents.org
Undercurrents News Network. UK-based network of video activists showing 'the news you don't see on the news'. Also produce video and DVD 'compilations of inspiration from a selection of radical video producers'.

http://911scholars.org and **http://stj911.org**
Websites committed to revealing and disseminating the truth about the incidents of that day.

http://www.warprofiteers.com
*Reveals whose fingers are in which pies.

http://www.swans.com
Insightful, thought provoking, and inspiring socio-political commentaries and essays from a variety of sources.

http://www.thomhartmann.com
Thom Hartmann is a Project Censored Award-winning best-selling author and host of a nationally syndicated daily progressive talk show in the U.S. Excellent 'Independent Thinker' Book of the Month Reviews.

http://tash.gn.apc.org/INDEX.htm
Photohistorian Alan Lodge's site containing a multimedia record of 'Alternative' and 'Youth' cultures of the last twenty-seven years. Received the 1998 Big Brother award for outstanding contributions to the protection of privacy from Privacy International for his work on surveillance.

www.poleshift.org/index.html
Informed debate about scientifically measurable mechanisms that might possibly cause events such as shifting or wandering of the poles, and displacement of the earth's crust.

http://www.astralvoyage.com
*Website devoted to out-of-body projection research and information dissemination.

http://www.survivalafterdeath.org
*Source of large quantities of research material on the subject.

http://www.livingthefield.com
Living the Field is a model based on the best-selling book *The Field* (see **Books** for details), a systemised course in expanding human consciousness based on hard science. Through the leading edge research of a variety of frontier quantum physicists, *The Field* tells a new scientific story, revealing our astonishing birthright and demonstrating how we are prisoners of an outmoded paradigm based on 300-year-old Newtonian thinking. Among things shown is that our human potential can soar far higher than what current science tells us about ourselves, and that we have the individual and collective ability to change our world. Essential reading for anyone interested in the emergent paradigm shift in consciousness, or anyone who wants to change the world.

http://www.imaginepeace.com
Yoko Ono Lennon continuing to spread the message: Think Peace, Act Peace, Spread Peace.

http://www.trufax.org
Website of the Leading Edge International Research Group. Research and socio-philosophy to open your eyes and <u>really</u> stretch your mind.

http://montalk.net
Information and advice from the leading edge of the fringe on Transcending the Matrix Control System. Those new to this level of thinking should read Fringe Knowledge for Beginners and Advice for Newbies. 'Take what makes sense and leave the rest for another time.'

Books
(A small selection connected with topics mentioned in the novel)

Freedom Is More Than Just A 7-letter Word by Veronica: of the Chapman family. One of the most important socio-political books you will ever read. The author has, as one person put it, 'given us the firm foundation upon which we can build a mass movement that will sweep away the Criminal Global Elite's influence and activities in Great Britain in a completely non-violent way.' The plain fact of the matter is that we have all been the victims of a massive deception – but the good news is we can all do something about it. Hardcopy and free PDF from: **www.lulu.com/items/volume_65/7313000/7313003/5/print/Fre edom.pdf

*The Law by Frédéric Bastiat
When a reviewer wishes to give special recognition to a book, they predict that it will still be read 'a hundred years from now.' *The Law*, first published 1850, is already more than a hundred years old. Frederic Bastiat (1801-1850) was a French economist, statesman, and author. As stated by one individual who hosts the classic on their website: *"If you believe - deeply, or generally, or even in passing - that the power of "the state" is beneficial to human beings, this book will challenge your premises. If your mind is open, you should not evade the challenge."* Downloadable from **http://bastiat.org/en/the_law.html**

They Thought They Were Free by Milton Mayer. A 'poignant and prescient' work showing how fascism took a hold in Germany before WWII, and how it can develop anywhere. Another 'must read'.

The Immaculate Deception: The Bush Crime Family Exposed by Russell Bowen. The retired Brigadier General with the Office of Security Services (OSS) reveals his former drug running activities on behalf of the U.S. government. *"This is perhaps the most shocking book written this century about treason committed by the highest leaders within the U.S. Government. This* *disturbing and thought provoking expose, which few Americans know about, shows the truth about the drug running activities on behalf of the 'secret government'. You will learn about the unsavory past of George Bush [Snr] and his family, as well as the unscrupulous activities in which he has been involved."* Amazon.com Book Review

And The Truth Shall Set You Free by David Icke. Labelled 'the most explosive book of the 20th century'. One of the most comprehensively researched works covering behind the scenes socio-political manoeuvrings. Say the name David Icke and nine times out of ten the response will be some asinine comment based on one of the biggest media smear campaigns ever. Icke is one of the most dedicated socio-political researchers of the past fifty years. The extent and duration of the campaign is an indication of how dangerous the man and his message were considered by the authorities. See also **Alice in Wonderland and the World Trade Center Disaster** and **The Biggest Secret** by the same author for more exceptionally researched evidence of, among other things, the connections between Halliburton/KBR and international drugs and arms dealing activities. As well as reams of information on other interconnected subjects, **Tales From The Time Loop** puts the author's much-publicised breakdown into context, and clarifies his theory about 'the reptilian agenda'.
www.davidicke.com

Virus of the Mind by Richard Brodie. Very detailed and readable work on the new science of mimetics by the author of the Microsoft Word program. Brodie's other work on the same subject can be found on the Meme Central website listed in **Section 1**.

Hands of Light: Guide to Healing Through the Human Energy Field by Barbara Brennan. Brennan, an ex-NASA scientist, has developed a perceptual and therapeutic system based around the human energy field. The book details the revolutionary way of seeing and healing the mind-body system.

76

The Dancing Wu Li Masters by Gary Zukav. 'An overview of the new physics.' Very readable and detailed explanation of quantum and relativity theories, and the comparisons between these, modern psychology, and eastern thought.

The Tao of Physics by Fritjof Capra. First published independently in 1975 it contested much of the conventional 'wisdom' of the day by demonstrating striking parallels between the knowledge of ancient traditions and the discoveries of 20th century physics. Published in 43 editions in 23 languages.

Mind Trek by Joseph McMoneagle. Written by an ex-U.S. soldier, one of the better-known military trained remote viewers. In his words: *"What must be remembered is that I'm not writing this in order to prove that psychic functioning or RV (remote viewing) exists. I already know this to be so. I am writing this in order to address what effect that knowledge has had on my mind and in my life and to share that information with others."*

Cosmic Top Secret by Jon King. Covers evidence of 'two intrinsically interactive phenomena: the extraterrestrial presence, and implications regarding the possibility of an imminent social, political and economic, and technological paradigm shift'. Includes a section on deep underground bases.

*Controlling the Human Mind: The Technologies of Political Control or Tools for Peak Performance by Dr N Begich. This is the century of the brain and the mind. The technologies that have advanced, under cover of secrecy and national security, now have the power to either enslave us or free us to our higher potentials. A real survival handbook.

Dark Mission by Richard C. Hoagland and Mike Bara. For most Americans, the word NASA suggests a squeaky-clean image of technological infallibility. Yet the truth is that NASA was born in a lie and has always concealed many truths about its occult origins. Mystical organizations quietly dominate NASA, carrying out their own secret agendas behind the scenes. This is the story

77

of men at the very fringes of rational thought and conventional wisdom, operating at the highest levels of our country. Their policies are far more aligned with ancient religions and secret mystery schools than the facade of rational science and cool empiricism NASA has successfully promoted to the world for almost fifty years. *Dark Mission* is proof of the secret history of the National Aeronautics and Space Administration and the astonishing, seminal discoveries it has repeatedly suppressed for decades. **www.darkmission.net/**

Fer De Lance by Col T Bearden. Comprehensive work on the subject of weaponised Scalar technology by a world authority in the field. **www.cheniere.org/books/ferdelance/index.html**

Mind Control Summary – The Secrets of Mind Control
This revealing ten-page mind control summary contains excerpts from three landmark books by top mind control researchers: *Bluebird* by Colin A. Ross, MD, a leading Canadian psychiatrist; *Mind Controllers* by Dr. Armen Victorian; and *A Nation Betrayed* by mind control survivor Carol Rutz. All three authors provide hundreds of footnotes for their research. Of those footnotes, 80 are included in this summary, many with links to original sources. Much of this research is based on 18,000 pages of declassified CIA documents on mind control. (The declassified documents can be ordered in CD format directly from the government. For details of how to request referenced documents using a FOIA (Freedom of Information Act) request go to **www.wanttoknow.info/mindcontrol10pg#ciadocs**)
For a two-page summary of this mind control material go to **www.wanttoknow.info/mindcontrol**

A Soldier's Song by Ken Lukowiak. Lukowiak served with 2 Para in the Falklands in 1982. Funny, sad, perceptive, and honest. The real story behind the news reports.

1984 by George Orwell. Worth reading again even if you already have. More relevant now than ever. Refer to C5 for the context of its mention.

and colleague Paul Beard through the medium Marie A. Baker.
Fascinating and touching.

Compassionate Justice by Dr Robert Dickson Crane. The
author, a one-time prisoner in Stalin's Gulag Archipelago, and
U.S. Ambassador to the United Arab Emirates, has condensed
hundreds of articles from the scholarly online publication The
American Muslim into a book on the traditionalist contribution of
classical Islam to human rights, which introduces a new
paradigm of compassionate justice as the source of convergence
between science and religion. Downloadable in sections from
**www.theamericanmuslim.org/tam.php/features/articles/comp
assionate_justice_table_of_contents/0014050**

Following on from the entry in **Section 1**, highly recommended
are three books by Sanderson Beck: **Best For All: How We Can
Save the World**, **Nonviolent Revolution for Global Justice**,
and the **Nonviolent Action Handbook**, all available in html and
hardcopy.
www.san.beck.org/BFA1-GlobalEmergency.html
www.san.beck.org/GPJ33-NonviolentRevolution.html
www.san.beck.org/NAH1-Nonviolence.html

The Field is a bestselling book by Lynne McTaggart that tells a
radically new scientific story. Called 'a book that could change
the world forever', it contains the work of a number of frontier
scientific explorers that suggests that at our essence, we exist as a
unity, a relationship utterly interdependent, with the parts
affecting the whole at every moment. The implications of this
new scientific story on our understanding of life and the design
of our society are extraordinary. If a quantum field holds us all
together in its invisible web, we have to rethink our definitions of
ourselves and what it is to be human. If we are in constant and
instantaneous dialogue with our environment, if all the
information from the cosmos flows through our pores at every
moment, then our current notion of our human potential is only a

glimmer of what it should be. If we're not really separate at our essence, we can no longer think in terms of winning and losing. We need to redefine what we designate as me and not-me, and reform the way that we interact with other human beings, prioritise capitalism, and view time and space.

www.intendingthefield.com

The Intention Experiment builds on the scientific evidence contained in *The Field* that we are on the brink of a new scientific age. The Intention Experiment is not only a book; it is the first worldwide series of double-blind experiments to test the power of intention. The studies, developed by McTaggart and a consortium of physicists and other scientists involved in consciousness research, invite thousands of readers around the world to send intention to several targets under controlled conditions through the Intention Experiment website. Thousands of people from thirty countries have already participated, producing evidence to show that group intention is powerful enough to affect targets more than 5000 miles away.

Because it can be so difficult to visualise the potential in positive alternatives open to society, I have included the following list of novels that portray 'utopian' society models. Those described are creative, adaptive, cooperative, non-exploitative, and advanced whilst retaining connections with the best parts of a variety of traditional cultures. If 'the map to a new world is in our imagination', works like these help to fuel that vision.

Woman On The Edge Of Time – Marge Piercy
Fifth Sacred Thing – Starhawk
The Dispossessed – Ursula Le Guin

All information seen to be correct at the time of writing. The author will be happy to consider any amendments. Please direct all communications, including notification of inactive links, through:

info@centreofthepsyclone.com

Appendix II
A Word on Cognitive Dissonance

This section is included in the hope of making people aware of processes which have the potential to keep them in the dark regarding some very important aspects of themselves and the natural and socio-political worlds, which, given the current state of things would be dangerous not only for themselves and their loved ones, but for every other person on the planet.

When discussing the information contained in Psyclone, I have found that, more often than not, people react in ways that after research I can now identify as 'dissonance mitigation'. Because of that I have included this section.

The theory of cognitive dissonance is based on the relationships between cognitions. A cognition can be described as a piece of knowledge. For example, the knowledge that your eyes are green is a cognition; the knowledge that you like the colour purple is a cognition; the knowledge that the Earth is round is a cognition. People hold a massive amount of cognitions simultaneously. These cognitions form relationships that are said to be irrelevant, consonant or dissonant.

Irrelevant means that the cognitions have nothing to do with each other. Most of the relationships among a person's cognitions are irrelevant. Cognitions are consonant if one follows on from, or fits with, the other. It may be part of the nature of the human organism, or it may be learned during the process of socialisation, but people generally prefer cognitions that fit together to those that don't. When a person's inner systems, their values, beliefs, attitudes, etc, all support each other and when these are supported by external evidence, including the person's own actions, they have a psychologically comfortable state of affairs.

Dissonance occurs when an individual must choose between attitudes, beliefs, etc, that are contradictory. A person who has

81

dissonant cognitions is said to be in a state of cognitive dissonance, which is experienced as unpleasant psychological tension. This tension state has drive-like properties not unlike hunger and thirst. When a person has been deprived of food for some time, s/he experiences unpleasant tension and is driven to reduce that tension. Reducing the psychological state of dissonance is not as simple as eating or drinking.

It should be noted here that although the words 'tension' and 'drives' have a relatively dramatic tone, the states described are very often experienced in very subtle ways. A characteristic of the process is that it happens largely outside of the person's awareness. Indeed, unlike hunger and thirst which are accepted tensions which can be endured for short or long periods, the psychological tension produced by a threat to one's existing beliefs or values can be so uncomfortable that the strategies for alleviating the discomfort are usually adopted swiftly and determinedly, and subconsciously.

As said, dissonance is experienced as an unpleasant drive, which motivates the individual to reduce it. The Asch study *(Solomon Asch, 1956)*, described in C5, showed what can happen when there is a serious inconsistency between one's own experiences (and the beliefs based on them) and those reported by others. But what happens if the inconsistency is among a person's own experiences, beliefs or actions? Many social psychologists believe that this will trigger some general trend to restore cognitive consistency – to reinterpret the situation so as to minimise whatever inconsistency may be there.

An example provided by a group of social psychologists *(Festinger, Riecken and Chachter, 1956)* is that of a study of a sect that was awaiting the end of the world. The founder of the sect announced that she had received a message from the "Guardians" of outer space. On a certain day, there would be a worldwide flood. Only the true believers were to be saved and were to be picked up at midnight of the appointed day in extraterrestrial craft. On doomsday, the members of the sect
82

gathered together, awaiting the predicted deluge. The arrival time of the craft came and went; tension mounted as the hours went by. Finally, the leader of the sect received another message: To reward the faith of the faithful, the world was saved. Joy broke out and the believers became more faithful than ever.

Given the failure of a clear-cut prophecy, one might have expected the opposite reaction. A disconfirmation of a predicted event should presumably lead one to abandon the beliefs that produced the prediction. But cognitive dissonance theory says otherwise. By abandoning the beliefs that there were Guardians, the person who had once held this belief would have to accept a painful dissonance between their present skepticism and their past beliefs and actions. Their prior faith would now appear extremely foolish. Some members of the sect had gone to such lengths as giving up their jobs or spending their savings; such acts would have lost all meaning in retrospect without the belief in the Guardians. Under the new circumstances, the dissonance was intolerable. It was reduced by a belief in the new message that bolstered the original belief. Since other members of the sect stood fast with them, their conviction was strengthened all the more. They could now think of themselves, not as fools, but as loyal, steadfast members of a courageous little band whose faith had saved the earth.

One thing worth noting was that while fringe members tended to recognise that they had made fools of themselves and to "put it down to experience", committed members were more likely to reinterpret the evidence to show that they were right all along (Earth was not destroyed because of the faithfulness of the cult members). This may have been because those who had invested everything in their belief would have experienced more dissonance than those who had not, and thus would have been more strongly motivated to reduce that tension.

The case in point is an extreme example of a process that happens regularly in much more mundane and subtle ways. As has already been pointed out, a characteristic of the process is that it happens largely outside of a person's awareness.

There are several recognised ways of relieving tension produced by two dissonant cognitions:

1) Reducing the importance of the dissonant cognition,
2) changing one to make it consistent with the other or
3) adding more consonant cognitions that outweigh the dissonant cognition.

(Based on my experience I would add simple ignoring to that list.)

Verbal indicators of the above have been:

- 'What a load of rubbish.'
- 'Not another conspiracy theory.'
- 'You're reading too much into things.'
- 'That's not the way things work/There must be some other reason.'
- 'Anyway, even if [what is postulated] were true there's nothing that we can do about it.'
- 'If that was true, someone would be doing something about it.'
- 'It might not be perfect, but it's better than…'

(See also **Seven Warning Signs of Bogus Skepticism** in **Appendix I**)

Earlier the example of a round Earth being a cognition was given. There was a time in history when large amounts of people believed that the planet was flat, a potentially understandable belief/cognition given the lack of knowledge of the time. (An interesting aside here is an article by Michael Roll (**www.cfpf.org.uk**), '**Uncomfortable Historical Facts That we are Never Taught at School in the Theocracy of England**' which shows that the round earth theory was actually proved by the Greek scientist Eratosthenes in the 3rd century BCE, and that information suppressed for theocratic/political reasons). When the news finally did get out, it took an inordinately long time for it to be accommodated by most. In that case the magnitude of the dissonance created, because the new cognition threatened some fairly fundamental beliefs, would have needed see-it-with-their-own-eyes proof or the combined weight of the beliefs of those around to change the cognition. Until that happened all sorts of wacky dismissals were put forward to reduce the dissonance produced.

Fast forward to modern day and, for example, the destruction of the World Trade Centre buildings. There is a substantial amount of evidence to prove that a) fires caused by the crashed planes did not demolish the towers, and b) there was foreknowledge of the event. One of the biggest difficulties that people have in accommodating those facts despite all the evidence (which many won't even consider for the same reason) is the dissonance caused by the thought that Americans, especially the nation's leaders, would do such a thing. The nature of the event, and the strength of the existing beliefs, makes accommodating the new cognition difficult to the point of impossible for many. Parallels can be drawn here with cases where, despite evidence and/or testimony, one parent is unable to accept the fact that the other parent has been abusing the children.

The process is equally observable when presenting, or being presented with, subjects like life after death, out-of-body projection, free energy, UFO's, etc. A good measure for predicting the stimulation of dissonance is a subject's relative social unorthodoxy. Which provides a clue to what is one of the biggest influences on the formation and maintenance of people's cognitions (see the Asch Study).

Part Two of Nick Sandberg's thesis Blueprint for a Prison Planet (see **Section 2**) describes in detail the conditioning process that most of us undergo in the course of a Western childhood that permanently alters the way most of us evaluate information.

85

KNOWLEDGE IS POWER.
YOUR IGNORANCE IS THEIR BLISS.